WICKED
FOREST

The Dollanganger Family Series
Flowers in the Attic
Petals on the Wind
If There Be Thorns
Seeds of Yesterday
Garden of Shadows

The Casteel Family Series
Heaven
Dark Angel
Fallen Hearts
Gates of Paradise
Web of Dreams

The Cutler Family Series
Dawn
Secrets of the Morning
Twilight's Child
Midnight Whispers
Darkest Hour

The Landry Family Series
Ruby
Pearl in the Mist
All That Glitters
Hidden Jewel
Tarnished Gold

The Logan Family Series
Melody
Heart Song
Unfinished Symphony
Music in the Night
Olivia

The Orphans Miniseries
Butterfly
Crystal
Brooke
Raven
Runaways (full-length novel)

The Wildflowers Miniseries
Misty
Star
Jade
Cat
Into the Garden (full-length novel)

The Hudson Family Series
Rain
Lightning Strikes
Eye of the Storm
The End of the Rainbow

The Shooting Stars Series
Cinnamon
Ice
Rose
Honey
Falling Stars

The De Beers Family Series
Willow
Wicked Forest

My Sweet Audrina
(does not belong to a series)

VIRGINIA ANDREWS®

WICKED FOREST

BCA

This edition published 2003
by BCA
by arrangement with Simon & Schuster UK Ltd
A Viacom company

CN 121128

Printed and bound in Germany by
GGP Media, Pössneck

WICKED
FOREST

Prologue

The sound of footsteps in the hallway shook me out of a deep sleep. The shuffling seemed to begin in a dream and continue even after I was awake, as if something dark and ominous and haunting was strong enough to crawl out of the graveyard of nightmares and follow me into reality. A hand of ice slid its fingers down the back of my neck. Under my breasts, shackles of cold steel tightened.

For a moment I didn't know where I was. I had driven nearly ten hours nonstop on the second leg of my journey from Spring City, South Carolina, intending to arrive at my mother's home in Palm Beach, Florida, at an early enough hour to have dinner with her and with my half brother, Linden. Because of some traffic delays due to road construction and a very heavy March rainstorm, however, I didn't reach the Flagler Bridge and cross into Palm Beach until nearly 11 P.M. Everything looked dank and depressed by the weather. Even elegant Worth Avenue reminded me of a glamorous woman caught in a downpour that ruined her expensive hairdo and soaked her haute couture outfit.

Both my mother and I were so excited when I arrived that we stayed up talking until a little after 1 A.M. Linden had gone to sleep before I arrived, and from what my mother had told me, he had not had any reaction to the news of my moving in with them and my decision to continue my college education in Florida. I thought that if there was any doubt in his mind that I was sincere about moving in with them, it would have been erased when my clothing and all of my personal possessions had arrived days earlier.

"Are you sure he understood what I have decided to do?" I asked her, disappointed. In my heart of hearts I had hoped that my decision would erase the gray depression clouding his mind and help cheer along his recuperation. Was it arrogant of me to believe I could bring sunshine into someone else's life just by being there, especially after all the overcast skies that had dominated my world lately?

What I feared the most was that now Linden resented me, resented what I represented in our mother's past. Fathered by a rogue, our mother's stepfather, who seduced and raped her, Linden was already a bitter, angry young man before he had learned all of it. My story and my mother's story simply had added salt to his open wounds by giving validity to the rumors and accusations flung at our mother. I could see the question in his eyes when he first learned the truth: Why couldn't I have kept my true identity a secret, buried forever and ever? An artist, Linden believed ugly secrets should be kept hidden with a stroke of the brush. Once buried in fresh paint, who saw it, who cared?

"Oh, yes, he understood what I was telling him about

your return, but very little gets him excited these days, Willow," Mother said sadly. She leaned toward me to whisper, "Sometimes his eyes are so empty that they are like glass. It's as if he's turned them around and looks only inside at his own dark thoughts." She sat back, shaking her head. "He never smiles. I haven't heard him laugh once since the sailing accident occurred," she continued, choking back a sob.

She always called Linden's sailing fiasco an accident, even though deep in our hearts we both knew he had set out that day deliberately to hurt himself. As a reminder of it forever, he had a deep scar at least an inch and a half long on his forehead where he had taken the blow from the boom. He had gone off in a depressed, suicidal rage after learning that our mother had given birth to me in my father's psychiatric clinic when she was a patient there and my father's lover, and that I was, therefore, his half sister. After learning all this, he was a lost soul just hoping to be hit by lightning. At minimum, his deliberate negligence and his anger at what he considered an unfair world put him unnecessarily in harm's way that dreadful day.

After I read my father's diary and learned who my real mother was, I was determined to get to know her and get her to know me. However, when I came here to meet my mother for the first time, I came incognito, pretending to be a graduate psychology student doing a study of Palm Beach society. I was afraid to burst on the scene and announce who I really was, afraid of what reaction my real mother would have, mostly afraid of being rejected.

At first Linden wanted nothing to do with me, even under my false identity, or perhaps because of it. He distrusted me and thought someone had sent me to talk to him and our mother as if they were some sort of Palm Beach curiosity to be exploited and made the subject of gossip and amusement, not only because of our mother's past, but because of his dark, somewhat eerie paintings. He eventually softened his reaction to me, and I agreed to pose for him and permit him to paint me wearing our mother's clothing, if he would permit me to meet and talk to her. He still didn't know who I really was, and even though it was a bit bizarre, I didn't think much about it. I was too happy about being given the opportunity to speak to my mother.

What I didn't realize was happening and what I should have realized was that he was falling in love with me, and when he discovered why we couldn't be lovers, his anger and rage were directed at a world of cruel fate, fate he believed he would never escape, never defy. Afterward, both my mother and I blamed ourselves for what he had done to himself, and that was a big part of why I wanted to come back here to live and to pursue my education in Florida.

"Well, we'll just have to change all that," I said, patting her hand. "We'll bring the smiles and laughter back to his lips." It was always easier to give someone else hope, to urge someone else to take a risk and believe in rainbows.

"Maybe," she said, nibbling on the brightness in my voice and face. "Maybe when he finally believes you're here, and here for good, it will make a difference." But her voice trailed off as if the whole thought were made of smoke.

"Exactly," I said firmly, building as much enthusiasm for the task ahead as I could. "We'll make him a happy and productive young artist again." It was an Olympian ambition, to restore someone's life and purpose, perhaps even an impossible dream, especially for me at the moment. I had enough to carry on my shoulders with the weight of my own problems, enough to sink another *Titanic.*

Even though I had come back to Palm Beach to live with my real mother and my half brother, I couldn't help feeling I was returning to an unfriendly world filled with people who would take pleasure in our struggles and our sadness. During my initial visit, I had developed what I believed was a serious relationship with Thatcher Eaton, a prominent young Palm Beach attorney and son of Asher and Bunny Eaton, the couple who were renting the main house on Mother's property. Now that the truth about my relationship to Grace and Linden Montgomery was public knowledge, however, I was no longer confident that the man with whom I thought I was falling in love and who I thought was falling in love with me would want to set eyes on me, would want me complicating his life by forcing him to choose between me and his own family, his position in Palm Beach society, and his ambition.

With all these worries putting folds in my forehead, it was no wonder my hands had trembled as I turned my car toward the gate of the estate Joya del Mar, the Jewel of the Sea. I could not help wondering if it would be a jewel to me or a home filled with "the dreads," as my nanny, Amou, had called dark premonitions.

My mother smiled at me across the table. My unrelenting optimism finally restored the warm hope in her eyes. Then she told me with glee how Thatcher's parents were in denial about her refusal to sell them the estate and to extend their lease for even another day. They had little more than two months to go, but from what she had seen and heard so far, it was a reality they still chose not to face or admit.

"It's gotten so they try never to look my way. As if I were now an eyesore," she told me. "Before this, Asher

Eaton would at least nod to me occasionally and ask me how I was."

"I wouldn't worry about it, Mother. That's the way of people here. They either ignore anything unpleasant or pretend it doesn't exist," I said. "If they could, they would hire someone to go to the bathroom for them."

She laughed.

"I have no doubt," she said.

"I'm sure they just can't stand the fact that you no longer need them," I said.

Ever since her stepfather had run her mother's finances into the ground, my mother had been forced to lease out the main building and live in the beach house, which also housed some of the Eatons' servants. Now that I had inherited my father's estate and sold our property in South Carolina, I had money that would free her from the financial shackles that made both her and Linden outcasts in their own home.

"Well, I suppose you're right. It doesn't take much to get them upset. You know Bunny Eaton," my mother said. "Just running out of caviar can put her into a deep enough depression to require a doctor's care."

We both laughed again, and then she looked at me with that soft smile around her eyes I quickly had come to cherish, the motherly smile every child basks in and from which he or she draws confidence and security. Pity the orphans who live in a world without such smiles raining down upon them, I thought, for I very nearly had been such a person.

"What?" I asked, already knowing her well enough to realize that behind that smile there was a thought itching to be voiced through those soft, loving lips.

"Thatcher is, of course, a different story altogether.

He was very interested in your arrival and peppered me with questions about you."

"Really," I said dryly, unable to prevent a skeptical smirk. "He hasn't called me since I left for home."

I had hurried home to help arrange and attend the funeral of my father's closest servant, Miles, who had been looking after the house and grounds since my father's passing. Now that he, too, was gone, I needed to see to the sale of the property as well. I then arranged for my transfer from the University of North Carolina, where I had begun my sophomore year, to a college in Florida. All that time I had expected to hear from Thatcher. He had promised to call, and I truly believed he would, despite his mother's disapproval of our relationship and me.

"He will call now," my mother assured me.

"I might not want to speak with him if he does," I said petulantly.

"Maybe not, and maybe yes," she teased. My eyes surely betrayed my hope that she was right. "I can see it in your small smile, Willow. You reveal your true thoughts with the same tiny tug in the corners of your lips that I have."

I shrugged, and then she and I both laughed, giggling like two schoolgirls. How wonderful it was finally to have a mother who could be as close as a sister or be a best friend. My adoptive mother could barely stand the sight of me and had never failed to remind me what a great favor she was doing for me to let me live in her home. She never knew I was living in my real father's home; she never knew the whole truth. Such a woman was better off buried with lies, I thought. I wasn't being vindictive. I was just rendering unto Caesar what was Caesar's. When she was alive, she had cherished deception, fabrication, and falsehood almost as much as she had cherished diamonds. She had a closet full of un-truths to pluck out and put to use at a moment's notice, even lies to tell herself. It seemed only just and proper that she take it all with her to the grave.

"I can barely keep my eyes open," I declared. Mother and I had been talking for hours.

"Me too," my mother admitted, and we put our dishes in the dishwasher and both went to bed, hugging in the hallway first.

"I'm so happy you're here," she whispered.

"So am I, Mother. So am I," I told her.

Up until now the word *Mother,* the very idea of hav-ing one, had been as mythical as a unicorn for me. I en-joyed saying it so much, I thought I would mutter "Mother, Mother, Mother" in my sleep forever.

When I finally crawled into bed, I felt like I was still riding in the car. The visions of oncoming headlights, rain pounding on the windshield, and globs of fog twirling be-fore me still lingered on the insides of my eyelids. Overtired, I tossed and turned for a while before dropping into what was more a state of unconsciousness than sleep. Then I awoke to the sound of those footsteps. I was sur-prised my ears had been capable of taking in the sounds in the hallway and delivering them to my groggy brain.

I lifted my head from the pillow and, after realizing where I was, listened keenly. The steps sounded more like someone shuffling along in shoes with sandpaper for soles. I heard the hinges of the front door squeak like impish tattletales. The whish of the wind rushed into the house, and then I heard the door close. I glanced at the illuminated face of the clock on my nightstand and saw it was nearly 3:30 A.M. Who would be walking about at this hour and for what purpose? Was my mother still going out to the dock at night with a lantern, dreaming of my father, who had promised to come to her someday? Such hope died hard, even in the face of the cold reality of his death, I thought, and my heart cried for her.

Despite my fatigue, I slipped my feet into my slippers and scooped up my pink and white velour bathrobe to hurry out to see what was happening.

The house was dark, but the rain clouds had been driven off by a stern easterly wind and there was enough of a first-quarter moon to illuminate the hall and entryway. On the other side of the house and above were housed the maids and the Eatons' butler, Jennings, but I knew it was our front door I had heard open and close.

I brushed back my hair and stepped out to the loggia, facing the sea. The water looked choppy, the starlit whitecaps higher than usual. At first I thought there was no one out here and perhaps I had imagined it all, but then, looking to my right, I saw Linden walking in bare feet slowly, very slowly, and wearing only his pajamas!

My first inclination was to turn back and fetch my mother, but Linden was moving closer and closer to the water. The frightening thought occurred to me that my return might have had a terribly negative effect on him, something my mother had not realized, so terrible in fact that it had revived his suicidal urge. Would I be responsible for another near-tragedy? Panic seemed to add a hundred pounds to my weight. Even so, I shot forward and hurried after him. The wind whipped my robe about my legs and threw sand up into my face as if nature herself wanted to keep me from reaching him.

"Linden!" I screamed. "What are you doing? Where are you going? Linden!"

He didn't turn, nor did he change his pace, which was a very slow, dreamy gait, his arms stiffly at his sides. I broke into a run, losing my slipper once, getting it back on, and running until I reached him moments later.

"Linden!"

There was no question I was close enough so he could hear me, but he continued to walk, his head lowered. I reached out and seized his right arm at the elbow. It was enough to stop him, but he didn't turn and he didn't speak. He just stood there, his shoulders swaying as if he were still walking.

"What is it? Why are you doing this? Where are you going?" I fired at him, yet he still didn't turn. "Linden!"

Finally, his shoulders stopped moving and he stood deathly still, his head down, the strands of his long, blond hair hanging limply like a small curtain over his face.

I moved around to stand in front of him and saw that his eyes were closed. In fact, he looked asleep!

"Linden? Are you all right?"

Without responding, he turned slowly and started to walk again, lifting his feet as though the beach were made of sticky tar.

He's sleepwalking, I realized. I had never seen anyone do it before and it was frightening. It was like being drawn into someone else's nightmare. I caught up to him again, my heart pounding.

"Linden," I said softly. "Linden, please wake up. You're outside, on the beach."

I shook his arm gently, not sure what effect an abrupt awakening might have on him and how he might react in light of his recent head injuries and subsequent operation to relieve the pressure the blow had put on his brain. Opening his eyes and finding himself on a beach and not in bed might trigger some horrible response. The doctor had spoken of posttraumatic symptoms, I recalled. Perhaps this was one of them. He might go into a hysterical rage and harm himself, and I wasn't strong enough to stop him.

He continued to walk toward the house, but I think if I hadn't nudged and turned him when we drew closer, he might have gone past it. Fortunately, he made it to the loggia and then permitted me to guide him gently down the hallway toward his bedroom. I anticipated my mother waking, but she didn't, and so it was left to me to get him back into his bed. He was stiff, but I was able to get him under the blanket. Amazingly, he never woke; he never uttered a sound.

Standing beside the bed and gazing down at him, I brushed his hair from his face and looked again at that scar, that horrible reminder of his sadness, anger, and loneliness. Linden's lips twitched and his eyes moved rapidly behind his closed lids. Then he opened his mouth and moaned softly. After that he was very still again, his breathing regular, quiet.

Satisfied he would be all right, I returned to my own room and tried to go back to sleep, but that wasn't to happen very quickly. Chasing after him and bringing him back to the house had put needles and pins in my stomach. It actually took hours for me to fall asleep again, and just as I did, the bright sunlight clapped its hands in front of me like a mesmerist snapping me out of a hypnotic state and made me open my eyes.

I could hear the muffled sounds of the servants above preparing to go to work at the main house for the Eatons, and I could also hear my mother talking softly to Linden. I did not hear him speak. My body moaned complaints from toes to the top of my head when I forced myself to rise. After I washed my face in cold water to shock out the sleepiness and brushed my hair so I could at least tie it back, I put on my robe and went out to the kitchen where my mother and Linden were having breakfast.

"Oh, Linden," she cried as soon as she saw me approaching, "look who has returned, just as I told you. She arrived last night after you went to bed."

He didn't turn his head or lift his eyes toward me at all.

"Hi, Linden," I said. "How are you feeling?"

He stared down at his oatmeal and then, as if he hadn't heard a word I said, he sipped some coffee.

"Willow is back, Linden," my mother said. "Don't you want to say good morning to her?"

He looked at our mother, but he didn't look at me. Again, he sipped some coffee.

My mother and I exchanged a look of concern, and then I smiled back, closing and opening my eyes gently.

"Are you hungry, Willow?"

"I'll just make myself some toast with jam," I said.

"I didn't expect you would be up so early after driving all day and late into the night, and especially after I kept you up so long talking," she told me as I went to make the toast.

"Neither did I," I said. "I was awake earlier," I added, wondering if Linden had eventually realized what had happened during the night. I glanced at him to see if he was going to sneak a glance at me, but he didn't. He pushed himself back from the table and stood.

"You haven't finished your breakfast yet, Linden," our mother said.

He shook his head.

"I'm not very hungry this morning," he said, still not looking my way.

I was beginning to wonder if he would speak to me at all. Why wouldn't he at least say hello to me? I guess he truly was angry at me simply for existing, for dropping my mother and father's past in his lap like a ball of cold lead. Perhaps it was the age-old fury that required recipients of bad news to kill the messenger.

He turned, his eyes brushing over me like a passing feather, and walked out and down the hallway.

As soon as I thought he was out of earshot, I told my mother about being woken by footsteps in the hallway.

"I came out because I thought it might be you and something was wrong. I discovered it was Linden and he was out there," I said, nodding toward the beach, "walking in his sleep."

I described what I had done and how he had remained asleep the whole time.

She pressed her lips together and closed her eyelids as if to keep the tears contained. Then she sighed so deeply, I thought she had cracked her heart.

"It's been one thing after another like this since he came home from the hospital. His therapist there predicted his depression would deepen and suggested a more intense therapy with medications. She wanted me to have him admitted to a nearby psychiatric hospital, but I could not do it, even though I have always wondered if he has inherited my manic-depressive condition."

"No, Mother. Your condition wasn't anything genetic," I said firmly. I had read my father's reports about her.

She nodded.

"I was hoping that the medicine they gave him would bring him back to an even keel, that somehow he would improve and we would at least have what peace we had before, but . . ." She swallowed hard and continued, "This is new, this sleepwalking, though." She shook her head. "What will we do? Lock his bedroom door?"

"Maybe it will pass. It might never occur again. It's

still too soon after the whole event," I suggested, buoying up her hopes. She nodded, her shoulders and back softening with another sigh.

"Yes, maybe, but I suppose we do have to consider what to do if it doesn't. In any case, I'll call his doctor and tell her about it, even though I know she will only repeat her suggestion to put him in the clinic."

We stopped talking when we heard him returning. He had put on his windbreaker and was headed for the door.

"Where are you going, Linden?" Mother asked.

As if the question required a great deal of consideration, he took a moment to respond.

"For a walk," he said.

"I'll come out to join you in a while," I suggested. "If you don't mind."

He paused. For a moment I thought he was finally going to turn and speak to me, but he didn't respond. He continued toward the front door.

"Don't go too far," my mother called to him with urgency in her voice.

"I've already gone too far," he said, opened the door, and left us both looking after him wondering what that meant or if there was any sensible meaning at all in that twisted cloud of thoughts, dreams, and memories that swirled about like a tornado in his troubled head.

As with the answers to so many new questions about my life and my future, it waited out there for me like the fruit on the forbidden Tree of Knowledge. *Pluck it at your own peril, Willow De Beers,* I thought.

And hope that, like poor Adam and Eve, you don't get driven out of paradise.

1

Return to Joya del Mar

Now that I was here, that I had made the firm decision to be involved with my real mother's life and family, I felt like someone who had gotten off the roller coaster. I was a bit shaky regaining my footing, but finally, time had slowed down for me. I could take a deep breath and let my memories, especially my most recent, the ones that had been stringing along behind me like so many ribbons in the wind, catch up and be stored in the safest places in my brain. They were no longer to be ignored, but I could draw upon them for lessons and wisdom to guide me through the days ahead.

Right before I left for my second year of college, Daddy and I had a wonderful after-dinner hour or so together on the rear patio of our South Carolina house. Quiet moments together like that were as rare as shooting stars. I hadn't the courage to ask for them. Puppies unabashedly snuggle at the feet of their loving masters, hoping to be stroked. I envied them for their obvious play for love. Growing up in a home in which my adoptive mother always made me feel like an uninvited guest made me timid and quite withdrawn as a child. It took very little to get her upset with me. I clung so hard and so close to my nanny Amou's skirt, I am sure people who saw us thought I was attached to her hip.

I remember I would try to turn and twist in a way that would keep me hidden from my adoptive mother's critical eyes whenever she was in the same room or passing by. Those eyes stabbed me with accusation and contempt. Amou was truly my shield, my protection. Her warm voice and touch gave me enough reassurance to challenge nightmares and keep the dark clouds away most of the time.

I wasn't afraid of going to Daddy for comfort, but now, of course, I understood that in those early years, when he was concerned about pleasing my adoptive mother and keeping his secret life and love just that, secret, he put up a wall of firm, correct authority between us and, especially in front of my adoptive mother, remained as aloof and objective as he could. He was, in other words, the psychiatric doctor first, the counselor, the therapist, and my father second.

Always the one who relied on reason and logic, he put me through the behavioral catechisms as soon as I was capable of answering a question with a yes or a no. My adoptive mother would rail against my sloppiness or my forgetfulness. She would pounce on my failure to keep my things well organized, even when I was only three. Even then I noticed how she would turn to my father and, like a prosecutor in a courtroom, make an argument for declaring me guilty of some horrid imperfection, some mental weakness, and demand a punishment. By the time I was five, I thought she would ask for the death penalty.

Daddy rarely contradicted her openly. He would show some form of agreement with a nod or a widening of his eyes and then turn to me, the defendant, and begin his soft but well-constructed series of reasonable questions.

"You want your room to look nice, don't you, Willow? You want to be able to bring your friends here? You want to make less work for Isabella, right?"

Isabella was Amou's real name. I called her Amou from the first day I could pronounce a word. She called me Amou Um, which in Portuguese means "loved one," and I just picked up on that. My adoptive mother hated nicknames and tried to get me to stop calling my nanny Amou, but I resisted, even in the face of her fiery eyes of anger that threatened to sweep over me, engulfing me in the blaze.

Of course, I nodded in agreement with every question Daddy would ask, and somehow, my acquiescing to that sort of reprimand satisfied my adoptive mother enough to lower the flames of her rage and enable me to escape from her circle of heat. My eyes were glassy with tears, of course, but most of the time I didn't permit a single one to escape. It was almost as if I instinctively knew as an infant that weeping in front of my adoptive mother was some sort of acceptance of how she characterized me, the child of a mentally ill woman, a bundle of promising new problems just waiting to give themselves expression.

Afterward, I sometimes caught the look of sadness and disgust on Daddy's face, but it was there for only an instant or so. He had to maintain his self-control. He had to treat me like the child of a stranger, the charity case my adoptive mother believed I was. I could only imagine what havoc she would have wreaked upon

Daddy if she had known the truth. Not only would she have put him through a nasty divorce, but she would have driven him out of his profession and, therefore, out of his reason to be. Keeping their love affair buried in their hearts was a price and a sacrifice both my father and my real mother knew they had to pay in order for me to exist at all.

I feel certain now that Daddy would have told me all of the truth in a face-to-face meeting eventually and not left it for me to read as part of some postmortem. He was just waiting to be sure I could handle it and not be harmed or horrified by it. In a real sense, he had to reinvent himself for me first, change from one sort of man to another, from a guardian to a father, from someone merely full of concern and responsibility to someone full of love. He was in the process of doing just that before he died. Perhaps he waited too long, but none of us ever really believes in the end of ourselves. We always feel there will be one more turn to make, one more mile to go, one more minute to enjoy, and the opportunity to do what must be done will not be lost.

Fortunately, after his death, Daddy had left me his diary, his insurance policy for the truth, and after reading it, I knew more about who I really was and what I had to do. My closest relative, Aunt Agnes Delroy, my father's widowed sister, tried to stop me. Like everyone around me, she wanted to deny reality and truth.

"I'm so glad you're enjoying college, Willow," Daddy began that warm spring evening that now came up vividly out of my pool of memories. I recalled how the stars had burned like the tips of candle flames growing stronger with every passing minute.

"I am, Daddy. I love all my classes and enjoy my

teachers. In fact, some of my new friends think I'm too serious about my work."

He laughed.

"I remember that I had to work so hard to enable my-self to attend the university that I would feel some sort of ridiculous guilt if I relished my studies and wallowed with pleasure in my assignments and challenges."

"That's how I feel."

"It wasn't supposed to be fun," he continued, gazing out at the fields and the lake and forest beyond as if he could look past the present, back in time to happier days. His smile said all that. "It was supposed to be hard work. What an incredibly unexpected reaction to it all. Like your new friends, some of my closer friends thought I was bizarre. 'Psychiatry is a good place for you, Claude,' they would say. 'Eventually, you can treat yourself and send yourself the bill.' "

We both laughed at the idea, and then he turned to me, his face as serious as it had ever been.

"If we don't love what we do," he told me, "then we don't love who we are, and the worst fate of all is not liking yourself, Willow, being trapped in a body and be-hind a face you despise. You hate the sound of your own voice. You even come to hate your own shadow. How can you ever hope to make anyone else happy, wife, children, friends, if you can't make yourself happy?

"It seems like such a simple truth, but it remains buried beneath so many lies and delusions for most people. I know now that won't happen to you," he said assuredly.

As I walked on the beach after breakfast this morn-ing, that conversation and those words of Daddy's helped me to understand Linden. He was out there, wan-dering, trying to find a way to escape from himself, from what he now perceived to be who and what he was.

Suicide was of course, one avenue to take, and he had evidently tried that, but there had to be something better. I was determined to help him find it.

Perhaps it was truly arrogant of me even to think I could be of such assistance to him. I was still quite a young woman, tentative and unsure of myself, of my own emotions, still haunted by my own childhood fears. For me, the daughter of a world-renowned psychiatrist, and someone who wanted to follow in his footsteps, it seemed like a natural thing to do. But would it be like the blind leading the blind? Would I cause him even more harm, drive him even deeper into that darkness in which he now spent so much of his time? How I envied my father for the confidence he had behind all his decisions. Most of those decisions could have a significant effect on other people's lives. How could you know that and still speak with such authority, such self-assurance? I wondered. When would it be like that for me? Would it ever be?

Laughter coming from the rear loggia of the main house pulled my attention from the ocean and my own heavy thoughts. I had just come up the small rise in the beach and I was nearly directly behind the loggia. To my surprise, Bunny and Asher Eaton, who usually partied late into the evening almost every night during the so-called Palm Beach Season, sometimes even into the next morning, were up and dressed in their pink and white, blue and white tennis outfits and having breakfast with Thelma and Brenda Carriage, two friends of Bunny Eaton's I had previously met. She herself described them as great gossips who knew where to look to find everyone's dirty laundry. She called them "core Palm Beach" and had told me their husbands were big Palm Beach developers, two brothers who had married two sisters, now both widows.

I knew they couldn't help but notice me. They were all facing in my direction. However, neither Bunny nor Asher said a word.

Even from this distance, I could see the displeasure in Bunny's face at the sight of me; she was probably, like me, recalling our nasty confrontation just before I left for South Carolina. She turned back to her guests quickly and, a moment later, released another peal of exaggerated laughter as if I were some sort of clown who had wandered too far from the circus. She mumbled something else and then they all laughed.

I was about to ignore them when Thatcher suddenly appeared, obviously dressed for work. He had his back to me so he couldn't have known I was here on the beach. Neither Bunny nor Asher was about to tell him, I thought, but one of the Carriage sisters must have asked about me because he quickly turned to look in my direction. For a moment we gazed at each other. My heart began to pound so hard and fast, I had to take a deep breath. He didn't call out and he didn't set out to greet me. As if it had a mind of its own, my hand wanted to lift and wave, but I kept it down and chastised my heart for its weakness, threatening my pride.

Thatcher said something to the group and then went into the house. As if to gloat, Bunny Eaton turned my way quickly and laughed again.

I lowered my head and continued to walk the beach, searching for Linden. I soon suspected he had gone in the opposite direction because I saw no sign of him ahead, even as far as the adjoining property. Suddenly, I felt terribly alone and again experienced those pangs of doubt that tormented every decision I was making.

I paused and looked out at the sailboats in the distance. The warm but strong easterly breeze paraded a line of puffy, milk-white clouds toward the horizon and a passenger jet lifted off the runway at the West Palm Beach airport. I watched it climb, turning toward the clouds.

"You look like you wish you were on that," I heard, and spun around to see Thatcher coming down a pathway between a row of bushes.

He had obviously gone out of the main house and then to the left to follow an approach to the beach. I glanced back in the direction of the house. I quickly realized that what he was doing was sneaking around to meet me. The heat of indignation built so quickly in my face, I felt as if someone had put a lit match close to my cheek.

"What is it, Thatcher?" I asked, folding my arms under my breasts and pulling up my shoulders. "Are you afraid you'll get a spanking or something if you're caught speaking to me now? The Carriage sisters will put it on the news wires?"

He had been heading toward me quickly to embrace and kiss me, but stopped and forced a smile and a laugh.

"I should know that there isn't any way to deceive the daughter of a famous psychiatrist," he said. He took the next few steps toward me cautiously.

I looked down at his polished new shoes picking up some wet sand. The breeze lifted his hair. There was no doubt Thatcher Eaton was a handsome man. He had just enough tan to highlight the blue in his eyes and the whiteness of his teeth. Not quite six feet tall, he was broad-shouldered and narrow-waisted enough to give the impression he was taller, bigger than he really was, and his air of confidence, bordering on arrogance at times, made him appear stronger yet.

It would be easy to fall in love with such a man, to surrender to his charm and cast myself with abandon into his waiting arms. But I didn't laugh at his silly quip. I was sure that the expression on my face told him I wouldn't tolerate any featherbrained excuses or half-truths and fabrications to justify his failure to call me after I had left Joya del Mar to tend to sad business back in South Carolina. I certainly wasn't going to ignore the way he was behaving now and feel sorry for him having to soothe and protect his spoiled mother.

The smile left his face, quickly replaced by that look of seriousness and assuredness that he habitually wore to face the public.

"I'm here to apologize for not calling you when I said I would, and I'm sorry about the things my mother told you the day you left. She recited the exchange to me word for word, although I'm sure she embellished your statements to make you appear harder and nastier," he said, smirking.

"No, I imagine she didn't exaggerate anything. Whatever she told you I said, I'm sure I did say. I wasn't going to permit her to make me feel like I was beneath the Eatons because of what my mother has been through," I assured him.

"No," he said, his expression softening into a smile. "I bet you weren't."

His eyes grew dark and serious again as he stepped closer to me.

"Look, Willow, there is no question about the right and the wrong here. Of course my parents are snobs. I never pretended they weren't, did I?"

"No, you didn't, but you left out your own snobbery, Thatcher. I was very disappointed in your failure to call me. You knew I wasn't going home for the fun of it, and you knew how terrible things were for my mother, Linden, and me back here. It broke my heart to have to leave her, even for a short while, but I'm beginning to wonder if you are capable of understanding how quickly such love and concern can develop and flourish when they're honest and true."

"Listen, listen," he said, pleading, "I really was getting ready to contact you. In the meantime, I was working behind the scenes to be sure Linden had the best medical attention possible if he needed anything, and to be sure your mother was all right."

"Why behind the scenes?" I fired back. "You're a grown man, a successful attorney. You led me to believe you weren't affected by the glitz and the opulent wealth down here and you had just as little respect as I did for the pompous asses who parade about as if they were some sort of gods and goddesses."

"That's true. It's still true, but . . ."

"But what?"

"Look," he said, stepping closer, "you have to compromise a little to succeed in this world, Willow. Those who won't, who insist on standing on high principles and won't compromise, are just as snobby."

"What?" I smiled incredulously. "Highly principled people are snobby?"

"That's right. There's another sort of arrogance, an arrogance of being right, of being perfect, of intolerance. Rich people can be pitied, too. For their failings, their insecurities, their imperfections," he added quickly before I could laugh or even widen my smile of incredulity at such a thought.

I wasn't going to. The truth was, I did pity people like his parents far more than I hated them or, of course, envied them.

"The successful person in this world is the one who knows how to compromise in such a way that he or she holds onto enough self-respect to enjoy the success. It's a matter of proportion, diplomacy, negotiations," he lectured.

"How does any of that justify your sneaking about your own property even to speak to me?" I threw back at him.

He sighed and shook his head.

"Look, it might not be obvious to you, but I do have a rather fragile family, especially when you consider my sister and her situation. My parents put up a good facade, but my father especially is carrying a great burden on his shoulders."

"What burden, the supply of champagne?"

"Ridicule if you want, but you're not the only one with a troubled past and present. My sister's marriage has been on the rocks for years. Her husband isn't as successful as he makes out to be. There's a lot you don't know, Willow. I saw no reason to add my dark shadows to your own house of dreads," he said, softening his lips. I had told him of Amou's sayings and ways. His using the expression did quell the flames of fury in my chest, if not put them out altogether.

"And then, all of this, these revelations about you and Grace, and Linden's actions . . . all of it coming at us so fast and so furiously . . . it takes time to adjust, to accept, to understand," he continued in a voice of pleading. "Despite how it looks, there is a very orderly, disciplined life here, at least for me."

I stared at him. How reasonable he sounded, how perfectly, damnably reasonable.

"I keep forgetting what a good trial attorney you are, Thatcher Steven Eaton, even though it's usually a trial over bad kitty litter or something similar," I said, and he laughed.

"Hey, don't knock it. It pays the bills and then some."

I took a deep breath and looked away. Was he right

about it all and the way he had behaved? I wanted him to be right. I needed him to be right. Did that make me weak? Was I willing to delude myself, accept lies so I could be happy, just like so many people here, so many people I knew, especially my adoptive mother? If there was anyone I didn't want to resemble, it was she.

I hated how I continually analyzed myself, but I couldn't help thinking I would always be weak when it came to facing a strong, confident man. Analysts would tell me I was constantly searching for a father figure.

Thatcher stepped closer, practically touching me. I turned away from him, afraid of looking into those beautiful eyes and weakening.

"You've got to believe I suffered, knowing that you were alone out there, dealing with all your problems without me at your side," he said in a soft, low voice.

I spun on him.

"Then why didn't you just call . . . just call me once!"

"I thought you would be on your way back sooner," he said. "Especially with Linden still in the hospital and all."

"That's such a lot of . . . hooey, Thatcher," I snapped back at him.

He stared at me.

"You're just fishing for excuses to rationalize your inaction. Your objections are too flimsy, counselor. They're overruled."

He nodded, then pressed his lips together and took on a different look, a darker look.

"You're right," he said. "There's more."

"What more?" I asked, taken back by his abrupt surrender.

"Something else happened very soon after you left."

"What?" I repeated with more demand.

He looked away, and the expression on his face made

my heart skip a beat. What else could have happened that was more difficult to accept or understand than all that had happened to me and to Linden and my mother?

"My sister realized how serious I was getting with you," he began.

"So? Why did that matter? You never let her opinions sway you before, did you?" I practically screamed at him.

He glanced toward the house as if afraid we would be heard and took a few steps farther down the beach so our voices would definitely not carry back there. I walked a little behind him, now almost as nervous as I was angry.

"No. You're right. Her opinions wouldn't matter. I don't adjust my life or change my plans to satisfy Whitney's view of the world. That's for sure," he said. "We're as different as a brother and a sister can be, but . . ."

He turned to me quickly.

"But what?"

"But that's the point, or at least the point she was making in her revelations."

"What revelations? What are you talking about, Thatcher? You're not making any sense to me and—"

"I was hoping not to have to tell you any of this yet, not until I investigated it for myself and either confirmed or disproved it," he said. "My sister is not above using a trick like this to get me to do something she wants or not do something she doesn't want."

"Like what?" I practically shouted at him.

He took a deep breath, bit down on his lip, and then brushed back his hair.

"You know, of course, who Kirby Scott was," he began.

"Yes. My mother's stepfather, the one who seduced and raped her, Linden's father. I know about all that," I said, waving away the words like so many sand flies.

Of course, I knew. The story was practically engraved on my heart. After my grandmother's husband, a naval officer, was killed in a helicopter accident, she and my mother, who was about twelve at the time, moved to West Palm Beach, where my grandmother, Jackie Lee Houston, worked in upscale restaurants until she met Winston Montgomery, a very wealthy widower twenty-five years her senior. He fell in love with my grandmother and married her, bringing her to Joya del Mar. After Winston died, my grandmother fell in love with a debonair Palm Beach playboy named Kirby Scott. They were married, and Kirby eventually took advantage of Jackie Lee. In practically no time, he gambled and spent my grandmother's fortune and left her nearly bankrupt. Before that, he had seduced my mother and she had become pregnant with Linden. It was a well-hidden pregnancy. My grandmother tried to convince the world that Linden was her child. For a long time, she even had Linden convinced of it.

"We've been through that sordid tale, Thatcher. I don't see how that matters at the moment."

After a moment more of hesitation, Thatcher said, "Your mother wasn't the only one he seduced, apparently, or at least according to my sister."

"What is that supposed to mean? Who else did he seduce, and what does it have to do with us, Thatcher? You're not making any sense and frankly—"

"My mother," Thatcher blurted.

I stared at him. Was this a dream? He was telling me his mother was seduced? And by the same man who had started this whole mess?

"What?" I asked. Surely the devil wind had been playing with our words, twisting and turning them to suit its impish pleasure.

"Let's continue to walk a bit," he suggested, as if he

had to put more distance between us and his parents with every small revelation.

"Thatcher—"

He put up his hand.

"Let me explain. Immediately after you had those nasty words with my mother, she called Whitney. She's closer to Whitney than she is to me. They have more similar goals in life, share values, are more sympathetic to each other's little disappointments."

"So?"

"My mother poured her heart out, which really means her fears, poured that into Whitney's receptive ears, complaining to her about the whole situation. Whitney claims she then told my mother she had to take me aside and tell me the truth. Apparently, if I am to believe any of this, it is something my mother shared with her many years ago, but kept from me.

"Right after that conversation, my mother had one of her more serious breakdowns. Let me quickly explain what that means. She goes into a deep depression, won't get out of bed, won't eat, sobs uncontrollably. . . . My father calls me whenever that happens, and we get her over to what's best described as a spa, where she is given exaggerated tender loving care, the works—mud baths, facials, massages, you name it."

"How fortunate for her that it takes so little to restore her happiness," I said dryly.

He nodded, but looked at me with a critical sideward glance.

"You know, Willow, if I can offer you some constructive advice for a moment . . . I'm sure what made your father the great success he was had a lot to do with his tolerance and compassion. I never denied my mother's weaknesses, and still don't, but I don't hate her for that.

In fact, even though I'm not a professional therapist, I sympathize and treat her as you will someday treat a similar patient, I'm sure. I humor her, cajole, reason with her.

"Yes, there are people here who are so wealthy, they make kings and queens in other countries look like paupers, and they can buy and own and do almost anything they want, but they still suffer depression, disappointment, doubt, whatever, and all their wealth doesn't make it go away forever. In short, you have to leave a little room in that heart of yours for the well-to-do as well as the unfortunate and poor.

"A doctor who treats a rich person with less compassion than he or she does a poor person isn't really a good doctor, right?" he asked me.

"Sometimes what you're saying is very right, Thatcher, and I would not be happy with myself if I couldn't offer compassion to everyone who needed it, but there are people who are simply spoiled rotten and just need a bit of discipline more than they need extra tender loving care. Their loved ones don't do them any good catering to their whims and moods. They just prolong the misery for everyone. I wouldn't send your mother to a spa. I'd make her work for a week in the supermarket packing groceries," I said.

He laughed.

"Okay. That's a debate we'll put on hold for now. Whether she should have been whipped or embraced, my mother went into one of her depressions after you left, and I was coping with that as well as helping your mother and Linden.

"One night after she returned, I visited her in her bedroom. She was better, but I could see she was still very distracted, especially for her. There were piles of

unopened party and dinner invitations on the nightstand. I asked her what it was that was bothering her so
much. I suspected it had to do with you and me, of
course, but I was prepared to discuss it reasonably. I
was planning, in fact, to call you that night, explain
what was going on, and find out how you were doing
and when you were returning.

"My mother took the wind out of my sails. She started
with her concerns that you were the daughter of Grace
Montgomery, that your half brother was Linden, that all
of the dark mental problems could be passed on to our
children . . . on and on like that. I didn't agree and I
talked about your father and did about as good a job on
her as I had ever done. In fact, I could see from her face
that I was crushing her arguments like bugs on the loggia.

"Finally, she sat back on her fluffy pillow, looked up
at me, and told me what Whitney had wanted her to tell.
It was like I was a priest in a confessional booth, Willow.
I was so stunned. I couldn't speak. My own mother was
admitting to adultery, and admitting it to me!

"The upshot of it all was she was telling me that
Linden's father and my father were one and the same,
that Linden is my half brother, too. She was telling me
that there would be even a greater chance of our having
a disturbed child—not only was your mother passing on
mental problems to you, but my father, as evidenced by
Linden, could be passing on his abhorrent behavior to
me. That was her great fear. Understand?"

I started to shake my head, to shake the words back
out of my ears.

"No," was all I could barely utter.

"She described Kirby Scott as a very romantic, se-
ductive man who took her one night when she had been
drinking too much champagne. Shortly afterward, she

became pregnant with me. She said the doctor gave her a ballpark time of conception, and she knew without a doubt that I was Kirby Scott's son. She and my father hadn't had any relations during that period. Or so she claimed."

He paused and, with great effort, as if there were a weight on his chest, took a deep breath.

"But you look like your father. I can see resemblances to him," I said. I shook my head. "It's not true. It can't be true."

"I know, but after she told me, I dug up some old newspaper photographs. I've looked at pictures of Kirby Scott, and I see resemblances between us as well. They aren't so strong that there are no doubts, but they are strong enough to make it seem possible."

"Even if such a story proves to be true, Thatcher, it wouldn't affect us. We still don't have any blood relationship," I pointed out. "My mother didn't inherit any illness. She was abused. There's no concrete evidence that a mental problem caused by social or environmental conditions will be passed on through some genetic strain. That's all ridiculous."

"I know, but all of it is a scandal nevertheless and it would create all sorts of complications. I just might have to kiss my legal career down here goodbye if such a story ever got out."

"What of it? You can have a legal career anywhere you want, Thatcher," I countered.

"So you would marry me and leave your mother and Linden the next day?"

I started to reply, and stopped.

"You see what I mean, Willow? It's not a black and white issue and not something we can decide instantly."

"Your mother would reveal all this, tell the world

about her disgrace?" I asked, incredulous. "Just to prevent you from being with me?"

"If this were twenty years ago, I would say never, but what was once embarrassing and devastating has become socially accepted dramatic fodder now. People are on television revealing deep family secrets every day. Shame is like a vestigial organ, no longer necessary. In short, maybe my mother wouldn't do it, but I wouldn't put it past my sister."

"Maybe it's all not true. Maybe it's a fabrication just to keep us apart. Maybe . . ."

"Yes," he said. "Maybe so. I need time to confirm all this for myself. In the meantime, I am asking you to be understanding and patient with me. For everyone's sake, not just mine or yours," he added. "Why risk the unnecessary critical attention and gossip? Some of us aren't strong enough to endure any more of that sort of thing."

I knew he meant my mother and Linden. He was right. What they certainly didn't need at the moment was more scandalous baggage placed on their shoulders. What's more, how would Linden react to such news? He despised Thatcher. How would he like to learn that Thatcher and he were related, were brothers!

And what would such a story do to my mother, whose mental problems had once put her in my father's clinic? These were very fragile people who could stand no added weight. What good would I have brought to their lives? Should I be selfish and tell Thatcher I didn't care about any of that? Should I be like his mother and insist on my own pleasure and satisfaction first?

"This isn't fair," I muttered. "None of this is fair, especially if it's true. Why do we have to suffer for their indiscretions, their weaknesses?"

"Sometimes there is a lot of wisdom in the old biblical sayings . . . the sins of the parents lie on the heads of their children," Thatcher said.

Now he was the one gazing at a commercial jet lifting toward the horizon and another world, somewhere far away from all our pasts.

"Wish you were on that?" I countered.

He smiled.

"Very often, yes—but," he said, drawing closer, "only if you were sitting beside me."

"Maybe we'd all be better off if we didn't have the ability to dream," I said.

"Then where would you psychiatrists be?" Thatcher kidded.

I laughed, and he reached out to take my shoulders firmly. For a moment we looked into each other's eyes.

"No matter what the truth is or what obstacles are placed in our way, we'll be together eventually, Willow. I swear," he said with such confidence and determination, he took my breath away. He brought his lips to mine. We kissed softly at first, then hard and long, as if we both wanted it to last forever and ever. I couldn't stifle a moan of pleasure, and he let his lips glide over my cheeks and around again to my lips.

When we stopped kissing, he put his arms around me and held me against his chest. We stood there silently for a long moment. I could feel his heart pounding and I'm sure he could feel mine.

"I've got to get to work," he said in a tight, cracking voice.

When I looked up at him, I saw his eyes were glossed over with tears.

"Okay."

"I'll see you every moment I can. For a little while, we'll be discreet about it, but I'll be working on this as much as I can, and we'll get to the bottom of it and to the solution as quickly as possible," he promised. "And without hurting anyone, if we can. Is that all right?"

"Yes," I said, not fully realizing what it was that I was agreeing to.

"When I saw you from the loggia before, it was as if the clouds had been blown away, as if sunshine had returned, and I knew why they call this Joya del Mar, the Jewel of the Sea. You're the jewel as far as I'm concerned, Willow."

I smiled at him through my own glassy eyes now.

He started back toward the path, then turned.

"You're still going ahead with all the legal motions to enable Grace to keep the property?"

"Yes. I'm seeing the accountant today and signing whatever has to be signed."

"Just be sure it's the right thing for them, Willow."

"It is," I said firmly.

He nodded.

"I'll speak to you later."

"In the darkness. You'll see me only in the darkness," I whispered to myself, and watched him hurry along until he was gone.

Then I turned and, with my head down, walked back along the beach. The sound of a tern swooping down on an unsuspecting fish drew my attention back to the sea. I watched and then I took a deep breath. As I started to walk again, something caused me to look off to my left.

At first, there was nothing to see—small dunes, bushes, a cloud of sand flies circling madly over something on the sand—but then, as if he materialized out of the air itself, Linden's body took form behind a bush where he sat like Buddha staring out at the sea.

He made no effort to attract my attention, nor did he call out to me.

How long had he been there?

What had he heard?

My first thought was to call to him, to go to him, but I hesitated. Maybe it was better to pretend I didn't see him just now. Maybe it was better to pretend he was as invisible to me as I apparently was to him.

At least for now, I thought.

I turned and started back toward the beach house. There was no one on the loggia of the main house anymore, except for some servants cleaning up after the Eatons and their guests. They looked my way, but just as they were supposed to behave, they seemed to see no evil, hear no evil. Servants were taught to be invisible here.

Maybe we were all invisible here.

Daddy, I thought, *how I need you now. If you're inside me, I've got to find a way to touch you and hear your wisdom.*

There was nothing more fearful than the thought that he was drifting away with every passing hour, every passing minute. Maybe the truth was that the dead lose interest in the living and not, as everyone thought, the other way around. We stop visiting graveyards and looking at tombstones after a while, don't we? We put away our family albums. We forget the sounds of voices we once loved.

And then what?

If we don't find love, we find we're alone.

That's where Linden was.

And my mother.

And maybe me.

2

A Lien Against the Property

Later that morning I drove into Palm Beach proper to meet with Leo Ross, my mother's accountant. He had an office on Via Encantada in a pearl-white stucco building that looked more like a Spanish hacienda than a business structure. It glistened in the sunlight as if it were really covered in pearls.

The accounting offices themselves were plush with a rather large lobby that had a marble floor, cream marble tables, expensive-looking settees and chairs, and prints of some of the portrait paintings of famous Palm Beach residents done by Ralph Cowan. Whether the implication was that these people used Leo Ross's firm or merely that people of this stature used it, I didn't know, but it had an impressive effect.

From what I could see, there were nearly a half dozen CPAs working in the office, any one of whom could have been assigned to us, I imagine. However, perhaps because my attorney back in South Carolina, Mr.

Bassinger, had set all this up, Leo Ross himself came out to greet me. He was a man about five feet eight inches tall with thinning gray-blond hair. Very fair-skinned, he had patches of freckles over his forehead and along the crests of his cheeks. His eyes were the faded blue of stonewashed jeans and his lips were so orange, they looked tinted. I imagined him to be well into his early sixties.

He extended his soft, well-manicured, strawberry-twirl-skinned hand to me and held on to mine as he introduced himself and spoke highly of Mr. Bassinger.

"I had the occasion to call upon his services once on behalf of a client of mine," he explained. "Small world, wouldn't you say?"

His polished smile was highlighted by his ivory teeth. I had the funny idea that in a previous life, he must have been an ice cream cone, cool, refreshing, and full of cherry vanilla.

"Yes, yes, it is," I agreed.

He ushered me back through the wide corridor to his private office. It looked immaculate, almost untouched and unused. Fresh flowers adorned the coffee table in front of the soft leather settee and the right corner of his desk as well. In this office was hung a portrait of himself with his standard poodle. Awards and plaques from various charitable organizations were arranged in the shape of an X on the wall to the right of his large, black-marble-topped desk. A set of what looked like gold-plated golf clubs in a rich leather bag stood against one wall.

I saw immediately that the files for Joya del Mar were spread over the coffee table and a chair had been brought around for him to sit facing the settee and me while we discussed the situation.

"Please," he said, indicating the settee. "Would you

like something to drink? Bottled water, coffee, tea, juice, soda . . . whatever."

"Nothing, thank you."

He looked surprised and waited for me to sit before seating himself. For a moment he stared at me with a wide, almost incredulous grin that made me a bit uncomfortable.

"I was expecting Grace to accompany you," he said. "I was looking forward to seeing her. It's been some time."

"She's not up to it just yet," I said, hoping I wouldn't have to go into a long explanation about Linden's condition.

"I suppose not. She has had a very tough time, very tough time. Well then, I'll tell you what I know. I know that you have a trust that will generate a fixed amount of income, and you have asked Mr. Bassinger to arrange for me to help you organize that income so you can cover all the basic expenses of Joya del Mar. Your funds will cover that monthly nut, as we say," he continued, flashing his smile.

"Good," I said, releasing the air I had trapped inside me out of fear I would learn my plan was impossible and all I had promised would be another broken rainbow for my mother and Linden.

"However, I don't know if you have been made aware of a sizable lien against the property."

"A lien?"

Little jolts of electric fear surged under my breasts.

"A lien is a legal maneuver a creditor will make to force you to pay what you owe him. In this case, your grandmother's third husband, Kirby Scott, pledged the property against a line of credit at the bank, which he then defaulted upon."

"Oh. What does that mean exactly?" I asked. My experience with financial matters was very limited. In fact, in the weeks following my father's death, I had learned more than I knew my whole life.

"It means that your mother cannot sell the property without first paying off this debt, and something has to be paid toward it on a regular basis."

"How much are we talking about?" I asked, and held my breath.

He closed and opened his eyes, indicating that it was going to be a painful response.

"A quarter of a million dollars," he replied. "And then there is the accumulating interest, of course. It complicates matters."

"What did he do with this money?" I asked, wondering if there was a way to get it back.

"Your guess is as good as mine, I'm afraid. Most likely lost it in Las Vegas or Monte Carlo. I'm sorry to give you this news."

"Does my mother know?"

"I send her reports, but we've never discussed it."

"Can I afford to pay it off and still generate enough income to take care of our needs?"

He smiled. I guessed I was asking the right question.

"Well, not with the full army of servants now employed. You can hold on to the landscaper, but I'm afraid not all of the household servants, the chef, the chauffeur."

"I understand," I said.

"When the rental income stops, you will have to create a sensible budget, until Grace sells the property, that is. In the meantime, I have all your accounts arranged, generating as much interest income as we can without experiencing too much risk. I understand you're going to attend college soon."

"Yes."

He sat back, looking like a disapproving uncle now.

"It wouldn't have been a bad idea to hold on to the Eatons," he said after a moment. "I still might be able to negotiate something with them."

"No," I said firmly.

"It's a big property for just you, Grace, and Linden," he insisted. "I would not be fulfilling my obligation to you, as well as to Mr. Bassinger, if I did not point all this out to you as clearly as I can."

"It's just as big for the Eatons."

"Yes, but the rent is no burden for them, nor are the servants and the maintenance. We might be able to get them to come up on a purchase price offer."

"I'd rather the bank took it over," I said dryly.

He shrugged.

"If it went into foreclosure, the Eatons, or any of a few dozen other families, could pounce on it and get it for even less, especially if you are unable to keep it up and it degenerates in any way."

"Buzzards with gold beaks," I muttered, and his eyes widened, his lips stretching into an amused smile.

"Well, I've never heard them referred to in quite that manner, but . . ." He left the rest of his words hanging. Nothing was as well hidden as a thought unspoken.

I sat back on the settee and thought about all he had told me.

"You've been the accountant for the Montgomery family for some time now, haven't you?"

"Oh, yes. I was Winston Montgomery's accountant for years and years before he died. I attended his wedding to Jackie Lee Houston. One of the few business associates he invited," he added proudly.

"You must have known Kirby Scott personally, then."

He nodded.

"It isn't something I admit with any pride, however. I had to sit behind this desk and watch him chop—not chip—chop away Winston Montgomery's fortune. I tried warning Jackie Lee, but Kirby Scott had her hypnotized and she seemed incapable of taking the actions that would help her, protect her and her daughter, at least until Linden was born. By then it was too late, I'm afraid. There were a number of liens against Joya del Mar back then, and not just the bank's. Kirby Scott was a piece of work, a true old-fashioned scoundrel."

"How do you mean, old-fashioned?"

"Well, he was as handsome and debonair as any man I've known here in Palm Beach, a cultured con man, if you will. A snake charmer in a tuxedo. Jackie Lee Houston Montgomery was not the first woman to fall for his winning smile and his promises, and I'm sure not the last."

"I suppose that sort of gossip makes its way into these fine offices as well as the rest of Palm Beach," I said, fishing for more information.

"Well, maybe not into the offices as much as the local watering holes, which we all frequent from time to time. Have to keep up appearances you know," he quickly added. Gossip and innuendo were just as nasty in the world of the wealthy as anywhere else in America, or anyplace, for that matter, even if they were planted in a bed of diamonds and watered with champagne.

"Was there any other Palm Beach family Kirby Scott messed up?" I asked.

He studied me a moment, obviously deciding whether or not to spread a story.

"I'm sure there are other victims, as I said, but I don't know anything specific. I guess if you like that sort of gossip, you're in the right part of the country."

"Any part of the country," I countered, and he laughed. "Do you know where Kirby Scott is now?"

He shrugged.

"I've heard rumors. One of my clients claimed to have seen him at the George V in Paris last year with a woman so bedecked in furs hanging on his arm that my client thought she was a fur trader from Alaska—not to mention the diamonds she had strung around her neck, sparkling on her fingers, and dangling from her ears." He shook his head. "How that man manages to pluck a fresh fish with such consistency is truly amazing. If he had put his talents to legitimate use, why he might today be the CEO of a major corporation."

"Sounds like he is," I said. "The Kirby Corporation."

Mr. Ross laughed harder.

"Well, there were darn few here who didn't invite him to their house parties and events in those days. Why, he even socialized with the Eatons, as I recall. In fact, now that I think of it, I'm sure it was Kirby who put it into Asher and Bunny Eaton's minds to consider renting Joya del Mar from the Montgomerys. If you can say he had a pang of conscience, I suppose that was it."

"What do you mean?" I asked with bated breath. Did he know of Bunny Eaton's affair? Was that what he meant?

"Realizing he would soon bankrupt the Montgomerys, he at least instigated the rental of their property so they wouldn't be chased off. Sort of like someone who beat you up and robbed you and then arranged for your hospitalization."

"Sounds like we're giving him too much credit for a conscience," I said. "Maybe he was simply trying to ensure a flow of income to exploit."

"Maybe. Probably so." He nodded, thoughtful for a

moment, then snapped back to attention. "Well, here are the documents for you to peruse and sign," he said. He rose. "I just want to check on one thing and then I'll return to answer any questions you might have."

"Thank you," I said, and began reading.

When he came back, I had a few questions about some of the investments; then I thanked Mr. Ross and left. Before returning to Joya del Mar, I decided to do a little shopping and pick up some toiletries at Saks. I was also searching for what Amou used to call a piece of *luz do sol,* a piece of sunshine, some pretty thing that could bring joy and brightness into a gray day. My mother probably hadn't gone shopping for years and still relied on the clothing, jewelry, and accessories her mother had left her. Of course, she would claim she had no use for any of it. She went nowhere, but even Daddy, who had little use for so-called romantic ideas, used to say a woman is more like a garden than a man.

"She needs a new flower or pruning and tender loving care far more than a man. A new piece of jewelry, a bouquet of roses, a box of candy can make a woman's face blossom, and the glow from that can light up the day, not only for her, but for everyone around her," he told me.

My mother was so fond of shawls, I decided to get her a pashmina. After I had picked out the things I wanted, the salesgirl asked me for my address.

"So we can send you notifications of sales and new items," she explained.

I saw no reason not to give her my address, and did so. Two women shopping together were standing nearby; they both obviously turned an ear in my direction and, as soon as I gave Joya del Mar as the address, smiled at me and approached.

"I couldn't help but overhear your address," the taller

woman said. She wore a leather outfit with a fur-lined collar and had diamonds dripping from her earlobes. "Are you staying with the Eatons? We're good friends of Bunny's," she added quickly.

"No, I'm staying with my mother and my brother, Grace and Linden Montgomery," I replied, smiling.

They both pulled back as if I were breathing the plague.

"Oh," the taller woman said. "You're the long-lost daughter."

The shorter woman, clad in a gray skirt suit, stared at me with furious eyes. She had coal-black, curly hair and was stouter, almost without a waist.

"I happen to work for Mangle, Orseck, and Lapolt as a paralegal," she said through barely opened, thick lips, "and I can tell you it's not only foolish but pathetic and cruel for you to be encouraging that woman not to sell her property to the Eatons."

" 'That woman'? 'That woman,' as you call her, is my mother, if you don't mind. She has a name, and she has more intelligence and compassion in her pinky finger than the two of you have in your whole bodies," I countered.

They spun around like tops and marched away. When I turned back to the salesgirl, she was staring with a mouth so agape I could diagnose tonsillitis.

"Anything else you need?" I snapped, and she leaped to finish my sale.

My heart was still pounding when I exited the department store. How cruel people could be, I thought. How difficult life must have been for my mother all these years, and how easy it was now to understand why she had chosen to remain like a hermit. I walked along, past the quaint shops and galleries, then stopped when something caught the corner of my eye.

Through the window of a small café, I saw Thatcher

at a table sitting across from an attractive dark-haired
woman, elegantly dressed, wearing designer sunglasses.
At first I imagined her to be one of his clients, but he
had his hand over hers and was looking so intently at
her, they appeared more like two lovers. For a moment
the sight took my breath away and drained the blood
from my face. Then he turned slowly as he leaned back
in his seat and started to bring his cocktail to his lips.
His eyes shifted toward the window, through which I
was sure he saw me. He froze for a moment, then turned
back to the woman as if he had not seen me at all.

Now I had two men treating me as if I were invisible,
I thought, and pounded the sidewalk hard as I marched
to my car, threw the packages into it, and drove home.

As I had hoped, my mother's smile was like a sun-
burst when I gave her the present. However, almost as if
she realized she had violated some bargain she had
made with a guardian angel, she quickly hid her joy
and declared I was doing enough for them, too much as
it was.

"You don't have to buy me presents, too, Willow."

"I know. I don't do it because I have to, Mother."

She stared at the pashmina shawl covetously, torn between her admiration for it and her guilt in accepting it.

"You don't have to be afraid to be happy, Mother," I
said. It was like tossing a dart and hitting the bull's-eye.
She looked up at me quickly, her face revealing the accuracy of my analysis. I could almost feel the patter of
her quickened heart. Sometimes, it was painful to be
right, especially if it was a heartfelt secret someone
would rather keep under lock and key.

"Every time I permit myself to enjoy something,
Willow, I can't help but feel like a little girl blowing up

a festive balloon with such excitement and enthusiasm, she causes it to burst."

"You don't have to feel that way anymore. We can blow up all the balloons we want. In fact, we'll bury this place in balloons," I declared with a furious air.

She brought back her smile, then put on the shawl and gazed at herself in the mirror. Suddenly, her face returned to that dark, pained look.

"What's wrong? Don't you like it?" I asked.

"Oh, yes, Willow. Yes, of course. It's beautiful. It's just . . . it seems like a waste, like putting a new window in a jalopy, a run-down junk heap of a car. Look at my dull hair, these streaks of gray, these split ends, and my complexion. I'm so pale, so sickly-looking. And this ridiculous old rag I wear."

She thrust her hands at me.

"I have fingernails like a garage mechanic. See! I hate mirrors. That's why there are so few of them in this house. All they do is remind me of what I've become," she declared, and started to whip off the shawl. "Why tease and torment myself?"

"Then don't," I said sharply, and seized her hand, stopping her from completely removing the beautiful shawl. It dangled off her right shoulder. "Let this be the beginning of a renewal, Mother. Let this be magical," I urged, stroking the shawl.

Then, instead of a bulb bright with a new idea, a string of Christmas lights went on inside my head.

"I know what we'll do," I said firmly. "We'll both go to the beauty parlor this week. We'll have it all: facials, body wraps, mud packs, paraffin baths for our hands and feet, pedicures, manicures, everything, and we'll do something exciting with your hair, too."

She started to shake her head and back away as if the

idea were so forbidden and terrifying, it could bring a
hurricane of new disasters to her doorstep.

"Why not? It will be fun to spoil ourselves and be
Palm Beach royals."

She stepped farther back, continuing to shake her
head while her eyes betrayed a wish to agree.

"I couldn't . . . I just wouldn't know how to . . ."

"I'll be there with you. I need to do something with
my hair, and I haven't spoiled myself for some time
now. Look at me." I stepped before the mirror and
tugged on the strands of my hair. "It isn't just a whim. I
have to do something if I'm to become competitive with
the women here, right? You've got to help me," I said,
making it seem as if she were going to do it all for me.

The idea was beginning to become a possibility. Her
eyes softened with memories and excitement.

"I can't remember when I last did anything like that.
It was obviously before I went to the clinic, but after
your father and I . . ." She paused as though she had said
too much. "I mean, that was part of our therapy, to permit the volunteer beauticians to come to the clinic and
help us feel better about ourselves, but afterward, when
I came home, I just didn't have any reason to continue."

"Now you do," I said. "Soon, we'll all be moving
back into the hacienda again. There will be people visiting, dinners and teas. All the good things will come
flooding back to you, Mother."

"Will they? Do I dare hope for such a thing?" she
asked, almost rhetorically.

"Why not?" I countered angrily. "Why should people
like the Eatons be the only ones who dance with happiness here? What makes them more deserving than
you?"

"They didn't live in so much darkness," she said

sadly. "Darkness they inherited from their own family, darkness of their own making."

"How do you know that? Everyone, especially everyone here, if you ask me, has his or her own closet full of dreads, Mother," I said, recalling the things Thatcher had told me. "They might be richly dressed and well attended, but they have to stand before mirrors, too, and wipe off their makeup, and take off their jewelry and their wigs. Naked, they are full of their own wrinkles of sin, and they drink themselves to sleep or take their little pills or pay people to create a world of fantasy for them so they can ignore and forget. That's why they are so frightened of you."

"Frightened? Of me?" She started to laugh.

"Of course they are," I said sternly, and her smile ceased. "You're right in their faces with the truth, and that forces them to look at themselves. In their heart of hearts, they all know they are just as vulnerable as you were and they could just as easily shatter like so much of their precious Tiffany."

"I never thought of it that way, Willow."

"Well, now you will, and you'll get strong again and be as beautiful as you want to be, as you are," I insisted.

She studied me for a moment, then nodded.

"There is a lot of your father in you. He used to tell me what I would do and what I would overcome with just as much confidence and even with just as much anger running beneath his words. He hated my illness more than I did, and made me think of it as something outside of me, something I could attack and defeat."

"Then don't stop now," I said.

"Okay." She smiled. "Okay, Willow De Beers, daughter of the doctor, I won't stop."

We both laughed.

"Do you have any preference in beauty salons?" I asked.

"I wouldn't even know where to begin."

"All right. I'll do my own research and make our appointments," I promised.

I left her turning back to the mirror, putting the shawl neatly on again and doing what every woman has done since the beginning of time: envisioning herself more beautiful. I felt like a Wiccan, a good witch who had truly brought her some magic woven in silk.

However, my powers weren't to be as great when it came to Linden.

I found him sitting by the window in the room he had used as his studio. I almost passed him by because he was as still as a storefront mannequin. He was staring out at the beach and the sea. He had left the door open. I gazed around the studio. Unfinished works were covered with cloth, and those that had been finished were piled against each other on the floor and against the wall. His paints and brushes were locked away. On an easel in the far right corner was a canvas covered with a sheet, standing like an obedient servant, waiting for orders that weren't coming.

I knocked on the door. It was time to confront him, I thought, to force him to see me, to hear me, but to do it as gently as I could.

"Hi, Linden," I said. "Do you mind if I come in?"

He didn't turn from the window.

"So this is where you do some of your work. It's a nice room, but you'll have a bigger and better place for all this soon, Linden, a real studio again."

I saw his shoulders lift, deepening the crease in the back of his neck for a moment. I ventured farther into the room until I was nearly beside him.

"It's really a very nice day, not too hot or humid, with

a beautiful breeze. You should go out, go fishing for that inspiration you talked about," I reminded him.

It was an analogy he had made when I had first arrived and he was eager to tell me about himself. He said he was like a fisherman cashing his creative line and waiting for some vision, some inspiration to take hold and be pulled into his mind.

He turned slowly toward me, so slowly it actually started my heart pounding.

"I can't go out there while they're whispering," he said, and turned back to the window.

"What? What did you say, Linden?" I stepped up so he would have to look at me. "Who's whispering? Who are you talking about?"

I actually gazed out the window myself, searching the beach for signs of someone. There was no one.

"There's no one out there, Linden," I said. "No one is whispering." I thought he must be speaking about the Eatons. "And anyway, they have no right to whisper about you or anyone else."

"Yes," he said. "Yes, they do."

I pulled a stool closer and sat. At least I had him talking to me, I thought, even if it didn't make much sense yet. He held his gaze fixed on something he was certain he saw on that deserted beach.

"What are they whispering then, Linden? What do they say that bothers you?"

"They are angry," he replied. "They are angry with me."

"Why?" I asked. He was silent. "Why, Linden? Why would they be angry at you? What right do any of them have to be angry with you?"

He turned again, slowly, his eyes dark and tired, looking at me but giving me the feeling he was not seeing me. It was almost like someone talking to a ghost or a shadow.

"Because I put them in my paintings," he said. "They never wanted to be seen. They never wanted anyone to know they were there."

I realized immediately that he didn't mean the Eatons or anyone alive, for that matter. It was chilling.

"That's silly, Linden. They would be happy you put them in your pictures. Your paintings are wonderful and very interesting. You have them in galleries, don't you?"

His eyes widened and he reached out and seized my hand, squeezing hard enough to make me wince.

"The galleries. I forgot that. We've got to get them back. You must help me do that!"

"Why?"

"We've got to get them back," he repeated with more insistence. "They will never stop until all the paintings are back."

I could see from the way the veins in his temples bulged and the muscles in his neck strained that he was very disturbed about it. He held on to me. .

"Okay, Linden. Okay. If that's what you want, that's what we will do."

"Promise," he demanded. "Promise."

"I promise. We'll do it together tomorrow, okay?"

"Yes," he said, relaxing his hold on me and lowering his shoulders. "Yes, tomorrow. We'll do it tomorrow. Tomorrow," he repeated, gazing out the window as though telling that to the spirits he saw.

How bizarre, how twisted and bizarre for him to think he had violated some trust by painting the images of what he envisioned when he was on the beach. Poor Linden, I thought. How would he ever be reimbursed for all that shadowed his eyes and darkened his heart? His injury and the aftermath had left him still falling through one tunnel of nightmares after another.

Maybe by tomorrow he would forget this whole horrible idea. Perhaps after a night's sleep and the start of a new day, it would be gone, whisked away like so many cobwebs. I watched him for a while. He barely blinked, but his lips moved ever so slightly, just like someone listening to voices and repeating what they told him.

"Would you like something to eat or drink, Linden?" I asked.

He didn't respond, not even to shake his head.

"If you want anything, please tell me. Come out as soon as you are able and I'll be happy to take a walk with you, if you like, okay?"

There was no visible sign that he heard me anymore.

I rose slowly, put the stool back, and watched him for a moment more before starting toward the door. I paused at the sight of the pictures piled against each other on the floor, all with their backs toward me. Something caught my eye, a seam in the top one. I looked back at him, and then I knelt and lifted the first picture from the pile.

The sight made me gasp.

It had been slashed in an X. So had the next, and the next, and the next. In fact, they were all slashed!

I stood up quickly and took the sheet off the one on the easel. It had been slashed even more viciously. I knelt and leafed through another pile of pictures stacked against the wall. They were in the same horrible condition.

"Oh, Linden, why? Why did you do this? All your work," I moaned.

He turned and looked at me on my knees, the ruined pictures in my hands.

"Why did you do this, Linden?"

"To stop the whispering in here," he said in a tone of voice that as good as called me stupid.

Then he turned back to the window.

"To stop the whispering," he chanted.

I stood up slowly, weighed down by the sight of the destruction. Then I went out to tell my mother, my own shoulders heavy with the burden of such news, and this, after I had just put some light back into her eyes.

She rushed into Linden's studio to see what I had painfully described, then burst into a torrent of tears. Linden looked her way, rose, and shuffled out while I held her.

"Linden," she called after him. He went to his bedroom and closed the door. "What are we going to do?" she wailed. "Thatcher was right. He should be in a clinic. Who knows what he will slash up next?"

"No, no, Thatcher's not right, Mother. I'm here now. We'll help him. We don't have to send him away," I insisted.

"But . . . he might need more than simply tender loving care, Willow. He might need medication and more vigorous therapy," she said.

"Perhaps so," I admitted, "but let's give him some more time. Once we're back in the main house and he sees the dramatic changes, he might have a better reaction, don't you think? It could revive him."

"I don't know," she said, sniffing back her tears and grinding her eyes dry. "Nothing seems certain in my world except that when I think things have gotten as bad as they can, they always seem to get worse."

I was about to reassure her when the phone rang. She sucked in her breath and answered it, then called for me.

I thought it might be Mr. Bassinger or Mr. Ross, but it was Thatcher.

"How are you doing?" he asked.

"Fine."

"I need only hear one word from your mouth to know you're angry," he said. "I'm sorry I didn't acknowledge you earlier today."

"Uh-huh."

"The woman I was with is a client. She's starting a very nasty divorce. I was in the midst of calming her down when you suddenly appeared in the window. It was such a surprise that for a moment, I actually thought you were a vision, some working of my imagination. In the middle of such domestic misery, you looked angelic to me."

"You could have at least nodded," I said.

"Get this straight, Willow, I can't just nod at you and then turn away as if you were just another person, another face, another name in my life. I'd rather not see you at all than suffer like that."

"Thatcher Eaton, you should be writing for *Hearts Entwined* or some other soap opera rather than writing those boring legal briefs," I quipped, which brought a laugh.

"You're right. You bring out the romantic in me. What can I say? It takes a good woman to make a man good."

"I'll remind you of that."

"Forever, I hope. Can I see you tonight?"

"I don't know. Can you?"

"You know what I mean, Willow. Will you meet me someplace, say about seven? I know where we can have an intimate dinner, and then later . . ."

"Yes, later?"

"I have the keys to a friend's beach house. He's in Europe at the moment. Actually, for a whole month or so. It can be our secret rendezvous. I'll have a key made for you. We'll set up our private world there and it will be like we've stepped out of this insanity, stepped onto a cloud or something," he continued, weaving the dream with the thread of his golden words.

"Sounds like we're a pair of spies or fugitives."

"Just a pair of lovers," he replied. "Well?"

"All right. A part of me says no, but . . ."

"Your heart says yes?"

"No, it says maybe," I said, refusing to be a complete prisoner of the dream.

He laughed.

"I'll fix that with candlelight, music, your favorite pasta, and wine. The restaurant is called Diana's. It's a very inconspicuous, unpretentious little family restaurant just north of Palm Beach Gardens. You can't miss it. It will be on your right with a simple neon sign above the door. The beach house is only fifteen minutes away. I'll meet you at seven."

"Okay," I said, unable to put up the slightest resistance now.

"How are things there?"

"Not good, Thatcher. Linden is not well at all. I'm worried for him and for my mother."

"He belongs under a doctor's care, Willow. Waiting is merely postponing the inevitable."

"That's something we all do," I muttered.

"Yes, perhaps, but it's far more costly and even dangerous for someone like Linden. I can help, if you want."

"We'll see," I said. I was still under the illusion of being able to change things dramatically myself.

"Let's not think about any of that tonight," he urged. "We've got some catching up to do, right? Right?"

"Right," I forced myself to say.

"Until then," he said, and hung up.

I found my mother on the loggia, sitting in her chair and staring at the sea. I sat beside her, both of us quiet.

"You and Thatcher," she began after another long moment of silence, "will see each other?"

"Sort of," I said. She turned, confused. "Inconspicuously, for a while. There are some new complications. His parents, of course. He wants us to be low-key for a while. Secret rendezvous, that sort of thing."

"Oh?"

"It might just be nothing," I said, already regretting saying as much as I had. Putting any more weight on her shoulders now would be disastrous, I thought. "I'll give it a little time and see."

"I hope it does work out for you, Willow. I hope your coming here wasn't a monumental mistake in your life, that my bad luck, my dark destiny doesn't infect you like some flu or bad disease."

"Oh, Mother, no. Don't talk that way."

"My mother, Grandmother Jackie Lee Houston, used to tell me everything is part of some grand plan, everything is meant to be, and in the end we can do little to change it. I guess it was her way of accepting some of the harder and sadder events in her life, and I guess she anticipated I would experience similar things and need the same philosophy to get through. But why, I wonder from time to time, do we bother to get through? Through to where, to what?"

"To something better," I declared.

"Yes. To something better. A sailor's dream," she said, looking out at the horizon. "He would have come one day, you know. He would have come to fetch me and take me away from all this, your father."

"Yes, I believe it, too, Mother."

She smiled.

"At least, in his way he did come. He sent you."

"Exactly," I said, grateful for a little light in her eyes, a little warmth in her smile.

"For some of us, it's almost sinful to hope," she said.

I took her hand quickly.

"Then let's go to hell together, Mother," I countered.

Her smile widened into a thin laugh.

"Come on," I said, tugging on her to rise. "Let's look at some magazines and think about a new hairstyle for you. We'll make appointments tomorrow."

"That soon?"

"Why wait any longer to start again?" I asked. "Hesitation just makes it all seem so serious."

"It is serious. For me," she whispered.

As if she were made of air, she rose at the end of my hand and let me lead her along like a balloon on a string, just as light, but just as fragile and just as vulnerable to a strong, stormy wind.

3

New Beginnings

Thatcher couldn't have chosen a more inconspicuous restaurant. I passed it twice, turned around, and practically crawled along the highway until I spotted it. The neon sign he'd described was so small, you really had to start down the driveway of the restaurant before fully seeing it, and the restaurant itself looked like someone's home, with a short walkway and steps leading to a small entry porch. The wooden cladding, stained by years of sea air, was a marine gray, reminiscent of a ship's hull. I recognized Thatcher's Rolls-Royce parked off to the right, sufficiently in the dark to go unnoticed by disinterested eyes.

I parked in a lot that contained a half dozen other vehicles and walked to the entrance. There was a short foyer with a dark oak desk on my right. The lighting was subdued, only a small lamp on the desk and a dull fixture above dripping just enough pale yellow glow to reveal a coatrack and a poster-sized map of Italy. I could hear some chatter coming from the room off to my left, but before I took another step, a short gray-haired lady in a black dress with a cameo on her bodice stepped in from the room on the right and went around the desk. She had a round face with Santa Claus–red cheeks and eyes the color of black pearls.

"Buona sera," she said, "and welcome to Diana's. Did you have a reservation?"

"I'm meeting someone who might have made a reservation," I said. "Mr. Eaton?"

"Oh, yes, of course. He's already here. Please," she said, indicating I should follow her.

We went to the right, but I glanced into the room on my left and saw a half dozen tables, all occupied. The recognizable voices of the famous three tenors— Carreras, Domingo, and Pavarotti—came over the sound system, but the volume was kept just low enough to serve as background and not overpower the conversations.

The room to the right was smaller, with only three tables. The one at which Thatcher waited was off to the left in the corner, screened by privacy walls on both open sides. He stood up quickly. A bottle of chilled champagne was beside the table and a bottle of red wine at the center, next to a basket of small rolls.

"Thank you, Mamma Diana," Thatcher said, and extended his hand to me. "Willow," he mouthed, kissed me quickly, and pulled out my chair.

"Buon appetito," Mamma Diana wished us.

"Grazie, ma con il suo cibo, non c'è problema con l'appetito," Thatcher said, and she laughed as she moved away.

"What did you say?"

"I thanked her and told her that with her food, there is no problem with appetite."

"I didn't know you could speak fluent Italian."

"Così, così, abbastanza d'arrangiarmi. So-so, enough to get by," he replied, and sat.

"You can get by quite a bit with that," I quipped, and he laughed.

Then he reached across the table to hold my hand.

"I missed you so much, Willow. Those days we had, the picnic on the boat, those nights, were so special, the memory of them was enough to sustain me until you returned. I thought we'd have a champagne toast to celebrate your coming back, back to me."

I tilted my head.

"Maybe you really are Kirby Scott's son, Thatcher."

His smile wilted.

"I mean what I say, Willow. Kirby Scott came here and used words like a magician uses the turns of his hand to distract and confuse and betray," he said sternly. "That's not my intent or purpose."

He looked indignant, hurt, and insulted. *Maybe I was being too harsh,* I thought.

"In a strangely ironic twist of fate, if what you have been told is true, you and Linden could very well share a similar anger at the world and fate," I suggested.

He considered the idea for a moment and calmed.

"Yes, perhaps so. I never think of things from his point of view exactly. I guess I should."

I quickly told him about my conversation with Leo Ross and his references to Kirby Scott, especially his belief that Kirby had introduced Thatcher's parents to the idea of renting my mother's property.

"I don't know. I can't recall any mention of him in that regard, but it might be true. I'll have to ask my father and mother. However, I think I would agree with you that if it is true, he had other than altruistic motives. What a piece of work he was."

"You realize that from what you've been told, you might be talking about the man who is your father, Thatcher."

He smirked and shook his head.

"If my legal experiences have taught me anything these last few years, Willow, it's that it takes more than blood to bond people. I've represented fathers against sons, sons against fathers, brothers and sisters against each other, everything. I hate to think I might share anything with such a person, even a single corpuscle."

"What are you going to do? How are you going to get to the truth, Thatcher? You can't live in limbo with this, and we can't let it hover over our heads like ominous storm clouds forever."

"I know. I know," he said, squeezing his forehead with his thumb and forefinger as though it all gave him a constant headache. I did feel sorry for him.

"Are you going to have a blood test or something like that?" I asked.

"I'd have to tell my father everything. How can I do that?" he practically cried. "How can I be the one to tell him that my mother was once unfaithful? Even if it was only once," he muttered as far under his breath as he could, realizing that the couple at the nearest table had turned our way.

He looked desperate, distraught, defeated.

"I feel like I'm boxed in, and that is not something I have experienced much in my life."

"I'm sure you'll find a way to make sense out of it all, Thatcher," I assured him, and put my hand out to touch his.

Here I was again, finding myself in the role of cheerleader, with all my heavy baggage to carry. Daddy once told me it was sometimes a blessing to have other people's problems on your mind—it kept you from fretting too much about your own. Solving someone else's difficulties often brings more pleasure than solving your own. Still, I felt a little bit like the patient telling the doctor he would be fine. Thatcher was the man of action here, the person with all the resources at his beck and call. Who was I to advise him or predict anything?

He leaned toward me to whisper.

"I'm tracking him down," he revealed.

"You are?"

"Yes. The day of reckoning will come soon," he promised, his eyes sharp with fury.

"How can you ever be sure that such a man will utter a single syllable of truth when you confront him?"

"I've had some pretty tough witnesses to cross-examine in court, Willow. I'll get the truth," he bragged.

I stared at him, admiring his self-confidence. A successful person had to have a little more confidence than other people, a little more ego, too, perhaps. When would I have it? Would I ever?

"But let's drop all this. I should have insisted we pretend we've just met or something, or we check our troubles at the door the way cowboys had to check their guns. This is a special night, a reunion, a renewal and new beginning for us, Willow," he said, reaching for my hand again. Then he poured us both a glass of champagne. "Let's start with the toast. To us," he said. "To our health and success and love. Let them rise above everything and everyone."

We tapped our glasses and sipped, fixing our eyes on each other over the tops of the glasses.

"These garlic rolls are homemade," he said, offering me one. "Wait until you taste the food here. It's like being in someone's home and not a restaurant."

"That's what it looks like from the highway. It's certainly a good hideaway. Why do I have the suspicion you've used it before?" I teased.

"I will bring you to special places only, and after you and I are there together, they will become off-limits to me unless you are with me. I couldn't imagine ever having a business meeting here again," he said.

"I wasn't speaking of those."

He laughed.

"You make me sound like a Palm Springs walker, like some international gigolo hovering around wealthy available women whether it be in Paris, on the Côte d'Azur, or on Rodeo Drive."

"You speak French, Italian, Spanish. You know wines, and you've traveled all over the world. You're like someone trained to escort sophisticated women, Thatcher. It would be a waste to have you sitting at home. I can't imagine you ever becoming a couch potato."

He laughed.

"Well, from now on, you're the only woman I've been trained to escort, Willow De Beers."

We tapped glasses again and sipped our champagne. He poured us each some more. Then the music became a little louder and we ordered our food and nearly finished the bottle of champagne before starting on a bottle of wine. Thatcher was right about it all. The food was delicious, and very soon I felt as if we were in some private place. The rest of the world drifted away. The music was just for us.

Afterward, he talked me into leaving my car in the restaurant's parking lot and going with him to his friend's beach house.

"I don't want you picked up for DUI. I would have to

defend you, and the judge would quickly see I have a personal interest in my client," he told me.

We kissed in his car and held each other closely before we drove off. I felt like someone being swept away, but I was allowing it to happen. I was caught in the wind of our passion. Resistance was futile. I hadn't realized how much I wanted to surrender to its power, but I did, I certainly did.

The beach house seemed closer than he had described. I closed my eyes and sat back, and in what seemed to be only a few minutes, we were turning down a gravel and dirt road and pulling up to a beautiful home with a large screened-in pool. The house itself was only a few hundred yards from the beach. It was done in a very modern decor and looked almost brand-new.

"Was it just built?" I asked, and Thatcher laughed.

"No, but like many of my clients, he has more money than he can use and would be better off staying in one of the finer hotels than actually owning a property he gets to live in only about two or three weeks a year. Some people collect houses the way people used to collect stamps."

"You mean some people you know, not people I know," I said, and continued my tour of the place. There was a large living room with a big-screen television set, and two bedrooms, one with a patio overlooking the water.

"Not too shabby, huh?" Thatcher said, coming up behind me and kissing the back of my neck.

As if his lips were magnets, I felt myself leaning back into him, holding on to the warmth of his kiss. He held me at the elbows and for a while we stayed just like that, planted against each other, listening to the surf and staring out at the starlight dancing on the water.

Special moments like this were as rare as precious jewels, I thought. So much of our lives were spent on one level, coping, attending to the mundane, the ordinary details and chores. Days, weeks, even months could pass before something so wonderful and true, something so memorable and unique would happen to us. Some memories did sparkle like diamonds in the darkness, restoring our hopes and dreams, but mostly telling us we were capable of love and being loved.

I turned and we kissed.

Passion rose in waves mimicking the sea, undulating up my legs, climbing with every touch, with every breath we took. He swept his arm under me and scooped me up, gently placing me on the bed. He gazed down at me so intently, my heart began to pound like a Caribbean steel drum. I reached up for him and he knelt beside the bed and slowly began to undress me, first removing my shoes, then unzipping the back of my dress and peeling it away. He took off my panty hose, then undid my bra and lowered my panties. Bare naked and spread before him, I felt my heart skip beats, my breathing grow so fast and furious I had to close my eyes to keep the room from spinning.

I expected him to be beside me in moments, naked and loving, but when I opened my eyes, he was still gazing down at me and he was still dressed.

"Thatcher," I moaned. "What are you doing?"

"I want to capture the vision of you forever and ever, just like this, delicious, waiting."

"That's unfair," I complained, and he laughed.

To continue the exquisite torment, he brought his lips to mine, but kept his hands away. I could feel every part of me tingling with anticipation, crying out for his touch, his lips, but he held back, restrained, controlled, prolonging the preamble to our lovemaking until I could bear it no longer and cried out with desperation.

He laughed, then brought his lips to my breasts and

followed down my body until he had me demanding him. He undressed as quickly as he could and crawled beside me.

"We're safe," I said. "I'm on the pill."

"Oh," he teased. "And how did you know we would be doing this?"

"I knew. Besides, a girl has to be prepared for a thunderbolt of love."

"I hope not with just anyone," he said.

"You know not with just anyone. You do, don't you?" I asked when he didn't respond quickly enough.

"Yes," he said, after teasing me again with that moment of pretended doubt. "I know who you are, and I love you for that."

This kiss was longer. We kept our lips pressed against each other's as he moved to put himself in me.

"Scream all you want," he told me when I muffled a cry of ecstasy. "No one can hear us but the seagulls, and they couldn't care less."

I did scream and cry and hold him until we were both panting with wonderful exhaustion, lying side by side, not speaking but saying volumes with our breath, our trembling bodies, and our entwined fingers. Outside, the sea continued to play its lullaby. I actually closed my eyes and drifted off with its soft, rhythmic murmur echoing in my ears.

When I opened my eyes again, Thatcher was up and getting dressed.

"What's happening?" I asked. "Did I fall asleep?"

"For a little while. I didn't want to disturb you, but we've got to get you back to your car. Are you all right?" he asked.

I felt like someone emerging from a dream.

"What? Oh, yes, right," I said, and began to fumble for my clothing.

"I just want to check out a few things in the house. I'll be in the living room," he said, and left me.

I was tired, but it was a pleasant sort of fatigue. It actually made me feel a little silly, and I couldn't help giggling when I gazed at myself in the mirror. Whoever owned the house had a collection of elaborate Mardi Gras masks displayed on a wall. I took one off its hook and put it on before I left the bedroom to search for Thatcher.

I could hear him speaking very low on the telephone.

"I'll be there," I heard him say. "Stop worrying about it."

I stepped into the doorway of the kitchen. He had his back to me.

"Of course I care about you," he said. "What a stupid question. I've got to go. Later. We'll talk about it later." He cradled the receiver, standing there and looking at it as if he had an afterthought he wanted to see if he could still include.

When he turned, he jumped. For a moment, I had forgotten I was wearing the mask.

"Very funny," he said.

I removed the mask.

"Who were you calling so late?" I asked in a much more demanding tone of voice than he obviously expected. It even surprised me, but I felt I had a significant enough investment in him and us to do so.

For a moment I thought he wasn't going to reply. Then he smirked.

"Who do you think would be up this late? My mother, of course."

"Oh. You sounded like you were arguing," I said.

"She does that to me often, turn me into a tight ball of nerves until I want to smash the phone against the wall."

He took a deep breath.

"Is it about us?" I asked.

"No, no. My sister is having a rather elaborate birthday party for my niece tomorrow night, and Mother dear is afraid I won't show up. Every birthday party is bigger than the previous one, both in size and expense. I don't know what they'll do for her sixteenth. Probably rent the White House," he said. "People here often compete using their children and what they do for them, and my mother knows I'm not terribly fond of being a part of all that. Anyway, why are you making me talk about it?"

"I'm not making you, Thatcher. I just asked because you sounded upset."

"Willow, when I'm with you, I don't remain upset about anything very long," he said, moving toward me. "Even if you wear the mask."

I laughed, and we kissed.

"Come on," he said. "We'd better get going. Maybe we can manage to spend a whole weekend here together soon," he added, gazing around. "What do you think?"

"Maybe," I said, without sounding too optimistic.

He studied my face for a moment, and nodded.

"Okay, tell me about Linden," he commanded as we headed out. "What did he do now?"

I described Linden and what I had discovered he had done to his paintings. Thatcher listened intently, his face grim. We got into his car. He sat there for a moment in silence and didn't start the car.

"Thatcher?"

"I don't like the sound of it, Willow. Art has been his

whole life. For him to turn his back on that has to be something very serious. I'm not the psychiatrist here, but to me it sounds like another attempted suicide. He's simply destroying himself in another way. Not only are you possibly endangering your mother and yourself, but you're certainly risking Linden's health and welfare by not committing him.

"I don't like to lecture anyone," he said. "I hate when anyone lectures me, but it seems to me this is just the wrong time for Grace and you to be taking on all the added responsibility of running Joya del Mar. Let my parents extend their lease for another year and get that off your head for now."

I thought for a moment. Maybe he was right; maybe I was pushing everyone too hard and this was all my fault. Maybe my mother didn't even want to go back into the main house.

"You don't even have to live on the grounds, if you don't want to," Thatcher continued as he started the engine and pulled away from the beach house. "I can help you find a place more suited to your needs and finances. It could do Grace a lot of good to have a fresh view of things, don't you think?"

"I don't know, Thatcher."

"That's just it," he pounced. "You don't know, but you're still taking all this action. It might not be too late for me to fix things for you. Should I?"

I was silent. All my life so far, I had always had someone else—my adoptive mother, Amou, Daddy—decide the bigger things for me. Even my old college boyfriend, Allan Simpson, tried to run my life and was angry when I disagreed with him. Taking advice and being a good listener was one thing, but making up my mind for myself in the end was another.

"No," I finally said, recalling the brightness in my mother's eyes today when we talked about going to the beauty salon together and getting back into the main house. "I think we'll be all right."

"You're making a mistake, Willow. Maybe you're taking on too much responsibility here."

"I don't think so," I said with more confidence. "I'm no longer an outsider, Thatcher. This is my family now and I've got to be a big part of what happens and what doesn't. No," I continued, convinced, "we're going ahead with everything, and I will spend more time with Linden. I always felt somewhat responsible for what he did to himself."

"That's ridiculous."

"No. It's not. I shouldn't have pretended to be someone I wasn't. He was very vulnerable and he trusted me. It was a form of betrayal that hurt him deeply. I have to make up for that, and sending him off to have someone else try to mend my fences is not my style."

Thatcher smiled.

"You might become a very successful psychologist or psychiatrist yet, Willow. I wish I had gotten to meet your father. I have a feeling I was just introduced anyway," he said. "Through you."

"I hope so," I said.

He reached over to pull me closer to him and kiss my cheek.

"Whatever you decide, I'll be there beside you."

"When?" I pursued with some aggression.

He laughed.

"Very soon. I promise. My problems will be over very soon."

Both of us hung on the silence that served as a period to his statement until the restaurant came back into view.

He waited for me to get into my car and drive off, promising to call me sometime during the afternoon the next day.

I found my mother hunched over a cup of tea in the kitchen when I returned. She was in her robe and her hair was down around her shoulders.

"What's wrong?" I immediately asked.

"Nothing, Willow. I just couldn't sleep, so I made myself a cup of herbal tea. How was your evening?"

I plopped in the chair across from her.

"Everything about it was wonderful, Mother. It was as romantic a dinner as could be. We had another special time together, but doing it all in a world of shadows, hiding, worrying about everyone who sees us, takes the glitter out of the stars, if you know what I mean."

"I think I do," she said with a very wide and deep smile. "I think I have a little understanding about what you are experiencing."

"Oh. Of course you do," I said. "How selfish of me to think of myself as the only one here who's been involved in a secret romance. You, of all people, know exactly what I mean. How did you and Daddy keep it so special, worrying about every look, every sound in that clinic?"

"I wouldn't say we had a routine, but we did have the benefit of cloaking everything with our clinical relationship. A patient fixating on her doctor is not unusual, don't forget; so that was easy to excuse, and your father . . ."

"What?"

She smiled at the memory.

"Your father could be 'the doctor' at the blink of an eye. The tone of his voice deepened. His eyes became those penetrating, perceptive orbs resembling two small X-ray lights. His posture firmed and straightened into his formal demeanor. Why, the very air around him changed."

I smiled, remembering.

"Yes, that was Daddy."

"As you know, there was only that nurse who had once come here, that Nadine Gordon who tried to blackmail us. She was the only one who knew or suspected anything. If anyone else did, he or she kept it under lock and key."

"I'm not as good as my father when it comes to hiding my true feelings," I said. "And the difference is, I don't respect the reasons to hide them. I can tell you this—I won't be doing it very long. Either Thatcher gets up the courage to face his parents, or . . ."

"He will," she assured me with a pat on my hand. "That's one very capable young man. I would trust his judgment."

"Maybe," I said. I skipped a beat and then added, "He wants us to have Linden committed immediately. I told him what happened, and he thinks we're playing with fire."

"I know," she said. "It's been on my mind ever since I saw what he has done."

"How was he after I left tonight?"

"The same. He ate a little better, but he was just as distant. What I found him doing on and off was going into my room and looking at the painting he had done of you."

"Oh, no, he wasn't going to tear it up, too, was he?"

"I don't think so. He seemed more intrigued by this particular work than anything else he has done. It was as if he thought there was some answer sleeping in it, something he could nudge awake that would solve his problems."

"Maybe there is," I said. "Did you ask him about it?"

"I kept asking him if he was all right. Most of the time he didn't answer, but sometimes he nodded, and once he said, 'Soon.' That frightened me a bit. You know, what did he mean by 'soon'?"

"I've decided to spend as much time with him as I can," I told her. "But let's agree about one thing, Mother. If he doesn't show any sign of improvement in the next few days or weeks, we'll get him into treatment."

She nodded and sighed deeply.

"But let's be optimistic," I insisted with a smile. "When he sees us, sees you changing, looking bright and hopeful, it will have a significant effect on him. You'll see."

"I hope so," she said in a small voice, so thin and fragile it brought tears to my eyes. "I don't know if we should leave him alone here while we're at the beauty salon."

"We'll see in the morning. He had been talking about my going with him to the gallery to retrieve his works. Maybe he'll forget about that."

"I suppose we can have Jennings keep an eye on him. He's the nicest of the Eatons' servants and he has done favors for me before."

"Good. Let's get some sleep," I suggested, and she nodded, rose, and put her cup in the sink.

Afterward, when I laid my head on my pillow, I listened to the sounds in the grand beach house, the creaks and groans in the building, the sea wind on the windows with a sound like fingers running back and forth over the panes. What a kaleidoscope of emotions ran through the myriad of dreams being dreamed in this building tonight, I thought. Everyone had his or her secrets unraveling and raveling like multicolored balls of yarn being tossed through the darkness above and around me.

Was there a place in the night where dreams crisscrossed, where people glanced into each other's minds and saw the fear or the sadness or the happiness for an instant, like passengers on trains passing in the dark?

And did that make us sympathetic or envious? Did we long for someone else's dreams, or were we grateful we didn't have those nightmares?

Somewhere surely there was a common place, a well from which we all, rich or poor, drew some strength, for when we all slept we were truly alone. And who was more alone than the three of us now, circling like small planets searching for a star we could call home?

When I closed my eyes, I thought I heard Linden's mysterious voices whispering outside my window. Were they asking me to stay or to leave?

The morning light waited behind darkness like a panther anxious to leap upon the shadows lingering in the corners of our minds. I was grateful for that, grateful for the new day. My hope now was that I could get Linden to feel the same about it all.

The next morning, my first attempts to find a beauty salon for my mother and me were dismal failures. One receptionist actually broke into laughter when I asked if there were any openings that day.

"We're booked for the next two and a half months," she said. "This is *Palm* Beach, not Miami Beach."

I thought about calling Thatcher, but decided that his receptionist or his secretary might make something out of it, despite their ethical responsibility to maintain confidentiality. Perhaps nowhere more than in Palm Beach was the old adage so true: Two can keep a secret if one is dead. I decided instead to call Mr. Ross. He had offered to be of any assistance to me, and I didn't think our need to get appointments with a decent beauty salon would be too insignificant to a man like him.

"I'll take care of it immediately," he said as soon as I told him what I needed. "One of my clients is Renardo de Palma. His salon is very prestigious and his client list is a veritable who's who of Palm Beach."

"We're not trying to impress anyone but ourselves," I told him, and he laughed.

"I don't know a woman here who would admit otherwise," he joked. "Let me see what I can manage."

Less than twenty minutes later, he called back to tell me we had appointments at two.

"It's like the best restaurants," he revealed. "They always hold an opening for a favor, and believe me, Renardo owes me a few."

"Now so do I," I said.

"It's my pleasure. Let me know what else I can do for you, Willow," he offered.

I couldn't wait to tell my mother, who, now that she realized it wasn't just our dreaming aloud to each other, really became quite nervous. I had to reassure her that we would be fine and I wouldn't leave her side for an instant. While I was doing so, Linden suddenly appeared in the doorway. He was dressed and had his hair brushed neatly.

"Linden, dear," Mother cried, "how are you?"

"Hungry," he declared.

I wondered if he had heard our talk about going to the beauty parlor and would then recall asking me to retrieve his paintings from the gallery.

"Good morning," I said, and he turned to me and nodded. His eyes looked clearer. His face had more color and he seemed more rested.

"I'm sorry I slept so late," he said. "I have been very confused and distracted and haven't been very hospitable.

I didn't even realize when you returned. Grace caught me up on everything that's happened. I feel so foolish."

For a moment I couldn't speak. It was as if a completely different Linden Montgomery had stepped out of that bedroom. He even stood straighter. Anyone who saw him now and heard me tell what he had been like before would surely accuse me of gross exaggeration.

"No," I said. "I understand how hard it has been for you, Linden."

He shrugged.

"I don't know why exactly, but I feel like some great weight has been lifted from my shoulders. So, Grace tells me you have enrolled in school here," he said, pouring himself a cup of coffee, then bringing it to the table and sitting across from me.

"Yes. I have found a program in a nearby college that will enable me to pursue my career."

"That's terrific. I know Grace is very pleased," he said, smiling at her.

She, too, stared with eyes wide with disbelief, but eyes full of happiness, as well. If anything was unusual now, it was Linden's apparent obliviousness to our reactions.

"Would you like some eggs today, Linden?" she asked him.

"I think so, Mother. That omelette you do with a little cheese. I don't know why, but I woke up absolutely famished today."

He smiled at me.

"So," he continued, "Grace tells me you two are thinking of going to a beauty parlor today."

"Yes, we have afternoon appointments. I'll be back to pick her up after I visit the college I am going to attend. I thought it might be nice to go to lunch first. You're welcome to join us, Linden."

"That sounds very nice, but I think I'm going to try to do some work today. Mother, pack me a lunch, if you will. I plan to stay out most of the day. It looks like a perfect day."

"But are you strong enough for that, Linden?" she asked him cautiously.

"Of course I am. Why shouldn't I be? Once I have one of your wonderful omelettes in my stomach, that is," he added, and laughed.

I think both my mother and I were holding our breath. Both of us looked about ready to explode. Still, he didn't notice. He went right on talking and was even chattier than he had been before his sailing fiasco. He was absolutely gleeful about our moving into the main house and the Eatons moving out.

"What a relief it will be to move about our property and not have them hovering above and around us," he said. "Do you know, Mother, I don't believe I have been back in that house since they moved into it. Have I?"

"No, Linden. Neither of us has, for that matter," Mother said.

He thought for a moment, then laughed.

"I think I'll plant myself at the gate and smile at them as they drive away. When will they leave exactly?" he asked, turning to me.

"May fifteenth is technically their last day here, according to what I understand," I said.

"Excellent," he said, and began to gobble down his omelette.

We both watched him in awe until I went to dress for my trip to the school, both of us afraid to say too much. It was like handling thin china, taking great care not to tap or bang anything too hard. A part of me worried that such a dramatic and radical turnaround could be the sign of something even more serious.

I noticed that all the torn paintings were gone from the studio, and when I gazed out of my bedroom window, I saw that sometime during the night or very early this morning he had taken them to the refuse area to be carted off. I had a chilling thought that the weight Linden talked about being lifted from his shoulders was the weight of the guilt he expressed in his madness. Since he had ripped up all his works and put them in the garbage, he no longer felt pressured and depressed. How would this affect his work? What would he paint? Would it all start again? Not wanting to detract from my mother's joy at seeing Linden's recuperation, I didn't mention any of my thoughts or fears to her when I stepped back into the kitchen on my way out.

She was preparing a lunch basket for him and he was talking about the studio he intended to set up in the main house when we were all finally living there. Her face was absolutely glowing. I was so happy for her, but as I stood there and listened, I noticed how Linden looked down at the table when he talked and how his talk was filled with such minute details, down to where he was going to keep his drawing pencils and how he would angle his table. How odd it was.

Now that I studied him some more as he spoke, I realized he was driven by a frenetic nervous energy. His eyebrows were like Mexican jumping beans and his hands never stopped moving. Mother wasn't really listening to the content of what he was saying or looking at him when he spoke. She was simply too excited and happy about his talking to care about anything more than that.

"I'm off," I declared, interrupting him. He hadn't

taken note of my return, barely pausing to take breaths.

Now he looked up at me, his eyes growing smaller, darker. He tilted his head as if confusion weighed too heavily on one side.

"When did you get here?" he asked.

Mother's hands froze. She looked at me, then at him.

"Get here? You mean, Joya del Mar?"

"Yes, of course. That is exactly what I mean," he replied.

"A few days ago," I said.

He nodded.

"Grace told me you were coming back. I understand you are going to attend a college here."

"Yes, Linden. That's where I'm going now—to meet with my assigned advisor and set up my schedule of classes. I thought you heard me say that before."

"You know we're moving back into the main house," he said, ignoring me.

Mother brought her hands to the base of her throat and released a small cry.

"Yes, Linden. I know and I am very happy about it."

"We never should have left it and rented it to those people," he said.

"Well, we won't have to rent it again, ever."

"Good," he said, and looked at the table.

"Linden, didn't you take your pill this morning?" Mother asked him.

"Pill? No. What pill?"

"Oh dear," she said, and went to get his medication. He watched her go.

"And then," he began where I had interrupted him, "I will keep my supplies in the closet on the right. I want to stock up so I don't have to depend on anyone. There's plenty of room. The stock closet has a great set of shelves, you know. I remember that. I remember the three light fixtures, brass, and there was a place for a safe, I think. Maybe it was just a mistake and they said it was a place for a mistake. Jackie Lee thought that, too. She always wanted me to call her Jackie Lee. Did you know that? Yes, Jackie Lee. Call me Jackie Lee. Don't call me Grandma or Ma or any other name like that. Let's just use our names, okay? You're Linden. I'm Jackie Lee. Okay, all right. Even if you have a bad dream, don't scream, 'Grandma.' Don't scream, 'Ma.' Don't scream anything, but if you have to scream, scream for Jackie Lee. Jackie Lee . . ."

His voice trailed off as Mother returned, and he sat back. After a moment he looked up at the two of us and smiled.

"I think I'll take a short rest before going out to work. I got up too early this morning. I've been up for hours and hours, haven't I, Mother?"

"Yes," she lied. "But first, take your pill." She handed it to him and gave him a glass of water, and he downed the pill quickly.

He looked at me.

"Will you be here for dinner?" he asked.

"Yes, Linden."

"Good. We can get reacquainted then." He stopped smiling and pressed his lips together as he stared at me. "I'm sorry," he said. "I've forgotten your name."

"It's Willow. My name is Willow De Beers."

"Yes, of course it is. Sorry. I've had a great deal on my mind these last few days. De Beers, De Beers . . . didn't we know a De Beers, Mother?"

"Yes, Linden, we did," she said, the tears filling under her lids.

"Of course. I'm sorry," he said, rising. "With all this

talk about moving. I've got so much to do. You'll have to excuse me. I'm sorry."

"It's all right," I said as he walked out of the kitchen and back toward his bedroom.

The tears, now free to move at will, charged down my mother's cheeks. She blinked through them and took a deep breath.

"For a while I actually thought . . . it seemed as if he was well again," she said, and moaned.

"I'm sure the forgetting and the confusion are just a normal and expected part of his condition, Mother."

"I don't know about going to lunch and then to a beauty parlor, Willow. I don't want to make a fool of myself and embarrass you, and with him like this."

"It will be fine, Mother. You've got to make an effort, too. Please try. Please," I pleaded.

She wiped away her tears.

"I don't want to disappoint you, Willow."

"Then just do it," I said firmly.

She nodded.

"Okay. I'll try," she said. "I'll speak to Jennings and ask him to keep an eye on Linden."

"Good. I'll be back in a few hours at the most, Mother," I said, and hugged her. "He's going to get better. This is some improvement, at least," I assured her, even though I had no idea if it really was anything but more confusion. "He has energy, an appetite. Be optimistic."

"I haven't been optimistic for so long, I don't know if I can."

"You can. I'm here now, and I'm here for you, Mother. You can," I insisted.

She smiled.

"Yes," she said. "I'll let myself believe in a rainbow or two again."

"Good. See you soon," I said, and hurried out.

I was going to attend the branch of Florida Atlantic University located on the John D. MacArthur campus in the heart of Abacoa, a residential community in Jupiter, Florida. The commute was not very far for me, and they had what looked like a good undergraduate program in psychology. I had received a letter instructing me to meet with Professor Miguel Fuentes, who had been assigned to be my advisor. The campus was relatively new, its groundbreaking as recent as February 1998. There were only about three thousand students, which was fine with me. I was looking for as much personal attention as possible.

This was a new beginning, I told myself. *We're all going to be fine,* I chanted insistently to myself. *We're all going to be fine.*

I paused when I heard a door slam and turned to look back at the beach house.

Linden was charging out and down the beach, a blank canvas under his arm, his case of paints clutched in his hand like a club. He looked like a man who was late for an appointment.

How I hoped it wasn't with some haunting memory.

4

The Talk of the Town

Professor Fuentes's office was small but very tidy. His assistant, a tall, thin, and prematurely balding psychology graduate student with dull brown strands of hair as thin as dental floss, was aptly named Norman, I thought, because he reminded me of Norman Bates in *Psycho*. He had similar vulnerable, lonely eyes and spoke with that same soft uncertainty as if he expected every syllable he uttered to be challenged for its accuracy or its appropriateness. He didn't shake my hand so much as simply touch my fingers and quickly pull his own back like someone who has committed a social violation.

"Professor Fuentes asked me to make you comfortable. He's going to be a few minutes late. Some last-minute business with the department head," Norman muttered, flicking his hand close to his ear as if chasing off a fly. "Would you like anything to drink? I can get you a soda or even a cup of coffee from the coffee machine."

His Adam's apple bobbed at the ends of his sentences, adding an extra period.

"No, thank you."

He looked completely lost as to what to do next, and I wondered what such an inarticulate, shy man could possibly do in the world of psychology.

"Well, then," he said. His eyes moved every which way to avoid direct contact with mine.

"I'm fine," I said. "I'll be all right."

He looked relieved and left me sitting in Professor Fuentes's office. Looking around, I saw a picture of an elderly couple on his desk and beside that a picture of a tall, dark-haired woman standing beside a man who held a fishing pole. They were on a dock with a boat in the background.

Professor Fuentes's diplomas and awards were in gilded frames and placed on the wall directly behind his desk chair. There was a bookcase on the right, a table with papers neatly piled on the left, a standing lamp, a copy machine, and a computer printer beside it. A laptop stood open on the desk itself, but it wasn't on.

On a small table beside my chair was a pile of *Psychology Today* magazines. I began to flip through them and came upon an article written about my father. It was entitled "Legacy of a True Analyst." There was a picture of Daddy in his office at his clinic. He looked about twenty years younger than when he died. My eyes immediately clouded over with tears, but I wiped them aside so I could begin to read the article. The author was lauding Daddy's many studies and articles, as well as his book on bipolar disorder.

"You know, I thought that might be your father," I heard a deep, resonant voice say from behind me a short while later, and turned to see a handsome man about six feet tall with a coal-black beard trimmed neatly down the sides of his face and around his lips and chin. He wore a light gray sports jacket and dark gray slacks. His shirt was open at the collar, and I could see a thick gold necklace that glittered against his caramel complexion.

"I didn't mean to startle you," he continued, a very friendly, gentle smile rippling up his lean cheeks to his ebony eyes. He had his hair swept to one side, but full in the front and well trimmed down the sides and at the back of his neck. "Didn't Norman offer you something to drink?" he asked, putting his briefcase down on the table beside the pile of papers.

"Yes. I'm fine."

"So, was that your father?" he asked, nodding toward the copy of *Psychology Today*.

"Yes," I said, and he widened his eyes.

"I read the book mentioned in the article. What a brilliant man he was," he said, moving around to sit at his desk.

"Thank you."

"Well, it will be an honor for me to be the advisor to Dr. De Beers's daughter. Are you a chip off the old block, as they say?"

"Let's call it a shaving," I replied, and he laughed. He had perfectly straight, bright white teeth. I saw that he wore a Rolex and also a beautiful diamond pinky ring in a gold setting, but no wedding ring.

"I have your transcripts, so you can't tell me you're an average student. You were doing so well there. What made you decide to transfer, if I may ask?"

I smiled to myself, thinking, *Imagine if I went into my story in detail.*

"My mother lives here with my half brother, and I've decided, since my father's passing, to live with them," I replied. It was a simple and true answer.

He nodded.

"Well, then, UNC's loss is our gain."

"I hope so."

He smiled at my modesty.

"I have your schedule here. I took the liberty of making sure you were in one of my classes, psych social science. You will be surprised at just how many psychiatrists I create in the first three sessions," he joked. "Before the semester ends, the whole class is analyzing itself, and everyone develops one complex or another."

I laughed and told him I was sure it was true.

"Are there any extracurricular activities that interest you? I saw that you didn't do very much in that regard at North Carolina."

"No."

"All work and no play, then, eh?" he asked with what I thought was a flirtatious grin.

"Let's just say I leave my playing for off-campus life," I replied.

He lifted his eyebrows and nodded.

"Muy bien. Sometimes, my Spanish inserts itself," he quickly explained. "My family is from Cuba. We came over right before Castro took the island. So I was born and raised here. These two are my parents," he added, turning the picture so I could get a better view, "and this is my sister and her husband the fisherman. He takes it very seriously. It's practically an art form. However, if I say anything about anyone in my family, they all pounce, accusing me of analyzing them. Did that go on in your home, too?"

"Sometimes," I said, smiling now at what had often been bitter moments between my adoptive mother and my father. Eventually, I came to realize he was often analyzing her.

"I assume you were born and raised in South Carolina, then?"

"Yes."

He nodded, a pregnant pause between us for a moment. The speed with which he had become personal at this first meeting impressed me and relaxed me.

"I'm curious," he finally said, "how do you see yourself, say, ten years from now?"

"Excuse me?"

"It's a little game I play with all my students, but a game that has value. It gives me some insight about them, what they expect from their education, their career goals, that sort of thing."

"I hope only that I will be half the success my father was," I replied. "I don't want to work in a clinic, however. I want to have a less structured practice. I am thinking more seriously now of working with young people, specializing in it."

He smiled and nodded as if he had expected that exact answer.

"Thank you," he said. "I feel certain you will like it here. We're all very new, the school being relatively an embryo compared to other universities and colleges in the state, much less the country, so you will find much less pretension. We're all students here."

"I was happy to find a school with a program for me so close to Palm Beach."

"Yes. Well, then," he said, nodding at the card he had given me, "how do you like your schedule?"

I read it, feeling his eyes on me.

"It's fine," I said. "Everything I wanted."

"Very good. I can ask Norman to give you a tour of the campus, if you like."

"No, that's all right," I said. "I have plenty of time before I begin. I'll be back."

"Please don't hesitate to call my office if you have any questions or if there is something I can help you with or explain further," he offered.

"Thank you."

"I have a similar commute. I come from Palm Beach Gardens," he said. "My parents have a rather well known restaurant in West Palm Beach. It's called Havana Molena." He smiled. "Molena is my mother's name. My sister and her husband, when he is not fishing, actually run the restaurant these days, but my father is never too far away and my mother is still the kitchen general."

"I'll have to try it," I said.

"If you mention my name, you get a free rum and Coke," he said, and laughed. "Well, you know when the next term begins. We operate on the trimester system. I have seen all your teachers, and here," he said, pulling a small packet out of his briefcase, "is the list of books you will need and the reading preparations."

"Thank you," I said, taking the papers.

"There's a map of the campus in there as well and my office hours, et cetera. Are there any other questions, concerns?" he asked.

"Not at the moment, no. You are a big help. Thank you, Professor."

I stood up, and he rose quickly to extend his hand.

"Welcome, and I hope you will have a very successful and enjoyable experience here."

"Thank you."

He nodded, and I left thinking that he had such an intense way of looking at me, I could still feel his eyes on me even when I got into my car and drove away from the campus.

Almost the moment I arrived back at Joya del Mar, I sensed that my mother was going to back out of going to the beauty salon with me. She wasn't dressed and ready as I had hoped. At first I couldn't even find her, and thought she might have gone off looking for Linden on the beach. I called for her as soon as I stepped into the house, but she didn't respond. She wasn't in the small living room or the kitchen, and when I peeked into her bedroom, I didn't see her. The bathroom door was open and she wasn't in there, either.

I stepped out on the loggia and gazed down the beach, but saw no one. Fortunately, out of the corner of my eye, however, I caught sight of her, her hair blowing in the sea breeze as she stood on the beach off to my left, barely visible behind a small knoll. I hurried to her. She didn't turn when I called to her. She was staring so hard at the sea, her arms folded under her breasts, her body so still, she could have been a statue.

"Mother!" I cried, inches from her.

She shook her head without turning to me.

"Why aren't you dressed and ready to go to lunch with me?"

"I'm sorry," she said quickly, then threw me a very troubled glance. "I can't do it. Go on without me, Willow."

"Didn't you speak with Jennings and ask him to watch over Linden?"

"Yes, but I still can't go, Willow."

"But why, Mother? Everything has been arranged for us. There is no problem."

"For you there is no problem, Willow. I've been here so long, I can't just pick up and go out there as if nothing happened these past years. Besides, why am I doing this? I don't intend to get into the social scene here, Willow. Let's not fool ourselves. Even when we move back into the main house, I'm not going to have those elaborate parties and do all those things."

"We're not doing it for that, Mother. We're not doing it for anyone but ourselves," I practically moaned. She smiled at me. "It will be good for you. I know it will. Please, Mother, try."

"You must not worry about me so much, Willow. I'm fine as I am. Really." She smiled at me again and patted my hand. "The truth is, I sat at my vanity table after you left to visit your college, and I realized I didn't want to change this face and this hair. This is who I've become, who I am, Willow. It's the woman your father fell in love with many years ago, the woman who stood on that dock and hoped and prayed he would come to her. I'm not ready to put her away. Do you think you can under-stand that?" she asked softly.

Of course, I understood. I was trying to do exactly what she didn't want to do: close the door on the past, shut out the darkness, almost re-create myself. I had so few wonderful memories to cherish, few reasons to hold on to my old world. She had every reason to hold on to the only happiness she had ever known.

"Yes," I said reluctantly.

"Do you mean that, or do you believe I am guilty of funny fantasy? Are you going to diagnose me with some mental malady and tell me I am only hurting myself?" she asked with a wry smile.

"No, Mother. Psychiatrists don't want you to put away your dreams. Your fantasies serve an important purpose. I wouldn't want anyone to be unable to imag-ine and dream. It's only when the fantasies take over your life, control it, that the psychiatrists become concerned," I said.

"I suppose my dream has taken over my life, has for some time now, but forgive me for wanting that and not wanting to come back to this," she said, gesturing toward the main house and the extravagant and opulent property that was representative of the kingly wealth of the people of Palm Beach. "All the beauty here, all the luxury, can't replace what I have lost or perhaps refuse to lose." She smiled. "Did you know that your father often read poetry to me?"

"No," I said, shaking my head. "I can't recall seeing him read anything but his scientific journals or books by well-known doctors in his field."

"Yes, he relied on literature often. He said he often found deep and complex ideas expressed simply and far more beautifully in poetry. When we parted, he quoted Dante Gabriel Rossetti and said, 'Beauty without the beloved is like a sword through the heart.' It was his way of telling me that once we parted, his life would be far less satisfying and he would never appreciate anything as much as he had with me. The same was true for me, only I didn't express it as well.

"In my way, I have kept him beside me all these years. To turn from that now, to start a new life with a new face and an entirely different pair of eyes . . . well, it would not leave me with as much satisfaction as you hope."

I didn't know I was crying until the tears actually tickled my chin.

"I'll be fine," she said, wiping them away and then kissing my forehead. "As long as you do what you are capable of doing and you find happiness, Willow. Please don't let me hold you back or be a reason for you not to

achieve it all. Please, go on and burn your way through
without me dragging behind you."

"You could never be a drag for me, Mother."

"I know. But I would feel that way if you worried too
much about me. I wouldn't be comfortable, and that
would hinder you and even Linden," she said, looking
toward the beach.

"Where is he?"

She sighed and shook her head sadly.

"He's out there, trying to paint something. He's
calmer now. His medicine kicked in, I suppose."

I took a deep breath. It was hard for her. It might always be hard for her, I thought.

"Go on. Don't miss your appointment. Come back
looking like a trust baby," she said, and we both laughed.
Many of the rich young people here and even the older
ones lived entirely off the fortunes their parents and grandparents had accumulated and were known as trust babies.

"We can still have lunch together," I suggested.

She shook her head.

"I've prepared egg salad for Linden. Even though it's
one of his favorite foods for lunch, he won't eat if I
don't hover over him."

"All right. Then I'll have lunch with you here first."

She scrunched up her face and pressed her lips together
as she shook her head, looking like someone in pain.

"I don't want to hold you back from doing things,
Willow. That would be so wrong."

"You're not. I haven't made any friends here yet, and
I am not fond of eating alone," I said. "I'll go find
Linden and tell him we're having lunch."

"Okay," she said. "I'll set the table on the loggia."

"Fine," I told her, and went down the beach to search
for Linden.

I found him sitting in one of his usual places, staring out at the sea. He sat at the foot of his easel and looked like someone in meditation. As I approached, I glanced at his canvas and saw it was still blank.

"Hi, Linden," I said. He didn't turn to me. "Mother sent me to fetch you. It's time for lunch and she's made the egg salad you love."

I held my breath in anticipation of his response, any response, but he remained silent.

"The sea air always makes me hungry. Doesn't it do the same to you?" I asked.

Finally, he turned slowly toward me, his eyes small, suspicious.

"Why did you come back?" he asked, but with such an angry undertone, it took me by surprise. For a moment it was I who couldn't speak.

"This is where I belong now, Linden. You and Mother are my family. I have nothing back in South Carolina. My father is gone and I've sold the property. Don't you want me here?"

He stared, his face not softening, but his eyes blinking rapidly.

"You think you'll get him to marry you? You think you'll win his devotion? He's not capable of it," he said, and smiled coldly. "I've grown up here in the shadows, watching him seduce and break the heart of one girl after another, all like you, each convinced she was the one who would make him a decent fellow. Like I said, he's not capable of it," he finished, his words filled with venom.

"Everyone is capable of it, Linden, because after a while, everyone gets lonely," I said.

My words were like well-aimed arrows hitting the center of the target. I could see it in the way he flinched and turned away.

"Besides, that isn't the only reason why I returned, Linden. I've come back to be with you and Mother and pursue my career goals. I want to help you both, too. We're moving back into the main house. It will make Mother very happy, don't you think?"

"No," he said sharply.

"No? Why not? You sounded so happy about it before, planning your studio."

"I was fooling myself. There are too many ghosts there," he muttered.

"We'll drive them out then, Linden. You and I," I said. "We'll drive them out."

He turned back to me, a new expression on his face, one that permitted a little ray of hope to pierce the mask of his unhappiness.

"You and I?"

"Yes, Linden. We'll set up a nice home. You'll have a wonderful studio and do great things. Oh, Linden, let's be happy. Let's try to be happy together, please," I pleaded.

He actually flicked a small smile, but then, as if realizing he was tolerating some optimism, darkened his face quickly and pressed his lips together hard enough to form a little white line under them.

"Come back to the house for lunch, Linden," I urged softly. "Mother is preparing the table for us on the loggia. It will be nice sitting out and having lunch together, don't you think?"

"I thought . . ." He shook his head.

"What?"

"I don't know. My thoughts get so confused, as well as my memories sometimes."

"What did you think? I'll tell you whether or not you're confused. I will," I said when he looked at me skeptically. "I'll always be honest with you, Linden."

For the moment, at least, I won his trust.

"I thought you were going to lunch on Worth Avenue and then to a beauty salon with Grace."

"She would rather not. We've got to go slowly with her," I said.

He raised his eyebrows at my including him in the plan. Easy as a mask to take off, he threw away his remnants of anger and antagonism and put on a dreamy-eyed look as he turned to gaze at his canvas.

"I don't like what I've done so far. It's not very good," he said, rising.

I looked at the blank canvas again to see if there was something I had missed, some lightly drawn lines, perhaps, but there was nothing there. When I turned back to him, I saw he was watching me expectantly.

"Well?" he asked. "What's your opinion? As I recall, you know something about art."

"I . . . I don't think you've done enough yet for me to form any opinion, Linden," I said.

He smiled.

"Very diplomatic. I guess you *will* be a good psychiatrist someday after all," he added, and marched past his empty canvas, stopping a few yards away. "Well? Are we going back for lunch or not?"

"What about your things?" I was staring at the canvas.

"It's all right. No one will bother with that," he said. "Well, are we going?"

"Oh, yes, yes," I said, and quickly caught up with him.

We walked along quietly for a while, and when my arm grazed his, he jumped. He stopped and stared at me.

"Are you okay?" I asked.

"I was going to do birds today," he muttered, continuing to walk along, "but they weren't being very cooperative. They know when I want to paint them and they are capable of teasing me. Tormenting me, I should say. Just like the sea and the sky and the clouds and the stars and you!" he finished, speeding up to stay ahead of me all the way to the house, his hair flying around his head, his arms swinging as if he were pulling a rope and climbing upward and away with all his strength.

Linden was quiet during lunch, looking like he was daydreaming as he chewed and swallowed. The way he gazed through us and not at us made Mother nervous. She talked, leaping into every quiet moment as if afraid Linden would do or say something terrible if she didn't. She spoke mostly about the main house and what it would be like to move back into it.

"Just about all of the furniture in there belongs with the house, you know. Even most of the art on the walls. It's a big house to take care of, Willow. We'll have to decide what we want to use and what we want to shut away, knowing how little help we can afford."

"That's fine with me, Mother."

"It's still going to be a very expensive house to keep up. The utilities and all, I mean," she said.

"We can manage," I assured her. "Besides, Linden is going to work and sell lots of his paintings." I smiled at him.

"Yes," my mother agreed, "he can do that if he puts his mind to it."

Linden lifted his gaze from the table and looked from her to me and back to her, his face full of surprise.

"I don't know if I'll sell any more of my work, Mother," he said.

"Of course you will, Linden. As long as you try. You'll try, won't you?" she asked him.

He nodded.

"Yes, I will, Mother," he said.

"Good." She sighed. "Maybe this is a new beginning, then."

Linden looked surprised again, and then he looked at me as if he finally had realized I had come back and we were all together. He nodded.

"Maybe," he said in a voice barely above a whisper. "Maybe."

I smiled, but he didn't. His smiles had become as rare as diamonds and, for us, more valuable and important.

Afterward, I went to the beauty salon by myself. I was still disappointed that my mother hadn't come along. I had so looked forward to a real day together as mother and daughter, but I realized now that I had to move even more slowly. There were many miles to make up, a great stretch of emotional pain to ease and stop. It wasn't going to happen overnight. It might never happen completely, but as Daddy used to say, "An inch at a time is still moving forward."

The beauty parlor was very busy. The receptionist was not at all diplomatic about her disappointment in my canceling Mother's appointment.

"Do you know how valuable that time slot is?" she chastised. She didn't look much older than I was, if she was older at all, but she had a very snooty attitude from the start.

She wore black leather pants and a white translucent blouse that did nothing to hide her small but firm bosom, and she had bleached hair. I thought she wore too much makeup and was especially heavy-handed with her lipstick. Her swollen lips looked like they were made of wax.

"I'll pay for it anyway," I said.

"That's not the point," she wailed with more volume

than necessary. I knew she was trying to attract the attention of those women in nearby chairs and their beauticians. "We have clients we had to turn away, and pleasing our clientele is our first priority," she recited.

"Oh really," I said sharply. "Well, I don't see how you succeed with your attitude."

"My attitude?"

"What is happening here?" I heard a male voice ask from behind me, and turned to see a man with his dark hair in a ponytail. He wore black slacks and a frilly red shirt with the sleeves folded back over his slim wrists. His black pearl eyes flicked from the receptionist to me.

"She just arrived and canceled one of her appointments," the receptionist wailed. "With no notice!"

"I see."

"It couldn't be helped," I said. "I apologized and offered to pay for it anyway. It was my mother's appointment."

"Oh, you are Miss De Beers?"

"Yes."

"I am Renardo de Palma. It's fine, Candace. There is no need to be histrionic," he added with a tone of authority and chastisement that brought immediate tears to her eyes.

"I'm just doing my job," she moaned.

"I'll take charge of this," he told her firmly. "Is your mother ill, then?" he asked me in a far softer, more concerned tone of voice, even though it lacked real sincerity. I thought he had a smile smooth enough to charm a cobra.

"Yes," I said, thinking that was the best and fastest explanation.

"These things happen. No earthquake. Please, let me take care of you personally," he offered, turning me toward the workstations. "Don't mind her. She's my brother's child so I have to employ her," he said with a wave of his hand. The receptionist smirked. His brutal honesty brought a smile to my face.

"Right this way," he said, and led me to a chair in the rear of the salon.

I couldn't help but feel everyone's eyes on me as I walked alongside him. Conversations were put on pause. Beauticians froze for a moment. It wasn't until after Renardo took my jacket to hang up and put my purse aside and I sat that the place seemed to come back to life.

"So," he said, stepping behind me, "let's see what we have here first."

He lifted my hair with his hands as if he were dipping them in a mound of diamonds and stared at my image in the mirror.

"Well, Miss De Beers," he began as if I were a four-year-old child, "you haven't been taking care of yourself as well as you should." He shook his head. "So many split ends, and your hair is too dry. I must do a complete treatment on you before we begin. We must wash it and condition it, and then we will decide on a cut."

"A cut? You think I need a totally different style?" I asked.

"But of course, *señorita*. You are not taking advantage of what your hair can do for your beautiful face," he said. "I think of a woman's hair as the frame for her face, which is the picture, and just like any wonderful picture, it can be enhanced or it can be diminished by a poor-quality frame, no?"

"I suppose so," I said.

"Muy bien. Then let us begin. You are in the hands of an artist. Don't worry," he said, and turned. "Trinity," he called to a young, dark-haired girl chatting with the receptionist. She stopped in what looked like midsen-

tence, excused herself, and hurried to my side. "A wash and condition," he dictated. "Use formula forty-two."

"Sí," she said. She had bright, eager dark eyes and looked not much older than seventeen.

"As soon as you are ready, I will be," Renardo promised.

He gave the young girl a very hard, almost threatening look, then left us. She looked like she was trembling as she pinned the protective sheet behind my neck and turned my chair gently so I could be lowered to the sink behind me.

"You are comfortable?" she asked as she did so.

"Yes."

She tested the water, then began to soak my hair, moving her fingers through it with long, even strokes like someone who had just been taught how to do it and wanted to be sure she had the technique perfect.

"It's not too hot?"

"It's fine," I said, and closed my eyes. "How long have you been doing this?" I almost expected her to say I was her first client.

"Five years," she said.

I snapped open my eyes.

"Five years? How could—how old are you?"

"I'm twenty-one," she said. "As soon as I was sixteen, my father put me to work in his salon."

"Your father?"

"Renardo de Palma," she replied. "I am his daughter."

"His daughter?" The receptionist was his niece. Was his whole family employed here?

She began to scrub more vigorously as if she was angry about revealing she was his daughter and put all her anger into her fingers. She was giving me a virtual head massage.

"He wants me to become a beautician like him, but I told him I had other plans for myself," she muttered well under her breath. "He keeps me here helping, hoping I will give in and graduate to cutting and styling. My father doesn't look it, perhaps, but he is behind the times. He believes in the old-fashioned idea that a parent should design his child's whole life. He has even picked out the man I should marry, a fifth cousin.

"You would think in this day and age, parents don't choose who their children will marry," she added.

You'd be surprised at how many parents still think of their children as their property, puppets to manipulate, I mused, thinking about Bunny Eaton, but I didn't say anything. I tried to relax instead and enjoy being pampered. After washing my hair, she put in the conditioner her father had prescribed and then told me it should sit for a full five minutes. I felt my scalp tingle delightfully.

"I can get you a magazine, if you like," she offered.

"No, I'm fine."

She stepped back but remained at my side. I opened my eyes and glanced at her.

"You're from Joya del Mar. My cousin was telling me," she said.

"Yes."

"You've never been here before, maybe on my day off?"

"No. I've just moved to Palm Beach," I told her.

"That's where Mr. Eaton lives. I know because I just shampooed his fiancée yesterday," she said with some pride.

"His fiancée? Who are you talking about?" I asked, lifting my head. Was she referring to Thatcher's sister?

"The lawyer, Mr. Eaton," she replied.

"Who told you he was engaged?" I asked, a little

more aggressively than I intended. She actually backed up a few steps.

"Well, it's in the paper. I'm not making it up. I shampooed Miss Raymond and she was talking about it, too. She comes here twice a month with her future sister-in-law, but I don't shampoo her. She always asks for Carol Ann," she said, glaring at another young woman across the way who was working on an elderly lady.

"You said it's in the paper? A recent paper?"

"*Sí*. You want to see it?" she asked me.

"Yes, please," I said, lowering my head. My heart felt as if it was sliding down to the bottom of my chest.

She went to the front of the salon and spoke to the receptionist, who reached under the desk and handed her a shiny newspaper. Then she hurried back as if she were delivering an important telegram to the Queen of England.

"Here. It's in 'Talk of the Town,' " she said, opening the Shiny, as I knew everyone called the glossy paper, to the proper page and pointing to a column written by someone called Suzy Q. Most of the column was devoted to a recent charity event given by a prince at the Flagler Museum. It listed people who'd attended, and one paragraph picked up on a recently knighted architect, Sir Floyd Raymond, whose daughter Vera was rumored to be ". . . expecting, but not a baby, not yet. Vera is expecting an engagement ring from one of the most eligible bachelors in Palm Beach, Thatcher Eaton. Sorry, girls, the counselor appears to be making a motion, and from what we've learned, no one in either family will raise any sort of objection."

There was a picture of Vera Raymond with Thatcher, and she looked very much like the woman I had seen him with in the café. I could feel the blood drain from my face.

"If you lived there, I thought you would know her

and know all about it," Trinity said, her curiosity now piqued.

"No. I just moved here," I replied, fighting to keep my voice from cracking. Managing a simple sentence was suddenly like unraveling twisted wire in my head. My fingers held the paper like pincers as I stared at the picture of Thatcher and Vera Raymond, his arm around her waist, both smiling for the camera. I'm sure I looked like I was trying to burn a hole through the page.

"You can keep that," she said, backing away.

"No," I told her, and held it away from me as if it had become contaminated. Gingerly she took it back, flashed a smile, and hurried to return it to the receptionist, who had been watching us the whole time. I saw them put their heads together to mix some new gossip.

I lay back. It seemed hard to breathe. Despite the air-conditioning system, the air was oppressive and heavy. I closed my eyes. When I opened them again, it seemed to me that everyone in the salon was now looking at me and whispering. Minutes later, Trinity returned to rinse my hair and wrap it in a towel.

"Are you related to Mr. Eaton?" she asked. She had obviously been given the assignment of finding out as much as she could about me and passing it down the line of gossips just waiting to cackle like hens.

"I'm here to have my hair done," I said sharply. "Nothing more."

Her hands lifted from the towel as if she had touched a hot stove.

I glared at her.

"I'll tell my father you are ready," she said, and hurried away.

Moments later, Renardo de Palma was at my side, that soupy smile spreading like hot butter over his face.

"So, now we do some cutting, no?"

"No," I said, sitting up.

"Excuse me?"

"I'm sorry," I said. "I've changed my mind. I don't want to do anything different with my hair."

I practically threw off the protective sheet, my heart thumping like a blown tire on a fast car.

"But, *señorita—*"

"I've got to go," I said. I moved quickly to get my jacket. Renardo's mouth hung open, his jaw slack, his arms up and frozen in position as he watched me put on my jacket.

"But your hair . . . your hair is wet, and—"

"I'm fine," I said. "Just tell me how much I owe you."

He simply shook his head.

"Very well. Send me a bill, then," I added, and marched down the center of the salon, passing all the gaping eyes. Everyone stopped talking and watched me hurry out of the place. When the door closed behind me, I felt as if I had just left a sauna. I took a deep breath and hurried to my car. Water was dripping from my hair down the sides of my face.

Vaguely, I realized how mad and wild I had appeared and still looked to anyone who gazed in my direction, but all I could think of was getting myself away from those dissecting eyes and those whispers that had looped around me like chains, causing me to feel trapped and so naked and exposed that everyone could see the cracks in my broken heart.

How could he do this? How could he take advantage of me this way and lie and betray me? I felt so violated. I couldn't feel any worse if I had been raped, I thought. I *had* been raped. Instead of force, he'd used promises and sweet talk. The rage continued to build inside me, expanding like a hot balloon that was on the verge of exploding.

I didn't recall getting into my car and starting the engine, but after I had, I lurched away from the curb, cutting off another vehicle and nearly sending it into an oncoming car. The driver pressed on her horn, the blaring noise causing me to go even faster. I shot forward, then had to bring the car to an abrupt halt at a traffic light. The moment I did so, a police car pulled up alongside with its bubble light going and the officer stepped out.

He gestured for me to roll down my window.

"What exactly do we have here?" he asked, gazing in at me.

I simply stared at him, my lips trembling.

He turned when the light changed and waved the cars behind me around; then he nodded toward the side of the street.

"Pull in there and let me see your license and registration," he ordered.

"I'm sorry," I said, hoping my apology would work like a magic wand and make him disappear.

He acted as if he hadn't heard it and walked back to his car. He got in and waited for me to pull over, then pulled up behind me and got out again. I fumbled through my purse for my license and reached into the glove compartment for my registration. He read them both and tipped his hat back with his right thumb. I thought he looked very young, too young to be an actual policeman.

"South Carolina, eh?"

"I've just moved here," I said. "I haven't had time to change anything yet."

"I see. You do drive like someone who hasn't got much time."

He stared at my soaked hair.

"I'm sorry," I repeated. "Something upset me and I wasn't thinking."

"I see. Is that some sort of new hairstyle?" he asked. The strands were glued to my temples and cheeks, the water still traveling down the sides of my face.

"No," I said, my lips and chin trembling.

"Are you at a hotel here?"

"No, a home," I said.

"What's the address?"

"It's called Joya del Mar. I have the address here somewhere," I said, reaching for my purse again.

"That's all right. I know that address. You're staying with the Eatons?"

"No, the Montgomerys," I corrected sharply, flicking the tears from my cheeks.

He nodded.

"One minute," he said, and returned to his car. Through the rearview mirror, I could see him talking on the car phone. A few minutes later, he returned.

"Okay, Miss De Beers. Despite its fame and the people who reside here, this is a quiet little community. We like to keep it that way."

"I understand," I said.

"Yes, I expect you do."

He handed everything back to me.

"You'll have to think when you drive and not drive when you're upset, ma'am."

"I know," I said.

"Ordinarily, I would issue a ticket for that sort of reckless driving in our city, but you have a good man vouching for you. You can thank Mr. Eaton for this one. Take it easier, and dry your hair soon," he added with a smile.

He started back to his car.

"Give me that ticket! I don't need anyone to vouch

for me, *especially* Mr. Eaton," I cried, but he either didn't hear me or ignored me and got into his car. He pulled away first, leaving me fuming. I shoved everything back into my purse.

I was about to start off again, but stopped before putting my car into drive and sat back, letting the fire inside me diminish. Then I looked at myself in the mirror. My hair was still quite soaked. I was a ridiculous sight. *That young policeman certainly got a shock when he looked in at me,* I thought, imagining what I looked like from his perspective. Suddenly, I began to laugh. I laughed so hard at myself, I couldn't stop even after my stomach started to ache. Tears rolled down my cheeks.

I choked and coughed and leaned against the car door until I was able to catch my breath. Finally, I started away again. Driving far more slowly and carefully now, I found a place where I could pull to the side and walk down to the beach. I sat in the sunshine and let my hair dry.

Sometimes, we're so eager for people to love us, we become so vulnerable, we're actually victims of our own hunger for affection, I thought, then vowed, *I am not going to play the wounded one and mope and cry.* Maybe I was out of my league here. Maybe Thatcher was truly no better than the man his mother claimed was his real father, but I wouldn't permit him to belittle and exploit me like this.

I rose, my thoughts and feelings more collected, and returned to my car where I brushed out my hair the best I could. I was ashamed of myself, ashamed of my emotional deluge. *I should be stronger if I want to be a therapist and help other people,* I told myself. Daddy was always stronger.

Or was he simply better at hiding his pain?

5

A Secret Ring

I think I've always hated secrets between people who really care about each other. They are like blemishes on a beautiful face, dark spots. Your eyes are drawn to them like magnets and for a while, if not most of the time, that is all you can see. But what I didn't want to do was let my mother know how upset I was and how betrayed I felt because of what Thatcher had done. Hiding that secret seemed to be the proper thing to do.

I felt I had gotten myself together enough to keep it all well concealed. We really had not spent enough time with each other for her to recognize when I was very upset, I thought—or I hoped. But I was soon to learn that there is something about a mother and a daughter, some mystical bonding that even time and distance cannot prevent. It is an insight that a mother has simply by being a mother, I imagine, for she took one look at me as soon as I entered the house and, despite my carefully constructed mask of happiness, immediately asked me what was wrong.

"Nothing," I said a little too quickly. Her eyebrows went up and her eyes narrowed with suspicion.

"Your hair doesn't look very different, Willow."

"I wasn't happy with the beautician after all that big deal getting us appointments. I didn't like anything he suggested. Why fix it if it isn't broken? Right?" I asked, trying to smile and joke my way out of the moment.

She kept her eyes dark and narrow. I wasn't doing a good job of concealing my feelings. I didn't want her to think I didn't want to trust her, to confide in her. I was in turmoil, being pulled every which way. Oh, what was the right thing to do, I wondered, keep my heartache a secret or fall into her arms, bemoaning Thatcher's betrayal?

"Thatcher Eaton has been calling for you," she said as if she knew anyway. "He's called three times during the last two hours. He asked me to tell you to call him at his office as soon as you got the message."

"I got the message, loud and clear. If he calls again, tell him I'm not here," I blurted.

She gave me that motherly, knowing look now and nodded.

"What's happened between you?" she asked.

I bit down on my lip and shook my head.

How horrible this was. I had come to help her, to help Linden, and here I was, barely living with them and I already had more sorrow draped over my shoulders. I felt like a doctor who had come to minister to the sick only to discover she was sick herself.

"Let's just say I've been disappointed and leave it at that for now, Mother," I begged.

"Whatever you wish, Willow. I don't have big shoulders. Maybe I never had, but I'm here for you if and when you need me."

"Thank you, Mother. Is Linden here or is he still on the beach?"

"He's still on the beach. I wanted to go see how he was doing, but I was afraid he would think I was spying on him. He's been complaining about my being too much of a mother hen," she said, and smiled. "He declared he wasn't an egg. He said he's already been hatched and that was that. It's difficult. Sometimes he doesn't hear a word I say, and then suddenly he is so sensitive, even catching my glances and accusing me of studying him like something under a microscope."

"He's going in and out of awareness at the moment. I'm sure he'll settle down soon. His doctor will arrive at the best doses of his medicines," I predicted.

"I hope so," she said.

I went into my room and changed quickly into a pair of jeans and a University of North Carolina sweatshirt. It brought back memories of my boyfriend, Allan Simpson, and how, like Thatcher, he had disappointed me in the end, pulling away from me as soon as he learned the truth about my father and mother and not supporting my effort to get to know my real mother. He was so selfish and so self-absorbed.

How confusing men could be. Either they were so shallow and obvious, they hit you over the head with their intentions, or they were so smooth and deceitful, they broke your heart with the truth.

Maybe we should create our husbands, I mused, pluck them out of a herd of boys and nurture them and cultivate them until they were perfect crops, then harvest them as husbands. The idea brought a smile to my lips and lifted the layers of gray from my brow.

While I was changing, I heard the telephone ring and went to the doorway to listen as my mother answered. It was Thatcher. I heard her tell him I wasn't here. Eavesdropping, I could tell Mother wasn't a very good liar. Her voice betrayed the untruth, and Thatcher must have sensed it as well and kept talking. Finally, I heard her say, "I'm sorry. All I can do is let her know you've called again."

She hung up. I slipped on my sneakers and joined her in the kitchen.

"I apologize for asking you to do that," I said. "I should have spoken to him myself."

She nodded.

"I don't know the details, Willow, but it's better to just let him know how you feel and get that over with rather than prolong the pain for both of you."

"You're right. I'll call him," I said.

She was right. What was the point of hiding and lying? This was his game, not mine, I told myself, and went to the phone. When I called his office, however, his secretary told me he wasn't there.

"He has to be there," I insisted. "He just called me. Tell him I'm on the phone."

"I'm telling *you* he's not here," she fired back. "As a matter of fact, he just left and he didn't leave a forwarding number." Before I could say another word, she cut me off.

Fuming, I slammed the receiver down. Rather than do any more complaining to my mother, I shot out of the house and went down to the beach, pounding the sand with every step. I found a nice, secluded spot and flopped down, closing my eyes and letting the sound of the sea calm my jolting nerves. It worked. The ocean could be mesmerizing, a true panacea for all mental pain. After a little while, I actually fell asleep.

I woke when I sensed a coolness over me. When I opened my eyes, I saw it was a long shadow. I sat up quickly and saw Thatcher standing there, looking down at me, a tight smile on his face. With the sun behind him, I had to shade my eyes when I moved an inch either way.

"I know why you're angry and avoiding me," he said quickly.

"Really, Thatcher? And why might that be?"

"I heard what happened at the beauty salon," he said, folded his legs, and sat beside me on the sand. In the purplish light of the failing day, his glimmering eyes met mine, but his good looks had an opposite effect on me at the moment. They merely made me feel even angrier. Those were the good looks he apparently shared with any and every attractive and available young woman in Palm Beach.

"What, did the little bird tell you?"

"News travels quickly in this town," he said. "GTS."

"What's that?"

"Gossip telephone system," he replied, and smiled.

"Nothing seems funny to me, Thatcher."

"I know. I know. Look, Willow, for years the Shiny has been featuring me in gossip columns. If you're seen with the same woman more than once and you're an eligible bachelor, rumors pop out like pimples everywhere. For some reason, I'm more of a prime target than most."

"I can't imagine why," I said.

"The point is, none of it is true. This last series of rumors has been spread mainly by my sister and my mother. They believe that if they get it in print, it will happen eventually," he said, and raised his hands. "It's nothing more than that."

"Really." I was quiet a moment, and then I turned on

him. "I saw her picture in the paper, and I know that Vera Raymond was the woman I saw you with in the café, Thatcher. She was not someone in the midst of a bad divorce. One lie by necessity gives birth to another and another until they're swirling around you like bees, and just like bees, Thatcher, they can sting."

He widened his smile.

"I don't know what possessed me to think that I could keep anything from you, Willow. Yes, that was Vera with me, but I *was* talking about a case, just not a divorce case. Her parents, especially her father, have been throwing her at me, if you want to know, and it just so happens he's a major client for my firm as well, so I humor him by escorting his daughter to affairs and letting the fantasy continue. But I'm bringing that all to an end. I swear," he said.

"Won't your mother and sister be heartbroken?"

"Not any more than usual," he said. "I should have warned you about the gossip columns and all that, but I didn't think you would take any of it seriously."

"This is a place in which the true and the false are sides of the same coin most of the time. Whatever way it flips is the way it's accepted. How would I know what is to be taken seriously and what is not?"

"Take this seriously," he said, and reached into his pocket to produce a robins-egg blue ring box with the word *Tiffany* scrawled over it.

I simply stared at it.

"Open it and see what's in it, Willow."

Gingerly, I did, and there inside was an engagement ring with a diamond that looked to be at least two if not three carats in a platinum setting. My heartbeat quickened so fast, I lost my breath.

"I took a guess at your ring size, but I'm usually pretty good at things like that," he said, plucking the ring out of the box and slipping it on my finger. It fit perfectly. "See?"

"Thatcher, an engagement ring!"

"That's what they call it," he said, and leaned back on his hands, closing his eyes and turning his body to bask in the late-afternoon sun. "I figure if all goes well, we can get married in a few months, six at the most.

"Of course," he continued quickly, sitting up again, "I don't want you to think I expect you to give up anything you want to do just because we get married, including school and your pursuit of a career. I think, as well, that we should have the wedding here, don't you? It seems, I don't know, proper and right. Don't you think?"

He was speaking quickly and so nonchalantly about the most important things in my life while to me it seemed as if the world had suddenly come to a stop. Even the ocean waves were on pause. The birds were all listening and waiting. The breeze held its breath.

"You're asking me to marry you?" I finally managed.

He laughed.

"That's kind of what an engagement ring promises for the near future, Willow, even here in Palm Beach."

"Oh, Thatcher," I said. I threw my arms around him. "I feel so stupid, so foolish for what I did and how I behaved. What an embarrassment!"

He kissed my cheek and forehead and pressed his to mine.

"You were perfect," he said.

"Perfect?" I pulled back. "How can you say I was perfect? I ran out of that place with my head soaking. I drove recklessly and was pulled over by a policeman. I made an absolute fool of myself."

"I know."

"I know you know that, but that is far from perfect behavior."

"What I meant was, it was the sort of dramatics Palm Beach socialites love. Who knows, maybe you'll be in the Shiny tomorrow."

"I'd rather not. Unless, of course, it's to announce this," I added, holding out my hand with the ring glittering on my finger.

"Yes, well . . . there's just one favor I need from you concerning that, Willow," he said, nodding at the ring.

"Favor?"

A small tickle, like the flap of a butterfly against the inside of my stomach, started and stopped.

"Yes. I have a few things left to work out, as you know, and for the time being, I think it would be best if you kept that out of sight."

"Out of sight? You mean, not wear it?"

"Not yet," he said. "I don't expect it will be that long, but—"

"You want me to keep our engagement a secret?"

"Just for a little while. As I said, I have a few things to work out."

"By things, you mean your mother and your sister and maybe even your father. Is that it?"

"It will help us, all of us, if I can do this so that no one is hurt, Willow."

I slipped the ring off and put it back into the box.

"Then why give it to me now, Thatcher?" I asked.

"I want you to know how committed I am to you and what you mean to me, Willow."

I thought for a moment, and then I handed it back to him.

"Don't give me an empty promise, Thatcher."

"That's not an empty promise. That's a three-carat class A diamond ring."

"This ring could be made of glass, for all I care, as long as it was for real and for now and for all the world to see. Other than that, it's just a fantasy, a dream, as stable as a bubble," I muttered.

"You're wrong, Willow. It means I love you and it means you mean the world to me. You were willing to be discreet about our romance before. Why not now?"

"It would be torture for me, Thatcher, to have the ring in a drawer, to look at it privately or in the dark. I'd rather not have it until you can give it to me freely and openly. And if you never can, you never can. Why fool each other?"

"I'm not fooling you. I'm only asking you to be a little patient!" he practically screamed.

"While you continue to be featured in the society columns with other women?"

"That means nothing. I told you. Your mother had a secret romance, didn't she?" he added pointedly.

"Her romance was an entirely different thing. It would have cost my father his career."

"Well, this is somewhat similar, Willow. I have to work some things out so that my career continues to prosper, for the both of us."

"It's not the same," I insisted. "When you can be honest about our love, I'll respect you more." I stood up.

He gazed up at me, then looked at the ring box in his hand and put it in his pocket.

"All right," he said, standing. "We'll wait until I can do that. In the meantime . . ."

"What? What, in the meantime, Thatcher?"

"I've got to see you, Willow. Please. Meet me tomorrow night at the house, our beach house. Be there at seven. I'll fix a pasta dinner for us."

"I don't know," I said.

"Please," he pleaded. He reached for my hand and pulled me closer to him. "Let's not lose what we have, what we'll build upon, Willow."

"Right now, that seems like a foundation made of chopped liver," I muttered.

"It's not. It's made of love, deeply felt love. Look, I'm not going to deny I've had some girlfriends, Willow, and even been serious with one or two, but you are the first woman I felt was substantial, the first woman I felt would complete me, make me substantial, too. With you, I can build something here, truly build a family and a life. I don't want to lose you. I know it seems quick, but I'd have to be a complete dodo not to realize you're the best thing that's come along. You believe me, don't you?"

"I want to believe you, Thatcher."

I really did, and he was as convincing as either the devil or an angel. I was still not sure which one.

"Good. Then meet me. Besides, I think I might have some news about Kirby Scott tomorrow," he added.

I looked up at him.

"Kirby Scott? Why?"

"I heard from a reliable source that he is in the Palm Beach area. I'm going to confront him tomorrow. Someone is working out the arrangements for me."

"What will you do?"

"Get the truth, or as much of it as I can, even if I have to choke it out of him—and not just about me, Willow, but about Grace and all that went on. Maybe I'll even learn something that will help Linden," he added. "Whatever I learn, it will bring some resolution to most of the problems that are interfering with us, maybe all of them. That's for sure. We'll have more to celebrate, okay?"

"I'll see. My head is spinning," I added before he could say another word. "I need to think, Thatcher. I need to think about everything."

"Okay, okay," he said, leaning toward me to kiss me softly. "I won't throw anything else at you today. But I will be coming at you fast and furious tomorrow." He started away, and stopped. "I mean that."

I watched him go. Then, as I went to turn away, I saw Linden stand. He had been crouching behind a bush. He gazed after Thatcher, then started toward me.

"I saw that," he said. "I saw him give you a ring and I saw you give it back. I'm happy you made the right decision." He turned in the direction Thatcher had gone. "He's probably got a collection of phony diamond rings in his dresser drawer. Who knows how many women he's given one to and promised things to?"

"It's a little more complicated than that, Linden," I said, "but thanks for worrying about me."

"It's not complicated!" he insisted, actually pounding the sides of his legs with his fists for emphasis. The look on my face calmed him some, and the redness began to recede. "You know, I grew up here on this property. I watched him often and saw how he seduced one innocent girl after another, each one buoyed by his promises, kept afloat by his oaths full of hot air. I told you that before, but you didn't believe me. You will," he added. "You will."

He paused and looked around as if he could still see the ghosts of all Thatcher's women.

"He had his favorite places. That gazebo was one. Whenever I saw a chaise lounge had been put in it, I knew Thatcher would be there late at night with another victim. Or he would go over to that little knoll by the beach house and spread a blanket that just happened to be hidden behind the brush. Once, I spilled turpentine over it, and the smell ruined his evening. After that, he would get them into one of the sailboats. He's just like his father."

Linden's last comment stunned me. It was almost prophetic—only, of course, Linden didn't know which father I was thinking of at the moment. Or did he?

"What do you mean?" I asked in a deep whisper.

"Asher Eaton's no better. I've seen him take a woman or two during one of their famous all-night parties, walking her away from the guests to some secluded spot. They have no shame. I've seen it all."

I nodded, thinking Linden probably had gotten a backseat Palm Beach education living on the fringes of the social world here. All of that was going on while they, the sinners and the promiscuous, looked down upon Linden and my mother. It was a world full of hypocrisy and deceit, peopled by sanctimonious liars who paid lip service to the truth and honesty while they worshiped self-indulgence and extravagance.

"That's probably true, Linden, but people can change, can realize that they have nothing meaningful in their lives and then try hard to find it."

"Not the Eatons," he declared, clenching his teeth. He pulled back his lips so hard, I thought he would tear them.

"Were you able to work today?" I asked softly, hoping to change the subject and get him less agitated.

"Yes," he said, then evidently realized he had left everything down on another section of the beach. He must have either seen or heard Thatcher and followed to do what he had apparently been doing for some time— spying on him.

He trekked off quickly and I walked behind. As we

approached his easel, I saw that he finally had begun to paint a new picture, one that resembled his style and previous work. It looked like the bow of a boat heading into a deep, swirling fog. As I drew closer, I could make out a face emerging from the fog or being swallowed up by it. It looked like me.

Before I could study it, he threw a cloth over it and finished putting away his paints.

"Can I help carry something?" I asked him.

He turned and gave me one of his vacant looks, his eyes glassy and distant, the look of someone who was a complete stranger.

"Linden? Are you all right?"

He blinked rapidly, and then his body snapped to firmness.

"What? Yes. Can you carry this?" he asked, handing me his paints.

"Of course," I said, and he put his easel over his shoulder, his picture under his arm, and began to walk back to the beach house, his shoulders turned in and down like some Neanderthal plodding to a cave.

"I'm glad you're working again, Linden," I said. "You have a great talent and it would be a shame not to use it."

He paused and turned to me, his eyes sharper, his gaze firmer and more scrutinizing.

"Maybe you'll pose for me again," he said.

How his mind worked amazed me. He moved in and out of his memories, moved in and out of time, lost an immediate moment and then later on picked it up like someone who had noticed what he had dropped along the way. His thoughts were like radio waves waiting for a receiver strong enough to hone them in and eliminate all the static.

"If you would like me to pose, I will."

He nodded.

"Good," he said, and marched on ahead of me mumbling, "Good."

I helped him put his things in his room, then went out to help my mother prepare our dinner. Linden remained in his room, so I was free to tell her all that had happened.

"I couldn't see myself taking that ring and living with it all like some dark secret," I said. "Was I wrong?"

"No, no," she said. "I can tell you what it is like holding everything in, wearing a mask of indifference while your heart cries for passion and love and truth. How many times your father and I would look at each other across a room full of other people and just for an instant reveal our hearts, only then to be terrified that someone had caught the glance, the tight, small smile on his lips or mine, the extra gentle and loving touch.

"No, secret love is a painful thing, torture. To find excuses to be alone, to steal a kiss and embrace, to hold hands behind walls . . . all of it is so difficult, so tantalizing.

"And then to say goodbye was the height of agony, goodbye not only to him but to you, for what I thought would be forever and ever. I used to tell myself I was surely being punished for sins committed before me or sins I would yet commit. Of course, your father used all his powers of persuasion to convince me otherwise.

" 'Love is often an accident of the moment,' he told me, 'an unexpected clap of thunder. I will not permit you or myself to think of it as anything evil, any sort of punishment.' As he quoted to me, 'it's better to have loved and lost than never to have loved at all.' "

"What a different sort of man he was with you," I said, unable to keep myself from being envious, jealous of her knowing so warm and wonderful a side of him. "He was just beginning to be that man with me."

She smiled and we hugged.

When we parted, Linden was in the doorway.

"I've made a decision," he began.

"Oh," Mother said, glancing at me in anticipation. "And what is that, Linden?"

"I've decided we definitely should go back into the main house, but only after it is thoroughly cleaned and all evidence of the Eatons ever having been there is expunged," he said.

"Okay," Mother said, pretending she and I were actually waiting all this time for his approval of the idea.

"And we'll start over, as a new family."

"That's what we want, Linden, yes. That's what we intend to do."

"And we'll help each other and trust each other and never betray each other."

"No, we never will," Mother said. He looked at me.

"We never will," I repeated.

He smiled and came toward us, stood before us a moment, and then threw his arms around both of us.

"My girls," he said. "I won't let anything bad happen to my girls."

Then he released us as quickly as he had embraced us, turned, and marched out of the kitchen.

Mother and I looked at each other, not knowing whether we should cry or laugh with joy.

"Maybe we *will* all be okay again," she said. "In time, maybe we will."

We had a wonderful dinner together. Linden listened with interest as I described my meeting with Professor Fuentes and my class schedule. The conversation was so bright and cheerful. He even expressed some interest in taking a class in art.

"That way I can sound as if I know what I'm doing as well as do it," he declared, and we all laughed.

Afterward, we sat on the loggia and had coffee. Mother talked about Linden's and my grandmother, Jackie Lee Houston Montgomery.

"She had a lot of self-confidence," Mother said. "I remember how strong she was after my father was killed. That early part of my life seems like a dream now. I sometimes wonder if it ever really happened or if I imagined it.

"My father doted on me, treated me like a little princess. Back then, I truly believed all of life would be like one long and perfect summer day, not too hot or humid, with a breeze that filled you with hope and expectation.

"It's so important to have expectations, to have something to look forward to," she continued, directing her words almost equally to Linden and me. "You have to make room for hope in your heart. You can't live in fear of being disappointed all the time. You have to take some risks. That's what I learned from your grandmother."

"It had to be hard for your mother to start all over in a new place with a young daughter along," I said. Linden nodded.

"Especially this place," he muttered.

"Jackie Lee, as she liked to be called, had more than just grit. She had a fire burning in her. My father's tragic death was devastating for her and she spent a long time in mourning, but she came out of it, I remember, with a blazing anger at the world that gave her the strength to meet one challenge after another.

"Once, she told me that she had pursued my first stepfather, Winston Montgomery, with a vengeance.

Marrying him and marrying into all this was her way of getting even with an unfair fate. She would show the world she would not be defeated."

"Then she went and defeated herself by getting involved with Kirby Scott," Linden said sharply. "She brought all the evil into the house. I'd rather not have been born," he added quickly.

Mother's joyful look of contentment quickly faded.

"I would go through all the pain and suffering again to have you with me, Linden."

He scowled, and glanced at me to see my reaction.

"Good things can come from bad experiences, Linden," I said softly.

"How do you know I'm a good thing?" he challenged. "He was my father, wasn't he? Something of him passed into me."

"There's more of Mother in you, and that's stronger," I said.

"And your grandmother, Jackie Lee," Mother said. "That's why I want you to know about her. Think of her as your heritage, and not him."

"I feel like I have a disease in me and I have to keep my immune system strong."

"You'll never be like him," Mother promised.

Linden gazed at me again.

"Maybe some of what he was isn't so bad. Women seem to go for that."

It seemed as if he meant Thatcher and me.

"He was a good-looking man," Mother said. "I'll give him that, and a charming man—but let's not talk about him. That's the painful past. Let's just talk about our future, our hope."

Linden grunted a reluctant agreement. I was beginning to understand him and what had turned him into the introverted man he was. For him, it was like being told the devil was your father. You were Satan's son and there were streams of evil flowing through your veins, evil that would take over and turn you into something terrible. He must have grown up looking for signs of that every time he gazed into a mirror.

How oddly different Linden's reaction to Kirby Scott being his father and Thatcher's were. Thatcher didn't feel personally threatened at all. Of course, if it was even true, Thatcher had learned about it at a much later stage of his life. His personality was already formed and solid. Such revelations were shocking, but easily tossed overboard.

Linden had carried the burdens of this knowledge from the moment he had learned what the word *father* meant. Just as I had grown up longing to have a real mother, he had grown up longing to have a real father. I understood some of his pain. I could empathize, and that gave me more confidence in my efforts to help him.

The ringing of the phone interrupted all our reveries. I rose first and went in to answer it.

"It's been arranged," Thatcher said as soon as I said hello and he recognized my voice.

"When?"

"Tomorrow about midday. I'm going to meet with him privately. Will you be at the beach house by seven?"

"Yes," I said.

"Good. You'll be wearing that ring sooner than you think," he predicted. "Willow Eaton. I like the sound of that, don't you?"

"I like what it promises," I said, and he laughed.

Mother took one look at me when I stepped back outside and knew I had spoken with Thatcher. Linden seemed to know it as well.

"I'm going for a walk," he said sullenly, and practically leaped off the loggia.

"He has such dramatic mood swings," Mother said, shaking her head and looking after him. "Even with his medication. I remember going through that same mental turmoil, and I vividly remember what it was like to see it in the other patients at the clinic, especially after your father had succeeded in making me well enough to have clear eyes. There was one suicide while I was there, you know."

"No, I didn't know that. Daddy never brought home his work experiences, and certainly wouldn't have mentioned something like that to me or in front of me. I kind of doubt he would have told my adoptive mother either. She wasn't very sympathetic when it came to his work-related problems."

"I know," Mother said. "He told me about her—or, should I say, complained to me about her—often. We all stumble into little traps here and there, he said."

"It was more than a little trap, at least to me. It was more like a pool of quicksand."

She laughed, but looked worriedly after Linden.

"I'll go walk with him," I said.

She nodded gratefully, and I stepped off the loggia and followed Linden into the night.

He was standing at the edge of the water as if he were teasing the tide that reached inches from his feet. He stood with his hands in his pockets.

"I love the warm evening sea breeze," I said as I approached him.

He didn't respond. I stood beside him and gazed out at the sea. An ocean liner was sliding across the horizon, its many lights festive. Although we couldn't hear anything, I imagined the music and the food and how excited and happy all of the passengers were, embarking from a Florida port on the start of their cruise.

"Do you ever want to go on one of those cruises?" I asked.

He turned slowly.

"I've been on a cruise with my grandmother. I was only fourteen. Grace wouldn't go. She hardly came out of the house in those days, much less mixed with people socially. Grandmother Jackie Lee loved parties, and a cruise like that was just a continuous party."

"Did you enjoy it?"

"No," he said quickly. Then he added, "Most of the time I didn't, but back then I still thought Jackie Lee was my real mother, so I did what she wanted me to do. Once," he said, gazing at the ship, "I met a nice girl who promised to write to me. She was from New York."

"She never wrote?"

"People make more promises on cruises, promises they won't keep. That's what Grandmother Jackie Lee told me."

"You must have been very fond of her."

"I was, but even a woman with her strength and insight could easily become a victim," he said through tight lips. "What happened to her, what Kirby Scott did, wasn't her fault. He could charm a snake. Men like him know what buttons to push in a woman, what fantasies to promise, and they always have a good and seemingly reasonable excuse for their selfish acts.

"He almost had Jackie Lee convinced he didn't rape Grace, you know. He almost had her believing it was Grace's fault. That was part of what . . . what drove her mad. How would you like it if your mother believed you were responsible for something like that? It wasn't what he had done to Grace that turned him out of the house; it was what he had done to our fortune. He left because there wasn't anything left to plunder here.

"Grace knew that deep down, and it broke her heart. It broke mine, too, when I learned it all," he said.

How clear and in control of himself he suddenly sounded, but he also sounded like someone speaking in a state of hypnosis. His eyes never left the ocean liner until it disappeared over the horizon.

"People are complicated, Linden," I said. "It seems we spend most of our lives forgiving someone for something. If we didn't, we would live with little balls of hate and anger choking us inside.

"It's easy for me to say, I know, but you've got to let go of some of the past, Linden. You've got to think about the future more and more."

"Future," he said, laughing. "What sort of future do I have?"

"A good one. You're going to do wonderful things artistically. We're going to create a new home for Grace, and you're going to get out and meet more people and travel and do all the things you've dreamed of doing."

He looked at me as if I was the one suffering mental turmoil.

"You will," I insisted, "but you've got to stop worrying about me so much. I'll be fine. I won't fall into any traps."

In the light of the stars, his face glowed, and I could see him raise his eyebrows and tighten his lips at the corners.

"Besides," I said, "I want you to get yourself strong and well enough so that if I do slip, you'll be there to pull me up, okay?"

He nodded softly.

"Be my big brother," I urged. "Be the brother I never had, but so desperately needed."

His smile widened and softened.

I put my arm around his waist and pressed my head to his shoulder for a moment.

When I raised it, he was glowing brighter than the stars.

"Let's keep walking," I said, taking his hand.

We said nothing more. We simply strolled along the beach and back. The silence was like a balm on our old wounds. That and the night filled with boat lights and starlight dazzled us. It was the warmest, closest time we had yet had together.

And when we returned, the healthy, happy radiance on Linden's face filled my mother's heart with joy.

"We'll be all right," I whispered to her. "We'll be just fine."

I kissed Linden's cheek and said good night, thanking him for the walk.

Later, when I laid my head on my pillow and gazed out my window, I saw the clouds rolling in from the west, unfolding like a dark charcoal blanket, reminding me that just like the promises made on cruises, promises made under the stars could be lost and forgotten if we weren't careful.

I felt like a little girl again and imagined Daddy standing in my doorway. He had come to take me through his catechism designed to bring me to some sensible conclusions.

Could you be taking on too much responsibility here too quickly, Willow?

I don't know. Maybe.

If you are, do you know how to retreat without hurting yourself or someone else?

I guess not, no.

Would you go walking in the darkness in a strange new place without any light at all?

No.
What should you do first, then?
Find some light.
Will you do that, Willow?
Yes, Daddy.
Before you go too much further?
Yes, Daddy.
Okay, then. Good night, Willow.
Good night, Daddy.

The door closed on my imaginary conversation, but it had been enough to send me back in time.

In my memory, the house turned down the volume of all its sounds. My adoptive mother's muffled voice came up through the floor like a bad record and then stopped.

Somewhere from the rear, I could hear Amou singing a Portuguese folk song as she folded clothes.

Then it was completely quiet.

And sleep, like the blanket of clouds outside the window, shut off the stars, even the ones I carried with me forever.

6

Dressed to Kill

Almost as soon as I woke up the next morning, I couldn't stop thinking about Thatcher and his meeting with the infamous Kirby Scott. If doctors could x-ray nerves, I was sure they would diagnose mine with split ends. To keep my mind occupied, I decided to return to the college campus, go to the bookstore, and get all the material Professor Fuentes had given me to read before my classes started. Once there, I found a few other books I had wanted as well, and in twenty minutes I had my arms so full, I felt like I would topple over if someone bumped me.

Someone didn't bump me. However, he tapped me on the shoulder, and when I turned, slowly and carefully I looked into the ebony eyes of Professor Fuentes.

"I see you had no trouble finding your way around."

"No."

"Here, let me help you with some of that," he said, and began taking books off my pile before I could object. He looked at some of them. "Ambitious," he declared, nodding. "Anyone else would be quite content with what is required. But this is a very good quality to have. Despite what everyone thinks," he added in a loud whisper, "the true student teaches himself."

He laughed.

"Don't let my colleagues know I said such a blasphemous thing."

"My father loved to say you can lead a horse—"

"—to water, but you can't teach it to drink," he recited with me.

We both laughed.

"Are you getting anything else? There are still a few thousand left to choose," he said, waving at the stacks.

"No. I believe I have what I need."

He stood by and watched me open my purse to get out my credit card while the cashier began to total my purchases.

"So," he said after I handed her the card, "how are you enjoying living here so far?"

"Except for the traffic and what I call Florida lights, fine," I said.

"Florida lights?"

"Those four-way traffic lights. If you miss the green, you're there long enough to read a chapter in one of these texts," I told him, and he laughed harder.

"But don't you have the same sort of traffic lights back in South Carolina?"

"Yes, but somehow not on every single intersection," I told him, and signed my credit card slip. As I reached for the bags, he seized one quickly.

"Let me help you to your car," he offered.

"Thank you. This really is personal service," I said. I thought he blushed a little, but he followed me out.

"Thank you," I said when he and I had put everything into the car.

"De nada. You're welcome," he said.

He stood staring at me, looking like he was thinking very hard about something. His eyes held me, and I waited with a small smile of amusement.

"Are you in a hurry?" he finally asked.

"Not in particular, no. Why?"

"I was supposed to have a luncheon with the dean of students today, but he had one of his small crises and just canceled on me. How would you like to join me for lunch? I know this little nothing place that serves the best chicken burritos and chiles rellenos in southeastern America. Unless you don't like Mexican food."

"I don't eat it very often, but when I've had it, I've enjoyed it."

"Is that a *sí?"*

"Sí," I said.

"Muy bien. You can leave your car here and come with me, or follow me in your car."

"Why don't we just go in my car?" I suggested.

"Now, why didn't I think of that?" he said, laughing. "Actually, I did," he admitted as he got in, "but I didn't think it was proper to ask you to drive me."

"The Latin male thing?"

"Old habits die hard—not that I am anything like a male chauvinist. I am the modern Latin man," he declared. "The truth is, I have to admit to an ulterior motive for asking you to join me for lunch."

"Oh?" I said, starting the car and pulling out of my parking space.

"I can't help being curious about you, your life with your father in particular. I hope you don't mind, but I have read everything he wrote, and I even have a letter

he sent me after I wrote to him, asking him about something in one of his books. I thought he had a very clear
and accurate view of human behavior. I imagine he was
a very calm, well-organized man, not easily shaken or
disturbed. Am I right?"

"Yes," I said. "My father was that."

"And yet capable of great passion—compassion, I
should say," he corrected.

I nodded.

"Oh, just make a quick left turn here and then take
the first right. Yes, that's it on the corner. Don't be discouraged by its outward appearance. This is a book that
definitely should not be judged by its cover," he added.

I parked and we entered a very small place. Although
it looked clean and well maintained, there were paper
tablecloths and even plastic knives and forks, which gave
it a truly unpretentious appearance. The menu was on a
plain sheet of paper and, according to the heading, was
changed daily. Everyone knew Professor Fuentes and
greeted him warmly. He introduced me as one of his
newest students. We took the table near the front window.

"Why don't you order for me, too?" I asked, seeing
that the menu was in Spanish.

"No problem."

He gave the waitress our order, then sat forward, his
face resuming an intense expression.

"If I ask anything that is impolite, please, don't hesitate to tell me," he said.

"Okay."

"I bet you will, too," he said with a smile. "Did your
father practice any of his theories about human behavior
on you?"

"If he did, it was so subtle, I didn't realize it," I said.
"When I was old enough to understand and appreci-

ate him more, I saw how cleverly and smoothly he used psychology on everyone, especially my adoptive mother."

"Adoptive?"

"Yes. I was adopted," I said.

"Oh." He sat back. "I see. I just assumed . . ."

I saw how disappointed he was that I was not a blood relation. I considered him for a moment, then decided to be forthcoming.

"However, I am my father's daughter."

His eyebrows hoisted.

"Excuse me?"

"My adoptive mother never knew, but I am my father's actual child. After both of them passed on, I learned the truth about my origins, and then visited my real mother and decided to live with her and go to school here."

"Oh. So that's why you told me you were living with your mother and half brother."

"Exactly."

"I am prying, but not as a busybody. I hope you believe that."

"Of course," I said.

The waitress brought us iced teas.

"There is and will always be that age-old debate about the relationship of heredity to behavior. A colleague of mine is developing a thesis that there is a so-called evil gene. Some people turn it into something society accepts, such as aggression in sports or the military or," he said with a wider smile, "politics."

I laughed.

"Daddy would never discount any theory out of hand."

"I know. He was the quintessential Renaissance man, the man with an open mind. I imagine he had no prejudices."

I thought for a moment.

"The only thing I know my father couldn't tolerate was prejudice. He was prejudiced against people with closed minds," I said.

They brought our food, and I immediately remarked on how delicious it was.

"I'm happy I didn't disappoint you," he said. "So, I imagine your adoptive mother must have been quite a woman as well."

"Quite," I said dryly.

He raised one eyebrow.

"Let just say that was where my father was a typical man first and the professor second, and leave it at that," I added.

He smiled.

"So," he said, dabbing his mouth with his napkin, "am I to assume you are romantically unattached, since you are recently arrived here?"

"No," I said.

"No, I shouldn't assume, or no, you're not romantically involved?"

"No, you shouldn't assume," I said.

He kept his smile, but I saw his eyes darken a bit.

"And you, Professor? I see no wedding ring."

"Close, but no gold ring, no," he replied. "It takes a special sort of woman to want to live with a man who is so dedicated to his work, especially because the work is so abstract. You don't see a finished product, like a house or a suit. Ideas are too mysterious."

"Yes. My adoptive mother never really took my father's work seriously—only seriously enough to see it as a form of competition for her attention and time."

He nodded.

"Are you working on some original theory?" I asked him, thinking I might just be a part of his research.

"Yes. I'm not sure how original it is, but I am explor-ing the influence of certain aspects of the physical envi-ronment on the psyche. The obvious things are already well accepted—people are more depressed in bad cli-mates, et cetera—but I think we have to continually evaluate the effects of technology on our personalities. But, please, don't let me get started and bore you with one of my lectures, at least not until you're trapped in my classroom," he added, and I laughed.

He was a charming man, I thought. Daddy would have liked him.

He asked me questions about my classes at UNC and we talked a bit about the school. I ate everything on my plate, not leaving a crumb.

"You did enjoy this. I'm glad. Would you like any-thing else? Coffee, some deep-fried ice cream, per-haps?" he asked.

"No, I'm fine," I said. "I have to get back anyway."

"Well, thank you for joining me and permitting me to ask you these questions."

"Thank you, Professor," I said. He signaled the wait-ress again, and paid the bill.

I drove him back to the campus. On the way, he told me more about his family, their restaurant, and his own college education. I learned he was actually as young as he looked, only twenty-eight.

"I was chosen to attend a school for special, ad-vanced students and graduated high school at age six-teen, college at nineteen, and I had my master's and then my doctorate by twenty-two," he told me. "That is why I grew this beard, to cover up what my mother calls her *cara del bebé,* her baby face," he confessed, then added after a moment's pause, "Thanks again for sharing with me."

"*São benvindo*," I replied.

"Huh?"

"Portuguese for 'you're welcome.' I'm showing off. If you're going to use Spanish on me, I'll use some Portuguese. I had a Portuguese nanny," I said, and he laughed.

"We'll teach each other languages, then," he said, and waved after he stepped out of my car.

What a nice man, I thought again, and then I wondered if it was proper for me to get so close and personal with my college teacher.

It's only a friendship, I told myself. *What's the harm?* There were far more serious problems to solve, most of them inside the gated property of Joya del Mar.

"Thatcher asked me to tell you to call him the moment you stepped in the door," my mother said, greeting me. "He sounded very excited."

"Oh?"

"He made me promise twice that I wouldn't forget!"

I put my bags of books down quickly and went to the phone. The moment his secretary heard my name, she put me through to him.

"I met with Kirby Scott," he said. "When I told him what I wanted to know, he was afraid I was coming after him as an attorney. He was so shaken by my directness, he was probably more forthcoming with me than he's been with anyone in his life. I learned some things about his relationship with Jackie Lee and with your mother as well. I'll tell you what he said that I think is true.

"But as far as what my sister and mother told me, the bottom line is, I have researched what he told me and I have confirmed it is impossible for him to be my father. He was a few thousand miles away from Joya del Mar and Palm Beach during the period when my mother would have conceived. It is as I suspected and hoped, a fabrication, a plot conceived by my lovely sister and my mother. I've already let Whitney know how upset I am by what they tried to do. My mother is next."

"I'm happy for you, Thatcher. You wouldn't want to be tied to that man in any way or form."

"Be happy for *us*. I'm no longer hiding anything from anyone here," he said with determination and fury in his voice. "I've changed our plans for dinner. You'll have to wait to enjoy my cooking genius. Instead, I've made reservations for us at Ta-Boo, the first place I ever took you and a virtual neon sign when it comes to announcing a relationship in Palm Beach. We can go to the beach house afterward. I'll pick you up at seven. Dress to kill," he ordered. "I don't want a single eye to miss you and me together tonight."

"Are you sure?" I asked. Actually, I was having trouble keeping my breath. Suddenly, my whole life, my future, was charging forward at a pace I had not expected.

"Am I sure? I tell you what, Willow De Beers, get that ring finger lathered up and ready. We're coming out. Tonight is our coming-out party!" he practically screamed into the phone.

The moment I hung up, my mother was there, holding her breath in anticipation.

"Is everything all right?" she asked, looking at my crimson face. I could feel the heat in my cheeks and at the base of my throat. "Willow?"

"I think so," I said. "I think I've agreed to become engaged tonight and for all the world to see and know."

She looked astounded, but cautious.

"Are you happy? It's what you want?"

"I think so," I said. "Yes, I think so."

"Then let's celebrate and be happy together," she declared, and rushed to hug me.

Regardless of the problems Linden continued to have, he didn't have to look at me twice to see and understand what was happening. Whatever perceptive and artistic ability he had to see things was well at work. He walked in on Mother and me still hugging and laughing, and when we parted and looked at him, his face registered his unhappiness.

"You're going to marry Thatcher Eaton," he concluded before I had spoken a single word.

"Be happy for her, Linden," Mother urged.

"Happy? More like feel sorry for her. What are we going to do now, permit the Eatons to continue to live in our house?" he said.

"No, Linden," I said. "One thing has nothing to do with the other."

He looked skeptical.

"Let's wait and see," he said. "Thatcher is a master at getting what he wants. He could sell anyone on anything, even Eskimos on buying ice."

"Please, Linden," I begged. "Give him a chance. He wants to be your friend. He's expressed his concern for you many times."

"Oh, has he? I wonder if he'll recall the many times he and his rich Palm Beach friends mocked me and ridiculed me. Ask him about the practical jokes they pulled on me," he urged. "Get him to explain all that while he's telling you how much he's concerned about me."

"Everyone grows up, Linden," Mother said softly. "I'm sure there were things you did as a young boy that you wouldn't want to speak about now."

He turned and squinted at Mother as if he wanted to be absolutely positive the woman who was speaking was indeed his mother.

"I don't understand how you can be happy about any of this," he told her, "especially after the way you've been treated by that family for years!"

"I'm tired, Linden. I'm tired of unhappiness, of anger, of sorrow. I want us to have some happiness now. I want us to look forward more than we look back. Please try to do what Willow asks and give it all a chance. Will you? Please."

He looked from her to me and then back to her.

"When it's over," he predicted, "when you're both sorry, don't apologize to me. Don't even look at me and expect any sympathy." Then he stepped toward me. "You know what it's like for me to wish you or anyone else good luck? It's like a crippled rabbit wishing another crippled rabbit good luck during the fox hunt. So, good luck, Willow," he said, and left the room.

"He'll come around," Mother told me, now sounding like the optimistic one. "When he sees how happy you are and how good things will be, he'll lose some of that anger."

"I don't know," I said. "Maybe I should wait until he shows more improvement."

"Don't be foolish. I told you before and I meant it, Willow, I don't want us to hold you back. If I ever feel we are dragging you down, I'll ask you to leave us," she threatened.

"That'll never be," I promised, and we hugged again, but not with as much vigor and excitement.

Later, I considered my wardrobe and what I would wear on this most special of all evenings out. Thatcher wanted me to wear something eye-catching. I did have a dress I was always afraid to wear because I thought it looked so sexy it didn't leave all that much to the imagination. It was a pleated snakeskin fitted tank dress, short enough to make it impossible to bend over. I had worn it only once before when I went out with Allan. He told me he had mixed feelings about it.

"On one hand," he'd said, "I'm proud to have you on my arm, but on the other . . . when I see the way other men gape lustfully at you, I am not comfortable."

In the end, I never wore it again when I went out with him, but somehow, looking at myself in the mirror and considering Palm Beach and Thatcher, I thought, *Thatcher will have a different feeling about it. He won't have any doubt or hesitation.*

I brushed out my hair. All at once, I did a double take, realizing that Mother had come in behind me and was watching me quietly.

"I'm sorry," she said. "I didn't mean to sneak up on you."

"You didn't," I said. "I'm just thinking and dreaming too hard. I'm in a daze."

"Standing here and watching you get ready, I was reminded of watching my mother when I was a young teenage girl. I would stand behind her and she would brush her hair and talk to me in the mirror. It was like we were looking at each other through a magic window. She would speak to me as if I were a full adult, never talking down to me. I suppose that was because we went through so much together, losing my father, moving here, starting new. Struggles like that mature you faster. I sometimes think I didn't have a girlhood.

"I did enjoy those moments we had together," she added, smiling at her reminiscences, "usually right before she went somewhere with Winston, some ball or el-

egant dinner. She was a very attractive woman, you
know."

"I know, I saw some photographs on your dresser."

"I think you look a lot like her."

"I wouldn't mind that," I said.

"She never did any of the things women do today to
keep their figures. She could eat the worst things and
not get fat, and she had skin like alabaster, so smooth
with just a slight peach tint in her cheeks, like you have.
She didn't wear very much makeup, either, just a bit of
lipstick and a little eye shadow sometimes, but she
loved expensive perfumes, and of all the jewelry she
had, she favored this," she said, and opened her hand to
show me a platinum hair clip set with diamonds.

"Oh, that is so beautiful," I said.

"It's one of the few pieces Kirby Scott didn't get his
greedy fingers around. This was made especially for
her. Winston commissioned it. I think it would look perfect in your hair," Mother said, offering it to me.

I started to shake my head.

"I know she would want you to be wearing it,
Willow. Something as beautiful as this doesn't belong
hidden under socks in the bottom of some dresser. And
besides, it's a special enough occasion to justify it being
worn. Go on, put it in your hair," Mother urged me.

I plucked it carefully from her palm and did as she
asked. Then I sat back and we both looked at me in the
mirror. I could see the look of pleasure settled in
Mother's face like strawberries sitting in whipped cream.
She bent down to hug me and press her cheek to mine.

"I'm sorry I wasn't there for your growing up,
Willow. I should have brought you back here with me,
but Mother was sick then. She had been fighting breast
cancer for two years and the battle took its toll on her.

She was like some beautiful flower, deprived of sunshine and water, fading, crumbling, with only a hint of its former beauty left for someone to see.

"It always bothered me that I wasn't here when she needed me the most in her life, and I regret not being there for you when you needed a real mother."

"You're here now," I said. "And I'm here, and we're together."

"I hope it's not too little too late."

"It's not. We have many years to enjoy together," I assured her.

Hearing Linden in the hallway, we both looked through the doorway. I wondered if he had been standing there and listening.

"I'll go spend some time with him," she whispered, and patted my arm. "Don't worry."

She left, and I looked through my wardrobe to find my black shawl. Then I gazed at myself in the mirror again and imagined Daddy standing behind me.

You look very nice, I thought he would say. I hoped he would say. He was never a prude, and with a wife like my adoptive mother, he was used to fashionable clothing and expensive jewelry.

Suddenly, I imagined his smile hardened into that psychiatrist's face of his. *Are you sure about all this, Willow?*

Sometimes I feel very sure, and then sometimes I don't.

Did you ask yourself why that is?

No, but I imagine it's not unusual. Don't we all have doubts when we make big decisions?

His smile softened.

Now who's being the psychiatrist, answering a question with a question?

I had a good teacher.

He laughed, and then his image faded.

"Daddy," I whispered to the mirror.

There was only I, looking hard, looking alone, looking afraid.

Linden and Mother were on the loggia when I came out of my room. The door was open, so I could hear their conversation. I heard Linden complain, "I bet you wish you had two daughters."

"Of course not. Why, most married people want to have one of each."

"You weren't married, either time," he said harshly.

"I don't love either of you the less because of that," she said.

"Willow was born out of a love relationship, at least," he muttered bitterly.

"I've told you a hundred times if I've told you once, Linden. I would go through all of it, the pain, the disgrace, the misery, if it meant I would have you."

"You're just saying that because it's too late to give me back," he snapped.

"No, that's not so."

"Right," he said.

"Hi," chimed in a new voice. It was Thatcher, approaching the house.

Linden rose immediately and came in, moving so fast he almost didn't see me standing in the entry. He stopped short and pulled himself up.

"Your Prince Charming has arrived. Have a good time," he said, and started by me.

I seized his arm, which surprised him.

"I wish when you said that, you really meant it, Linden."

He blinked and relaxed his shoulders. Then he

looked down, ashamedly, I thought, before looking up at me again.

"I do. I'm sorry. I do," he said.

I smiled.

"Thank you, Linden," I replied, and he nodded and walked more slowly away from me, looking suddenly years older.

I stepped outside. Thatcher, wearing a gold sports jacket, black slacks, a black shirt, and a black tie, looked up at me and whistled. Then he turned to Mother, laughed, and shook his head.

"Grace, the hens will be cackling about this for a month."

"As long as they don't lay any eggs on my front steps," Mother said, and Thatcher laughed again.

He held out his arm.

"Mrs. Future Thatcher Eaton," he said in an exaggerated southern accent, "may I escort you?"

"Why, Mr. Eaton, I thought you'd never ask," I said, and Mother laughed harder than either of us.

On such a wonderful, happy note, how could anything bring back the clouds of despair? I thought.

7

Tea with Bunny

Everything Thatcher did that night seemed designed to flaunt our relationship before Palm Beach society. He'd reserved a table that put us in the front so that we would be constantly on display, and when we entered, he made sure to pause to introduce me as his fiancée to anyone and everyone he knew. I was already wearing the ring. He had presented it to me again as soon as we were in his Rolls.

"I'm giving it back to you a lot sooner than you expected, I know," he said as he took my hand and slipped it over my finger.

"Yes."

He kissed me.

"That's the way it will be from now on, Willow. You give me a task and I'll get it done. Your happiness is my happiness," he told me.

I know it was only my imagination, but my hand felt heavier, especially after he began to introduce me as his fiancée. Whenever I shook hands with anyone, I watched the way his or her eyes and the eyes of those around us were drawn to the glittering diamond. By the time we reached our table, the whole place was chattering about us. I caught bits and pieces of phrases: ". . . never thought Thatcher Eaton would get serious about anyone . . . it can't be true . . . Grace Montgomery's daughter?"

People who hadn't been in the "receiving line" made their way to our table to be introduced and to hear Thatcher say "my fiancée," as if the ring itself were no guarantee or proof of anything. It had to come from his lips as well.

One woman who looked about my mother's age but dressed as if she were my age surprised me by seizing my hand and holding it up so the ring was clearly visible to anyone nearby. Then she blurted, "Do you realize what you have done? You have lassoed the wildest stallion on the beach!"

"Really?" I said, sounding as unimpressed as I could manage as I retrieved my hand. I looked at Thatcher. "He's so polite and civilized when he is with me, I never would have known it."

He roared, and the woman, who'd been introduced as Muffy Anderson, dropped her jaw so quickly it looked like it had unhinged. Her escort, a thin, small, dapper man, held a frozen smile. I thought they made a most unlikely couple. She looked like she could absorb him with a mere embrace, especially if he was drawn into the valley between her two bulging breasts.

"Who was that?" I asked Thatcher as soon as they left our table.

"Muffy? She's the widow of Lowell Anderson, who patented and manufactured a plastic wine bottle cap that sold like hotcakes throughout western Europe. Her escort is just some Palm Beach walker, another Kirby Scott," he said through the corner of his mouth.

I wanted to hear more about his meeting with Kirby Scott, but I knew almost from the moment we had arrived at Ta-Boo that we wouldn't have much time to talk seriously at the restaurant. There was a constant parade of Thatcher's friends and acquaintances marching to and by our table. Before the evening ended, a woman who looked like she had just come from a costume ball, wearing a jeweled cowboy hat, a beaded blouse, a pink quilted skirt, and a pair of what looked like alligator boots, came charging into the restaurant with a young man at her side who carried an impressive-looking camera. She made her way directly to our table. We were just having our dessert.

"Thatcher Eaton, you rogue," she shouted. She nodded at me. "How dare you do something like this without giving me fair warning?"

Taken aback, I looked to Thatcher, who sat with a wide, self-satisfied grin slashed across his face.

"Somehow, I knew a little bird would be whispering in your ear, Suzy. Willow, this is Suzy Q, the most important and influential society columnist in Palm Beach."

"I'll need a picture or two," she said as if we had nothing to say about it. She nodded to her photographer, who started to snap the photos. "Put your arm around her shoulders, Thatcher. Make it look as real as you can," she ordered.

"It is real," he said, and lifted my hand to show her the engagement ring.

She tilted her head and pulled in the corners of her thickly painted lips. I thought she looked like a walking billboard advertisement for cosmetic surgery. Her nose was clipped. Her eyes were pulled so tightly, I wondered if she was able to close them at night, and her chin looked tucked under so snugly, I had real doubt that she could swallow anything. Her gaudy blond hair hung straight down beside her cheeks like strands of plastic.

"All right," she told the photographer, "that's enough. So give me the scoop, darling," she said, shoving what looked like a miniature tape recorder in our faces. "Where did you two meet?"

"Wasn't it in southern France? Nice?" he asked me.

"It was nice, but it wasn't Nice," I said, and we both laughed.

"I'm going to get all the nitty-gritty anyway, darling, so why play games with Suzy Q?"

"She's right, Willow. There is no point trying to hide anything from her. She has eyes everywhere, behind the highest walls. Even Donald Trump isn't safe." He turned back to her. "Willow is my landlady," Thatcher said.

Suzy raised her eyebrows and looked at me.

"Really?"

"She owns Joya del Mar. I figured if I married her, I'd get a break on the rent," he said.

Suzy Q dropped her gullible expression quickly, and dropped her tape recorder into the small black leather purse hanging at the end of a strap over her shoulder.

"All right, Mr. Smarty-pants. I'll go round up my usual sources and get the truth, or something that closely resembles it. You'll have to take your chances."

"Isn't that what everyone appearing in your column does, Suzy?"

"Cute. Very cute. My dear," she said, turning to me, "you have my condolences. And my best wishes," she added with as warm a smile as she was capable of producing, I thought.

"I'll be seeing you . . . everywhere." She made it sound more like a warning than a promise. She nodded to her photographer, and left the restaurant as quickly as she had burst into it.

Thatcher laughed.

"Is it over yet?" I asked him.

"I think so, for now," he said, nodding, and signaled for our check.

Leaving was more difficult than entering since more people had arrived, seemingly because they had heard about Thatcher and me. I was introduced to nearly twice as many people on the way out as on the way in. By the time we got into the Rolls, I was exhausted and pretended to collapse.

"I feel pinched and squeezed, examined under microscopes, and tested for every known social disease. There are eye prints over my whole face," I complained, scrubbing my cheeks.

"I assure you, they weren't looking only at your face," Thatcher said.

"We might as well be in a giant fishbowl!"

"That's exactly what Palm Beach is," he said, laughing, "high society under glass."

I groaned and sank deeper into the seat.

"I hope you'll get your second wind," he said as we drove off. "The night is early, especially for us."

"Oh, Thatcher, we're not going to another Palm Beach nightspot, are we?" I moaned.

"No, we've done enough damage here," he said. "My mother and my sister will be on the phone all day tomorrow trying to field the questions and the comments. I've already made arrangements to be out of town so they won't be able to reach me. I'm taking a deposition down in Miami. Of course, with the speed of gossip reaching supersonic in this town, they could already be on the telephone, especially with each other.

I can just hear Whitney calming and comforting our mother deary. Dear old Dad will comfort himself with a Grey Goose vodka cosmopolitan on the rocks." He laughed.

"You're enjoying this too much," I said with suspicion. "Is it because of me or because you're getting sweet revenge?"

"Mostly because of you," he replied, "but I won't deny I'll enjoy the sweet revenge."

"That's just great, Thatcher. How am I ever supposed to get along with your family if you rub me in their faces like so much hot pepper?"

"Oh, they'll get over it and take you in with as much sincerity as they are capable of showing," he replied. "Besides, Willow, you're marrying me, not my whole family."

"You know that's not realistic, Thatcher. Let's make a pact right now and promise to try never to fool each other," I told him.

He nodded.

"Okay," he said softly. "You're right. I won't gloat. Once my family understands I am serious and we are for real, things will change. That's realistic," he assured me. "Speaking of which, we should think about a wedding date."

"I'm starting college soon," I said. "I've met with my advisor and I have my schedule. The semester ends in early June."

"Good. So let's use that as a plan. Why don't we think of a late June wedding? I want to make a honeymoon reservation for us in Eze village in southern France, at a place called the Château de la Chevre d'Or. It's like being in a storybook world, but I've got to do it well in advance."

My heart began to thump at the thought of planning it all. There was so much to do.

"Maybe it's all happening too fast," I said. "We're moving back into the main house in May, and—"

"You could always postpone that," Thatcher said quickly.

"No," I practically shouted. That would be all that Linden needed to hear, I thought. It would confirm all his dreads. "I've promised my mother and Linden, and they are looking forward to it now, Thatcher. I'd much rather postpone our wedding a few months," I told him firmly.

"I understand," he said. "Well, I don't think it will present any serious problems anyway. We have plenty of time to do everything."

"We could always just elope," I said, and he laughed.

"We could, but we'd have to have a real wedding anyway."

"Why?"

"Why? This is Palm Beach, Willow. Get used to it. You're a part of Palm Beach society now. That will be confirmed and stamped in tomorrow's papers."

"Is that all it takes?" I asked.

"All? You heard Suzy Q. You've corralled the most eligible stallion on the beach. Get ready. Your phone's going to ring off the hook, too."

"Why?"

"Invitations," he said. "Everyone is going to want a piece of you. You'll see. We're both going to be the most sought-after guests of honor."

"Is that good?"

"It's good for me and my career, and what's good for me, Willow, will be good for you," he replied.

I sat back wondering if I'd really and truly understood what I was getting into when I agreed to marry

Thatcher. I looked at him, smiling and happy, a handsome and accomplished young man whose love for me was apparently so overwhelming, he couldn't tolerate the thought of any delays.

"Don't look so worried," he said, and reached out to take my hand. "I'll always protect you from the sharks that swim on shore. What good is having a husband who's an attorney if he can't do that?"

"I'm not worried for myself," I said.

He nodded with understanding.

"We'll take care of everyone now, Willow, you and I. We'll bring the glitter of joy back to Joya del Mar, where it belongs, where it should be forever and ever." He smiled. "Did I tell you how sexy you look in that dress tonight?"

"Not enough," I said, and he laughed.

"Hey, the night is just beginning," he told me, and turned onto the road that would take us to our beach-house rendezvous.

His pager rang as we entered. He looked at it and nodded.

"Your mother?" I asked.

"I'm surprised it took this long. Must have been a jam up on the phone lines or something."

"Are you going to call her?"

"No, not tonight. We're closing the door on all that out there. In here, it's just you and me," he said, and pulled me to him to kiss me. "I couldn't think of anything else if I tried. Not with you in my arms looking like you do." He kissed me again, then scooped me up and carried me, laughing, to the bedroom.

"What's left for the honeymoon?" I asked as he began to undress.

He paused and smiled.

"Wait until we're there on that mountain looking down at the sea. Then you'll know that every day we're together will be better than the day before. This," he said, kneeling beside the bed, "is just the coming attractions."

"Sounds more like a movie than a marriage."

"Our marriage will always be a romance, Willow," he promised, and kissed me on the tip of my nose as he rose slowly to lie down beside me and make love to me.

I once overheard my adoptive mother tell one of her closer friends that when you made love with your eyes closed all the time, you were trying to forget the man you were with and replace him with either some fantasy or someone you wished you were with. Her friend said if that was true, she hadn't made love with her husband for years. They both laughed, and then my adoptive mother shocked me by saying she'd *never* made love to her husband: "Even on our honeymoon, I replaced him behind my eyelids."

Their laughter felt like bee stings.

If my adoptive mother was right and was at least to be trusted when it came to something like making love, I had nothing to fear about my feelings for Thatcher.

Yes, his kisses and his caresses closed my eyes, and his hot breath on my neck made me tingle with pleasure and anticipation, but I loved looking at him. He was truly a handsome man, and when I watched him soaking in pleasure, he would open his eyes, too, and look into mine and smile and say, "You're so beautiful, Willow. You're so fresh and special."

If something were to happen and we were not together forever and ever, and if I was with someone else, I thought, I would most likely close my eyes all the time and behind my lids see Thatcher Eaton.

Such was the magic that ignited between us. We were

like two sticks rubbed together to spark a flame that grew so hot and bright, it threatened to consume us in ourselves. Afterward, both of us needed a few minutes to catch our breath, to cool down our bodies and come back to earth. Still embracing me, he held me against his body and breathed normally. I had my back to him.

"Tell me about Kirby Scott now, Thatcher. What was he like? What did he say about my mother and Linden?"

Thatcher slipped his arm out from under me and turned onto his back to look up at the ceiling. I spun around to face him and propped myself up on my elbow.

"I will say this," he began, "there is something to be said for the life of a rake. Never really worrying about anything, living the free life without responsibility or conscience, has kept him looking remarkably young. What aging there is in his face just distinguishes him. When I first set eyes on him, I thought this must be a different Kirby Scott. The man I was looking to meet had to be in his early sixties at least. I mean, he was married to your grandmother.

"Then I remembered he was about five years younger. Maybe he was even younger than that, but lied about his age. Who knows? The reality was, I could understand how he continues to charm and beguile women years and years younger than he is.

"He is presently the escort of Jill Littleton, Hunter Littleton's widow. Hunter was CEO of Mars Industries, the company that specializes in constructing airport malls. I did some work for her two years ago, and that's how I arranged to have the face-to-face with Kirby."

"But what was he like?" I pursued, impatient.

"He was a cocky, confident son of a bitch. He had some idea about why I wanted to see him, but that didn't shake him a bit, at least so I could see. He wore a blue sports jacket, white pants, and Italian loafers without socks. He flaunts his gold in a thick necklace and a gold bracelet that looks like it could be used as the anchor of a battleship. He had a pinky ring with an emerald the size of a Ping-Pong ball."

"I'm happy you noticed all of his jewelry, Thatcher, but what was he like?"

Thatcher laughed.

"Hey, I can't help being impressed with all that, especially on a thief. That's all he really is, a glamorized thief.

"He was crafty and oh, so polite and refined. He tried to show his concern about Grace. How was she? He wished he could visit her and see Linden, but he didn't think it would do either of them any good. The way he spoke about those days, he has either convinced himself or perfected the fabrication that he was young and innocent and impressionable. According to him, Jackie Lee took advantage of him, used him, and then, as if he were something disposable, threw him aside to have extramarital flings.

"Frustrated and alone, he claims, he was vulnerable to Grace's young charm. She worshiped and admired him so much it made his head spin, and he gave in to temptation. Yadda, yadda . . ." Thatcher added, waving his hand in the air.

"I got into the business about my mother, and that's when his disposition and confidence took a nosedive. His lips actually began to tremble with his denials: If I was seeking to start some sort of lawsuit . . . on and on, until he produced some hard evidence that I could follow up and, as I told you, confirm.

"We returned to talking about Grace and Jackie Lee. He claimed Grace was always quite an introverted girl, had few friends and hardly socialized. She was content living through his experiences and would sit for hours and hours to hear him describe his travels, his adventures. He made himself sound like Othello charming Desdemona with tales of battle and journeys to exotic lands.

"Of course, according to him, he never realized how attached to him she was becoming. She was a very beautiful young woman, and when she enticed him, he weakened. Once he realized what he had done, he says, he made the decision himself to leave Joya del Mar.

"I told him if he continued to spread such a fantastic tale, especially now, I would indeed take him to court. He surprised me by knowing all about you and confidently declared that your existence and Grace's affair at some clinic demonstrated the truth of what he was saying and had been claiming as a defense. In other words, he wasn't a bit frightened of me when it came to that and, instead, suddenly showed great interest in you."

"In me?"

"He was intrigued and began asking all sorts of questions."

"Like what?"

"Just questions," Thatcher replied quickly. "I told him if he should so much as come within ten yards of you, I would personally put him in a permanent coma. I wanted to leap over the table at that point and choke him, but Jill came out and I had to be civilized. My eyes continued the hot threat, and I'm sure he understood I was serious.

"Anyway, I followed up on his information, leading me to the wonderful conclusion that he is by no stretch of the imagination my father. After having met him and seen what a shrewd, conniving, and unfortunately charming rogue he can be, I was happy to disprove what my sister and my mother were trying to convince me to believe. It made me even angrier, and I told my sister off like I have never told her. By the time I was finished, she was crying over the phone."

"I hope they weren't crocodile tears," I said, and he laughed.

"Anyway, for now it might be better if you didn't tell Grace and especially Linden that Kirby is in Palm Beach. I'm sure he won't be here long. Jill has her own luxury ship and was already talking about going over to Barbados," Thatcher said.

I agreed.

Afterward, when we returned to Joya del Mar, he walked me down to the beach house. We kissed and said good night. He told me that as soon as he returned from Miami, he would call and we would begin to plan our wedding.

"I want Grace to do as much as she wants," he said, "but let's keep the pressure off her, too."

"Will your mother want anything to do with it?" I wondered aloud.

"You can be sure she will," he assured me. "It's a Palm Beach high event. She won't be able to ignore it. In fact, I'll make this prediction right now: We'll have our hands full keeping her from taking over the entire affair."

"Don't worry. I'll see she doesn't do that."

He laughed.

"Don't underestimate the tenacity of a Palm Beach socialite when the opportunity to ring bells, direct spotlights, and impress the town comes up," he warned.

"I should think our wedding will be more special," I said.

"That's the point. So will she. You'll see," he said with a chuckle. He kissed me again, and returned to the main house.

When I stepped onto our loggia, I almost didn't see Linden sitting in the corner in the shadows. He didn't acknowledge me. He sat so still, I was afraid he had wandered out in his sleep again and was actually asleep in the chair.

"Linden?"

Slowly, he turned, but he didn't speak.

"Why are you out here so late? Are you all right?"

"I'm fine," he said with remarkable alertness. "Sometimes, I like to stare out at the sea. Most people think it looks the same all the time, but they don't see the changes in the water, the movement of starlight and moonlight and even the fish. You can tell the future by studying the sea at night."

"How?"

"It takes practice. You learn by watching how far away the darkness stays, where it is. It comes from the horizon," he said, nodding toward it. "It's coming closer and closer. That's not good."

"Linden, you must not dwell on dark and sad things," I told him.

He gazed at me. I couldn't see his eyes, but I knew they were unmoving, intense.

"One way or another, he's going to remain in that house," he said. "Thatcher is going to remain. That's a good reason why he proposed to you."

"Really, Linden, I don't think Thatcher's purpose is to keep living in Joya del Mar. Surely there are homes just as beautiful, if not more beautiful, here."

He turned away.

"We're all going to be happy together, Linden. You'll see."

"I see the darkness coming closer," he said. "That's what I see."

"Aren't you tired? It's getting late."

"I'm all right." He turned back to me. "Don't worry," he said in a harder, firmer voice. "I won't hurt myself anymore. I've got to remain strong."

"Good."

"To protect you," he added. He turned away again. "I've got to remain strong."

He was silent again, again like stone. I debated staying out there with him, then decided it would be better to leave him be and hope that with the morning and the light, the darkness in his mind would go away.

Mother was asleep. I went to bed, but I couldn't help lying there and listening for Linden. Finally, nearly a half hour later, I heard him come in and walk softly through the hallway, pausing at my doorway for a moment before going into his own room.

He was, surprisingly, far more cheerful in the morning. His talk was about the main house and our moving back into it. There was such a nice, positive energy about us. As if Thatcher had his ear to our wall, he surprised me with a call from his car on his way down to Miami.

"I couldn't wait to tell you," he began. "I just got off the phone with my father. They know everything, of course, and as I told you, they are going to accept it in their inimitable way. They have decided to move out of Joya del Mar sooner than anticipated. In fact, my usually laid-back father surprised me. He has been plotting and planning all this time, and they have made an offer and agreed to purchase a home that's turnkey ready."

"Really?"

"Yes. I have a feeling my sister had something to do with it, too. Anyway, I thought you and Grace and Linden would be pleased to know. They are moving within the month and paying you whatever they still owe. That gives you more time to get organized and think about our wedding," he said.

"That's wonderful, Thatcher."

"I'll call you as soon as I'm done here, Willow."

When my mother and Linden heard the news, Linden was the happiest I had seen him since my return. He spoke eagerly now about setting up his studio. I, too, felt much better about all I was planning to accomplish in the next six months. My wedding, the moving, starting a new school, all of that boosted my mother's spirits as well. She had a great deal with which to occupy herself.

However, thinking about an event such as a wedding in Palm Beach also made her nervous.

"We'll take it a step at a time," I told her. "Just think of all we'll be able to do together."

That thought put the smiles back on her face, the lightness in her step, and the hope in her eyes.

Was it too much to believe that we would finally be a real family?

Later that afternoon, Jennings, the Eatons' butler, came to our front door and told me Mrs. Eaton would very much like to speak with me this afternoon. Would I be available for tea at about four? I was so tempted to say no, I was too busy. Mother gave me a look when she saw my hesitation, which was more or less a look that asked me to be nice, so I agreed to be there.

"We've all got to make an effort if this is going to work," she wisely advised. "The past is the past. We should worry only about our futures."

I felt ashamed that she had to be the one to tell me that, especially after all she had been through.

So, with as much enthusiasm as I could muster, I went up to the main house and rang the bell. Jennings greeted me with what I thought was a look of sympathy and led me to the sunroom, where Bunny was on the telephone. She waved for me to enter and take the seat across from her while she continued her conversation.

"Don't tell me you need more time, Angelo. This is Mrs. Eaton," she screeched into the phone. "I know what you need and what you don't need, and I expect as wonderful a menu as you did for the Turners. No, amend that. I expect something better. Bring me a list of new dishes not ever served at a Palm Beach affair. . . . Of course we are talking about seven to eight hundred. How could it be any less? Really, Angelo, I'm worried about you," she said, and followed it with her little hollow laugh. "I expect to see you before the end of the week," she ended with the sharpness of an army general. "Thank you. *Arrivederci.*"

She hung up and flashed a smile at me, then signaled the maid who was standing so still she looked like a store mannequin. The maid moved quickly to pour the tea from the silver pot and uncovered the petit fours.

"Thank you, Mary," Bunny said, which really translated to, "Leave us."

The moment she did so, Bunny's smile faded.

"Well, I must congratulate you, my dear. You are far more clever than I ever imagined."

"What does that mean?"

"Nothing, except for you to have so captivated my son after all that has happened is rather astonishing. I mean that as a real compliment. Actually, it encourages me to know that you are that clever. I would have hated for Thatcher to end up with one of those many airheads he dated."

I smiled to myself at her backhanded compliment. This was her way of turning an about-face. I reached for my teacup.

"It wasn't so much my being clever, Bunny. What

brought Thatcher and me to this point is love, a deep-seated and all-encompassing affection for each other," I defined for her.

"Love," she moaned as if it were a mythical idea. "Just an excuse for two people using each other."

"I'm sorry you believe that, that you are so cynical."

"I'm just wiser than you, but let's not debate some soap opera. The fact is, we're here together, thanks to Thatcher, and I have decided we shall start anew, as if nothing has ever passed between us. Is that all right with you?" she asked. "It's so much easier than reviewing this and that and apologizing and explaining, don't you think? Who needs that useless aggravation, and especially who needs it at a time like this? Thatcher just simply insists on this quite unrealistic marriage date and consequently, as men are wont to do, has left the impossible task in our hands."

"If it's impossible, how can we do it?" I countered, still smiling. She was truly a character. How could I remain angry at her?

"That's just it. We can do the impossible and we will. I'll do everything in my power to help, of course. I know the burdens under which you live at the moment, and I realize how much time you have and how many other responsibilities you have, whereas that's all I do have . . . time," she said, and sipped her tea. "Please have one of these. They are fresh and sumptuous."

"No, thank you," I said.

"Oh, eat one," she cried. "I can't stand eating something fattening in front of another woman who has such self-control. You ruin it for me."

Reluctantly, I plucked one of the cakes from the plate. I nibbled on it and sipped some tea. She looked contented, as if she were the devil in the Garden of Eden and had gotten me to eat the forbidden fruit.

"What exactly is it you think you will do, Bunny?"

"Thank you for not calling me Mother right off the bat. How I hate those young women who just can't wait to label their mothers-in-law. It makes them sound like parents to everyone around them. I refuse to let Whitney's husband Hans call me Mother or Mom or any such ridiculous thing. He's not all that much younger than I am, for that matter, and it would look absolutely ridiculous for him to refer to me as anything other than Bunny.

"So call me Bunny forever," she said, and bit more aggressively into another petit four.

"Okay, Bunny forever, what is it you are planning to do?"

"Well, as you heard when you walked in, I just spoke with the caterer. We have to get onto these things ASAP. We have a ready-made list of guests to invite. I keep it updated. Nowadays, you can actually have the envelopes preaddressed and waiting. I've always anticipated Thatcher's wedding, of course, and have a whole file drawer filled with ideas, not to mention the ideas I've accumulated over the years from attending other weddings here.

"As you know," she continued, barely taking a breath, "we're leaving the property quite soon, so it would be wise to plan out the location of everything immediately. You've attended a party here already, so you know how wonderful it can be if it is set up correctly.

"I thought you should be married on the lower patio," she rattled on, as if she had indeed been rehearsing it for years and years. "We'll construct an altar of flowers. There'll be flowers everywhere, of course, but something special for the altar. I'd prefer a mix of red and white roses. What do you think of that?"

"Perhaps we should get married in a church and come here for the reception," I suggested.

"Oh, what for?" she cried, grimacing like someone who had just bitten a rotten walnut. "There isn't a church that can hold all the people I want to have attend. Besides, that's such a droll setting for a wedding."

"A church?"

"Of course it is. They hold funerals in it, too, and everyone is so serious in a church. Make the minister come to us. Oh, dear," she said suddenly. I thought she truly had eaten something bad. She held the petit four at the edge of her lips.

"What?"

"It just occurred to me that I don't know your religious affiliation. Do you follow your father's faith? Are you Catholic? I know you can't be Jewish. Can you?"

"My father wasn't very religious, but my adoptive mother was Episcopalian, as I believe my mother's family is."

"Yes," she said with relief. "Well, that avoids anything vulgar. Now, as to the guest list," she pressed on, running away with my life and my future, "my advice to you is to have it made up as quickly as you can. With Thatcher's business acquaintances and our own friends and acquaintances, we simply cannot invite fewer than five to six hundred people. I'm assuming you will have half that many."

"Nowhere near it," I said.

"Oh? Well, whatever. Well, then, I've made up a list of things to do and I've underlined in red those things I can arrange," she said, handing me a sheet of her personal stationery.

"This is all very interesting," I said, glancing at it. Practically everything on the sheet had been underlined in red. "Thank you. I'll take it back with me and discuss it with my mother."

"What?"

"To see how this corresponds with her own ideas, of course," I replied.

"But . . . your mother? Is she capable of such decisions? She's been out of society so long. She wouldn't know where to begin."

"Oh, Bunny, a woman always knows where to begin when it comes to the wedding of her daughter, don't you think? Especially a wedding like this. We'll get back to you," I added, and rose.

She sat there, looking stunned.

"Actually, lilacs," I said.

"What?"

"An altar made of flowers? I think I'd prefer lilacs. I'll see what Mother thinks. Thanks for the tea—and you're right, those little cakes are sumptuous."

She looked like she couldn't swallow. I flashed a smile at her and left her sitting there with a petit four pinched between her right thumb and forefinger.

Willow De Beers, I heard my conscience declare as soon as I stepped out of the rear of the house and started down to the beach house, *you little brat. You enjoyed that too much.*

But I was nice about it, wasn't I?

I can do this. I can handle them all, I thought confidently.

Do you think you're being too arrogant? Daddy would ask.

No, I told him in my mind. Just confident. . . . It's the right answer, isn't it, Daddy?

We'll see.

We'll know sooner than later.

Won't we?

8

Lunch with Whitney

My life began to move as if God had pressed a button and shifted it into fast forward. Despite my reaction to Bunny's heavy hand in my and Thatcher's wedding plans, Mother and I decided it was not so bad to permit her to make most of the arrangements. For one thing, Bunny wasn't wrong about the fact that Mother was out of touch with Palm Beach society and the people to contact; for another, with all I had to do to prepare for school and we had to do to prepare to move into the main house, it was wise to place the heavier burdens on the Eatons, people who had nothing to do with their lives but frolic.

"Besides," Mother pointed out, "we have to give the devil her due. She will know more about arranging a formal wedding than I will."

And so, despite my instinctive belief that Thatcher and I should simply go off somewhere and get married, I agreed with Mother and we sent word through Jennings that we would like to discuss it all with Bunny.

Just like two warring parties negotiating a peace treaty, we met on neutral ground about halfway between the beach house and the main house, the pool patio. Bunny had already gone ahead and hired herself a temporary secretary-assistant, which should have given Mother and me fair warning as to just how elaborate and involved this was all going to be.

"This is Patricia Prescott, my temporary personal assistant," Bunny began. "She'll take notes and follow through on our decisions."

Patricia looked like she was in her early to mid-thirties, dark-haired with a pale complexion. She smiled in flashes, making it seem like any expression of joy or relaxation was forbidden. She mouthed, "Hello," and quickly took a seat, opening a briefcase and extracting a long legal pad.

"I am happy you have decided to move as quickly as possible on all this, Grace," Bunny told my mother, and then she turned to me to aim a missile. "I hope we're not rushing about madly because you're pregnant. Thatcher wouldn't tell me if that was the case. He's too much of a gentleman."

"What makes you think I'm not too much of a lady to even treat that question with any dignity?" I fired back.

Her assistant looked like she wished she could shrink under the table.

"I just wanted to get that aired," Bunny said, as if she were talking about hanging out smelly clothing. "There is nothing so embarrassing as a bride in a white wedding gown with her stomach protruding."

"This stomach won't be protruding," I said, stabbing her with my eyes.

Nothing flustered Bunny Eaton. She released one of her hollow little laughs and turned to Mother.

"Young people today have no concept of what they

get into, it seems, and it is usually left to members of our generation to do all that is necessary."

"All that is really necessary," Mother said softly with that gentle smile on her lips, "is for them to get their license and pronounce their vows before someone licensed to marry people. The rest is often more for us than for them, don't you think?"

Bunny looked devastated for a moment. I watched her with interest as she struggled to regain her composure.

"No, I don't think that. Years from now, they will thank us for doing it so well and giving them such a wonderful memory. I've always appreciated what my parents did for me, and I know Asher does as well. But let's not quibble over philosophical things. We have too much to do." She turned to her assistant. "Patricia."

"Invitations," she recited like a trained parrot.

"Right. They will have to be engraved with insert cards and return cards, of course, although I feel pretty certain we'll have a minimum of regrets for this occasion," she said, sounding as if she was at the top of her ego meter. "This community has been waiting for some time to see Thatcher Eaton settle down. Everyone is surprised at how fast he decided, of course, but what will be will be," she finished with dramatic resolution.

Mother and I looked at each other, both battling the hysterical laughter that wanted to rise like a burp.

"Engraved?" Mother said instead, and Patricia reached into her briefcase quickly.

"We've begun the search. Here are some samples I thought would be fitting," Bunny said as Patricia spread them before us like tarot cards on the patio table. "A wedding like this needs a theme, don't you think? So we have coordinated the invitations with the guest book, the photo album and the memory book."

"This is a rum pink peau de soie accented with sculptured matching roses," Patricia began. "And this is a delicate organza bow wrapped over moire and highlighted by a satin rose. This one is done with a satin ribbon accented by hand-sewn pearls, or you could choose a satin brocade with gold accents on off-white."

Mother and I stared down at the display.

"How did you get all this together so quickly?" I asked Bunny.

"Oh, really, Willow," she said with a small laugh trailing, "you don't think I did it overnight. As I told you, I've been thinking about Thatcher's wedding for some time. He's been quite serious with a number of debutantes and young women from distinguished families. There have been many times I thought he was on the threshold of marriage vows."

Even if you had to push him there yourself, I thought, recalling the society pages.

"In any case, I wasn't going to be caught by surprise. The truth is," she said, directing herself more to Mother than to me now, "I've kept all this updated constantly. It is simply something I've always felt obligated to do. I'm sure you understand, Grace. You were living here when we had so many wonderful occasions and events, parties that made the front pages of the society papers all the time. We've always made it a point to keep up with styles, fashions, et cetera."

"It all seems the same to me," my mother said in a dreamy, distant tone.

Bunny's eyebrows hoisted. She glanced at Patricia, who concentrated on keeping the samples straight.

"Yes, well, you know what I mean," Bunny said. "I do favor the organza bow with the satin rose. What do you like? Remember, we'll carry it through all the printed materials, the invitations, the napkins, favors, everything."

"It is pretty," Mother said.

"Exactly. Now you see why I suggested roses for the arch, Willow?" Bunny practically sang. "Theme, theme, theme."

"Fine," I said. I was beginning to worry a bit about Mother. Her eyes were blinking and she suddenly was looking less energetic, even melancholy.

"Good," Bunny said, nodding to Patricia, who made a notation and put the samples back in her briefcase. "As Willow probably has told you, we've already begun to research the catering. We'll have an elaborate buffet, of course. You can meet with me and Angelo Di Vita to-morrow, if you like, and go through the menu item by item."

"That's all right," Mother said. "Food is food."

"Oh, no, Grace. Food is never just food at Joya del Mar. I hope you don't really believe that. We're going to insist on having—"

"Whatever you choose is fine with us," I interrupted. "I'm sure you will pick what is appropriate."

"Oh. Well, good," she said. She took a breath. "When do you think you'll have your guest list available?"

"Tomorrow," I said. I looked at Mother.

"Yes, tomorrow," she agreed.

"I'll have a rush put on everything," Bunny said. "With the way people here plan their social calendars, this is going to be difficult."

"Somehow, I think you'll be up to the task, Bunny," I said. She missed my sarcasm and took it as a compli-ment.

"Yes, I will certainly do my best. Now, do you want help in choosing your bridal gown? I can get you an appointment tomorrow at Rose Le Carré. Everyone is using her, here and in Monte Carlo."

"No," I said. "I think that's something my mother and I will do ourselves."

"Oh, I see," she said, not hiding her disappointment. "Well, do remember this is a very formal affair. You need a floor-length gown, either short-sleeved or sleeveless, with a long train, a long veil, and long gloves. Your bridesmaids will need floor-length gowns, headpieces, and gloves as well."

She paused and stared at me a moment.

"You do know that you should have a minimum of four to twelve bridesmaids, don't you?"

"I don't know who I would have except for maybe my cousin from Charleston," I said. "I was unable to attend her wedding recently, so I'm not sure she will want to attend mine."

"Of course she will. But one bridesmaid? That's ridiculous. Don't you have any close girlfriends, college friends, anyone from home you want?"

"No," I said. There were girls with whom I had begun to get close at UNC, but I felt funny sending them such an invitation, and I had lost contact with my closer high school girlfriends.

"Well, we'll provide additional bridesmaids. I have friends with daughters who will simply climb over each other to be here and be in this wedding," she said. "I was thinking of Whitney's children to serve as flower girl and ring bearer. Asher's brother and his wife will come from Texas, of course, and bring their two married children, one of whom has a simply angelic little girl who will make a delightful train bearer. Don't worry about any of that, in fact," she concluded.

"Okay," I said. "Is that it?"

"What?" She looked at Patricia, who quickly lowered her eyes. "Of course not. Next, we'll discuss the music. I have someone working on getting us the Bill Renner Orchestra. It's a twenty-six-piece. They are usually booked for a year in advance, but there is a chance we can get them.

"We'll have to think about elaborate floral arrangements, of course, the favors, and the photographer. I think for this wedding we'll need at least two photographers. You'll have so many pictures. You know how weddings are," she said. "They bring people together who rarely get to see each other. It's nice to have pictures of relatives, and there will be a number of VIPs at the wedding. You'll want a visual record of all that.

"Then there will be the limousines to pick up members of the wedding party and to take you and Thatcher to the airport afterward. I'm sure there is much more. I'm overwhelmed myself. Patricia?"

The assistant reached down into her briefcase.

"Bunny, this sounds like it will cost a fortune," I said.

"Of course it will, Willow. It's your and Thatcher's wedding. I don't think you'll be doing it that often. Or at least, we hope you won't, right, Grace?" she said, and laughed.

"No, but we do have a limited income."

"Yes, I know you do, especially with us leaving and your loss of rental income. However, I simply can't have Thatcher married in an inferior affair, can I? We'll talk about the finances later. I think that's the most boring and droll part anyway, don't you? Asher will handle it."

"Yes, well . . ." My mother's voice trailed off as if it couldn't carry the weight of her thoughts.

"I don't want to sound rushed, Grace, but have you begun to think about her shower?"

"Shower?" Mother looked at me. "No, I—"

"Well, that's nothing. I can have it all arranged before we leave the main house and hold it there. I'm sure Whitney will help and perhaps even have it at her magnificent home."

"Are you sure?" I asked bluntly.

"Of course. Whitney is always there to help me. I don't know what I would do without my daughter. Someday, I hope you'll feel the same way, Grace."

"I do already," she said, speaking firmly and sharply for the first time.

"Yes, well, that's nice." Bunny turned back to me. "Do run your wedding gown choice by me when you think you've decided," she added, and rose. "Patricia, we have to get right on all this."

"Yes, Mrs. Eaton," she said. "It's nice to have met you," she told Mother and me. "Good luck with everything."

"Oh, it's not a matter of luck," Bunny insisted. "It's a matter of good planning, logistics, timing, negotiating. Usually it's wise to have the proper time for good planning, but who can anticipate the intensity and passion with which two young people fall in love? We're just a bit pressured, but we shall endure and achieve," she vowed, sounding as dramatic as an over-the-top high school actress. "I'll be in touch, Grace." And she walked off, talking nonstop at her assistant.

"Sounds more like she's planning a Civil War battle," Mother muttered.

We both laughed.

"Let her do it all," she said. "It gives her life some purpose. But I must confess, Willow, I do look forward to our choosing your wedding gown. It's something I never had a chance to do, but now, I'll be doing it through you."

"Okay, Mother. I'll get right on it, as Bunny would say."

Later that afternoon, Thatcher phoned, only he didn't ask for me. He asked to speak with Linden, who just happened to have returned from painting on the beach and was in his room.

"He wants to talk with Linden," Mother said, and called to him.

"What?" he cried from his doorway.

"Thatcher Eaton would like to speak to you on the phone, dear."

"Thatcher Eaton?" He came into the kitchen. "Why does he want to talk to me?"

"I don't know, Linden," Mother said. He looked at me.

"I don't have a clue, Linden. I swear," I said, raising my right hand.

Skeptical but curious, he went to the phone.

"Hello," he said, and listened. "Me?" we heard him say after a moment. "I don't know. Why me?" Then he turned to look at me. He nodded as if he were standing in front of Thatcher. "Okay. I'll think about it. . . . I said I would think about it. . . . Right. Goodbye. . . . What? Yeah, she's here. He wants to talk to you now," he said, holding out the receiver.

I crossed the room and took it. Linden avoided my eyes and hurried out, not pausing to tell Mother anything. She waited.

"Thatcher?"

"Hey, how are you doing? I heard Mother met with you guys today."

"Yes, it was a summit meeting. We planned the Battle of the Bulge."

He laughed.

"She'll do a great job. Don't worry about that."

"I'm not. I'm worrying she'll do too great a job. Thatcher, she's planning an event that will probably costs hundreds of thousands of dollars."

"I would expect so," he said without sounding a bit impressed.

"Well, we can't afford—"

"Don't worry about the costs. Just buy your own wedding gown. My parents will take care of everything else. They would insist."

"But I don't . . . I don't think we need such a wedding."

"We'll talk about it later, honey. I've got to get back to the office."

"What was that all about with Linden?"

"I asked him to serve as my best man," he replied.

"You want Linden to serve as your best man?" I repeated for Mother's ears.

"Yes, I thought that would be nice and might do some good to help bring us all together. Was it all right?"

"Yes, of course. I'm just surprised."

"Listen, there was a point there where I was nearly convinced he was my half brother. I want him to think of me that way."

"That's very kind and considerate of you, Thatcher."

"Talk him into it, then," he said.

"I'll try."

"I've been able to get us the reservations in Eze, France," he said.

"That's wonderful."

"It's exciting," he said. "All of it. Isn't it?"

"Yes," I said, reluctantly agreeing. Seven hundred or more guests, elaborate flower arrangements, a twenty-six-piece orchestra—how could it not be?

"I'll call you later," he promised, and hung up.

Mother and I just looked at each other.

"I don't think he'll do it," she finally said. "Do you?"

"Maybe," I said, and headed for his room.

He was sitting on his bed staring down at the floor. I knocked on the open door and he looked up slowly, so slowly it made it seem as if his head were made of stone.

"You put him up to that, didn't you?" he accused before I could say a word.

"Absolutely not, Linden. I was just as surprised as you were. I do think it's a very nice thing, and I hope you will do it," I said.

"He's a schemer, always plotting, conniving," he muttered.

I drew closer to him.

"Can't you give him a chance, Linden?"

"Give him a chance? You forget, I've lived here all my life and so has he. I've given him hundreds of chances."

"Please try," I begged, and sat beside him. My action widened his eyes. "I so want us all to get along, to be a family. I know deep down you want it, too, for Mother as well as for us, don't you?"

He studied me for a moment, then looked away.

"Best man. Me, a best man? I suppose I'll have to wear a tuxedo and all."

"Of course. We're all going to be quite dressed up. Mother's going with me to pick out the wedding gown, and I'll get her to choose a beautiful new dress. I'd be happy to go with you to help you get fitted for a new tuxedo, too," I offered.

He couldn't help but look interested.

"When is this world-shattering event, anyway?"

"The last weekend in June," I said.

He looked thoughtful.

"I'll do it if you will let me give you a wedding present," he said.

"Let you? Why shouldn't I let you give me something?" I asked.

"You have to help me create it," he said. "It will take up some of your time."

"You want to paint me again?" I asked, realizing. "You've already done a beautiful picture of me, Linden," I said softly.

"This one will be different," he insisted. "I was looking at you with different eyes then. Well?"

"Of course," I said. "Thatcher will be very happy to hear about it."

"I'm doing it for you," he said.

"But it's a wedding gift, right? That means it's for both of us."

He thought a moment.

"I suppose so," he said. "He's never really commented about my work except to say it's really something, whatever that is supposed to mean. I always felt he was laughing at me behind my back."

"That couldn't be so. Don't forget, he helped get your work into some galleries, Linden. Right? Right?" I pursued.

"Yes, I suppose."

"Just give him a chance, a real chance, okay?"

He nodded.

"Thank you, Linden," I said, and kissed him on the cheek. He brought his hand up to touch it as if the kiss still lingered there.

There were moments when Mother and I both wished we had left the choice of my wedding gown and the bridesmaids' gowns to Bunny Eaton after all. What we had assumed would take only a few hours took all afternoon the following day—but it wasn't only the time, it was the feeling we had truly fallen into the fishbowl. Thatcher was certainly right about the speed of gossip and social news. I wondered if there was anyone within fifty miles who didn't know by now that I was his fiancée and we were planning our wedding. Just the mention of my name put more hurry into everyone's steps, more excitement and interest in everyone's voices.

For one thing, we didn't even have to begin to research where we should go to choose a wedding gown. Less than an hour or so after our meeting with Bunny Eaton, our phone began to ring. Three bridal shops called within ten minutes of each other, one of which was the shop Bunny had recommended. Being skeptical of Bunny's motives all the time, I suspected she had her spies there and would somehow overpower Mother's and my opinions with her own. We decided on the third shop, simply because we both liked the name, the Bride's Nest. Even before we stepped up to the door, it was opened for us, suggesting the saleswomen had been told to keep an eagle eye out for our arrival.

Fawned over and treated as though we were both royalty, we were quickly led to a showroom where three women modeled one wedding gown after another. The manager of the shop, a French woman named Monique Patachou, delivered continuous descriptions of the gowns and commentary including mentions of prominent women who had worn dresses by the various designers. After the fifteenth gown, both Mother and I were exhausted by the choices. We conferred and, amazingly, both centered on a silk chiffon over silk shantung gown that had beaded lace covering the bodice and an off-the-shoulder sweetheart neckline. The beaded lace also traced the hems of the skirt and the detachable chapel train. Both of us also preferred it in ivory.

Then began the fitting. Once I came out in the gown, I could see the pleasure and excitement in Mother's eyes. Her face took on a healthy, happy glow that put the flutters of joy into my own heart.

"I would recommend you buy your shoes now," Monique suggested. "You can wear them a bit to break them in and wear them at all your fittings. Get something you're used to wearing, too. I see you favor flats," she added, and suggested a satin shoe with soutache, which was a type of narrow braid.

After that we chose the gloves, settling on operalength. Nearly four hours after we'd started, we were too exhausted to begin choosing a bridesmaid gown, but Monique addressed Mother and offered some opinions about what she should wear.

"Mothers are always putting their dress choice off until the last moment. I wouldn't recommend that. You want something that complements your daughter's choice. Bone and off-white remain the most popular colors for the mother of the bride, and I have selections that are anything but matronly. In fact, a pretty halter dress with a jacket might work. You will certainly look young and trendy."

"Later," Mother pleaded. "Please."

"We've accomplished what we set out to do today," I explained. "We'll be back soon."

"*Oui,*" Monique said. "But remember not to wait too long and be too rushed. You might think you have a great deal of time, but with fittings and all the other decisions to make—"

"I understand," I said. "Thank you."

"We'll call you for the first fitting. Maybe then, madame," she told Mother, who eagerly agreed.

"How exhausting," Mother cried when we were in my car and heading home. "I can't imagine doing all the things Bunny Eaton has taken on."

"What else does she have to do with her life? Still, I hope I'm not making a big mistake having such an elaborate wedding. I could be more insistent with Thatcher and have a small affair, maybe just the immediate family."

"No, no. Bunny Eaton's right. You'll never forget it."

"I wonder if a big wedding adds any strength to a marriage," I said. "Does it make your vows seem that much more lasting and serious? Is it like a coronation?"

"I used to fantasize about your father and me getting married. It was always a simple ceremony, but somewhere beautiful, not in the back room of some justice of the peace's house. I think deep down, no matter what face we put on to the public, we all want something romantic and wonderful, Willow. It's a chance to be a star, to shine and glitter, to be queen for the day."

"Here you can't be queen for the day, Mother," I said. "It's either a lifetime appointment or nothing."

Mother laughed.

"Won't we have fun though," she said.

I glanced at her as we drove on. She was looking out the window, but I could see from the way her eyes took on that dreamy far-off look that she was gazing inside herself rather than at the scenery. She was remembering good times, wonderful times, loving times. I had helped her revive that. At least for now, in doing all this, I had given her something, I thought.

I felt very good about it all. Nothing Bunny Eaton could throw our way would change that, I concluded.

We would bring the jeweled glitter back to our home, Thatcher and I, and Mother and Linden.

Weddings were times when people believed with all their hearts in the line, "And they lived happily after."

Let it be true for us, I prayed.

Now that Thatcher's and my wedding was a reality, I was not surprised to receive a phone call from Thatcher's sister, Whitney. It came just before we were about to begin dinner. Thatcher had called to say he was going to be involved with a dinner meeting, taking on some interesting new clients. Mother and I were having so much fun preparing dinner that Linden came out to see what was causing all the commotion, and I put him to work peeling potatoes. Mother and I performed imitations of Bunny Eaton for Linden, and we had him roaring with laughter. It was the warmest, happiest time all of us spent together yet. It was so good to hear the sound of Linden's laughter. Mother and I were so bright with happiness, we didn't need lights.

Then Whitney called.

"Now that this all appears to be a reality," she began, "I suppose you and I should have lunch."

"Yes, lunch usually follows," I said, my voice dripping with sarcasm. It was the way she pronounced 'reality,' making it like a disease had been diagnosed and confirmed and not a wedding and a marriage.

She missed my tone, perhaps deliberately. I had met Whitney only a few times before and always found her to be cold and aloof. She was a tall woman, actually as tall if not a bit taller than Thatcher. She had a long, lean face with thin lips that fell into a habitual slash of pale red with the corners tucked in tightly as she contemplated someone or listened to someone speak. In just the short period I had been in her company, she'd struck me as one of those people who are always looking for flaws and weaknesses in others, taking pleasure in pointing them out because it made her feel superior.

I had to admit she had striking rust-tinted eyes that were so powerful they glued her gaze to the face of whomever she was speaking to, commanding them to pay strict attention to her valuable comments and criticisms. She was the type of person in whose company you were never really comfortable, but if you were in her company and she wasn't singling you out for some criticism or another, you felt grateful, even a bit superior to the others who were victimized.

Whitney's husband, Hans Shugar, was, as Bunny had told me, years older than Whitney, actually old enough to be her father. They made such an unlikely couple, showing no warmth or affection toward each other whenever I saw them together. I would have suspected that their two children, Laurel, age fifteen, and Quentin, age thirteen, were adopted, if they didn't look so much like their parents, Laurel more like Whitney's side of the family, Quentin almost a clone of Hans.

I agreed to meet Whitney at the Brazilian Court's Chancellor restaurant at one o'clock the following day. It was on Australian Avenue, only two blocks from Worth Avenue, so on my way there the next day, I stopped by the bridal gown shop to pick out two dresses for Mother to consider, which Monique gave me to take home so Mother could try them on in the comfort and security of her own house. Monique understood we would make more progress that way.

Whitney wasn't there yet when I arrived, but the hostess brought me to our table in the courtyard near the grand fountain. After fifteen minutes, I ordered a glass

of white wine. It was a pleasant and actually quite romantic place, but being made to wait like this began to
stir up my insides, making my stomach feel like a concrete mixer. Nearly twenty after one, Whitney sauntered
in, paused to greet a number of people and then, finally,
turned her attention to me.

"Hello, Willow," she said.

"I thought you said one o'clock," I snapped. I could
see she had no intention of apologizing for being so late.

"Were you here at exactly one? Everyone from Palm
Beach knows to be twenty minutes late."

"I'm not Palm Beach. I'm from a place where people
make an effort to be on time."

She raised her eyebrows. I thought whoever advised
her about her makeup believed in a heavy hand. She
used too much rouge and painted her lips too thickly,
probably to make up for their thinness.

"I was hoping we wouldn't start off on the wrong
foot," she said. Before I could respond, she turned to the
waiter and ordered a champagne split. "I have decided
to have your shower at my house," she blurted, turning
back to me. "You can give me a list of the people you
would like to invite."

"I don't know anyone here yet, really, and I don't
think anyone I know from back home or even my relatives would fly down for a shower."

"Why not?" she demanded. "It's not like traveling in
a covered wagon. They're on a plane for a few hours at
the most, and then here. I'd think they'd love to use it as
an excuse to come to Palm Beach."

"Not everyone is so fascinated with this place,
Whitney. I think too many people who live here are
under that illusion. I mean, we don't exactly have the
world's most fascinating natural scenery, and you can

look at the homes of the rich and famous in dozens of places nowadays, as well as on television and in magazines."

"If you think so little of Palm Beach, why did you decide to make it your home?" she snapped.

"I didn't say I thought so little of it. I'm simply realistic about it, and I'm here because it's my mother's and my brother's home—and, now, the home of my future husband as well," I told her.

The waiter brought her champagne split.

"Do you want to wait to order?" he asked.

"No. I'll have my usual," she said with a flip of her long hand.

I glanced at the menu, and ordered a shrimp salad.

"That's my usual," Whitney remarked as if I had won a contest.

"Lucky for me," I quipped.

"I thought you would sound a bit more grateful concerning your shower, Willow."

"I'm not asking you to do anything for me, Whitney," I said. I leaned across the table to return one of her intense stares and lock eyes. "I know how hard you tried to prevent Thatcher and me from becoming engaged and married. I know all about the Kirby Scott fabrication."

"I didn't know it was a fabrication," she replied. "But I'm not making any excuses for my mother or myself. For a long time now, I have had to look after Thatcher when it came to his involvement with women."

"Excuse me?"

She sipped her champagne and then leaned forward, too.

"I have to look out for my brother. When it comes to women, Thatcher loses his superior intelligence. His hormones overcome his reason. He thinks with his penis," she said.

"And what makes you so superior that you know who is best for him and what is best for him?"

Whitney smiled coldly.

"I know him better than he knows himself. Who do you think mothered him when he needed it the most? Bunny? Hardly. It was left to me, only a few years older chronologically, but years older mentally and physically.

"I can't tell you how many times I've gotten him out of trouble with the wrong woman," she bragged. "Little does anyone know, but I was the one who saved him from Mai Stone. I told her things that kept her from closing her grimy hands around him."

"You're lying. He would have hated you."

She laughed.

"Hated? In the end, he came to thank me. Perhaps you don't know my brother as well as you think you do, Willow. Maybe my mother is right: The two of you are rushing into this too quickly."

Could she be telling the truth? I wondered. She was so sure of herself, so arrogant and confident. Maybe there was a part of Thatcher I didn't know or would never know.

I sat back, silent.

"I will say this for you," she continued, "my brother never moved so determinedly and so quickly before. You have him hypnotized."

"I think of it as love, not manipulation, Whitney."

"Whatever," she said. "The point now is, we have to learn to like each other for the good of the family. I asked you to lunch so we could get to know each other better and, also, to advise you not to try to pry Thatcher away from his family."

"I have no intention of doing that. Thatcher's unhappiness with things you and Bunny have done appears to have a history that predates me, Whitney."

Again, those eyebrows rose.

The waiter brought our salads.

"I imagine you're planning on setting up house at Joya del Mar."

"Yes."

"You don't think it might be too hard living on top of each other like that? I mean, with your half brother's special problems?"

"I hardly think it's possible to live on top of one another at Joya del Mar. It's as big as many hotels. From what Bunny has told me, she could go days, even weeks, without seeing Thatcher."

"Frankly speaking, I couldn't imagine living with my mother in the same house."

"That's your mother, not mine," I retorted.

She winced, but didn't pick up the hatchet.

"You're still intending to pursue a college education and a career?"

"Of course."

She smiled to herself as if I were the one deluding myself now.

"We've already talked about that, Whitney. There's no problem."

"I always think of promises between men and women to be of the same timber as the promises we made to the Indians," she quipped. "Most men, my brother included, speak with forked tongue."

"I don't pretend to be an expert yet on human behavior or relations, but I think it's pretty safe to say that any relationship has to begin with a high degree of trust. Don't you have that with Hans?"

She started to laugh so hard, she had to sit back.

"Hans? Hans Shugar? My husband has brought deception to an art form. He carries it over from business into his personal relationships."

I shook my head. How could a woman speak so critically of her husband and still be married to him? As if she heard my thoughts, she leaned forward again.

"I simply don't permit myself any fantasies, Willow. I'm a realist, a cold realist."

"Are you happy?" I countered.

She blinked rapidly, dug her fork into her salad, ate some, sipped some wine, nodded to someone at another table, and at last replied, "Happiness is too high a goal to set for ourselves. Moments of contentment, satisfaction, pleasure, and absence of pain are about all we can hope to achieve. Anyone who thinks otherwise is . . ."

"What?"

"Walking a tightrope without a net beneath. It's a hard fall," she declared.

Suddenly, I understood her completely, I thought. Whitney was afraid. Perhaps she had been afraid all her life. When I considered the home in which she had been raised and the experiences she had witnessing her own parent's marriage, it was understandable, but I wasn't going to permit her to put the dark clouds over my days and into my future.

"Do you know what having trust means, Whitney?"

"I have the feeling you're about to tell me," she said.

"It's being willing to take a risk. Yes, it's like walking on a tightrope and maybe it is without a net, but if you put yourself in a cocoon of thick cynicism, you'll never know what it's like to be up there, to be free, to feel the wind in your hair and the love in your heart."

She smiled coldly at me.

"You're exactly what I expected," she said. "With all

the vulnerability to be a Thatcher Eaton woman. I wish you luck." She raised her glass and downed the remaining champagne. "But let's forget about all this," she added quickly, "and talk about your wedding plans." She reached into her purse. "I have some suggestions for you after speaking with Bunny."

Now it was my turn to smile to myself.

Thatcher could be marrying the devil, for all she and Bunny cared. It was the affair, the reception, the event that mattered the most.

After all, they would say it themselves: This is Palm Beach.

9

The Club d'Amour

There were times when I stopped to consider what I proposed to accomplish within the next six months and found myself breaking out in a cold sweat of absolute panic. For a few moments I would become almost catatonic, unable to swallow, my body trembling. I was, after all, no longer responsible only for myself. I had convinced Mother and Linden to take this journey with me, buoying them up with as much of my inflated confidence as I could spare, helping them to see every formidable task as manageable.

First, I had to find the time to prepare all of the preliminary reading for my college classes. Professor Fuentes was right when he called me ambitious after he saw the pile of books I had gathered at the college bookstore. It was going to be difficult enough to get all the required reading completed, much less do anything extra. One of Daddy's characteristics was his ability to always be realistic about himself and others. It frightened me a bit that I had overestimated my capability and underestimated the tasks I had to accomplish in the time allotted. I felt like the pilot of a plane who only after takeoff realizes she isn't as capable of flying and navigating as she first thought. And there were precious passengers aboard!

Reading, taking notes, and organizing myself to start an entirely new college experience, I had little time and no tolerance for frivolous things, and Bunny Eaton seemingly had no end of those when it came to tossing them my way.

At least two or three times a day, our phone would ring and she would be on it with a question or a request for input about such earth-shattering things as the shape of the chairs for the tables at the wedding reception, the design of the chair covers, and the color of the servants' uniforms. She always insisted that both Mother and I be on the phone if we didn't want to come right up to the house for another planning session. We usually opted for the phone, Mother on the one in the kitchen, me on the one in my bedroom.

She justified this persistence and intensity by continually bemoaning how pressured she was because of what she described as her imminent evacuation from Joya del Mar: Not only was there packing to do, but also decorating for her new home. Despite this claim of heavier burdens, she wanted to stick her nose into everything we did by ourselves and, I found out, actually visited the dress shop to see the gown I had chosen and inquire as to what I had brought home for Mother to try.

"I don't mean to be an interfering mother-in-law before you even get married," she told me, "but I do wish you would consider Rose Le Carré's selections before settling on something. A wedding gown stays with you forever."

"I'm happy with my choice," I said firmly.

"Oh, I'm sorry," she said as if someone had died. She paused and then skipped to another topic, never discouraged.

One week she went on and on for days about the wedding favors.

"Wedding favors should be thought of as thank-you gifts to our guests for coming and for supporting our children's commitment to each other," she lectured first. "They'll serve as memories, but they can also be part of our decorations and they can be something of lasting value.

"In fact," she went on, laughing, "many wedding favors outlast the marriages around here."

"What is it you want us to choose now, Bunny?" I asked, quickly losing my patience.

"Do you want bookmarks, key rings, pencils or pens, magnets, letter openers? Candles are big. I don't approve of those cheap disposable cameras. We have professional photographers and don't want to detract from that. Well?"

"Mother?"

"Pens are practical," she said.

"Yes, but bookmarks can be very elegant," Bunny said.

"All right, then, bookmarks," I snapped. I had to get back to my reading for social psych.

"You and Thatcher will have to pose for some preliminary photographs so we can get them on the bookmarks. Now, what colors do you prefer? These aren't going to be those cheap paper things. They'll be leather."

"Why don't you choose the color, Bunny?" I said. "You know so much more about it."

"Yes, well, I was thinking we'd keep it in line with our theme, the same shades as the invitations."

"Perfect," I said.

"At most recent wedding receptions I've attended,

they had golf tees. Perhaps we should have golf tees for the men and bookmarks for the women, or would that be too chauvinistic? Many women play golf here. I do, whenever I get the time."

My stomach was churning.

"Mother . . ."

"You go off and do what you have to do, Willow. Bunny and I can work this out," Mother mercifully volunteered.

"Really?" Bunny said. "I mean, if a bride doesn't give her full attention to these things—"

"She trusts my judgment," Mother interceded. I couldn't see her, but I imagined her smiling.

"I do. Thank you," I said, and hung up before Bunny could utter another annoying syllable.

Ten days later, I began my first college semester at my new school. I had Professor Fuentes's class at 11 A.M. Tuesdays and Thursdays. There were only fifteen students. All were friendly, one boy in particular, Holden Mitchell, quite a bit more attentive than anyone else. He and I shared a second class, a required English literature course. Tall and dark-haired with features nearly too perfect to be natural, Holden had unusual blue eyes, cobalt blue with a shade of green. Most of the time, this extraordinary feature was hidden because he had a habit of squinting when he spoke directly to someone, as if he were trying to see some scene scorched on his brain. He sat behind me in both classes.

Professor Fuentes gave me a big hello when I first entered his classroom. Then he saw my engagement ring and widened his eyes with amused surprise.

"Is that what I think it is?" he asked while the others streamed in to take their seats.

"Yes."

"I guess I underestimated how involved you were when I asked. Congratulations. When is the wedding?"

"End of June. You'll be invited," I told him, and he laughed.

"Wait awhile before sending it out. You may hate my class and decide to have nothing more to do with me."

"I doubt it," I said, and his eyes warmed.

I enjoyed his class right from the beginning. He had an informal way of teaching and seemed to work from invisible notes scribbled on his lectern. After the first few sessions, I began to feel as if we were all just a group of people very interested in the subject who gathered twice a week to have a good discussion. Even when he scheduled a test or made an assignment, it didn't impose a heavy burden, at least not on me.

I enjoyed all my teachers and all my classes. The first week, I grew friendly with a pair of twin sisters, Loni and Petula Butterworth. They were attractive women with strawberry blond hair and patches of freckles in exactly the same places on their creamy faces, on the crests of their cheeks and along their temples. Both were about my height but with more petite figures, making them look years younger. I quickly learned that Petula had been nicknamed Pet by her father and was called that by most of her friends, but not by Loni. There was significant sibling rivalry, and Loni was quick to tell me, "Petula is my father's pet." Pet denied it, of course, but seemed to enjoy the accusation anyway. I thought they would make for a great psychological study and even, when I felt comfortable enough with him, mentioned it to Professor Fuentes, who said he couldn't agree more.

"Take mental notes," he advised me. "You might use

it someday. I think I read somewhere in your father's pa-pers," he added, "that he said for anyone in psychology, there are no wasted experiences. We're always in the midst of some research, something to add and to use."

"That was the way my father lived," I agreed.

Most of the people I met at the school, especially my teachers, were interesting to me. If I had inherited any-thing from my father in that regard, I guessed it to be his insatiable curiosity about people, especially people he had just met. He would go after them like some sort of mental cannibal, devouring their life histories, with an endless appetite for tragic, emotional, or significant events in their lives. I suppose his genius came from his ability to question wisely and make efficient use of every moment he spent with someone, no matter how difficult the situation or how short the time.

I was curious about Holden Mitchell. He was outgo-ing and talkative, yet seemed to have a strange restraint about him as if he was afraid of revealing something dark about himself. I quickly learned that no one, not even those who'd known him before, got too close to Holden Mitchell.

He came from a well-to-do family and lived in what Palm Beach residents would call a modest home, but most everyone else in the country would call a mansion. What I did learn was that his father had been married before and divorced with no children and was nearly twenty years older than his mother. Although Holden was just twenty, his father was sixty-eight and now a fully retired dental surgeon who had enjoyed a very suc-cessful practice. I got most of this in dribs and drabs from Holden himself, although socializing at college was no longer of much interest to me.

My college life and my life back at Joya del Mar

were so different from each other that at times I felt I should be carrying a passport because I was moving between two separate countries. The people I associated with at college were almost another species from the socialites who, as Thatcher predicted, began to chase after me.

It began with an invitation to lunch at a private Palm Beach club. Manon Florette, the owner's daughter and the granddaughter of the originator of the club, first sent me a written invitation and then, before I could RSVP, phoned to be certain I had received it and was going to attend.

"You should be flattered," Thatcher told me when I described it all to him.

"Why?"

"Club Florette is the most exclusive of all the private clubs in Palm Beach. Each year upwards of seven to eight hundred people apply for membership, and Henri Florette admits ten."

"Ten? Out of that many? How does he decide, net worth?"

"No. Actually, he told me he looks for the most interesting people to add to the mix and doesn't concern himself with their net worth. To join, you have to pay five thousand dollars, and then the yearly dues are three thousand."

"Just to eat at this place?"

"And be known as a member. It's like getting another ribbon to put on your chest," Thatcher said. "Anyway, the fact that she called to follow up shows you how much they want to know you."

I tilted my head suspiciously.

"Are you a member of this club?"

"Never applied, never was asked to apply, but maybe now we will be," he decided.

"I'm sure we'll find better places to waste our money," I muttered, and he laughed.

"Waste not, want not is different here. It's waste not, why not?"

We both laughed.

As long as we both could laugh at the world we were in, I guessed it would be all right.

At first sight, Club Florette looked like it fit its reputation for being exclusive. It was well off South Ocean Boulevard and tucked neatly behind very high hedges and a gate with a security guard. Even the gate wasn't just an ordinary gate: It was gilded and scrolled with palm trees. My name had been left at the gate, which was then opened, moving as slowly as I imagined the gates of heaven would. The grounds were beautiful, with a large pond populated by swans and pink flamingos. Everywhere I looked, flowers bloomed radiantly and uniformed gardeners pruned and nurtured the fauna.

The building itself looked more like a small beach hotel than a restaurant. It was a plush, sprawling Mediterranean-style structure in mauve stucco with a white marble portico. The valet stepped out to receive me as I drove up. He opened my door and welcomed me to the club. Almost every other car parked there was either a Mercedes or a Rolls. I saw a Lamborghini side by side with a Porsche. No wonder the valet smiled when he got into my car, I thought. It was a new experience for him to park something worth less than fifty thousand dollars.

The moment I entered the club, a gray-haired man in a tuxedo approached. He surprised me by addressing me by name as if he'd known me for a long time. Was my picture already in the Shiny?

"Miss De Beers," he said with a smile blossoming as

he drew closer. He extended his hand. "My name is Jorge. Welcome to Club Florette. Your hostess and her guests are already seated. Please, let me show you the way."

He took me through the small but elaborately appointed lobby with its oil paintings in gilded frames, its rich-looking leather settees and glass tables set around plush Persian area rugs, and brought me to a small but lavish dining room, the windows all draped in red satin and gold curtains. All of the tables were occupied, but everyone was speaking softly as though no one wanted to be overheard.

For a few seconds all conversation stopped and all heads turned my way. Then the conversations resumed as if I were too insignificant to require another second of pause and attention.

Manon Florette sat with three other women, all about the same age, mid- to late twenties, perhaps early thirties. She was an attractive light brunette about five feet eight with cerulean eyes. Like the other women at the table, she wore far more jewelry than I would ever think necessary, especially for lunch: diamond teardrop earrings, ropes of pearls, a cameo with a diamond set in the face pinned above her right breast. All the fingers of her left hand bore rings, and she had an engagement ring nearly twice the size of mine, as well as a diamond-studded gold band. The belt of her black pantsuit glittered with jewels as well.

"Willow, how nice of you to come," she said, extending her hand.

"Thank you for the invitation," I told her, which were apparently the exact words she was waiting to hear. She nodded softly at her companions, who looked just as satisfied.

"Let me introduce you to a few of my friends. This is Liana Knapp," she began.

Liana was a much taller woman with short, dark brown hair and green speckled eyes. Her eyes were her best feature. Her mouth was wide and her lips uneven. She had an abrupt chin and a long neck that brought back visions of the flamingos I had just seen.

"Pleased to meet you," Liana said, giving me her hand, but holding it out limply as if I was to take it and kiss it as someone would kiss the hand of a queen.

I gave it a quick shake, and her hand fell like lead to her lap.

"And this is Sharon Hollis," Manon continued. The much shorter woman with ebony hair and a dark complexion rose a little from her chair to extend her hand to me. I thought she had a pleasant, friendly smile and cute features, including a button nose and nearly gray pearl eyes.

"Hi," she said quickly.

"Finally, Marjorie Lane," Manon said.

"Why do you always manage to introduce me last, Manon, and always preface the introduction with 'finally'?" Marjorie asked.

"Simply alphabetical order, Marjorie. No insult intended," Manon said with an impish grin. The other two widened their smiles, but Marjorie shook her heavy shoulders as if she were ruffling feathers and then turned to me.

She was the stoutest of the group, with a round face and thick lips. Her eyes were a dull brown that seemed to be infected by the flat coloring of her light brown hair, the strands of which hung limply down to her jawbone. She wore the least amount of makeup and, although also dressed in a black suit with almost as much jewelry adorning her as Manon wore, she didn't look as elegant.

"Happy to make your acquaintance," she recited like some young girl ordered to say it and told exactly how to say it. She glared at Manon, then looked at the menu.

"Please, sit," Manon told me, and I sat between Liana and Marjorie.

"We've all been anxious to meet you," Sharon Hollis said. "Naturally, we hear a great deal about everyone in Palm Beach, but so much about you."

"Really? I don't know why," I said, pretending surprise and ignorance.

"You don't?" Marjorie said, looking up quickly from the menu.

"Well, I know Thatcher is a respected attorney, and I imagine there would be interest in our wedding," I suggested.

"Yes, yes," Marjorie said impatiently, "but surely you must know your family is one of the most famous in Palm Beach?"

"I had no idea," I said, my eyes as amazed as I could make them.

Manon laughed.

"Marjorie has a way of getting right to the heart of things. She doesn't enjoy preambles."

"Does that mean she doesn't enjoy foreplay?" Liana asked, and everyone but Marjorie and me laughed.

"Well, Marjorie?" Sharon followed. "Do you or don't you?"

"Stop acting like a bunch of teenage girls," she snapped. She turned to me. "I just don't see the point in beating around the bush or being a hypocrite," she added, glaring back at her companions.

"I probably agree with that," I said, "but I do enjoy foreplay, too."

Now they all laughed, even Marjorie.

"I don't want you to think of us as gossips," Manon said. "That isn't why we invited you to lunch."

"Oh, then why did you?" I asked.

"We four consider ourselves a sort of welcoming committee, don't we, girls?"

"Absolutely," Liana said. "We won't be bringing a basket of fruit or a cake to your door, but we do like to greet new residents properly."

"Everyone could use more friends," Sharon said, nodding at her own statement to get everyone's agreement.

"A friend is something special," I said, "and so rare."

"Precisely," Marjorie said. "That's why it's so important to make the effort to gain them, good ones, that is."

"What would you like to drink, Willow?" Manon asked. She signaled the waiter with a movement of her eyes, and he turned from the table he was serving and hurried to us. "We're all having cosmopolitans."

"Sounds good," I said, and she told the waiter. "Is everyone here a member of Club Florette?" I asked.

"My father is," Sharon said.

"No, none of us are actual members. We're Manon's guests. She invites us at least twice a year, but no more than that," Liana said pointedly.

"You know I don't like to take advantage of my position, Liana," Sharon said.

"No," Liana quipped, "I don't know that. In fact, as long as I've known you, you've taken advantage of your position."

The others laughed, Manon joining them.

Were they actually friends? I wondered. They each seemed anxious to jump on any opportunity to ridicule or criticize another. It was like some sort of socialite parlor game.

"Do you plan on living at Joya del Mar after you're married?" Marjorie asked.

"I can't think of any reason why not. It's so beautiful," I said.

"Yes, it is," Sharon agreed.

"What about the Eatons? Are you all going to live together, one happy family?" Marjorie pursued.

"Eatons? Thatcher and I are the Eatons," I said, pretending not to understand.

"I meant his parents," she said sharply.

"I don't know where they've established themselves, but I understand it's not far. Why?"

"In-laws have a way of not letting go," she replied dryly.

"Marjorie is recently divorced," Manon explained. "At the moment, she is quite bitter about marriage, in-laws, all of it, right, Marjorie?"

"Just my ex's," she muttered, and the others laughed.

Neither Sharon nor Liana was wearing a wedding or engagement ring. Manon caught me glancing at their fingers.

"These two were married as well, Sharon twice and Liana only once. My husband is Earl Lapel, of the Lapel jewelry family," Manon said.

"But you don't refer to yourself as Mrs. Lapel?"

They all laughed.

"You don't give up your name when you get married, unless your husband's name has more cachet and importance than your own, that is," Marjorie said. "I can understand your wanting to be known as Willow Eaton."

"Really? You obviously don't know then that my father was Dr. De Beers, the renowned psychiatrist," I said with a smile that could work for the devil. "De Beers is far better known than Eaton."

"I was thinking more of the Montgomery connection," she said in defense.

I turned to her, my eyes firm.

"I am not ashamed of my mother or my brother. They happen to be wonderful people, sincere and caring people."

"That's wonderful," Manon said quickly. "I'm sure Marjorie would agree, wouldn't you, Marjorie?" she asked with the force of a sledgehammer.

"Yes," Marjorie said. "Of course."

"So you've invited me here because you're all very curious about me and how I came to win the heart of Thatcher Eaton," I said. "Is that it?"

"That's certainly a big part of the reason, yes," Sharon said eagerly. Marjorie raised her eyebrows.

"Why beat around the bush?" I asked.

She glanced at the others. They were all smiling now. I sat back.

"It was like walking into a fairy tale," I began. "The air itself was electric between us. We could see nothing else but each other. I've always been skeptical of romantic love, but there it was, vibrant, pulsating, full of passion and not to be denied."

Their attention was glued to me, no one stirring.

"We courted, I left, but we couldn't keep apart. I think I said yes because I was afraid he would die on the spot if I didn't. That, as well as the fact that I was head over heels in love with him as well. We've done many romantic things together, and we look forward to doing them again and again for the rest of our lives," I concluded, looking from one to the other. They all looked incapable of speech.

"Wow," Sharon finally said. "I don't think I felt that way with either of my marriages. It's so unusual."

"Unusual?"

"She means here," Manon said. "Here, we see marriage as a result of good planning more than hot romance. First, we don't trust men very much, do we, girls?"

"Very much? We don't trust them at all," Marjorie corrected.

"For men, lying, betrayal, deceit, self-gratification are more natural than they are for women," Liana added.

"So we've formed something of an alliance, and we have invited you here today not, as you think, purely out of curiosity, but more to see if you are a good candidate for our club, which we call the Club d'Amour, the Love Club."

"What is it you do in this club?" I asked.

"First, we vow to always be honest with each other, and second, we vow to look after each other's, shall we say, romantic interests?"

The others nodded.

"Think of us as a sort of insurance policy, a Palm Beach insurance policy," Liana said, and they laughed.

"I still don't understand," I said.

"Each of us has a different piece of the pie here," Manon continued, leaning over the table. "We all attend similar functions, socialize with many of the same people, but each of us also has a different specialty, an area of expertise, if you will, and that helps us to bring together a more complete picture of things, events, especially events that could and often do impact on one or another of us."

"Precisely," Marjorie said.

"For example," Liana continued, "it was Sharon here who first brought Marjorie's former husband Hugh Durrel's infidelities to her attention."

"And then we helped her gather the information she

needed to pin the tail on the donkey," Manon said, and they all laughed again.

I stared for a moment, their words sinking in.

"You mean to say you function as spies, private detectives for one another?"

"Exactly," Manon said, nodding and sitting back. "We've just come to the realization that by ourselves, alone, we are not capable of competing with the men we marry. Say what you will about our husbands and former husbands, they are all quite established, confident, and capable men, and all part of the good old boys' club."

I shook my head.

"Thank you for considering including me, but this all sounds too diabolical for me. If a man and a woman cannot have trust, they can't have love."

"That's exactly what we think, too, Willow," Liana said. "It's why we think of ourselves as a sort of insurance policy."

"What is it that you do exactly?" I pursued. Did they actually have some sort of spy network, hire detectives, follow husbands? Bug rooms?

"When we learn of a betrayal or a potential betrayal, we make sure we inform our sister, and then we help or do what we can to give her the facts she needs," Liana replied.

"In short, we do whatever is necessary to accomplish the goal," Manon said.

"I'm sure Thatcher will have you sign some sort of prenuptial agreement," Marjorie said. "Especially since he is an attorney."

"Marjorie's husband tried to pin an infidelity on her to keep her from her fair share of their estate," Sharon said.

"But we had him dead to rights, and she was able to turn the tables on him and hold him to the fire instead,"

Manon explained. "Now, you and Thatcher will social-ize and get to know people here that we don't, perhaps. You'll bring another area under the radar for us, and in return, we'll share whatever we have with you."

"Why me?" I asked, still astounded. "What made you decide to ask me?"

They glanced at each other.

"We've known Thatcher Eaton longer than you have, Willow," Manon said.

"You're younger than any of us were when we got married," Sharon said.

"And like I said, it's a two-way street. You have something to bring to the table, too. Thatcher has done some work for my husband," Manon added. "Sharon is dating Franklin Bradley, and he is an attorney, too. She might very well be soon thinking of marrying him."

"What do you think?" Liana asked.

"I don't know what to say. I confess I thought this was just going to be a Palm Beach lunch, social chitchat, amusing, but . . ."

"Aren't you happy that we are all more substantial than that?" Manon said, smiling. "We're modern women, and since you're going to be a career woman, a profes-sional, we thought you would appreciate it."

"Let's face it," Marjorie said, "relationships between men and women today are more of a battleground than ever, considering all the legal ramifications, the oppor-tunities for betrayals and deceit."

"We have to stick together," Sharon pleaded.

"Just because you are in Palm Beach doesn't mean you have any more guarantee of a successful relationship and life than other women in other places," Liana said.

"In fact, maybe far less because of being here," Marjorie insisted.

They all nodded.

"Let's have our lunch," Manon declared, "and let poor Willow think about it all."

"Just think of this," Marjorie said, drawing closer to me. "If your grandmother had had friends like us and an organization like we have, do you think Kirby Scott would have been able to do all the destruction he did to your family? We would have been there for her, and we would have helped her prevent what followed."

"In the end, we have to stick together," Sharon said. "No matter how wonderful it seems at the moment, or how many bells you hear ringing, the day will come when you will hear more echoes than actual voices, and if you have to hold a marriage together on the basis of merely good memories—"

"You're like a bird who has lost all her feathers," Manon finished. "You sink into the sea."

Everyone nodded, each woman's eyes dark. It all made me feel very sad.

"Daddy!" Manon cried suddenly. "Come and meet our newest Palm Beach resident, Willow De Beers, Thatcher Eaton's fiancée."

The announcement brought the room to silence again as Henri Florette, a distinguished-looking, handsome man in a blue sports jacket that picked up the blue in his eyes, came toward our table.

"*Enchanté*," he said, reaching for my hand. "Welcome to Club Florette and to our little community." He turned to Manon. "She is as beautiful as they described, *mais oui, chérie?*"

"Yes, Daddy."

"Please, give my congratulations to Thatcher and tell him for me, he is a very lucky man," he said to me, then to all of us, "Enjoy." He moved on, visiting the members at each and every table, working the room with his charm like someone who could sell happiness in a bottle.

The waiter returned to our table and the conversation turned to food, but the real reason they had invited me never left my mind while I was there, nor for some time afterward. On one hand, I thought of it as a deceit, doing something very sneaky behind Thatcher's back, and that wasn't the way to begin a marriage and a life together; but on the other hand, their logic and their purpose was appealing.

I promised them to give it all serious thought, but even that promise made me feel guilty. Life was only simple for the blind and the deaf because they saw no evil and heard no evil. They lived in a state of trust. They never knew when they were being betrayed or laughed at and mocked. But they never saw the sunset and they never heard the songs of birds and that was too high a price to pay, especially for happiness that was totally dependent on the kindness and charity of others.

I told myself that perhaps I could join the Club d'Amour as part of my psychological research. It could become very valuable to me later on in my studies. It sounded like a great reason, but it also had the hollow ring of rationalization. After all, I didn't want to admit to them and especially to myself that I had any doubts about Thatcher. How could I do that and still love him?

Or was it impossible to love anyone that completely?

On my way home, I could hear Daddy step into the room of my thoughts.

Can you live with someone and not love him that completely? he asked.

I don't know. I haven't any way of knowing yet. It's

all too soon and happening too fast. But you did, Daddy, didn't you?

You were there, Willow. You tell me. Was I happy?

I don't think so. But later, with my mother, you were. Did you have that complete trust?

You know a great deal about it now. What do you think?

I think you did, and I think she did, too.

Even if that is so, that was us. I've taught you that everyone is different. One size doesn't fit all, Willow.

But you provided something, a goal to which I should aspire, didn't you? You were perfect.

No one is perfect, Willow. Remember that.

Then love can't be perfect.

Does it have to be? Maybe real love is knowing it's imperfect but still going on, still pursuing and supporting it with all your heart.

You're talking about forgiving.

You're trying to get Linden to see that, aren't you? You know you can't have love without it.

Yes.

Should you hold up a mirror for someone else to look into if you are afraid to look into it as well, Willow? Should you ask him to accept a world you can't or won't accept?

No, Daddy.

Then you have your answer, Willow. Don't you?

Maybe. I don't know.

I could see Daddy smiling.

You will know when you do, Willow.

You will know.

10

Advice from the Palm Beach Women

I began to think that Linden had forgotten about his request and my promise to pose again for him so he could do a portrait to present to Thatcher and me as a wedding present. Perhaps he saw how busy I was attending college and attending to the wedding plans, as well as socializing with Thatcher, meeting more and more of his friends and associates. Feeling guilty about not spending more time with Linden, I approached him to suggest he and I go looking for his tuxedo soon. That was when he reminded me about the portrait. He decided it would be the first project he would attempt as soon as he had his new studio ready.

In the meantime, Whitney scheduled my bridal shower at her home just a week before the Eatons were to move from Joya del Mar. Of course, Bunny complained at every opportunity, moaning and groaning about all the pressures Thatcher and I had put on her and Asher by insisting on getting married so soon.

"Some people here think you're pregnant," she managed to insert one day.

"They'll be quite disappointed," I told her. I could see she was one of those people.

My denial didn't slow her down. I began to see the rear loggia more as a theatrical balcony from which she could rant and rave, throw up her arms, and sigh deeply to any audience she managed to trap. As if she wanted the entire Palm Beach social community to witness her travails, she had a constant parade of afternoon tea guests, by no means the least of whom were the infamous Carriage sisters, who were probably as capable as UPI or AP in spreading news around the world.

Thatcher had a great tolerance for his mother's histrionics. I noticed that he favored referring to her as Bunny in front of people rather than as Mother. I imagined that in his mind's eye, he really did see her as a character in a play and therefore tried to avoid taking anything she did or said very seriously. He was adept at handling her, humoring her, placating her, even more so than his father, who at times seemed like an outsider, a guest in his own marriage, willing to leave the handling of Bunny, as I thought of it, to his son and his daughter. I couldn't decide who was more self-centered, Asher or Bunny.

There was so much to think about. It was nice to have someone with whom I was comfortable enough to discuss much of this, and Professor Fuentes turned out to be that person. From time to time he and I had one-on-one sessions, as he did with all his students, but somehow mine ran longer and occurred more frequently. I grew to like him increasingly, and found myself revealing more and more of my personal life to him. He laughingly accused me of using him as my personal therapist. I smiled, but thought, maybe it was true.

"Not that I would shy away from it in the least," he told me when he saw my smile harden with the realization. "I would love to be of any assistance to you, Willow."

I described my future in-laws to him, and we began to discuss Thatcher's attitude toward his parents.

"He sounds like a very wise man who long ago, probably in his youth, arrived at a certain acceptance. He balances it all quite well, from what you tell me, never denying who and what they are, but yet handling them with love and respect. He was born to be a lawyer, I'd say, a good one, I'm sure. He knows how to arrive at a good compromise.

"Remember that old saying," he added with a smile, "you can choose your friends but not your relatives."

"I can choose by marrying or not marrying."

"From what you have told me and from the glow in your face these days, I'd say you've lost that option, Willow."

I laughed.

"Maybe so, Professor."

"It's a nice wind that carries us off to such a blissful journey. I look forward to being so swept away myself," he said. He gazed at me for a split second or so longer than I expected, and just as unexpectedly, I found my heart tripping and my face growing warm.

Can you see the affection and warmth someone has for you in his eyes? Can you fathom how deep it is, and does it frighten you or does it excite you and stir up places in your own heart that you have reserved for someone else? I wondered.

Sometimes, I thought, it was better to leave some questions unanswered, leave some doors unopened. Too much light could also blind you.

I never mentioned to Thatcher my tête-à-têtes with Professor Fuentes, except to tell him I had a teacher's conference occasionally. He was happy I was enjoying school and kidded me about eventually earning more money than he did and supporting him like some Palm Beach walker.

"I'll be a kept man."

"Could you be satisfied doing nothing but play?" I asked.

"I'd like to be given the challenge," he replied, and laughed when I tilted my head and looked at him curiously. "No," he added quickly, "I enjoy my work more than most people enjoy their play. Don't worry about that."

This was during one of the frequent times we spent at what was now our romantic nest, the beach house.

"I'm beginning to wonder if this friend of yours even exists, Thatcher. When does he plan on using this place?" I asked him one night.

"Whenever he does," he replied, "he'll let me know well in advance."

"Will he be at our wedding?"

"Of course. Do you know anyone who won't?" he countered, and we laughed.

How happy these days were for me, enjoying college, enjoying Mother's newfound happiness and Linden getting stronger and stronger. Not a day went by that he didn't have some new idea about the main house, things we should do, especially to eradicate any trace of Bunny and Asher's presence.

"I must confess to you," Mother told me as we started out for Whitney's home on the day of my shower, "I had grave doubts that we would get this far. For weeks and months, I've anticipated a phone call that would tell us it was all off, even the move back into the main house. I was afraid to hope, to believe. You have brought us such joy, Willow. I am so grateful to your father for having the courage to tell you the truth and in his own way to send you to me. What a gift of love he made."

"To both of us, Mother," I said. "To both of us."

We pulled up to the gates of Whitney's estate. The twenty-foot hedges blocked any view of the interior and the gates themselves seemed to rise into the clouds. Someone must have been watching on a video security system because we were stopped only a few seconds before the gates, as if by magic, began to open.

"I wonder if the president of the United States is as well protected," I muttered.

Whitney's husband, Hans Shugar, was truly a trust baby, inheriting the Shugar detergent fortune. It was a German company that sold its products throughout Europe and the Far East. Whitney, Hans, and their children lived on El Vedado, one of Palm Beach's three Els, three streets that ran parallel from South Ocean Boulevard to Lake Worth—the neighborhood for the bluest of the blue bloods. Thatcher told me Hans had bought a mansion for four million and ripped it down to build their Georgian estate.

I already knew that it had more than thirty rooms and stood on twice the acreage of Joya del Mar, but I wasn't prepared for the immensity of the property, the gardens and mazes, the walkways and palm trees that lined the property like sentinels. It looked more like a palace. *No wonder Whitney feels so superior to everyone else,* I thought. *She must fantasize daily that she is indeed a princess ruling over some principality.*

There were at least two dozen luxury automobiles

parked in front, as well as two limousines with their drivers chatting.

"The yearly upkeep for this estate is probably close to the GNP of most third-world countries," I muttered as we parked.

"When Jackie Lee and I first came to Palm Beach, we were invited to parties in homes similar to this because of my mother's involvement with Winston. Jackie Lee used to say, 'Close your eyes, Grace, and pretend you're Alice dropping into Wonderland. The trick is never to show them just how impressed you are. Keep your eyes from getting too big, and never put an exclamation point at the end of any sentence while you're here.' "

"It was good advice," I said.

"Let's follow it, then," Mother declared, and although I saw she was trembling a little, having to submerge herself into the pool of high society after so many years estranged from it all, she managed a smile and walked with her head high as we were greeted by Whitney's daughter, Laurel.

"Please come in," she said, stepping back. "My mother and her guests are waiting for you." She made it sound like a reprimand for tardiness. She had Whitney's way of turning her eyes into critical orbs of cold gray and pursing her lips in a stern expression of disapproval.

"Hello, Laurel," Mother said, smiling at her. "It's been a while since I've seen you. You've grown so tall."

"It's not necessarily bad for a woman to be tall," she retorted. "My mother is tall."

"No, it's not bad at all," Mother said, holding on to her pleasant tone and smile. There was something in Laurel that stirred some memories, I thought, memories of herself, perhaps, although I couldn't see how.

Nevertheless, Laurel appeared to warm a bit under Mother's glow.

"Normally, our butler would greet you, but my mother thought it would be nicer for me to greet the guests," she explained.

"It is," I said.

She looked like she wanted to smile, but had been told not to smile too much, which she took to mean not to smile at all.

"I know that everyone else is here. All the other guests have already arrived."

"That's good," I said. "Then we've timed it just right."

She turned her head stiffly toward me.

"You're going to be my aunt," she declared. "Do you want me to call you Aunt Willow or just Willow?"

"Whatever you wish," I said.

"I like just Willow."

"Then just Willow it is."

"Please follow me, Willow," she said, and pivoted like a military parade guard, her posture perfect but as stiff as someone with an imaginary book balanced on her head.

Mother and I smiled at each other and walked behind her.

She led us through the wide and long entryway, down the marble hall to a grand room almost as large as some palace ballroom. The guests were all sipping champagne and plucking hors d'oeuvres from silver trays offered by three waitresses. Two waiters kept everyone's champagne glasses filled.

"The guest of honor has arrived!" Whitney cried, and the crowd of at least two dozen or so women stopped talking and turned our way. I saw that everyone from Manon Florette's Club d'Amour was present. Bunny, the Carriage sisters, and some other women I had seen at Joya del Mar from time to time were seated on the baroque-style settees, each woman looking more wrapped up in her jewelry than the next.

Someone began to applaud, and then they all joined in. Whitney crossed the room quickly to greet us.

"Thank you, Laurel," she told her daughter. "You're free to do what you wish now."

"Can't I stay, too?"

"No," Whitney said sharply, then smiled at my mother. "How nice to see you someplace else than the back of Joya del Mar, Grace, and you look so pretty, too. What a nice dress."

"Thank you, Whitney," Mother said. Her lips trembled a bit, but she held her smile. I squeezed her arm gently.

"Let me get you two some champagne." She turned and with a simple glance started the closest waiter in our direction. We took our glasses.

"The first toast of the day," Whitney cried, and everyone raised her glass. "To my brother's bride-to-be. Welcome to the looniest family in Palm Beach."

There was only a ripple of laughter, as though some thought Whitney had made a faux pas referring to anyone being loony.

"I know there are many people you don't know here, Willow, and even you don't know, Grace, so we have designed a fun way to introduce everyone to you. Girls," she cried.

Everyone began to form a circle around the large table between the settees on which Bunny and her friends were sitting. A large straight chair that looked more like a throne was brought up and placed next to the table, upon which was placed a silver bowl. In it were pieces of folded paper.

"Willow," Whitney said, indicating I should take the seat.

I looked at Mother, who shook her head and smiled.

"It's all in good fun," Whitney emphasized. I approached the chair and looked toward Manon and the others as I sat. They were all staring at me with tiny smiles on their lips, except for Marjorie, who looked as angry and critical as she had at lunch at the club.

"What is this?" I asked.

"We have asked everyone here to jot down a suggestion as to how to make your marriage successful. You have to pick each one out and read it aloud, and then we'll all try to guess who wrote it. That will give you an instant idea of what this new friend of yours is like, what she considers important in a marriage," Whitney said, turning and panning her gaze over the guests.

To me they all suddenly looked like little girls at a pajama party about to disclose their heartfelt secrets. I could see the anticipated titillation in their eyes.

"Not everyone here is married," I pointed out, gazing at the Club d'Amour.

Whitney pursed her lips, then smiled again.

"But everyone here has her idea of what it takes to make a marriage successful, even the divorced ones. Or should I say, *especially* the divorced ones?" she added, and everyone laughed.

"Can't everyone simply introduce herself?" I asked.

"Don't tell us you're afraid of good advice," Whitney challenged. "A little thing like that can't frighten a Palm Beach woman, and you're soon to be a Palm Beach woman, right, ladies?"

"Right," they cheered.

I glanced at Mother again. She was still smiling politely, but I saw the look of anxiety in her eyes. She didn't want me to be as uncomfortable as I knew she was. I decided to play along and make it seem as harmless and silly as I could, more for her sake than my own.

"Very well, let the games begin," I declared.

Whitney looked very satisfied. She glanced at Bunny, who nodded at the Carriage sisters. The two looked like they were about to take notes.

I plucked out the first slip of paper and unfolded it.

"Read it aloud," Whitney ordered.

"Make him sleep in a separate bedroom so he has to get permission to enter twice," I read, and they all laughed.

"Ladies?" Whitney cried.

"Lucien Castle," they cried, fingers pointing at a woman who looked well into her fifties, despite her obvious face-lift and platinum hair.

"Well, it works for me. Never let them take you for granted," she advised, shaking her head at me. "Obviously, my advice has stuck or they wouldn't have known it was my suggestion," she concluded with pride.

"Next," Whitney ordered.

I pinched another slip and opened it.

"At least once a month, have him wear your nightgown and you wear his pajamas to bed."

After the laughter, there was silence.

"Ladies?" Whitney asked the guests. Eyes searched faces. "The rule is, if we can't guess it in thirty seconds, you have to step forward."

The most unlikely suspect in the group did so. She was a short, plump woman who looked every bit of sixty-five to seventy.

"Oh, I told some of you about that," she declared. "My first husband and I followed it religiously, and we had a lovely marriage until he died. I'm Jean Blackman. My first husband, Wesley Shaw, had some business dealings with your stepfather Winston, Grace."

"Oh, yes," Mother said, although I could see she didn't recall.

"I'm happy to be the one who's the most shocking so far. Apparently, you younger ladies can still use some good advice and are not as exciting in the boudoir as you would have us older ladies believe."

There was laughter, but still restrained by surprise.

"You sure this is a good idea?" I whispered to Whitney.

"Absolutely. Look how quickly you're getting to know everyone. Next," she cried, and sipped some champagne.

I chose another and opened it.

"Every time he neglects you, spend twice as much as you did the time before."

"Heather Dresser," the Carriage sisters chanted before anyone else.

"Guilty," a tall, dark-complexioned woman cried, her hands up. She stepped forward. "I've bankrupted two husbands and I'm terrorizing a third. I think he's a faster learner and this one will survive." Even Mother was laughing at that.

"Heather's wardrobe, if hung in a straight line, would reach her hometown in Canada," Jean Blackman quipped.

"Look who's talking."

"Next," Whitney ordered over the laughter.

I opened another. My silence sent a nervous titter through the party.

"Even if you do the exact opposite of what she suggests, 'yes' your mother-in-law to death."

"That's mine," Marjorie Lane cried before she could be accused. "Willow and I have already met, so she would probably have guessed. My analyst warned me my ex-mother-in-law would get between me and my husband, even in bed."

There was a pregnant pause.

"Willow doesn't have to worry about that," Bunny finally declared. "My son isn't my type. He's much too serious and responsible."

Laughter of relief followed. Whitney gazed down at me, her eyes sparkling with mischief and glee.

"Go on," she said. "We have to get to the brunch soon."

More reluctantly than before, I took out another.

"Always pretend to have multiple orgasms, even if you don't have any. Their sensitive egos need it."

"That fits us all," Heather Dresser declared.

Everyone laughed, but no one was accused, and no one came forward to claim it.

"Well?" Whitney asked the group, her hands on her hips after nearly a minute of silence. "If your husband doesn't satisfy you and you were ashamed to have written it, why did you?"

"Go on to the next one, Whitney," Bunny ordered.

"No. Someone is breaking the rules. It's not fair. Let me see that," she demanded, seizing the slip from me. She studied it. "All right. We'll leave this out on the table by the door. Everyone look at it and put down the name of the person you think matches the handwriting and drop it in the bowl. We'll announce the vote before we leave. Last chance not to be embarrassed," she warned.

"I would rather no one be embarrassed, Whitney," I said firmly. "This is supposed to be a nice time for me and for all the guests."

"She's right, Whitney," Manon Florette agreed. "Besides, I'm hungry. Isn't it time to eat?"

A wave of agreement followed. Whitney threw me a glare of anger and disappointment, but quickly changed it to a syrupy smile and relented.

"You'll each just have to introduce yourselves to Willow the old-fashioned way, then," she said. "Let's move into the garden for our brunch and, following that, we'll have the opening of gifts in the parlor. I have the patio set up for a Viennese dessert feast afterward, and let's not have anyone pretend to be loyal to her diet.

"Why don't you hold on to the rest of those slips, Willow?" she told me sotto voce. "Some of them probably do have good advice written on them."

I put the bowl aside and stood up.

"You should probably save them for someone who will actually need them," I told her.

I saw the way Mother swelled with satisfaction and pride.

Whitney gave me a hollow, thin laugh, and turned to see to the brunch. The guests who hadn't spoken converged on Mother and me, eager to introduce themselves and, to my mind, to speak with Mother almost as much as they spoke to me.

One of the women introduced herself as Arlette Mitchell and told me she was Holden's mother.

"What a coincidence that you have the same college classes as my son. He's told me all about you."

"Oh?"

She leaned in so those nearby couldn't hear. "He fell into a nearly fatal depression when he realized you were already engaged to be married. He would die if he knew I'd told you," she added.

I wanted to ask, "So why did you?" but I swallowed the words.

"He's very shy. I told him he just has to keep looking until he finds someone just like you. I didn't get to marry the man I adored when I was Holden's age. You know what they say, you fall in love over and over with the same man, the man who first captured your heart.

"But I suppose that's all nonsense," she said quickly.

"Just romantic nonsense. I wish you the best." She left to speak to someone else on the way into the brunch.

The brunch itself was wonderful and in my mind probably rivaled the wedding feast itself. There were lobster, shrimp, and fish dishes, a variety of meats and poultry, each at a table with someone there to slice and serve. The platters of vegetables were beautifully displayed, many covered in sauces that made it impossible to know what they were until you asked. The champagne continued to flow as well as wine.

Mother and I sat with Bunny and the Carriage sisters, who provided an ongoing commentary about each and every guest at the shower. In minutes we knew whose marriage was in trouble, who had problems with her children or siblings, whose husband was in some financial trouble, and who was richer than she was a year ago.

Before we were herded into the parlor for the opening of my gifts, Manon Florette approached me.

"You see from that little bridal-shower game how catty most of them can be. You need allies here, Willow. You need friends like us. I'll call you and let you know when we're meeting again," she added before I could respond one way or another.

From the way Mother looked at me, I thought she might have overheard, but she said nothing. I was happy at how busy she was, at how many women, for one reason or another, wanted to speak with her. Whether she liked it or not, she was famous to them. They seemed to bathe in her notoriety. She was surprised at how many invitations she received. As Thatcher had predicted, we were suddenly "the flavor of the month."

The stack of gifts in the parlor looked big enough to require a decent-sized pickup truck to deliver. While we were having brunch, Whitney had assigned a servant to pile them neatly, the larger gifts on the bottom, so that it looked like a pyramid. The shower guests all sat in a circle and waited for me to unwrap each before they chanted their oohs and aahs.

There were silver and gold candleholders, jewelry boxes, and expensive vases. The girls from Manon's Club d'Amour gave me all sorts of lingerie—even leather!—which brought lots of laughter and comment. Opening each gift and hearing commentary about it was tiring. I was happy when I was finished. Whitney told me it would all be delivered to the house.

"I imagine you will want it delivered to the main house," she said, "since it's only a matter of days now until my parents move out and you and your mother and brother move in. I understand Thatcher is going to stay rather than move out and then back in again."

"Yes," I said, holding my smile and not blinking. "Delivering everything there sounds sensible, then, doesn't it?"

"That's why I thought of it," she said. Turning to the guests, she cried, "Onward to dessert, ladies."

If any guest was worried about her diet, she did a fine job of hiding that fact. Most of them had to have a taste of everything. The setting was magnificent. Under a blue sky with a few puffy clouds moving lazily from the south, I couldn't have had a more beautiful afternoon on which to celebrate the event. Whitney and Hans had an English maze below their tiered patio. The flowers and trees were breathtaking. There were two pools, one for adults and one for children, cabanas, and barbecue pits. She had a trio playing light classical music. It was very difficult to do as Jackie Lee had advised Mother and keep the exclamation points off the ends of my sentences. Whitney moved about like a queen. At one point,

I gazed up at the house and saw Laurel, her face framed in a slightly opened curtain, looking down at us like an imprisoned child.

Daddy once told me there were all sorts of prisons: "People you think have the most freedom are often incarcerated by their lifestyle or their own nightmares and thoughts. They move about in cages, and it is my job, and someday perhaps yours, Willow, to help them step out."

He would certainly say that here, I thought.

Just before it all ended, Thatcher made a surprise appearance, charming everyone with a little thank-you speech, thanking his mother and sister for welcoming me to the family so enthusiastically. Bunny soaked it all up and spoke as if it was her original idea for Thatcher to ask me to marry him. Mother and I could only glance at each other and smile.

"I guess we made quite a haul here," Thatcher commented. "I saw the pile of gifts being loaded into a van."

He kissed Whitney, then said he had to fly off and get back to earning enough money to keep me in the style to which *he* was accustomed, which brought lots of laughter. Just before he left, Manon Florette called out to him and asked if I was going to be welcomed as a surprise guest at his bachelor party.

"What's good for the goose is good for the gander, Thatcher," she said.

"I think if she takes a gander at that party, she'll want to cook the goose," he replied, and gave me a quick kiss on his way out.

It would have been a long, exhausting shower party, even without the added tension both Mother and I felt, so neither of us was surprised at how tired we were when it all finally ended.

"All I want to do is sleep," I told her as we drove out the gates.

When we arrived home, Linden greeted us with a phone message my cousin Margaret Selby had left. She and my aunt, Agnes Delroy, had decided they would attend my wedding after all, and Margaret would be one of my bridesmaids.

"Thatcher called, too," Linden said, "for me. He wants me to go to his bachelor party."

"Oh, that will be nice, Linden. What did you say?"

"I said I'd think about it. Do you want me to go?" he asked me.

"Only if you want to, Linden. I don't want you to do anything that you think will make you unhappy or uncomfortable."

He nodded, thoughtful, then said abruptly, "I'll go."

"Remember, you shouldn't drink with your medication, Linden," Mother warned him.

He grunted and left us.

"I'll remind Thatcher," I told her. "He'll look after him."

"I know we want him to get out, to mix with people, but I can't help but worry," she said. Then she sighed and added, "I suppose that's a mother's curse, always to worry. Wait until you're a mother. You'll understand."

"I understand now," I assured her.

One week later, the moving van arrived to pack up Bunny and Asher Eaton's things. I was at college, but when I returned the truck was still there. I spotted Linden on the sidelines, watching the moving men load the van. The pleasure in his face was quite evident, and I thought he resembled someone whose country had been under occupation for years now watching the defeated army in retreat. After all, for most of his life, he had been relegated to the back of the property and treated like an unwanted, weird person to be ignored and avoided as much as possible. How often had he looked up at the main house, perhaps the windows of a specific room, and thought about his and my mother's situation? Years of resentment festered in and around his heart.

Bunny had assured my mother and me that her maids would leave the house immaculate. Linden said we should have it fumigated.

"She'll be too proud and too afraid of any criticism to leave it any other way, Linden," Mother assured him.

Thatcher and I had discussed the costs of running the grand home, and he had decided that since we were making it our home, he would take over the upkeep and we would maintain the two maids, Joan and Mary, and, at his own request, Jennings, who was not eager to be packed off with Bunny and Asher. There would be little, if any, transition problems.

Jennings and the two maids then came to the beach house to begin to transfer our things. We had already determined that Thatcher's suite would become our suite. Mother would have what was once Bunny and Asher's suite, and Linden would have the bedroom next to the room he was going to use as his studio.

One room that had remained untouched, even when Bunny and Asher lived here, was the bedroom that my mother had when she was living here with Jackie Lee and Kirby Scott. The Eatons had treated it as if it were the scene of a murder. It was while she was in that room that my mother had been seduced and raped by Kirby Scott. I could see from the way she glanced at it and how her steps quickened when she passed it that it still carried the weight of those horrid memories for her. Linden mumbled that it should probably be walled up.

As Whitney had made a point of remarking, Thatcher was staying. Even though we weren't getting married for almost another six weeks, there was no point in his moving himself out and then moving himself back in. We didn't expect it to be any great shock in Palm Beach.

"I'll be so busy getting ahead on my work to make time for our wedding and subsequent honeymoon anyway," Thatcher said, "that I'll practically be nonexistent."

During the first week of our settling in, he was going on a fishing trip with a client. It was something he had been promising to do for some time, and he'd decided it might be a good time to do it.

"To give you, your mother, and Linden a chance to get settled in and adjusted without me hovering about," he explained. "Although I'll miss you."

He was to be gone four days. They were going down to the Keys and then around through the Gulf and back. Between my college work with finals approaching and our moving into the house, I didn't have all that much time to spend with him anyway.

If we thought that Bunny's having moved away would slow down her planning and plotting of the wedding, we were in for an immediate surprise. She actually returned the day we moved in to discuss the bridesmaids' gifts. A friend of hers whose daughter had married in Rome recently had what she thought was a wonderful idea: a picture of the bride and the groom and their immediate families put on the face of a table clock.

"Every time they check the time, they'll be reminded of your wonderful affair, and instead of an ordinary alarm, it will play your wedding song. What do you think?"

"I think a picture of the wedding party itself would

make them happier. Then they could see themselves in the photograph," I offered.

Her face flooded with disappointment.

"Oh. But wouldn't that be too many?" she followed up quickly, hoping to change my mind.

"We'll just get a bigger clock, Bunny. No problem," I said.

She thought a moment, then smiled and said, "I might do one of the immediate family, just for myself, as well."

There was no defeating her if it came down to simply a matter of spending more money, I thought. All of her life she had bought happiness.

But would there be a time years and years from now when she would be surrounded only by things, when she would realize something important was missing?

What was it? she would surely wonder. Was it more jewelry? More high-style clothing, new furniture, a painting, a new car?

Wrapped in her furs, she would still shiver. The chill of something dark and dreadful would pass through her bones, and she would look out at the sea from her mansion or from her expensive patio and see a flock of birds moving as one, sailing with grace against the azure sky.

And suddenly she would know.

It was loneliness.

That deep darkness in her heart was loneliness.

And nothing she had bought and nothing she had been given would take it away.

11

My Own Boo Radley

A week after we moved into the main house, Linden finally brought up the new portrait he was going to do of me and how he was going to do it.

"I know how busy you are with your schoolwork and getting ready for this grand wedding ceremony," he said. "I have therefore decided not to ask you to spend hours and hours posing for me in my studio."

"Really?"

"Yes, but what I have to do is develop an idea and plant it in my mind, and do you know how I am going to do that without your posing?" he asked. He was so excited and enthusiastic about it that all I could do was shake my head and smile.

"How?"

"I'm going to take dozens and dozens of candid photographs of you. I've been reading about some other artists and how they work," he quickly continued before I could respond. "This one artist I admire, Arliss

Thornbee, believes you have to submerge yourself in your subject, eat, sleep, and breathe nothing else until your artistic subconscious forms an image so powerful it cannot be denied and you as artist are merely a communication device, a transmitter bringing the idea out and onto the canvas. Isn't that a truly interesting and exciting idea?"

"Yes," I said, but I also felt a bit of a twang in my heart. Some tiny alarm, like the *tweep* of a baby bird alone and vulnerable in its nest. "But is that healthy? I mean, to permit yourself to be consumed by one thing?"

"It's only until the artistic subconscious has completed the vision," he explained.

"Why do the photographs all have to be candid?" I pursued.

He shook his head, his face filling with disappointment.

"I would have thought you of all people would know why, Willow. When people pose, when they are prepared, they do things to hide their true inner selves. You're the daughter of a psychiatrist and you want to be one, too. You should know that, should know that first you have to strip away all the subterfuge, the masks and devices people use to hide their true selves. The best photographs are the ones a photographer takes of an unaware subject."

"But now that you've told me what you intend to do, won't I be aware?" I asked softly.

He smiled.

"Now you are, but you won't be like me. You won't be thinking about it day in and day out, and I'll know when to snap that picture," he said with more confidence than I had ever seen him exhibit.

"How long will this preparation take?"

"Maybe a week or so. I don't want to give you an

exact time frame or you will be anticipating. One day soon I'll let you know the portrait is ready. Okay? You still want me to do it, don't you?" he added when I hesitated.

"Oh, yes, of course," I said.

"Good. Good," he muttered, and went off with a tight smile on his lips like someone who has just gotten his opponent to agree to something that would place the opponent at a disadvantage. It troubled me, but he was right: I was too busy and too occupied with other things to think about it all the time.

He went off to complete the setting up of his studio. Linden had ordered new supplies and decided to change the color of the walls and improve the lighting. Mother was encouraged. The dark thoughts that had troubled his mind so often since his injury and operation seemed to have gone. He moved about with more energy, smiling, eager to help her and take on more household responsibilities. When he wasn't working on his studio, he oversaw the work of the gardeners, and even got into some of that work himself, planting new flowers, trimming hedges, trying, I thought, to restore a look he remembered from before his world had turned upside down.

His doctor was satisfied with the results she saw and reduced his medication. She told Mother she was happily surprised and confessed that she had expected his condition to grow worse before it improved. The result was that she gave her permission to let him drive again. The first trip he made was to take Mother and me to help him get fitted for his tuxedo. He even agreed to go to a hair salon to get his hair cut and styled by a professional rather than have Mother trim it as usual. I thought he looked handsome and told him so.

"Even with this ugly scar?" he asked.

"It's so slight now, Linden, it doesn't detract at all from your good looks," I told him. "It even adds some character. Why, just think of the war stories you can tell some unsuspecting, innocent young woman when you go out."

"I don't know if I can do that," he said, looking away quickly.

"Oh, I mean just in fun, Linden. You can tell her it was just a boating accident afterward."

"I don't mean the story. I mean go out, date," he confessed. "I've been out of that game so long, I don't even know how to begin."

"Thatcher will give you some pointers, I'm sure," I said.

His smile dissolved.

"I don't need Thatcher's pointers. I'd rather stay home," he muttered.

"Maybe some night we can all go out on a double date," I suggested. "I know some very nice girls at college."

He kept his eyes down.

"When you're ready," I said softly, but I made a mental note to invite some of my college friends over one afternoon, thinking that if he could just begin to socialize, even slowly, he would gain self-confidence.

The opportunity came a few days later at lunch after Professor Fuentes's class when Loni and Petula Butterworth, Holden Mitchell, and I were talking about studying for upcoming exams. I suggested they come to Joya del Mar the following afternoon when we all had free time. I really only wanted the twins, but Holden was there and I didn't have the heart to exclude him. Loni seemed to be taking a fancy to him, anyway, and working at getting his attention and interest.

"I know he's shy," she whispered, "but I kind of like

that in a man. Most of the men I know want me to think I should be grateful they want to get into bed with me."

I told Linden they were all coming the next day and asked him to join us for coffee on the rear loggia. At first he was reluctant.

"I have nothing in common with any of them," he said.

"You don't know that, Linden, and besides, if you're still planning on doing my picture and working everything into your artistic subconscious as you told me, you should try to participate in everything I do, even if just as an interested observer."

He stared at me, his eyes narrow with suspicion.

"Are you using psychology on me?"

"I'd use anything I could to get you back into the world, Linden," I admitted. My honest reply brought a smile to his face.

"Okay," he said. "I'll meet your friends, but I'm not saying I'll hang around to chitchat while they talk about college life or something silly."

"Fine. Meet us at four," I said.

The twins and Holden arrived in separate cars. He was more than fifteen minutes late, and Pet thought he wasn't going to show. Loni was gleeful when he finally did appear.

"You're late, Holden. We started without you," Pet snapped at him.

"I'm sorry. I had to do something for my mother," he said, and quickly looked to see if I was angry at him, too.

"It's all right. We barely got started," I revealed.

"We've got a lot to do," Pet insisted.

"So let's do it," Loni said. "Here, sit next to me, Holden. I'll share my notes with you."

"I have my own notes," he said, but sat next to her anyway and we began to review.

It was a good study session. Every time Loni tried to bring up something that wasn't part of our work or get Holden to be warmer and more interested in her, Pet would jump down her throat and bring us back to the point. Holden himself seemed incapable of anything else anyway. His shyness was manic at times. Whenever Loni said anything that was in the slightest way complimentary, his face would flush a dark ruby red and he would start to tremble. It was evident in his lips. When she touched him, he practically jumped out of his seat. Finally, she gave me a look that said, "He's hopeless," and devoted her full attention to the work.

At four, Jennings appeared and asked what sort of coffee we all wanted. The twins wanted cappuccinos, Holden asked for tea, and I thought I'd have a caffé latte. I tried to delay it all, watching the door and hoping for Linden's appearance. Just before Jennings turned to go inside, Linden stepped onto the loggia.

"Oh, there you are!" I cried. "Wait, Jennings. What would you like, Linden? Loni and Pet are having cappuccinos. I know you like that."

"Fine," he said.

"Come meet everyone, then," I told him, and moved my chair so he would have to sit between me and Loni, whose eyes brightened with new interest. Holden was fading fast on the right, I thought, and smiled to myself.

"Holden Mitchell, this is my brother, Linden, and Linden, this is Loni and Pet Butterworth."

He nodded at them and sat.

"We know you're an artist," Loni pounced. "What are you working on now?"

Linden glanced at me to see if I had said anything about his wedding present. He could see that I hadn't.

"I'm doing a special portrait," he replied.

"Oh," she bubbled.

"I don't usually do portraits. I think portrait artists are just glorified photographers. Real art needs much more than just a face on a canvas."

"Then why are you doing this one?" Pet asked with a tiny smirk on her lips.

"It's special," Linden said.

"Why?"

"It's not something easily explained. You'll have to wait until I do it," he said sharply.

"What a good answer," Loni cried. "It is, Petula. I read somewhere that artists and writers who describe what they are doing lose their creative energy and their passion to do it."

"That doesn't make sense, does it?" Petula asked me.

"Actually, I think it does," I replied. "As Professor Fuentes was saying a week ago, I think, the creative impulse comes in the form of pressure, an obsession for the artist in which the only release comes in creating, releasing it in artistic form. Remember?" I started to thumb through my notes.

"Page 402 in the textbook," Holden said dryly. "The footnote to therapy and art."

"Right. Very good, Holden," I said, and he beamed.

Petula looked unimpressed and turned back to Linden.

"Where did you go to school for art?" she asked him.

"CU," he replied.

"CU? Where's that?"

"Right here," he said, gesturing at the beachfront.

For a moment no one said anything, and then Petula got it.

"You mean the sea. Sea U? This is your university?"

"And my universe," he said, glancing at me. "Nature

has much more to tell you than any college professor," he added sternly, dropping the corners of his mouth.

"Oh, I like that," Loni squealed. "I like it a lot."

"Good, then become a beach babe and leave," Petula told her.

The maid arrived with our coffee and some chocolate biscuits. The conversation soon turned to my upcoming wedding. I had asked Loni and Pet to be bridesmaids, not because I had become so friendly with them as much as because I didn't want Bunny Eaton dominating the wedding party with her choices and guests. The twins were very excited about it and made me give them an update on the arrangements. They had already been fitted for their gowns and had seen mine. Both Holden and Linden looked like they were getting bored, and to my delight, Loni picked up on it quickly and asked Linden if he would show her his studio.

The request seemed to put him in a little panic, however.

"I . . . don't think it's ready yet," he said.

"Oh, nonsense, ready-smeady. I just want to see where an artist works."

"I work out there," he said, sharply, and gestured at the sea again.

"But I thought . . . you have a studio. You said—"

"That's just—I do most of my work out there," he said more calmly, then rose. "I've got to get back to my work. It was nice to meet you all. Good luck on your exams." He barely gave them time to respond, making it look as if he couldn't get away fast enough.

"Is he all right?" Pet asked first.

"Yes," I said. "You know how artists can be moody and temperamental. Professor Fuentes said they spend so much of their time in the comfort of their imaginary

worlds, they have little tolerance for the static and conflicts in the real world."

"You quote him as if he were an internationally
renowned philosopher," Pet said. "I don't remember
half the things you do from his classes."

"She's just paying better attention than you are,"
Loni told her.

"To what? The professor's words or the professor?"
Pet asked with a playful smile.

I could feel myself blush.

"Oh, stop it, Pet. Willow is soon to be a married
woman. She's not interested in another man."

"Yet," Pet muttered.

Holden raised his eyebrows and looked from her to me.

"Let's get back to what's important," I suggested.

"I thought I was," Pet quipped. Loni laughed and I
thought I detected a smile in Holden's eyes, but just for
a moment, like a flash, something reflected and gone so
quickly you weren't sure it was ever really there.

An hour later we ended, and they thanked me for
hosting the session.

"In such beautiful surroundings, too," Loni said. "No
wonder Linden calls it his university. I can't wait for
your wedding. It will surely be the event of the season."

"At this point, I simply can't wait for it to be over
with," I said.

"Oh, I wouldn't be like that. I want to keep it forever
and ever on the brink of happening." She leaned toward
me so Holden couldn't hear. "Like an orgasm."

He did hear it, however. He had that beet-red look
again.

"Get out of here, you idiot," I told her, and laughed.
She and Pet said goodbye and started out. Holden lingered, gazing at the sea.

"Your brother is right about this place," he said. "I can see why he finds it stimulating. Artistically, I mean."

"Yes."

"How far does your property go?"

"Just over that ridge," I said, nodding to the left, "and up until the undeveloped beach on the right. It's very private."

"Beautiful. I wish we lived on the beach. I don't get to the beach as much as I would like. Everyone who knows you live here thinks you're on the beach every day. I don't even have a proper tan," he added mournfully. It was the most he had ever said to me in one breath.

"They say the sun isn't all that good for you anyway, Holden."

"The fox and the grapes again. Another one of Professor Fuentes's allusions, remember? The sore-loser mentality?"

"I remember, Holden."

"It's interesting how he works fairy tales and nursery rhymes and poetry into his lectures, isn't it?"

"Yes. He's a fine teacher."

"Maybe that's what I'll end up doing . . . teaching."

"Nothing wrong with that, Holden."

"Can we go for a little walk on your beach?" he asked, adding quickly, "Not long." He swallowed, his Adam's apple bobbing. He looked like a little boy whose hope hung on my every word.

I glanced at the time. Thatcher wasn't going to be home for another hour and a half at least.

"Okay, but not for long. I have to get some things done before dinner."

He nodded and moved down the steps quickly, hurrying like someone who was afraid I might change my mind. It made me laugh, but I kept it under control and followed, walking slowly with my arms folded under my breasts and my head down most of the time. He was so quiet, for a few moments I felt I was alone.

"Loni is very immature for her age," he blurted. "Don't you think so?"

"Loni? No, not really. She's just a fun girl with a gregarious personality. You should try to spend more time with her. I think she likes you, Holden."

He pulled his chin in and down and pressed his lips together so hard his cheeks bulged.

"Hardly," he said. "She's the kind of girl who has a brain made of lollipops."

"Lollipops?" I paused and smiled.

"Yes. It's my mother's idea. She likes to point out girls in the mall when she and I go shopping and describe what their brains are made of. Some are lollipops, some are jelly beans, some are just marshmallows. She says you can see it in their eyes. She calls them 'confections' and says the man who marries one of them will be talking to himself before the honeymoon is over."

I shrugged and continued walking.

"My mother likes you," he said. "She met you at your bridal shower."

"Yes, I remember."

"She says she could see you were not a 'confection.' "

"Well, thank her for saying that," I told him. I was biting down on my lower lip to keep from bursting out in hysterics.

"I think so, too," he continued. "I think you're the most stimulating girl on the college campus. I love when you speak in class. You always say intelligent things or ask intelligent questions, unlike Loni and the other 'confections.' "

"Maybe you're just being too harsh in your judgments of them, Holden."

"No, I'm not," he insisted.

He surprised me by reaching out to seize my arm at the elbow. I turned in surprise.

"I know you're engaged and all, but you've got more in common with someone like me. I think like you do. I'm interested in the same things. You got engaged too fast. My mother says that your mother-in-law even says so."

"I don't like that, Holden. I don't think it's anyone's business, and your mother has no right to say such a thing."

"Yes, she does. She's right. You need to, to wait . . . to meet someone else . . . to kiss someone else . . ."

Before I could respond, he grabbed my shoulders and squeezed so hard, I started to cry out in pain. He smothered my cry with his lips. I struggled to break free, but he was incredibly strong, much stronger than I'd imagined him to be. His lust and desire had given him power.

"Think about me!" he cried. "If you just think about me—"

I squirmed to get out of his grip.

"Stop it, Holden!" I shouted.

He leaned forward to kiss me again, opening his mouth so wide that he covered my mouth and jetted his tongue into it. I thought I would asphyxiate when, suddenly, I felt him torn away from me and looked around to see Linden, his camera on a strap around his neck.

Before Holden could catch his balance, Linden swung his forearm out and caught him square in the mouth, driving him back. Holden stumbled and fell over into the water, sitting down quite unceremoniously and, for a moment, looking absolutely stupid.

Linden appeared to swell in size between Holden and me.

"How dare you?" he spit at him. "Get the hell off our property before I bury you in it!"

Holden struggled to his feet and then shot away, his clothing soaked, the sand kicking up behind him. As soon as he was out of sight, Linden turned to me.

"Are you all right?"

"Yes," I said. "I don't know what came over him. He's been such a shy, withdrawn person."

"You shouldn't have gone for a walk alone with him," Linden chastised.

"I had no idea he would behave like that. I just thought—"

"You've got to be more suspicious of the men you meet."

He looked in the direction of Holden's flight for a moment, then back at me.

"Thank you for helping me, Linden. I was lucky you were nearby."

"I told you I would be," he said, his eyes still filled with anger. He held up the camera. "I've got a picture of him accosting you if you want to press charges against him."

"No, that won't be necessary. Thanks. I'd better get back to the house. What a terrible finish to a nice afternoon," I muttered, and repeated. "Just lucky you were here."

He stepped closer.

"It wasn't a matter of luck," he said assuredly. "I'll always be here for you, Willow. Even when Thatcher is not. Especially when Thatcher is not," he added, his shoulders back proudly. "You can depend on that." He started toward the house, then paused when I hadn't moved. "Coming?"

"What? Oh, yes, yes," I said, and hurried to join him and get inside.

Later, I wasn't sure whether I should tell Thatcher about the incident. I was afraid he would get very angry and might do something like press charges against Holden, but then I decided keeping things from one another wasn't a good way to begin a relationship. His reaction surprised me.

He shook his head and smiled.

"What is so funny?"

"The way you describe him reminds me of Boo Radley in *To Kill a Mockingbird*—you know, the disturbed man who protects the young girl, who comes out of the shadows to kill her assailant and saves her life. Linden is our own Boo Radley."

"Oh, Thatcher, don't ever say anything like that to Linden."

"I won't. But I can't help thinking it," he said, and laughed again. "And I can see from your expression that you can't help it either."

I shook my head.

I wasn't thinking that, was I? I wondered.

But I tucked it away in my closet of little worries, promising to take it out soon and give it the time it needed to be understood.

Before it grew into something I would regret.

As funny as it seems, studying for my exams and then taking them was actually relaxing for me. I found myself under more pressure at home as Thatcher's and my wedding day drew closer and closer. College became my escape. Bunny and usually one or two of her friends were at Joya del Mar so often, it almost didn't seem like she had moved away. She was planning the lo-

gistics, the scheduling of events, every single arrangement as if she really was staging a battle—and then she
added the most bizarre element of all by bringing in her
feng shui master to evaluate everything.

Feng shui, an ancient Chinese discipline focusing on
bringing everyday life into harmony with nature, was
the flavor of the month in Palm Beach, and Bunny was
always one to get on any bandwagon, no matter what, as
long it was "what everyone was doing." Time, space,
and action, according to this practice, had to be coordinated to increase energy, harmony, healing.

When she introduced Master Tee to Mother and me,
we had no idea what she was up to now.

"The wedding day is like the launching of a ship, the
birth of your new life," Master Tee explained. "You
want to begin with the most positive energy you can."

Then she and Bunny went out to review the locations
of everything. Using Thatcher's and my astrological
signs, Master Tee decided the flower altar had to face
the direction opposite to the one that had been previously chosen, and we should have our backs to the setting sun when we sat to eat our wedding feast. This
meant Bunny had to rearrange the dais as well. It put her
into a frenzy. The caterers were called back to redesign
their arrangements, and the decorator was informed that
the chairs he had suggested were the wrong shape.

On her way out, Master Tee, who had been taken to
look at what would become Thatcher's and my suite,
told me to get rid of all the mirrors in the bedroom.

"Mirrors mean troubled sleep," she said. "And you
must change the color of the ceiling. Just like the earth
and the sky, it must be different from the walls."

When they left, Mother and I had a good time imitat-
ing both of them. Linden walked in on our hysterical

laughter, and when he asked what was so funny, I broke into more laughter trying to explain.

"Poor Thatcher," Mother said. "She'll be on the phone with him warning him that he won't sleep well."

Linden didn't understand yet, but our giggling brought a smile to his face.

"I don't know what it's all about, but whatever it is, I'm glad it's about that," he said, and left shaking his head.

And so it was easy for anyone to understand how locking myself away to study and then taking my exams was truly an escape.

That weekend at home, however, I received the most wonderful news of all. Just before Thatcher and I were going out to dinner with two of his associates and their wives, Jennings informed me there was a call for me from "some woman who calls herself Amou," and I squealed with delight and rushed to the phone.

"Amou, is it really you?"

"Sim, Willow. *Como são?"*

"How am I? How are *you,* Amou? When you didn't respond to my last letter, I was so worried."

"I was traveling with my sister. We went to Brazil. I have decided I will make the trip to Florida and be there for your wedding."

"Oh, Amou, that's wonderful. I'll have the guest room prepared."

"Don't fuss over me."

"I will too fuss over you. I miss you."

"Yes, and I miss you. I'm very happy for you, Willow. You deserve happiness after so much sorrow and hardship. I am looking forward to meeting your real mother. It will help me forget the other."

"I already have," I said.

"That's good. Tell me more about Thatcher," she

said, and I described him with such hyperbole, she laughed and said, "Is he a man or a Greek god?"

"You will have to tell me, Amou."

"When you are in love, your eyes are full of roses," she reminded me. "But you are your father's daughter, too, and I am confident you have your feet on solid ground."

"Send me the details of your flight, and I'll be sure to meet you at the airport, Amou."

"I will. I can't wait."

"Me neither. Stay well."

"You, too, Amou Um," she said, and said goodbye. When I hung up, my cheeks were streaking with so many tears of happiness, Thatcher thought I had received some terrible news.

"Oh, just the opposite, Thatcher," I cried. "Just the opposite! Amou is coming!"

"The woman of the dreads," he teased.

"We won't let the dreads come into our world, will we?" I asked him.

"Never," he promised.

He kissed away my tears of joy.

Were my feet still on solid ground? Were my eyes full of roses?

Soon, Willow, I told myself, *soon you will know.*

Two days later, Thatcher's friends held his bachelor party. He reminded Linden, who was not eager to go. Thatcher insisted, however, and got me to join in encouraging him.

"Just don't let him drink, Thatcher," I begged. "Remember his condition and his medication."

"Of course. He's my hero. He saved my woman in distress, didn't he? I'll look after him," he promised.

When they left that night, Linden looked back at me with such dark, fearful eyes, I nearly rushed out after them to stop him from going. My heart actually stopped and started again after the cold wave of fear washed over my breasts. I avoided my mother, afraid she would see my anxiety and it would heighten her own.

Making excuses, I went to bed early, but I didn't close my eyes. I wanted to be awake when Thatcher and Linden returned, no matter how late. My determination wasn't strong enough, however, and my eyelids turned into lead, shutting and dropping me back on the pillow, where I was drifting away until I heard the first scream.

I practically flew out of my bed and out the door. Hurrying down the hallway in my nightgown, barefoot, I stopped at the top of the stairway and called down. Mother, who apparently had waited up for Linden, had been there when Thatcher and he came through the front door. It was more like Thatcher carrying him through the front door. He had his arm around Linden, whose head bobbed and swayed on his neck like one of those funny animals people put in the back of an automobile, its head on a spring.

Mother had her left fist pressed against her mouth to stifle another cry. I came down the stairs slowly. Thatcher looked drunk himself, his eyes silly and wild, a wide grin on his face.

"He's all right," he said. "We're both all right—right, Linden, buddy?"

It was then that I saw the small trickle of blood that had come out of Linden's nose and dried over his upper lip. He barely opened his eyes, then closed them again.

"What did you do, Thatcher? He wasn't supposed to drink at all!"

"It was a bachelor party. They got me drinking and I lost track of our boy. I didn't know he was in the sauce until I heard him topple over a chair. He's all right. He's all right. He'll just sleep it off, like everyone else. He's one of the boys now, finally one of the boys. Everyone was calling him Superman because of the way he saved you from an ugly fate."

"What?" Mother managed to ask.

"Nothing. Thatcher's being an idiot."

"Let's get him to his room," Thatcher cried, and moved toward the stairway, tripping and nearly bringing himself and Linden down. I rushed to Linden's other side and took most of his weight onto my shoulders.

"Tha's a good girl," Thatcher declared. "Worry not, Grace. He's fine. I'm proud of him. Everybody likes him, especially the belly dancer." Thatcher smothered a giggle with his free hand.

Mother moved up behind us as we climbed the stairway.

"I'll tend to him," Thatcher declared upstairs. "This isn't for you women to see."

"Forget it, Thatcher. You've done enough tending to him. Go to bed," I ordered.

"Ex-squeeze me?"

"You heard me, go to sleep," I cried, and pushed him away from Linden. Mother took up the slack and we guided Linden to his bedroom.

"Unhand that Superman and let him go down with pride," Thatcher screamed.

"Go to sleep!" I screamed back at him.

He fluttered about, then turned and stumbled his way to our suite.

Mother and I guided Linden into his room and managed to get him on his bed. She went into the bathroom to get a washcloth and cleaned away the dried blood while I took off his shoes and socks.

"I'll take care of him, Willow," she said, stepping back and gazing down at him. "I've done it all his life."

"I'm sorry, Mother. I'll make sure Thatcher is sorry, too."

"It's all right. Don't do anything more tonight. He isn't in a condition to understand you anyway. Men are often boys. Maybe it wasn't so bad for Linden to have the experience," she concluded, "as long as it doesn't set him back."

"Okay," I said. I watched her for a moment as she lovingly washed off his face and unbuttoned his shirt.

When I walked back to our suite, I found Thatcher sprawled over the foot of the bed, lying on his stomach, his arms dangling over the edge. He was fast asleep.

Mother has her little boy to put to sleep, I thought, *and now I have mine.* After I struggled with Thatcher, who periodically woke to giggle and kiss me, I managed to get him into bed. The moment his head settled on the pillow, he was asleep, snoring away as loud as a tugboat. He reeked of alcohol. To get some sleep myself, I retired to one of the guest rooms.

I awoke shortly after darkness began to pull its blanket of stars back, retreating before an insistent sun that promised a bright, hot day. The house was still quiet. I looked in on Thatcher. The way he was wrapped around the blanket and the pillow, he appeared to have been struggling with some demon and collapsed in exhaustion. His eyes were shut tight, his mouth slightly opened.

I left him and went to check on poor Linden. Mother, exhausted from worry and concern, was sleeping soundly, as was Linden, his arms still at his sides. I looked at his nose and saw it was a little swollen. He looked like he had spent the night in battle rather than in reverie with Thatcher and his friends. I did hope Thatcher was right about Linden enjoying himself and being accepted as one of the boys at last.

I smiled to myself, recalling how one of my teachers, Mrs. Foggleman, had once compared our socially accepted rituals, such as bachelor parties, to primitive tribal events.

"The line between what is primitive and what is not is often blurred by who is deciding," she lectured. "Sort of like history being written by the conquering army."

Maybe what was basic and natural to humanity made us all more alike than we would like to think, I concluded, although to compare people here to people in primitive lands would surely cause a social nuclear explosion. I laughed to myself, thinking how Bunny Eaton would react to such an idea.

As I turned to leave Linden's room, I caught sight of a stack of photographs on his dresser. Curious, I walked over and looked at them. They were all pictures of me, his famous candid photographs. I was astounded not only at the number of pictures he had taken, but at the variety of locations, the things I was doing at the time, the times of day, the people I was speaking to when he'd snapped them. It was as if he had been truly a fly on the wall, invisible and so inconspicuous. I couldn't recall his presence at a single one of these occasions.

He had me sitting at a table on the loggia, bent over my notebook, my face intense as I read and reread notes. He had me eating, speaking with the servants and with my mother; to my surprise, he even had pictures of the Butterworth twins, Holden, and me studying before he had arrived to join us for coffee that day. There were many close-ups of me, catching almost every expression on my face.

But it was the second pile of pictures that shocked me the most. These were taken of me in my room during various stages of undress. Somehow, like some voyeur, he had snapped photographs of me totally naked. There were even pictures of me taking a bath and stepping in and out of the shower stall, as well as bending over the sink, fixing my hair, putting on makeup, in every conceivable place and position—even going to the bathroom.

After my initial astonishment, my first reaction was a blood-angry rage. I wanted to tear each and every picture in two and throw the pieces at him. When he had told me he wanted to take candid photographs, I had no idea that meant he would invade my most private moments as well. There was just so much abhorrent behavior I would tolerate in deference to his emotional and psychological problems. This was totally unacceptable and inexcusable. I couldn't wait for him to recuperate enough to be chastised.

After my boiling anger receded somewhat, however, and I looked at the pictures again and then at him still dead to the world in his bed, I had a secondary reaction, one based upon a more thoughtful and objective analysis. This wasn't just annoying and infuriating; it was also somewhat frightening. To what would Linden's obsession with me lead? Was he capable of ever accepting who and what we were to each other? Could he ever have a substantial and satisfactory relationship with another woman?

If I ranted and raved at him and threw these photographs in his face, would he charge madly toward some dark abyss again, and would I then have to live with the knowledge that I had driven him there? Would

I stand over his gravesite with my mother beside me and feel it was all my fault? Here I was, a student of psychology, someone who, if anyone could, should be able to step back, calm down, and first seek to help him, not punish him.

I once asked my father how he was able to maintain his objectivity and remain calm enough to help his patients after hearing about some of the terrible things they had done to themselves as well as to others.

"It's a balancing act," he explained. "A surgeon performing a heart transplant on a convicted killer can't think of who he is. He has to think of the medical issues, the problems to solve, and treat the body, not the man.

"People often accuse doctors of being too cold, too indifferent, but sometimes they have to be that way to survive and to perform without prejudice. Caring too much for your patient might make you tremble at the wrong times, just as caring too little might make you negligent.

"I have had patients so full of belligerence and rage, they want to leap out of their seats and choke me to death. Their eyes are sending darts at me, but I can't show them I see that as a threat or see them as so terrible I won't want to help them.

"So, I think of the mind, the condition, the mental problems, and try to isolate them first." He smiled. "I don't always succeed at being so objective, but I have to try and to at least appear as though I have succeeded.

"We're all actors in a sense. We're all wearing masks, Willow. Just choose your masks carefully," he told me.

I looked down at the pictures again, then at Linden, asleep.

What mask do I choose now, Daddy? I asked him in my imagination.

You'll know.

What if I don't know? Daddy?

I heard nothing in my mind.

Some answers I had to find for myself, I thought. I was a little girl again with my daddy holding the bike as I learned how to pedal.

Suddenly, he let go.

He stepped away.

And I was on my own to ride.

Or to fall.

12

A Routine Organization of Assets

I didn't say anything to Linden about his pictures all day. When he finally awoke, he had such a bad hangover he spent most of the day sleeping in his room with Mother pampering him anyway. I took Thatcher to task again when he rose and came down for breakfast about noon. He apologized profusely and assured me repeatedly that Linden really did have a good time.

"My friends made him feel at ease immediately, Willow. They were all sensitive to him. There were so many guys there, it was impossible for me to keep an eye on him continually, and besides, I thought if we treat him like an invalid, he'll behave like an invalid. Now he is at least aware of what he should and shouldn't do at events like this."

"I doubt that he'll attend another."

"Oh, don't be so sure. You want him to break out of his doldrums, don't you? You know how unhealthy it is for him to have no one but you and Grace all the time.

He has to meet other people, do other things. Otherwise, he might as well be in some clinic," Thatcher insisted.

I didn't dare mention the photographs, but they surely underscored what he was saying. Linden needed to develop other interests, new friends.

"I'm upset more for my mother than for Linden," I told him, and he did look very remorseful then.

"I know. I had no idea Grace would stay up and wait like some parent of a teenager, otherwise I would have taken him to a motel and sobered him up first—not that I was that sober myself," he admitted with a grin. "This little drum in my head convinces me of that. I'll apologize to her.

"You know what I want to do today?" he said, looking down at the pool. "Just vegetate. We've got to train for our honeymoon, you know," he told me, and kissed me.

Even with his hangover, a light of excitement sprang into his dark-blue eyes, bright like golden candles seen through a window on Christmas Eve. How could I stay angry at him long?

"Consider all that we are doing now as merely our training. The main event is yet to come, Willow," he said, reaching for my hand.

"First you made our marriage sound like a movie, and now you're making it sound like a prizefight."

He laughed.

"That's why I tell everyone and everyone tells me you're a knockout," he said, and I laughed too.

We spent the rest of the day as he wished, lying by the pool, sipping cool drinks, listening to music, swimming and enjoying each other's company. With my exams over, my first college term here completed, the wedding now looming before me, this was a welcome interlude of relaxation.

Afterward, he went up to nap and I looked in on Mother, who was much calmer and philosophical about what had happened. Thatcher had gone in to speak with her and apologize once again.

"Maybe Thatcher is right, I'm being overprotective," she said. "Linden is so much like a little boy to me, I forget how old he really is."

"It's understandable," I told her.

"Yes, but it's time to let go, actually past the time to let go."

She looked so tired. I knew she had spent a restless night.

"Go rest, Mother," I said. "I'll see to Linden's supper."

"No, I—"

"Go on, Mother," I insisted. "Get some rest. We've got a very, very busy few days ahead of us. My final fitting. Your preparations, the arrival of guests."

"Amou?"

"Yes. I'm so excited about it."

"I can't wait to meet her. Your father spoke so highly of her and so often, I feel I've known her for years," she said.

"I know."

We hugged and she went off to rest. I went to the kitchen and had the maid prepare Linden's dinner. Then I took it up to his room myself. He was sitting up in his bed, his eyes half-closed, still looking a little pale, with a small bruise on the bridge of his nose. When I appeared, his face took on some color and he tried to be more animated.

"I guess I made a fool of myself last night," he said. "I've told Grace how sorry I am, and I am telling you."

"It's all right, Linden. As long as you had a good time. But you knew with your medication, you shouldn't drink at all, much less drink too much. It could have been far worse for you."

"I didn't take my medication," he confessed. "I'm tired of feeling like a leper."

He looked at the food.

"I'm not very hungry."

"Eat what you can," I said.

I glanced back at the dresser and saw that the pictures were gone. I couldn't imagine Mother having seen them and not mentioning them to me.

I watched him eat and saw that every bite he took looked painful.

"How did you fall and smash your nose, Linden?"

"I don't remember," he said. "I'm sorry if I made a fool of myself and embarrassed Thatcher."

"That's not what I care about. I'm sure at a bachelor party, everyone makes a fool of himself."

He nodded.

"Including Thatcher," he said. "I was surprised at some of the things he and the others did."

"I don't care to hear about it, Linden, but I do want to talk to you about something else," I said, and pulled the desk chair up to his bed. He ate a little more, then put the tray aside.

"What?"

"This morning when I looked in on you, I saw the pile of photographs on the dresser."

He nodded, showing no signs of apprehension.

"I was surprised at how you invaded my privacy, Linden. Do you think that was right to do?" I asked. I felt like Daddy speaking to me when I was just a child and my adoptive mother had brought some minor infraction to his attention.

"What do you mean? I told you I was going to take candid photographs of you. It's not like you didn't know," he defended himself.

"Candid is one thing, Linden; invasion of someone's most private and personal moments is another. How did you do that?"

"I'm an artist. I don't think of that as invasion of privacy. I wanted to get a complete image in my mind, and I've got it now. You'll see."

"I hope you're not painting a portrait of me sitting on a toilet, Linden," I said sternly.

"Of course not, but everything we do reveals another aspect of who we are. This is how Arliss Thornbee went about it. I told you that."

"I never heard of Arliss Thornbee, Linden, and even so, just because he did it doesn't make it the right thing to do, or even the artistic thing to do."

"I'm an artist. I don't think of you as a naked woman when I paint you. I see the beauty in you, and that beauty appears in everything you do, even when you go to the bathroom."

"I'm embarrassed by that, Linden. I hope you destroy those pictures."

"Sure," he said. "I don't need them anymore."

"You don't invade someone's privacy without his or her permission, Linden. Art isn't a good enough excuse."

"You will do it when you practice psychotherapy, won't you? You'll justify it by claiming it's part of what you need to know to do your job properly."

"That's different."

"No, it's not. We're all artists of one kind or another. That's what they call it the art of practicing medicine," he said, smiling.

I stared at him and then I stood up.

"I'm not happy about it, Linden. I'm disappointed in you."

"You won't be when you see the portrait," he insisted, refusing to see or admit to my points. "You'll for-give me," he added confidently.

"There are things that, no matter how beautiful they may be, are not worth the price, Linden," I warned him.

"Including love and marriage?" he shot back, his eyes so full of fury I couldn't help trembling.

"Including everything," I said as firmly as I could. I stood up and returned the chair to the desk. "Drink your tea," I advised, and left him, wondering if the cure I hoped to see occur in him wasn't worse than the illness after all.

My confrontation with Linden set off all sorts of alarm bells, but the impending arrival of Amou, my aunt, and my cousin, not to mention the army of people Bunny brought to the house to prepare for the wedding ceremony and reception, occupied too much space on the stage of my attention for me to think about Linden. He withdrew to the sanctity of his studio, claiming he was down to the actual creation of a work now and had to give it all of his time and energy. He kept the studio door locked and some days didn't even come out to eat. Joan and Mary were instructed to bring his food to him, knock, and wait for him to open the door.

I saw how much this troubled Mother, so I tried to di-minish her concern by assuring her that it was a good thing for him to have something he loved occupying his time. Meanwhile, I couldn't help trembling every time I thought about what his painting would be like. If he dared do a picture of me in the nude, Thatcher would be more upset than I would be, and no matter how good were Linden's intentions, it would in the end cause more problems for us than we presently suffered. A neg-ative reaction on our parts would surely send Linden into a deeper depression as well. Sometimes, when I moved through the house and passed his studio door, I found I was holding my breath.

And then, it seemed to me, the famous second shoe dropped.

The women of the Club d'Amour had been so confident when they predicted Thatcher would insist on setting up a prenuptial agreement between us. I had nearly forgotten all about that, and when I did think of it once or twice, I smiled to myself because we were so close to our wedding date and he had not yet even broached the subject.

Then, five days before our wedding, he paused at the door as he left for work and, as if just remembering something, asked me to stop by his office that afternoon.

"Why?"

"I have something we should discuss," he said. "Don't look so serious. It's routine, but I'd like to do it right and get it over with quickly. You'll see." He kissed me quickly before leaving. I stood there at the door thinking about it, and my anxiety mounted all day until it was finally time to go to his office. Maybe it was something altogether different, I told myself.

He made such a big show of greeting me in front of his secretaries and assistants, I couldn't imagine him bringing up anything that would put tarnish on the brightness of our love. Then he closed the door behind us in his office and sat me down at his desk, where he had a small pile of papers set aside.

"I would be one stupid lawyer if I hadn't done this," he began. "Sort of like the shoemaker without shoes."

"What is it, Thatcher?"

"Well, the legal term for it is a prenuptial agreement, but this is nothing like those stiff, formal contracts I prepare for some of my clients. This is just what we need to be sensible, and nothing else."

"Sensible?"

He sat back, pressing the tips of his fingers against each other.

"I know I have lived the life of a bon vivant, hedonistic and at times reckless. I have earned my reputation here in Palm Beach. Some of it I can blame on my parents and my sister and their damn concern about the social register, but for most of it, I have only myself to blame.

"However," he continued, sitting forward with an intent, dramatic look on his face, "it's no secret that after I met you, Willow, I was like someone who finally took a good look in the mirror and realized who he was and what he was and what he should be. I've said it before and I'll say it again, with you I want to be responsible, mature, and productive." He smiled. "You bring the best out in me, the man out in the boy."

"What's that have to do with all this, Thatcher?" I asked, nodding at the papers.

"Everything. We will have a family someday, maybe sooner than we think, and just as the family is the foundation of society, the marriage is the core of the family, the spine, and if it's not strong, protected, the family is weaker. By reducing or eliminating potential conflicts that could arise in the future, we diminish and eliminate stress, and you know what stress can do to people. You know better than anyone, Willow, or as well as anyone could."

"I don't need all this preparation. I don't like feeling like one of your clients, Thatcher," I said sharply.

He winced and nodded.

"I'm sorry. It's just habit for me to talk this way."

"What is it you want me to do?" I pursued.

Disappointment, like leaks in a boat, could threaten to sink a love and relationship, I thought.

"Getting married means more than just pledging to live together and consenting to have sexual relations. Getting married is entering into a serious legal relationship, Willow. It has diverse consequences on your ownership of your money and possessions, the way you raise your children, our relationship to each other."

"Don't you think I know all that?"

"Of course, but when people talk and work out issues before they get married, they have a greater ability, better tools to use to remain happy.

"I tell my clients to consider all this the way they consider life insurance. You don't buy it intending to die, do you? You buy it to provide for your loved ones in the event of death. It's just good planning. You want that, too, don't you, Willow?"

"Yes," I admitted, but I couldn't keep my voice from sounding small nor my heart from tripping beats.

"These papers just organize our assets and set up a method by which they are distributed should we find our marriage to be a mistake, which I don't have any expectation of happening. Not to be boring, these papers elaborate on what our individual debts at the moment are, how we'll handle gifts given to each or both of us, elaborating on what are our nonmarital assets and how we want to treat them, et cetera.

"You understand what I mean by all this, don't you? You realize it doesn't diminish my love for you even an iota, right?"

Rather than nod, I closed and opened my eyes.

"But, as I said, what would it look like if I never had this done for us? What a laughingstock I would be, and how would that be viewed by my clients and prospective clients, huh? You don't want to go to a doctor who neglects his own health, do you?"

"I don't need any more rationale, Thatcher. I'll read the papers," I said bluntly, and picked them up.

"I've upset you," he said, sitting back. "I would rather have looked the fool."

"No. You're right. I'll read them. In fact," I said, smiling, "I'll have them all faxed to my attorney, Mr. Bassinger, who is coming to our wedding, and get his comments, too. How's that for good, sensible preparation?"

He stared at me.

"I just mean to do the right things for us, Willow, to protect you as well as myself and our family."

"And I'm grateful for that. You won't charge us for it, will you, Thatcher?"

He looked startled, then laughed when I smiled.

"Now I know more about why I love you so," he said. "You are the most mature and sensible young woman I have met yet. What a bonus to add to your beauty."

"Compliments will get you everywhere," I said. He smiled and then kissed me.

"You can use my fax machine, if you like, and get it to Mr. Bassinger right away."

"Good. Let's do that."

He called in his secretary and had her carry out the arrangements.

"Well, then," he said, "that's over with. We won't mention it again."

"Unless my attorney has something to suggest," I said.

"Of course."

He told me he had a very important dinner meeting to attend and asked if I wanted to join him.

"No, I think I'd better stay home tonight. I'm picking

up Amou at the airport tomorrow, and my mother is nervous about everything."

"Sure. Okay. I'll see you later, then," he said, and I left.

No matter what his reasoning and the reasonableness of his voice, and no matter how many times I told myself he was only doing what he thought was right for us, I couldn't prevent something hard and heavy from growing in my chest, making it ache. I glanced up at a sky turned stormy and foreboding, heralding rain and wind. It sent me home faster.

"Are you all right?" Mother asked as soon as she set eyes on me.

"Yes," I said, but then began to cry. She sat with me and listened as I described my session with Thatcher in his office.

"It doesn't sound very romantic, I know, but the world has become so complicated, I suppose," she said. "I can understand him feeling that, as an attorney, he should take care of these things, but it does take a bit of the glow from the candles. It's not something Romeo and Juliet would have considered."

I laughed.

"Yes, I can see that scene in the play. The monk advising the two of them to see a lawyer, especially because of the animosity between their two families."

We laughed, and I wiped a fugitive tear from my cheek.

"I'm too busy to think about it anyway."

"Of course you are, and I'm sure it will never be an issue between you again."

Was she, I wondered, or do we all say the things to people that we know they want to hear? We ignore so much about ourselves, especially our own mortality. Maybe the Bunny Eatons of the world were better off after all. See everything through rose-colored glasses, deny the dark clouds their hold over us, spend your life avoiding sadness and depression. Dedicate yourself to it with such energy and vigor, you never have a reason to stop and think and mourn lost childhood faiths.

The storm brought rain and shut out the stars. I went to sleep early and didn't wait up for Thatcher, who came home late anyway.

What a welcome brightness it was for me, therefore, to be at the terminal gate the next day, waiting for Amou to deplane. I had not seen her for so long, and I was happy to see immediately that she had put on some weight. At five feet nine, she had always been on the thin side. When I was a little girl, I worried that she would wither like fruit on a vine and get blown away by a fierce wind. My adoptive mother was also tall, but so much more substantial-looking, perhaps because of her hard demeanor. Amou always looked like a lightweight in the ring with a heavyweight when my adoptive mother confronted her. Why Amou stayed with us so long, I'd never know. Anyone else serving such a demanding mistress would have long before found excuses to leave. I told myself it was only because of me. At least, I hoped it was.

Amou wasn't as beautiful as my adoptive mother, but my adoptive mother was jealous of Amou's vibrantly red hair, which she kept long, down to her shoulder blades. Often I would sit beside her in her room while she untied her hair and brushed and brushed it, telling me how important it was to care for your hair. She had a secret formula for natural shampoo that involved olive oil and eggs and other things she wouldn't reveal, especially to my adoptive mother, who constantly nagged her about cutting her beautiful hair.

"Why do you bother keeping it so long if you always

wear it tied up anyway? What a waste of your time!" she would tell Amou.

Amou always nodded as if she agreed, but ignored her. It was the way she handled my mother, a way that made me smile to remember now. In her own way, Amou was a better psychiatrist than my father, or at least as good when it came to dealing with my adoptive mother. She once whispered her secret to me.

"Remember, Willow, a branch that does not bend will always break. Bend with the wind to fool the wind. Let the wind think it is the master, and when it stops, go back to being what you were. In time the wind will grow tired and pass you by."

She was right. My adoptive mother eventually stopped criticizing her, claiming it was a waste of her time if Amou wasn't going to take her good advice. Amou said nothing. She kept those rosy, full lips in a tight, small smile and shifted her brown-speckled green eyes at me. We were conspirators by then, allies in a war within my own house, she and I against my adoptive mother, neither of us daring to challenge her face-to-face, but instead snaking ourselves around her, burrowing beneath her, flying over her, avoiding her, treating her as if she were invisible as much as we could until, like some exhausted conquering army, she decided to retire from the field and not be bothered any longer. Her indifference became our victory.

"Amou!" I cried, and ran to her.

She hugged and kissed me, the tears streaming down her face.

"Look at you. *Lindo! Muito lindo.* My beautiful Willow."

"And you, Amou. You have finally gained some weight."

"Don't remind me," she said, her eyes wide. "My sister thinks I have two mouths and two stomachs when she cooks, and you know how I hate to waste food."

"It looks good on you."

"Never mind."

"Let's go. I can't wait for you to meet Mother and Linden and especially Thatcher."

We picked up her luggage and headed back to Joya del Mar. During the trip I told her about Miles, my father's loyal servant, the funeral, how I had sold the property; and then I told her more about Linden and his problems.

"Heartache for *seua mãe,* for your mother."

"Yes, she has suffered in so many ways, but she is happy now, Amou. I think that for the first time in years, she is truly happy."

"She has you. Why not? You brought the light into the house. *Seu pai,* he always said so, if not in words, with his eyes."

"How long did you know the truth about my father and my mother, Amou?"

She glanced at me.

"You knew for a long time, didn't you?" I guessed.

"From the beginning. *Seu pai* honored me with his deepest secret and knew that I would never betray it or him or leave you until I was sure you needed me no longer."

"I'll always need you, Amou."

"Yes, but from a distance now, Willow," she said, and we both laughed. The sound of her laughter was like a wave of warm love, remembrances, cherished memories raining down on me, bathing me in hope and happiness again.

"I can't believe you're here, you're really here!"

"Stop. I am just an old lady. Make nothing more of me," she warned.

"Believe what you want," I said. "I'll treat you like the wind and I'll bend."

She laughed harder and shook her head.

"If only the doctor could be here, too."

"He is, Amou. I believe he is."

"So do I," she said, and we drove through the gates of Joya del Mar.

"What a place!" she cried. "You have become a princess."

"Hardly," I assured her.

The moment Mother met Amou, I could see they would be friends forever. As was Amou's way, she kissed Mother on both cheeks. They looked like they would both begin to cry.

"Thank you for being the mother to my daughter that I was unable to be," Mother told Amou.

"It was easy with such a child," Amou replied.

"I wasn't always easy, Amou. What about the time I painted the kitchen walls with honey and you had ants forever?"

"To this day, I think of that whenever I put honey in anything," Amou admitted.

Jennings took Amou's things to her room, and Mother and I showed her Joya del Mar.

"Um palácio!" Amou exclaimed. "This is truly a palace. One would think there are kings and queens in America."

"Some of the people who live here in Palm Beach believe they are royalty, and some really are related to royal families in Europe," Mother told her.

After we showed her about, I took her to her room so she could rest and dress for dinner, when, I hoped,

Linden would appear to be introduced. Thatcher was in court but had promised to be back in time.

"Obrigado, Willow," Amou said.

"No. I am the one who should thank you, Amou. Thank you for making this trip and being here for me, to stand beside my mother and be part of my family."

She smiled softly.

"Seu pai described her to me, not in detail, but just as a beautiful woman, someone who had put music and light back into his life. That's what he said. 'She is the woman who gave meaning to the word *angelic,'* he said. When he spoke of her, he had tears in his eyes."

"Thank you for telling me that, Amou. Rest," I said, and kissed her softly.

My heart was so full, I thought I would explode with happiness.

To my joyful surprise, Linden came down to dinner. He had dressed well for it and brushed his hair, and even participated in conversation, asking Amou questions about me as a young girl, some of the answers embarrassing.

After they were introduced, Thatcher couldn't wait to tease her about the dreads.

"To this day she worries about them," he joked.

"Stop it," I warned him, and glared at him with hot eyes.

"No, no, it's all right," Amou said. She gave Thatcher one of her famous intense looks—famous, at least, to me. "May you always be able to make fun of the dreads," she told him after a long moment.

He held his smile, but it was as if a prophet had spoken, and he couldn't wait to change the topic and talk about his mother's newest idea for the wedding. Afterward, he confessed that Amou was more than he had expected.

"She's nobody's fool, wise and very sensitive. You

were lucky to have had her," he told me. "Why, she even got Linden behaving like a normal person."

"She's always been magical for me."

"Maybe we'll take a trip to Brazil next year and visit her," he said.

"Oh, will we?"

"What's to stop us? Just your work schedule or mine, and we can find a way around that, most of the time," he promised.

That night, my heart so full of joy, we made the most gentle and yet passionate love we had yet. We fell asleep clinging to each other as if we were both afraid sleep would take us too far away.

The next morning, Aunt Agnes and Cousin Margaret Selby arrived. Aunt Agnes was astounded when she saw Amou and couldn't believe she had come all the way from Brazil to attend my wedding. She was cordial to Mother, but anyone could tell from the way she spoke to her and looked at her that she could never be very close or very friendly to Mother. The only reference she made to my father was a confession of surprise.

"All my life I thought of my brother as the most correct, proper man I knew. He was even serious as a little boy, so concerned at how he looked to people, he would wipe his mouth with his napkin practically after every bite at dinner. To think of Claude having an affair with a patient!

"On the other hand, I suppose I should be grateful," she said with as plastic a smile as I had seen her wear. "After all, if it wasn't for you, we wouldn't have Willow, now would we?"

Mother took no offense at anything Aunt Agnes said. Afterward, she whispered to me and revealed that my father had "described your aunt to a T."

When Bunny arrived, she and my aunt took to each other immediately, siding with each other at every opportunity. That, too, brought smiles to Mother's and my faces. Amou couldn't be idle and went into the kitchen to prepare one of her Portuguese chicken dishes with piri-piri sauce, a hot sauce so delicious that everyone raved about it.

Margaret followed me about all day. She explained at least a half dozen times why her husband was unable to attend my wedding. Pressing business concerns kept him from leaving Savannah. From the way she spoke of him and their marriage, it seemed that he devoted 90 percent of his time to his work and 10 percent to her, but she didn't seem to mind. She went on and on about her social activities, her charity functions, her full life, which to me sounded like a life full of activities designed to avoid facing reality.

Margaret was intrigued with Linden, who didn't give her a moment of attention, however.

"Is he dangerous?" she asked in a whisper.

"Only if you pester him," I said. She believed me and kept her distance.

To keep her occupied and get her out of my shadow, I introduced her to the Butterworth twins and later to most of the Club d'Amour. She got along well with all of them, although I thought Manon and her group were really humoring and toying with her most of the time.

With all my last-minute preparations, I had no time to be concerned anyway. Both Mother and Amou hovered around me. Bunny had asked to be called to my last gown fitting, but I conveniently forgot, imagining that she would find fault with something simply because we hadn't taken her advice and used the people she wanted me to use.

Thatcher had decided that he would spend the night away. He told me he was going to sleep at the beach house and that his friend, Addison Steele, had, as promised, flown in from his home in Paris to attend our wedding.

"Since we spent so many wonderful nights there," Thatcher told me, "I think it's only fitting I sleep there the night before our wedding."

I was too nervous to care or even to listen to half the things he was telling me. For someone who had avoided the wedding altar as if it were the guillotine, he, on the other hand, seemed very cool and collected.

When we kissed good night, I asked him why he wasn't at least as nervous as I was. He paused to consider, then shook his head and shrugged.

"I think because it still feels like it's happening to someone else. But soon enough, the reality will strike home and then you'll hear my knees knock," he promised, kissed me on the tip of my nose, and left.

An hour or so later, I had a phone call from Mr. Bassinger, who had just arrived in Palm Beach and was calling from his hotel.

"I must apologize, Willow. I was away from the office on a business trip, and my wife and I had arranged to fly directly here for your wedding. Only an hour ago, they faxed me your documents, and I've just completed reviewing this prenuptial. The only thing that seems out of the ordinary is Thatcher's working himself into your property because of some agreement you and he made about the upkeep. Is that correct? He's paying for that?"

"Yes. Since we're making this our home."

"That's fine. But the way this is written, it's the same as him levying a lien. Do you want me to get into it and have the wording revised? There are a few other minor things I would change."

I thought for a moment.

"No," I said. "I'm sorry I bothered you with it. I don't even want to think about it, especially tonight."

"I can understand. These things are usually done a lot more in advance. We can revisit it later, if you like," he added softly.

"Good."

"We're so looking forward to your wedding and seeing you."

"Thank you. I'm looking forward to seeing you," I told him. I was, because he had been one of my father's closest confidants, and having him there was having a little more of my father, too.

"Well, rest up," he said, and hung up.

I thought about his comments for a few moments, then drove them out of my head with a vigorous shake and denial. I would let nothing do what my mother had warned this could do. I would let nothing diminish the glow of our candles.

Not tonight.

Not ever.

Not if I could help it.

Do you think you are being realistic, Willow? Daddy would surely ask.

Must we always? You weren't realistic all the time, Daddy. Especially when you fell in love with my mother.

Was I right to be that way?

Yes. Yes! I screamed back at him.

He popped out of my mind like a soap bubble and left me staring at myself in the mirror. Wondering.

13

A Most Wonderful Wedding

How do you sleep the night before your wedding? I wondered when it came time to do so. I had periodic feelings of numbness alternating with an electric sensitivity at my nerve endings that made me jump and flinch and have shortness of breath every time I brushed against something or stopped and let myself dwell on the ceremony and reception. I don't know how many times I looked at my wedding dress, my shoes, my veil, questioning whether I had made the right decision or whether I should have listened to Bunny.

Stop this, Willow De Beers, I told myself. *Stop this second-guessing.*

However, with Bunny Eaton still hovering about the property and the sounds of men and women below setting up the tables and the decorations, I couldn't imagine closing my eyes. I was certainly not going to take any sleeping pills. All I needed was to wake up groggy on my wedding day.

I had just changed into my nightgown and pulled back the blanket to crawl into bed when I heard a knock on my door. Thinking it was Mother, I went and opened it quickly and found Margaret Selby in her robe and slippers.

"What's wrong?" I asked.

"Oh, nothing. I just remember what it was like for me the night before my wedding and thought I would stop by to see you. I'm sure your stomach is full of pins and needles. Mine was."

"Yes," I said, "but I'm going to try to get some sleep."

"Oh, you won't," she said with a wave of her hand, and marched into my room. "This is such a magnificent house and property. I can tell you, Mother was very impressed and is still babbling about it. She had no idea. What sort of a home could a mother who had been in Uncle Claude's mental clinic possibly have, she would ask all the time."

"Well, now she knows."

"Yes, and your mother is so lovely. I don't see how anyone could tell she was mentally ill."

"She was helped many, many years ago, Margaret. She hasn't had those sorts of problems for a long time. It's not something you see in someone's face forever."

"I know," she declared, and looked at my wedding dress. "Your dress is much prettier than mine was. Ashley's mother really was the one who picked out my dress. She and Mother, that is. They both thought the dress I wanted was inappropriate because it showed a little more bosom than they thought was proper. Imagine. Like it's against the law to look sexy at your own wedding or something. How about all those people who are seven or eight or even nine months pregnant at their weddings? No one seems to complain about that. And they wear white, too!

"At least I was really and truly a virgin when I got married in white. I bet you're not, are you?" she asked, after a moment of building some courage.

"Times have changed, Margaret. That's not something on everyone's mind at the moment."

"I just didn't think I should give myself to any man unless he was going to be my husband and give himself completely to me," she declared with a bit of a pout. "Your virginity is your most precious gift, your jewel, and you can't cheapen it by giving it to just anyone. And besides, later, when your husband makes love to you, he'll feel you're like a used car."

"Who told you that?" I asked, fighting not to break out in laughter.

"Mother and I have discussed it many times," she said with big eyes.

"I don't think all men feel that way, Margaret. This isn't some very restricted society in which women are treated like second-class citizens. If it's all right for men to be lovers, why shouldn't it be for women?"

"We're different."

"That's for sure, Margaret, but we're not less."

"Well . . ." She looked down and then up with an impish smile smeared like hot butter across her chubby face. "I almost did it with someone else once," she confessed in a loud whisper. "I came this close." She pinched her thumb and forefinger together. "I was only sixteen and Randy Karlan had me pinned down in the backseat of his Lincoln Town Car, so there was lots of room, and he pulled down my panties and pushed his thing against me. He called it 'knocking on the door' and made me say, 'Who's there?' He said, 'Open,' and I had to say, 'Open who?' And he said, 'Open sesame,' and pushed until it almost happened, only I kept thinking about what Mother had told me and I screamed and turned so quickly and forcefully, I spilled him off me and he got very angry. He said he would tell everyone he had done it anyway. I cried, and he made a deal with me. I have never told anyone else about it."

"What was the deal?"

"I had to relieve his agony, he said. Men suffer so much more because of sex, don't they?" she asked me, and I shook my head and smiled.

"What do you mean? Why?"

"I don't know. They get like a bomb or something and if you don't help them explode, they could explode inside, I suppose. Ashley told me that. He said men need more attention than women and need to pretend things more."

"Pretend? Like what?"

"On our honeymoon, he made me sit on him and bounce and recite, 'Jack be nimble, Jack be quick, Jack went over the candlestick' over and over until he screamed. And now that's the way we do it all the time. Sometimes I recite it twenty times, sometimes as high as fifty, and once less than ten times. Do you do things like that with Thatcher?"

"No, Margaret," I said. "And if I did, I wouldn't tell you."

"I just do what I have to do to make my husband a happy man so we can have a happy marriage."

"Do you have a happy marriage?" I asked.

"Yes," she said quickly and firmly.

"Then that works for you, Margaret, and I'm happy for your happiness."

She nodded and rose, walking slowly toward the door.

"All through the night before my wedding, I thought

only about the honeymoon night. I was so afraid I wouldn't be good and Ashley would hate me." She paused and looked at me with the eyes of someone who was ready to confess a great sin. "I even practiced," she revealed.

"With 'Jack be nimble, Jack be quick'?"

"No, silly. I didn't know about that yet. I practiced with a pillow. To this day," she whispered, "when I go home, back to Mother, I mean, I look in my room at that pillow I call Ashley, and I get a little excited and go home and wait for Ashley and hope he wants to play 'Jack be nimble.' There, I've told someone, but you're almost a therapist so it isn't so terrible to tell you, and we're cousins anyway and should be like sisters, right?"

"Your secret is safe with me, Margaret."

"Good." She opened the door. "I feel a little sorry for you."

"Why?"

"You won't have any surprises tomorrow night. You already know what it's like."

"That's not true, Margaret. It's never quite the same every time, and love is something you build upon. You don't get married, and then that's that. Marriage is really only the beginning."

She stared at me.

Then her lips began to tremble.

"For me," she said, her eyes glassing over with tears, "it was really the end."

She closed the door between us, and I thought how deep and secret is the pain some women carry at the very bottom of their hearts.

The day began with the musical sound of bells, bells, bells. Bells were everywhere, including in my imagination. Doorbells, rehearsal bells, the ringing of phone bells. The house soon resembled the backstage of some Broadway show. Bunny had asked for a guest room for herself and Asher to use as a changing room and also as a salon to greet people during the day. She brought along her hairdresser and someone to help with her makeup. A small army of valets arrived to handle the parking of cars. The caterers set up and began to dress up the various food stations. A half dozen bartenders arrived, and then a meeting was held with the waiters and waitresses, spelling out how they were to serve and clean up. Bunny insisted that not an empty glass or a discarded dish be left on a table more than a minute.

I didn't hear from Thatcher all day, but Whitney and Hans and their children arrived early and came to see me, "before it all begins, while we still have the proper time to wish you well," Hans said. Whitney remained silent, looking at me as she would through a mask. "Welcome to the family," Hans added. Whitney muttered an assent and gave me the coldest, quickest hug, one that left me questioning whether or not it had even occurred. The children were polite but so stiff they seemed propped up like pieces of scenery. It was a relief when they all left.

I wanted air, but every time I emerged from my suite, Bunny pounced on me, insisting I remain in seclusion.

"Tell her, Grace," she cried, enlisting Mother as an ally. "Tell her how she has to remain fresh and calm."

For once, Mother sided with her. Even Amou agreed I should not involve myself in anything but myself.

"Today is a day to dote on yourself, Willow. You're truly queen for a day today," Bunny cried, and waved her hand as though she held a magic wand in it to carry out her wishes.

I retreated. I was too nervous to greet people and be

involved in any last-minute decisions anyway. Time felt like maple syrup, dripping its seconds and minutes along so slowly, I could look at the clock twice and see the hour and minute hands on the same numbers.

I ate very little, and what I did eat threatened to march right back up and take its original place on the plate. It was hard enough to hold down a glass of water. Amou nursed some food into me, telling me if I tried to do everything on a completely empty stomach, I would surely faint away.

"Just last year I saw a bride pass out at the altar," she said. "My cousin's daughter. It took nearly half an hour to get her back on her feet, and she was wobbly throughout the rest of the wedding."

"That sounds like one of your famous stories, Amou, the sort you would lay on me when I was a little girl and resisted eating or taking a bath, like that little girl you knew who had a nest of beetles under her dirty arm."

She laughed, and swore it was the truth about the bride fainting. In the end, I ate something and held it down.

Suddenly, I realized I had neither seen nor heard anything about Linden all day, so I asked Mother about him. She smiled, but her eyes revealed some concern.

"He's been secluded in his studio. I know he had some lunch," she added. "This is not a day for you to be worrying about him anyway, Willow. Let me do that. I'll help him with his tuxedo and bow tie. He'll be fine," she assured me, but it came out like a prayer.

Finally, it came time to do my hair and makeup and get dressed. I tolerated only Mother and Amou in the room and locked the door against any other entrant, especially Aunt Agnes and Margaret. By now, Bunny was too involved in herself to care about anyone else, and for once I thought her selfishness was good.

Periodically, I gazed out the window at the reception

area below and began to see guests arriving, all the men in black tie, the women in gowns fresh from Paris, New York, and London. I spotted Manon and her husband and the women of the Club d'Amour with their escorts. Then I saw Professor Fuentes arrive alone, Mr. Bassinger and his wife, and Mr. Ross with his. I felt like a performer peeking through the curtains at the audience. The orchestra began to play. My heart began to pound so hard, I thought I would surely be just like the woman in Amou's tale of warning and faint at my own altar.

The woman Bunny had hired to supervise the wedding reception, Robin Monroe, knocked on my door and declared, "It's time for the bride to make her way down." Her voice was so deep and formal, it sounded like I was being called to an execution. I had already had my last meal.

Both Mother and Amou turned to me and smiled. I rose and, with my head bowed, began my walk.

"You look so beautiful," Mother whispered. She squeezed my hand.

Amou walked beside us. Never had she looked more stately and strong to me. How lucky I was to have her at my side again. I heard the wedding march begin. Mother and I hugged Amou, who went out to take her seat, and then we started down the steps to the aisle. I'd had no concept of what six hundred people would look like, all their eyes turned on me. For a moment I thought all the air had gone out of my lungs. I don't know how my legs held me up and were able to continue moving forward, but they did.

There, ahead of me, was Thatcher with Linden at his side, both looking handsome in their tuxedos.

"Here you go," Mother whispered. It almost sounded like she was saying it to herself.

I took another deep breath and stepped forward, entering the glow of Thatcher's smile and just glimpsing Linden's eyes a-dazzle with a glow of wonder. For a split second, I had the feeling he thought it was he who was the groom and not Thatcher. It was like a finger tickling behind my heart, and then my eyes went forward, the minister began, and all else, everything I had thought and worried about all day, disappeared in the rhythm of his voice and the meaning of his words.

"Congratulations," Professor Fuentes said. He hesitated a split second, then leaned forward to kiss my cheek.

I introduced him to Thatcher.

"You are the only man who has spent more time with her than I have," Thatcher declared. "Of course, I approve."

"Thank you. It has always been a pleasure to spend time with Willow," Professor Fuentes replied.

Before Thatcher could respond with one of his witticisms, Bunny pushed forward in the greeting line to introduce some distant relatives, "who have come directly from a vacation in Hong Kong," she emphasized. "But that's our family. No cost is too great when it comes to celebrating such an important event."

I greeted them and turned to the next guests. Out of the corner of my eye, I could see Professor Fuentes talking to Manon Florette and Liana Knapp. His eyes went from them to me, and I could see in them his cry for help. It made me laugh. I shrugged, indicating the line of guests that snaked around the entire patio. He was on his own. I wouldn't be able to rescue him until much later.

It was exhausting, and of course there was no way I could remember all the names. Some people simply wished us the best, while others had to talk about their own weddings or tell us where they had been on their honeymoons. Finally, we were able to retreat to the dais and get off our feet, but almost immediately there was a call for us to kiss, and then we were invited to get up and dance to our chosen song. Actually, it was *my* chosen song. Thatcher had left it up to me, and I'd chose "Love Is a Many-Splendored Thing." It was Daddy's favorite.

The food was served and the music played on. How happy Mother looked. Every once in a while, I caught her staring at us, her eyes so full of light. She and Amou had similar looks, both sharing their joy, and both telling me at different times how proud my father would have been.

Before the reception ended, Professor Fuentes asked me to dance. Thatcher was already dancing with Sharon Hollis. In fact, every member of the Club d'Amour danced with him at one point or another before our wedding party had ended.

"This is truly the most wonderful wedding I have ever attended," Professor Fuentes said. "Not that I have attended all that many, mind you, but I can't imagine anything grander than this."

"Much of it was done to please Thatcher's family. I would have preferred eloping."

He laughed.

"Me, too, whenever I marry," he confessed. "But so much of what we do in our lives is done to please the people we love and who love us. Is that not so?"

"Very so," I said.

"I'll be going soon," Professor Fuentes said after the dance. "Have a wonderful honeymoon. I do hope you will continue with your studies afterward."

"Of course I will, Professor."

"That's good," he said, nodded, and walked off. As I headed back to the dais, Linden stepped in my way. I had been so distracted and busy during the reception, I hadn't noticed him. I realized quickly that I hadn't because he hadn't been there much.

"Linden, where have you been?" I asked. "Did you eat?"

"I've been putting the finishing touches on your gift," he said. "It's ready."

"That's wonderful," I said.

"I want you to see it before you leave."

"That's all right. We'll see it as soon as we return, Linden."

"No," he said firmly. "You must see it before you go."

My heart started to trip. I looked to Mother, who was watching us with worry while she tried to pay attention to whatever Whitney's husband happened to be saying to her.

"All right, Linden," I said calmly. "I'll tell Thatcher."

"You could come look first, if you like. Or you could bring him, too. I don't care. It's a wedding gift."

"All right, Linden. Just give me a little time to get his attention," I said.

"That shouldn't be hard. Ever!" he snapped, and walked back to the dais to take his seat. For the next half hour, he sat there glaring at the guests like he was in a sulk. Mother spoke to him and I saw both the Butterworth twins talk to him, but he never took his eyes off me for long. I could feel them even when I had my back to him—especially when I had my back to him.

"Linden wants to give us our wedding present before we leave, Thatcher," I told him when I was able to pull him aside. He looked a little bleary-eyed from toasting with one group of friends and associates after another.

"What wedding present?"

"A picture he's painted," I said. "You know. I've told you about it before."

"Oh, boy. I can just imagine what it will be . . . two skeletons in bed, or a woman on fire and her husband trying to douse it with gasoline."

"Stop it, Thatcher. We'll just go and look at it and make him happy by telling him how wonderful it is."

"Okay, okay. Whatever you say, my love. Your wish is my command."

"You're not drunk, are you?"

"Absolutely not." He raised his right hand and pretended his left was on a Bible. "I solemnly swear I am as sober as a Palm Beach magistrate."

"You idiot," I said, laughing at him.

When I turned back to Linden, he had his head down.

"I'll get him and we'll sneak off for a minute, Thatcher."

"Right," he said. "Then we sneak away. The limo is waiting to take us to the airport. Jennings saw to our bags."

I went to Linden, who shot up out of his chair so dramatically, it stopped some nearby conversations. I smiled at Mother to indicate it was all right, and he and I joined Thatcher.

"So, it's time for the unveiling, then, eh, Linden?" Thatcher asked him.

"It's not a gravesite monument," Linden muttered.

Thatcher smiled at me, and we hurried up the walk and into the house.

"It's nice of you to have devoted so much of your time and effort to a gift for us, Linden," Thatcher said.

Linden gave him such a look of "oh, please" that I couldn't contain a small laugh. Thatcher actually blanched, his lips a bit white in the corners.

We paused at the studio door to wait for Linden to

unlock it. The room was dark, and Linden made no effort to turn on any lights. He walked across to an easel with a sheet over the picture. My heart began to pound. What had he taken from the pictures that had invaded my privacy? Would Thatcher lose his temper?

"Close the door," he said. "It's better if you see it this way first."

Thatcher did so, and we were in total darkness. Linden removed the sheet, then he turned on a small light above the easel, bathing the picture in its glow. I was in a sheer white dress, but it was in no way a pornographic depiction. My figure was clearly delineated, but the way he had painted me, the colors he'd used, gave me an angelic glow. He had placed me on the beach at night. As we drew closer to it, I could see that I was supposedly coming from the water, but I didn't look frantic or afraid. I was smiling, my eyes excited, happy, and I was reaching out for someone or something. On closer inspection, there was the vague outline of a hand reaching out of the darkness for me. My hair flowed off my shoulders, giving the sense of movement. He had done my face in such detail, we could even see the thin peach fuzz behind my ear.

"This is the best thing you have ever done, Linden," Thatcher declared. "You've captured the most beautiful things about Willow, and it's so tasteful and interesting. It makes you feel good. Most of your work addresses the darker side of our consciousness," he added.

Linden wasn't paying any attention to him. His eyes were fixed on me.

"You've made me too beautiful, Linden," I said.

"That's how I see you."

"I imagine that's my hand there, barely seen," Thatcher said.

Linden didn't reply. It was as if he and I were alone in the room.

"We'll put it right over our bed, right, Willow?"

"Yes. Thank you, Linden. It's the nicest gift of all." I leaned over and kissed him on the cheek.

"I'll see to getting it hung for you," he said.

"Great," Thatcher said. He shook Linden's hand vigorously, too vigorously, then turned to me and said, "We've got to get moving. You know how long it will take to say goodbye to my mother."

"Right. Take care of Mother while we are away, Linden," I said.

"I always do," he replied.

When Thatcher opened the door for me, I looked back at Linden. He was standing proudly beside his picture and smiling. There was no doubt in my mind and no doubt in my heart that the hand coming from the darkness toward me wasn't Thatcher's. It was his.

That small cloud of concern was wiped out of the diamond-studded sky of stars the moment we got into our limousine. Mother, Bunny, Asher, and Amou came out to see us off, everyone wishing us a wonderful time.

"It was a spectacular wedding after all, wasn't it?" I asked Mother.

"Yes. We'll have to give the devil her due. Bunny pulled it off in true Palm Beach spectacular fashion. Did everything else go all right?" she asked, meaning Linden's picture.

"Yes. It's really beautiful, different from anything else he has done."

"Good. He needs some success."

We hugged. I hugged Amou, the tears running down both our cheeks intermingled.

"We'll come to see you next, Amou," I promised.

"I hope so," she said. *"O deus abençoa-o."*

"God bless you, too," I said, and Thatcher and I got into the limousine. I looked back at them all and waved one last time.

"Stop crying," Thatcher said, laughing. "You're not going to prison. You're going to the Côte d'Azur."

"These are tears of happiness, Thatcher."

He laughed.

What else do we do that has such diametrically opposite meanings besides cry? We cry when we're happy; we cry when we're sad. Someone looking at us from afar might not know which we are feeling. Maybe we're always feeling a little of both. On this most important of days, I was saying goodbye to the little girl left in me. It was time to let go of most of that.

But I saw her standing there with Amou, waving to me, crying herself.

How do you feel about that? I heard Daddy ask.

I ache inside, Daddy. Why can't we keep it all, our innocence and our dreams, keep them alongside reality and maturity?

Why do you think we can't?

Responsibilities, responsibilities for others. But sometimes I think it's too high a price to pay.

I could see him in my mind, nodding, looking thoughtful, thinking about his own life and those dreams he he'd had and lost.

"Hey," Thatcher cried. "Stop looking so serious already. We're free of it all. For a week we'll be in paradise, okay?"

"Okay," I said, cuddling up to him and under his arm. We kissed, and I looked ahead and tried to do just what he wanted, forget everything but ourselves.

*   *   *

In Eze, France, that was not a hard thing to do. After we landed in Nice, we were driven for about twenty-five minutes up to the walled medieval hill village with streets too narrow for cars. The limousine stopped at the parking area just outside the ancient walls and the château. Converted from eleventh-century houses—which meant some bedrooms were in separate buildings—the château looked old but had very modern conveniences, including fax and Internet lines in the suite, which made Thatcher happy, even though he had been the one to demand we throw off the world and step into this storybook place.

I felt sorry for the bellhops who had to carry the luggage all the way up. I made sure Thatcher gave them a bonus tip. The view from our balcony was truly breathtaking, overlooking the coast and Cap Ferrat. The water was a turquoise shade I had never seen, and with the sailboats, ocean liners, and motorboats out there, it was like looking through a magic window into a make-believe world.

The first thing we did was order in some food, and then we crawled into bed to deal with our jet lag, but we weren't beside each other long before we began to make love. I kept thinking about my cousin's revelations concerning her honeymoon and sexual relations. Thatcher was not perfect—no one could be—but he was not a selfish lover. At times I suspected that came from his male pride. It was always important to him to hear that I was satisfied. He made it seem like a performance.

There you go, Willow, I told myself, *always analyzing, even your lovemaking.* I tried to shut myself up and just enjoy our days.

How wonderful they were. Breakfast on a patio that overlooked the bay. Walks through the ancient village with its little shops full of handcrafts, the gardens, the restaurants in town, the perfume factory where we behaved like two teenagers spraying each other with the test bottles until the saleslady pleaded with us to behave.

"People on vacation always feel younger and act younger," Thatcher declared. "There's this sense of abandon, of freedom, don't you think, Doc?"

He had begun to nickname me "Doc," teasing me about the way I studied people and analyzed their behavior.

"I can see now who will be the one who doesn't leave her work at the shop," he said.

"The world is my shop," I told him, and he said, "Touché. I'd better watch myself."

It was he, however, who surprised me with a strange announcement after the phone in our room rang the morning of our fourth day. He thought I was still asleep so he spoke very softly. When he hung up, I stirred and asked who that was.

"I've been tracked down," he said.

"What do you mean?" I sat up.

"I have this big client in France. He owns property in Palm Beach and he is heading up a conglomerate to invest in and build a new hotel there. It's very involved, but it looks like it will happen and yours truly will reap mucho moola for us."

He went to the closet and began to choose his clothes.

"Where are you going? It's so early."

"I have to meet him and two of his associates in Nice." He smiled. "I'm giving you this little intermission, this little break from being totally consumed by Thatcher Eaton, but it won't be for long."

"Break? How long will you be gone?"

"It's a meeting and then lunch. I'll be back by midafternoon," he said. "You wanted to do some shopping for gifts anyway, and I was never very good at that, never had the patience for it. I'd only be a drag and spoil it for you. We're having dinner here tonight," he added quickly. "I've arranged for the best table, one by the window with a view that will knock your socks off."

"But this is our honeymoon, Thatcher. How can you have arranged for a business meeting?"

"I didn't exactly arrange it. As I said, they tracked me down, and there is some urgency to it all. It's actually a great idea to take advantage of my presence here. I can meet with some of the other partners, and it would save me a trip back to France in a few weeks. This is definitely the lesser of two evils, Willow. I'll be back as soon as I can."

"How are you getting to Nice?"

"They have sent a car for me. These are heavy hitters, honey. They spare no expense, and that, my dear, includes my lofty legal fees as well as a piece of the action."

He kissed me on the cheek.

"Don't look so down. Remember what they say, 'Absence makes the heart grow fonder.' "

"I thought our hearts were fond enough of each other," I retorted.

"Never too much fondness. It's always good to have some to spare. Don't pick up any handsome young Frenchman while I'm away," he warned, and headed out.

"Thatcher," I moaned, but he was gone.

I fell back on my pillow and pouted for a while before deciding he was right. A little private time was probably healthy, and I did want to get the shopping done. I ate by myself on the patio, read the *International Herald Tribune,* and then got dressed and began to walk the cobblestone streets, visiting shops, thinking about gifts that would please Mother, Amou, Linden, and even

Thatcher's parents, not that there was anything they would appreciate for more than a fleeting few seconds.

In one shop where they made interesting signs and little posters, they had a quote taken from Sigmund Freud. I thought Professor Fuentes would love to hang it in his office, so I bought it and had it sent to him.

It read, "The great question that has never been answered and which I have not yet been able to answer despite my thirty years of research into the feminine soul is, 'What does a woman want?' "

I laughed to myself, imagining the look on his face when he opened the package and read that, especially considering the female students he had in his classes, including me.

After shopping, I sat in a small courtyard restaurant and had a salad, some wonderful French bread, and a glass of merlot. Below the patio a young man was sitting on a bench and playing an accordion. I thought he was very good, although most of his tunes were melancholy. It left me thoughtful, and I hated being dropped into a pit of pensive and philosophical thought on this happiest of all holidays.

Afterward, I went to the pool and sunbathed on a lounge. The people around me were from Germany, other parts of France, and even Japan. The mixture of different languages, the spools of laughter that unraveled from the happy couples around me, soon became background music to my ears, and before I realized it, I dozed off. I didn't wake until I felt a nudge and looked up to see Thatcher smiling down at me.

"You're getting a little too much sun, Willow. Your face is very red."

"Oh," I cried, sitting up quickly. "I must have fallen asleep. Maybe the wine at lunch—"

"So that's what you do when I leave you for a little while? Drink yourself silly, huh?" he teased.

I glanced at my watch. It was a little after four.

"You haven't exactly been gone for a little while," I complained.

"I know. This became a little more complicated than I had expected. Did you get your shopping done?"

"Yes."

"Then you didn't waste any time," he said. "I would suggest you come inside, take a cool shower, and get something on your skin before you peel and suffer."

"Okay," I said, and got up quickly.

We returned to our suite and I did exactly what he had suggested. Then we had a cocktail on the patio and I described some of the gifts I had bought. I didn't tell him about the gift I had sent to Professor Fuentes. Instinctively, I felt he might be a little jealous about it, although he had no reason to be.

That night we had a wonderful dinner. Thatcher was right about the view. Afterward, we sat outside and looked up at the stars and down at the water. It was a very romantic end to what had started as a disappointing day.

When we left Eze, I truly felt as though we were returning to the real world. We had been in a dream, floating on love, touching the stars. Our plane would bring us back to earth. I remember thinking as the wheels touched down that this was it, the beginning of a new life with all the questions to be answered, the roads to travel.

A whirlwind of events and revelations had brought me to this place. In a sense, I'd had little to do with it. I was born to it. Now, perhaps for the first time, I had something to say and some control of my own destiny. Into what kind of world would I bring my children?

What gifts and what burdens would I bequeath to them? How many questions would I leave unanswered, and how daunting would be their effort to answer them?

I loved Thatcher. He was the most exciting, handsome, and confident man I had ever met, other than my father, but there were so many dark areas in him I had yet to explore and to understand. It takes a long time to get to know someone, even someone you love very much. There are layers and layers to lift away, and all you could do and all you could hope for was that when you went deep enough, you would discover wonderful things and not something that made you regret ever having begun to explore and discover.

Most married people don't bother. They live on a superficial layer of thin ice and skate carefully around each other. They don't ask. They don't think about it. They turn away and distract themselves, and if one day they fall through, they pull themselves up and skate off to find another companion on another layer of thin ice, a companion just as eager not to look too deeply at them.

How do they sleep? What do they dream? My adoptive mother surely must have known how far out of love with her my father had fallen, but she chose to pretend it wasn't so or it wasn't very important. Just before she died, did she have a suddenness of regret? Did she remember her fantasies, those romances on the screen and in books that she had hoped would be true for her? Is it more painful to die with disappointment?

That will never be me, I thought with confidence.

I reached for Thatcher's hand, and he smiled.

"Happy to be home?" he asked.

"No," I said, and he laughed.

"We'll go back someday," he promised.

No, I thought. You could never go back. Every moment was fresh and special. You could only go ahead and hope to have similar ones or better ones.

Love is like a good book: You turn the page to go on and wish it would never end.

I turned the page.

14

Brothers and Sisters

When we arrived home, we discovered that Linden had gone ahead and arranged for the hanging of my picture above our bed. He had also done what I thought was a strange thing—he had moved out of the room he was in and into the infamous room in which Kirby Scott had seduced Mother. It was closer to Thatcher's and my suite, actually right behind our bedroom, but with all the bad energy and memories associated with that room, it was curious that he had done so.

I had an opportunity to ask him about it that very day. We arrived fairly early, and Thatcher went off to his office. He had been on his cell phone almost the moment we entered the airport, and told me he had a list of problems an arm long to solve.

Mother, Linden, and I had lunch together. I thought Mother looked tired, but I didn't say anything about it until we had a chance to be alone. She was interested in hearing about our trip, and she loved the hand-painted silk skirt and blouse I had bought her, as well as the glass figurines. I had found some interesting hand-crafted and hand-painted leather masks for Linden. I thought they were unique, and so did he.

Despite moving into Mother's old room, Linden seemed chipper and more alert than before Thatcher and I had left for our honeymoon. He talked about new works he was contemplating and some more ideas he had for sprucing up Joya del Mar, always thinking about ways to restore its previous character and eliminate any trace of the Eatons.

After lunch Mother told me Linden was doing well and had shown no signs of the melancholy that had so worried her and threatened to drive him to the brink of some new disaster.

"I did try to stop him from moving into that room, but he was determined. He said we have got to eliminate all the old ghosts, confront the past and bury it once and for all. He claimed it was something you had once told him. I was surprised at his show of new strength, so I didn't put up any more opposition and, as you can see, he's happy. Maybe he was right, but it did worry me for a while."

"I can see that, Mother. You're not getting enough rest. Are you sleeping enough?"

"Yes." She looked down and then up at me; her eyes had never been so full of fear and pain.

"What is it, Mother?"

"He's all right in that room, but I still can't go into it. It used to be such a warm and beautiful room. I had all my dolls, my precious gifts. Jackie Lee had that canopy bed custom-made for me. I felt so safe there, so cuddly safe and warm all the time." She paused, caught up in her memories, then went on.

"The first time he came into that room alone, he sat on my bed and talked about himself as a young boy. He was a good raconteur, weaving stories like fairy tales. I was so innocent, he had little difficulty taking my hand and leading me down the primrose path. Whenever he touched me then, I thought it was the touch of a loving parent, a caress to soothe and comfort.

"He began by holding my hand or putting his on my shoulder. Sometimes, when he told me a tale, he fingered my hair, and he always kissed me good night, starting on my forehead, then my cheeks, and one night a quick peck on my lips that came as such a surprise, I barely had time to react. I thought about it all night because it had left me feeling so different.

"It was a very slow, careful seduction, you see. I trusted him. If he came upon me when I was still in my undergarments, I had no fears, no inhibitions about it. He didn't seem to have any reaction. He led me to believe he saw me as asexual, saw me the way a parent should see his daughter," she said.

"One night he came in while I was still in my bath, in fact. I had a sufficient blanket of bubbles and suds to feel okay about it, but he lingered, deciding to wash my back for me. I kept my hands over my breasts, but he talked about so many things while he did it, I relaxed, thinking he didn't see me as a naked young woman. But after he finished and I submerged myself, his hand managed to graze my breast. He smiled down at me and left.

"Two nights later he returned. Jackie Lee was out with some of her friends. I had just crawled into bed and was reading when he came in, telling me he was lonely, that my mother had left him again.

"He talked about how hard it was for a man, harder

than for a woman, he claimed, to be lonely. He told me men have greater needs.

" 'Women find it easier to be nuns than men do being monks,' " he said. He had such a confident, assured way about him and was so worldly, I believed everything he told me.

"He asked me about my relationships with boys and if I had ever gotten excited in a female way. I knew what he meant, of course, but all I could do was blush. He took it from there, telling me how natural it was and how I shouldn't be afraid.

"Men, he said, get excited faster, easier, and for a longer period. He told me it was better that I understood it than be caught unaware· what sort of stepfather would he be if he didn't prepare me for all this? My mother, he claimed, was just too distracted and missed seeing how grown-up I had become.

"Then he flattered me so, talking about my looks, my body, and finally confessing that I aroused him. He made me see it was true.

"I was terrified, of course. I remember I could barely breathe, and then he crawled into the bed beside me and began to caress me and coax me until . . . it happened.

"The moment after it had, my room changed for me. It was the setting for all that, you see. Like me, it had lost its innocence, its magic. I couldn't sleep. My heart would thump the moment I entered.

"It still does," she confessed. "And now Linden is in it, and I feel such trauma every time I go to him. Maybe that's why I'm so tired."

She looked at me and saw some of the shock in my face. Her story made me tremble to the bone.

"I'm sorry. I shouldn't have told you all that. I have

never told anyone except your father when I was in the clinic."

"No, I'm glad you did, Mother. But I'm worried about you. I'm taking you to the doctor first thing tomorrow. You need a good physical."

"No, no. There's nothing wrong with me, other than having these recurring memories and my getting older," she insisted. "I'll be fine. Time will heal. I'll get over it, you'll see. Besides, you're just starting a new and wonderful life here. Let's not put any new problems on the table. Are you still going to attend some summer-school classes?"

"Yes. I'm looking forward to that."

"Good. Then no more talk of doctors. I've had my fill of doctors, and so has Linden," she declared firmly.

"If you continue to be tired—"

"Then I'll go."

I wasn't happy with the compromise, but I let it be rather than see her disturbed any more. I left her. I was still trembling inside, thinking about Kirby Scott and how he had painstakingly worked on her until he had seduced her. But she was right. We had to put it all away, bury the past. It made me realize how wounded she was, however, and how wounded Linden had been, too.

No psychology student had as much work at home as I did, I thought, trying to put a little lightness into the dark.

I went to talk to Linden, who had returned to his studio. He was sitting before a canvas outlining some new idea.

"I'm sorry to disturb you," I said after knocking on his open door.

"No, no, please come in. I'm just doodling at the moment, trying to find the center of something. You look tanned and rested. I guess you had a wonderful trip after all."

"Why shouldn't it have been wonderful, Linden?"

"Oh, I don't know. Just a manner of speaking, I guess."

He stared at his canvas.

"I hope you will do some traveling, too, Linden. There is so much more to see and learn out there, and that's especially important for someone who wants to be an artist."

"Right, right."

"I am curious as to why you moved into another bedroom," I said. "Especially that bedroom."

He turned, stared a moment, then shrugged.

"It's a bigger, brighter room. How foolish it is to waste it just because it was once the scene of some unpleasantness. It's not the room's fault, is it? There's no evil power living in it, right?"

"Of course not."

"And you were the one who convinced me that we could move back into this house and do away with all the old, troubling memories, the old ghosts, so to speak. I would think you would be very happy about it."

"I am. I was just curious."

"Worried, you mean," he said, with eyes so narrow and dark they looked like slits for a moment. Then he smiled. "Worry no more about me. I'm fine. I feel like I am getting stronger and stronger every day."

"Good. That's wonderful, Linden. How was Mother while I was gone?" I asked, checking to see how aware of her reactions he was. "She seems tired to me."

"Well, if there is anyone who is putting on an act about being back here, it's Grace. I find her sitting and staring at nothing a good deal of the time, and I know what that means—she's reliving the past. I'm doing my best to get her to put it behind her. Now that you are back," he said, smiling, "we'll work on it together."

"Yes," I said.

"We'll take care of her. It will be our little project, okay?" he asked. "Just you and me."

I smiled, but the way he said it made it sound as if he and I would have some secret mission, secret even from Thatcher.

I had to admit that in the days and weeks that followed, however, Linden was the dutiful son, actually more like the doting son, rushing ahead to do anything and everything he could for Mother. If she headed toward a door, he was there before her to open it for her. If she started to clear a table, he leaped up to take the dishes or cups out of her hands. The roles they had been playing were reversed. Now he was the one chiding her for not eating enough or not eating the right things. He was the one making sure she took her vitamins, the one who would rush off to fetch some ibuprofen for her arthritic aches.

Usually, I was included in any activity designed to assist Mother. If he suggested she go for a walk with him to get fresh air, it was always a walk with us.

"Willow wants to go, too," he would say, and throw me a glance to be sure I nodded or seconded his suggestion quickly.

On the nights Thatcher was tied up with a business dinner, Linden recommended we all go out to eat.

"Thatcher's not coming home. Let's not have dinner made just for ourselves," he would say. "Willow will drive us to some restaurant we haven't been to, Mother. Won't you, Willow?"

At first Mother was amused by all this, just as I was, but the intensity and the insistence with which Linden made his suggestions began to ring small alarm bells inside us both. He had changed from someone who was so introverted he would rarely laugh aloud, especially in front of strangers, to someone who was starving for activity, for attention, for society—only, however, as long as I would include myself. That wasn't always easy to do, and every time I had to decline one of his invitations, even as insignificant a suggestion as having coffee on the rear loggia with Mother and him, I felt deep pangs of guilt. I certainly didn't want to be the one to send him reeling back into his maelstrom of depression and suicidal rage.

I had returned to college and on a few occasions, during lunch, I had an opportunity to speak with Professor Fuentes. By now he had enough of an outline of my family problems to appreciate some of my concerns. He was always willing and eager to give me his time and expertise.

"What is he like when Thatcher is there?" he asked after I had related our latest episode.

I had already described how Linden seemed to hear Thatcher's every word whenever he explained or revealed that he would be late for dinner or tied up with clients. Most recently, without my knowledge, after hearing Thatcher say he was going to be down in Miami and home late, Linden went out and bought three tickets for Mother, himself, and me to attend a performance of the Palm Beach Philharmonic.

Never before enjoying getting dressed up and being with crowds of people, he was obviously very excited about it, so excited he got Mother laughing, agreeing to dress up and attend.

"See," he told me afterward, "we're having a good influence on her. We're getting her to forget the past and enjoy her life now. We're a team."

I couldn't say it wasn't true, yet it bothered me. Why? I hoped Professor Fuentes could help me answer that.

"What happens when you go somewhere with Thatcher and Linden is not included?" Professor Fuentes asked me.

"He doesn't sulk like he used to, but he looks . . ."

"Angry?"

"Upset. I don't know if it's out-and-out anger."

"You're still his whole life, Willow. It is so important he develop other relationships. Coming out of his depression, his difficulties, he resembles a young teenage boy doting on the first warm and pretty face he encounters. I suppose it's similar to a schoolboy's crush on his teacher. I don't think it's anything terribly serious, but I would do what I can to get him meeting other people."

"He's working hard again. He's done some new pictures, and Thatcher brought them to a friend of his who thinks he might sell them in Europe."

"Really? Well, there you go. Get him involved more in the art world. Maybe he'll meet people that way," Professor Fuentes suggested. "And encourage him to do what he said he would—take a course or two on art here."

I repeated Professor Fuentes's ideas to Thatcher, who then asked Linden to go with him the next time he was invited to a gallery exhibition.

"You should see the work of other artists, Linden. You'll get more inspiration."

"Thatcher's right, Linden," I said.

"Are you going, too?"

"I have to do some studying," I said, eyeing Thatcher, "but Thatcher is going."

"I've got work to do myself," Linden said.

"Oh, come on, old man, you can spare an hour or so.

You'll see. It will give you encouragement because you'll see how much better an artist you are."

"I'm not an old man," Linden snapped.

"Just an expression, Linden. Nothing nasty intended. What do you say?"

"You should go, Linden," I urged.

"All right," he relented. "But I don't want to waste the whole day."

Later, when they returned, Thatcher told me Linden had stood in a corner most of the time, "looking like he just dared anyone to say hello.

"I introduced him to some attractive young women, but he wouldn't give them the time of day. Maybe he needs hormone shots, the youngest man on Viagra, something like that," he joked.

"It's not funny, Thatcher. I'm worried about it now, and I don't want Mother to worry."

"Okay, okay. I'll dig up some female companionship for him."

"I'm not asking you to do that."

"I know, but what kind of brother-in-law would I be if I didn't make sure he got his rocks off once in a while?"

"Thatcher!"

He laughed and went off. However, I had to wonder if he wasn't right. Maybe a female relationship, no matter how short and sweet, was what Linden really needed. On the other hand, I thought, why was it men thought of sex the same way they thought of an aspirin?

The time I was spending with Linden, attending social events, shopping, eating dinner, or simply taking long walks on the beach, even with Mother along, was, to my surprise, becoming the subject of some nasty gossip. The second surprise was how it was all being spread. I wouldn't have known if I wasn't invited to another luncheon of the Club d'Amour. I should have realized they had good reason to beg for my attendance.

We didn't meet at Club Florette again. This time we all gathered at a popular Palm Beach restaurant and sat in the rear, as far away from everyone else as we could. That was Manon's arrangement. I was still very interested in them from a purely scientific point of view. I had told Professor Fuentes about them and he agreed that they were intriguing.

The luncheon began with chat about fashions, the latest Palm Beach charity event, people they had all just seen, and some of the latest party jokes that were being circulated. Finally, Manon turned to me and said, "There is something we've all heard and we thought you should know."

"Oh?"

My heart began to tick like a Geiger counter over radioactive material. Everyone's eyes were on me, waiting to see my reaction to whatever Manon was about to reveal.

"We all have good reason to say that your sister-in-law is making innuendos about you and your half brother. She's been complaining about all the time you spend with Linden, and she's left the impression that it isn't all brotherly and sisterly."

"What? Whitney is telling people things like that?"

"Absolutely and without a doubt," Liana said. "Our sources are the most reliable in Palm Beach."

Sharon and Marjorie nodded in agreement.

"What exactly is she saying?"

"She told someone we know well that your brother moved his bedroom closer to yours. Is that true?"

"Yes, but—"

"She said he had painted a picture to give you and Thatcher for a wedding present, but it's a picture of you only and it's done in a very sexy way. She said he put it over your bed himself, and one of the maids told her he goes there often to look at it. She said he looks at it as if he were looking at the Virgin Mary. She could see no reason for all this, other than something unnatural, perverted."

"Is there something weird going on between you and Linden?" Marjorie dared to ask. Everyone else held her breath.

"That's a disgusting question, an insulting question," I snapped back at her.

"I had to ask," she said defensively. "If we're going to stand by you, we should know the truth. Just like a good defense attorney."

"I'm not asking you to do anything," I said even more sharply. "There is nothing like that going on. I have no reason to need any defense."

"You know what they say about people who protest too much," Sharon quipped.

"Well, it's degrading to hear such things, disgusting, filthy and—"

"We agree," Manon said quickly. She looked around to be sure no one was in earshot before adding, "And we want to help you."

I settled back and stared down at the table.

"Why would she do such a dirty thing?" I muttered.

"Maybe she's the one who has something unnatural for her brother," Marjorie suggested. "The way she looks at Thatcher when they are together, I mean."

"Sounds like a plan," Manon said, nodding.

"What? What are you all saying? There's nothing to that filthy smear, either."

"Doesn't matter," Manon said. "You've got to fight fire with fire. Don't worry, we'll handle it."

"No. I don't want to get into some backstabbing gossip feud with my sister-in-law. I'll confront her directly and make sure that if it's true, it stops."

"Don't underestimate Whitney," Marjorie warned. "You're just an amateur when it comes to the Palm Beach Game and she's an expert. She'll have you for breakfast."

"I'll be fine," I said.

"We're just trying to help you," Manon repeated.

"Thank you," I said, but I could see they weren't motivated by a sense of right and wrong so much as they, too, enjoyed playing what they called the Palm Beach Game.

"Tell us about your honeymoon," Sharon said. For a moment I felt like a patient in a therapist's office. I'd shut one pathway to my inner self, so they moved on to travel another.

"Yes, every detail you can remember," Liana added.

"Or want to reveal," Sharon said.

"Was it everything you expected?" Manon asked.

I laughed loudly in their faces, and they all seemed to have their spinal cords snapped sharply, making them sit up.

"What's so funny?"

"You all sound like you feed off of other women's love lives," I said. "Vicarious sex."

Never had I seen smiles evaporate faster.

"Obviously, our psychology student is unable to leave Mr. Freud at home when she goes out with real people," Marjorie said through clenched teeth.

"If things aren't what you hoped they would be, they won't get any better if you take it out on us," Manon added. "You, a student of psychotherapy, should know that better than us."

"I'm not taking anything out on anyone, and who said things aren't what I expected?"

"Protesting too much!" Sharon sang.

"You're all being quite ridiculous," I said. "I've got to go."

I started to dig into my purse for money to pay for my lunch.

"Don't worry about money, Willow. We'll take care of the bill. I wish you wouldn't go off in a huff," Manon said.

"I'm tired and I have some studying to do. Thanks for all the dirty revelations."

Marjorie reached up to grasp my arm. It took me by surprise.

"Someday, maybe someday soon," she said, "you will be sincere when you thank us like that."

I pulled my arm free. Tears were burning under my lids, but I fought hard to keep them there.

"I hope I have more important things with which to concern myself," I said. "Thanks for lunch. That's sincere," I added and stormed away.

For a while I just drove, not paying much attention to where I was going. I made some wrong turns and went in circles. The tears streamed down my face freely now. Why would Whitney do such a thing? Why would family members try to tear their own family apart like this? What did she hope to accomplish?

How could I go home and face Mother and Linden, knowing what people were saying about us, about me, and all because of Whitney?

Anger quickly replaced emotional pain. In a snap, I made a decision. I turned the vehicle sharply and headed for Whitney's mansion.

It took so long for me to gain entry through those fortress gates, I thought I would be turned away. Finally they were opened and I drove up to the mansion. A maid greeted me at the door. She had a dust mop in her hand and looked annoyed that anyone would dare an unannounced visit and interrupt her important work.

"Mrs. Shugar is on the terrace," she said. She nodded down the long entryway. "You can go out the French doors on your right."

"Thank you," I said, and marched over the tiles, my heels clicking like tap shoes, the noise echoing up the walls and bouncing down from the high ceiling.

Under a large umbrella, Whitney was lounging in a pair of shorts and a white halter. The book she had been reading was beside her on a table, next to a tall glass of what looked like a piña colada. It even had the small umbrella sticking up. In my mind a thought flashed: *She thinks of her home as a hotel and herself as a perennial guest.*

As I approached, she opened her left eye, then closed it and, with a sigh of annoyance, sat up, fixing the chaise behind her.

"What brings you here, Willow?" she asked. "I thought you were so busy with your college and your brother."

"That's what brings me here, Whitney."

She raised her eyebrows and reached for her drink.

"Do you want something to drink?"

"No, I'm not staying that long."

"Oh. Well, you can sit so I don't have to keep looking up at you, can't you?"

I sat on an upright chair by one of the tables.

"So? Where is the fire?" she asked with a crooked smile.

"Better you should ask who is the arsonist," I retorted.

She put down her glass.

"What's that supposed to mean?" she demanded.

"It has been brought to my attention, painfully brought to my attention, that you have been saying nasty things about Linden and me."

"Oh?" she asked, without attempting to deny anything. "Have you?"

"I haven't said anything that everyone else around here doesn't think or believe," she replied with her haughty tone.

Whitney saw herself so high up on a pedestal of her own making that she had no fear of being challenged, and had too much arrogance to ever feel shame or defeat, I thought.

"What kind of stupid, filthy logic is that, Whitney? I'm Thatcher's wife. This is your family now, too. You should be protecting us, not helping spread disgusting gossip."

"I don't spread gossip," she snapped. She looked away for a moment, then turned back, her face not so much red as brassy, her eyes blazing. There were forces in her I couldn't even begin to fathom, I thought. "I am always looking out for my family."

"Looking out for your family? First you tried to ruin our relationship by concocting that stupid story about Kirby Scott, and now that we've married, you're doing something even worse."

"You can't blame me for trying to open Thatcher's eyes. You came into our lives like some northwester, blowing everything onshore. Who but Thatcher would marry someone with all the baggage you carry?"

"You still think you're so superior that you know what's best for everyone?"

She smiled coldly, her eyes so gray she looked like someone without a soul.

"I see you're not denying the stories."

"Of course I'm not denying them. I don't intend to

give them the dignity of even being considered seriously. Who but someone sicker than my brother would tell people such things?"

She winced, but didn't change expression.

"I have pictures," she said.

"Pictures? What pictures?" I asked. All the air seemed to have gone from my lungs.

She smiled again and lay back on the chaise.

"You should have realized that the people who worked for the Eatons all these years developed some sense of loyalty to us. Maybe not Jennings so much, but the maids you kept—and don't you dare go home and fire anyone!" she warned, her eyes wide with fury.

The blood had drained from my face.

"What are you talking about?" I asked, hoping she was talking about something else.

She smiled again.

"The disgusting photographs you permitted your sick brother to take of you." She thrust her body toward me. "You posed nude for him, too, didn't you?"

"No, I did not. I can't believe you had one of the maids do such a thing. Spying on us. It's so despicable, I can't even find the words to do it justice."

"I'm only protecting my family," she said dryly, and sipped her drink again. "Now that you have had the nerve to bring this to a head, I must insist you have your brother committed."

"What?"

"I want him out of that house," she ordered. "It's the best thing for Thatcher. This way he won't be harmed by any perversions that could go on there. His reputation is everlastingly bound to my parents' and my own reputations. No one lives in a vacuum here. What you do now reflects on me and my parents, too."

"What about what you do?"

"I doubt," she said with that crooked smile again, "that you will hear one substantiated piece of filth as dirty about me as people are spreading about you.

"You come from a family of disturbed people. What frightens me the most, if you want to know, is what sort of children you might have. I hope Thatcher gives that some thought and goes to a reputable adoption agency when the time comes to have children, if it comes. If your marriage survives."

She sat back, confident.

"I told you once before how I have had to come to Thatcher's aid to save him from one romantic disaster after another."

I shook my head, the words of anger choking in my throat.

The faces of the women of the Club d'Amour flashed before me. How right they were when they warned me about Whitney and the Palm Beach Game.

But I refused to be as helpless as everyone thought, especially as Whitney thought.

"Why would you do that?" I said, filling my voice with new strength and assurance.

"What?"

"Interfere in your brother's love life so often."

"I told you. To protect him. To protect my family."

"Really? Could it be that *you* are the one with a sick fascination for a brother? That *you* are the one who dotes unnaturally on him? Despite what you think of yourself and your precious Palm Beach reputation, I have just come from lunch with a group of women who think that of you."

"You're lying."

"I can see to it that you hear it from some of them, if

you like. You're frustrated in your own marriage. Your husband has been heard saying things about your cold bed. You're driving me out because you want Thatcher for yourself."

"You sick, evil—"

"Me?"

I stood up.

"Hardly me. I don't hire the maid in your house to listen in on conversations and steal things to give to me. But, I venture to say, some of the servants here don't feel all that devotion to you that you think they do, and they could be coaxed to talk about how you show excessive affection for Thatcher," I said in a threatening tone.

"You wouldn't dare attempt such a thing. I'll tear you to bits out there."

"Maybe and maybe not. Maybe we'd both be bloodied beyond repair, but don't worry. I'm becoming a therapist. Years from now, I'll treat you pro bono."

She stared at up at me, the doubt, the indecision and insecurity finally getting a beachhead on the shores of her evil mind.

I glanced at my watch.

"It's a little after three. By six o'clock today I will expect those pictures to be delivered to me. If I ever hear mention of them again or any more slimy rumors about my poor brother and me, I'll become a one-woman tabloid newspaper. You won't be able to go to a single charity ball, a single dinner party, a single restaurant in this town and not wonder about the eyes on you and the whispering behind your back.

"I could live anywhere," I said cheerfully, "even Boca, but you, you'd die if you left your precious Palm Beach home."

The expression on her face made me smile.

"That's right, Whitney. Think of it. Both Thatcher and I could practice our professions anywhere. Where can you practice your profession, Whitney, except here . . . and hell?"

I turned and walked away, paused and looked back at her.

"Six o'clock, and I mean not a minute after," I said.

My heels clicked on the tiles, sounding like bullets of rain behind me.

15

A Second Honeymoon

"**I** find myself continually underestimating how complicated and complex family relationships can be," Professor Fuentes said after listening to me describe my conflict with Whitney. We were in a café near the campus. "In fact," he said, looking up from his cup of coffee and smiling at me with that gentle ripple that traveled from his lips up into his eyes, "I daresay Whitney doesn't understand her motivations herself.

"Without even having met her," he continued, "I think she really believes she is doing something good for her family, her brother in particular. If I was practicing therapy and had her as a client, I would probably suggest she is using that as a rationalization for darker purposes, and it would be best for her to admit that, to stop lying to herself."

"Yes, eventually you might help her, if it's possible to help her, but by then it would be too late for poor Linden and myself," I said.

He nodded.

"Probably. I think you were right to face up to her, to confront her and demonstrate that you are not some helpless pawn. At least you will get her to retreat to whispers, but I'm not optimistic that she will stop altogether," he said.

"I know that."

"For now, it would be wise to continue to work on Linden's development of outside interests. Nothing would work faster and more successfully than his finding someone else in whom he could invest his interest and attention."

"I know that, too."

"I'm sorry," he said, smiling. "I'm not being all that brilliant and helpful to you."

"Oh, no," I protested. "You don't know how much I appreciate your listening and giving me your opinions."

He nodded and looked down at his coffee.

"Does Thatcher know how much you confide in me?" he asked, still looking at his cup.

"Now, Professor Fuentes," I said, "doesn't every psychotherapist advise the spouse of his client to permit that client to have his or her space? If the sessions aren't inviolate, they can't be effective."

He laughed.

"Always the doctor's daughter," he declared.

"I have no choice. It's who I am."

"I know. I just don't want to be misinterpreted."

"You won't be. Thatcher has his confidants and I have mine. I consider you more than my teacher now. I consider you a good friend," I said.

He nodded.

"Thank you. It is an honor I accept. Is your mother aware of any of these goings-on?" he asked.

"No, not unless she has overheard some servant gossiping about us. Despite our moving into a much more comfortable home and her having some help, she seems more tired. Her brows are furrowed more often, her shoulders slumped. She falls asleep in her chair, and she is not eating as well as I would like to see.

"But I haven't given her all the time and attention I would like. I haven't spent half as much time as I know I should with Linden, either. Thatcher has kept me pretty busy with his social schedule. The lines between what is social and what is a business affair are so blurred in his world, I don't know what's important and what isn't anymore. I'm afraid to say no to anything. I don't want to disappoint him or do anything that would hurt his business efforts."

Professor Fuentes held his smile.

"Aren't you also afraid of lending even a tiny suggestion of credence to the nasty rumors Whitney has engendered?"

I looked down and then up again, nodding.

"I feel like Audrey Hepburn in *The Children's Hour,* questioning every thought, every action and look, wondering if there isn't a seed of truth to the nasty tales, doubting herself.

"When I walk with Linden now, I look everywhere to see if a maid is watching us. If he touches me, I practically jump, and every time I look up at that picture above our bed, I see more licentiousness in it. If anyone else is brought to see it, I blush as if he or she is looking at me nude.

"And then I think, poor Linden, he doesn't deserve all this. *She's* done that to him, to us both! My father used to say the power is in the accusation, not the conviction. If I didn't understand him then, I certainly understand him now."

"Thatcher has said nothing relating to any of this?"

"He's said nothing directly, but sometimes he says things that could have underlying meanings, or I look up and catch him studying Linden and the way Linden is looking at me. Our eyes meet for a moment, and I feel this suspicion. It's only for a fleeting second or two, but nevertheless, it's there. I think. Maybe I've just become paranoid. In either case, Whitney would be satisfied."

"You should discuss it with him, Willow. You should do it as soon as you can and eliminate all that before it takes hold like termites and eats away at the foundation of your marriage," Professor Fuentes said.

"Yes, that's good advice. I know I should. I must. See," I said, smiling, "you are a big help. I don't know it all. I don't know even a quarter of it all."

He laughed.

"The truth is, Willow, none of us do," he said. "Some of us just do a better job of hiding that fact."

We both laughed, and so ended another of our precious tête-à-têtes over coffee. I went to my class. Later that afternoon, when I started for Joya del Mar, I vowed to do what the professor had recommended—have a heart-to-heart talk with Thatcher and tell him all of it.

Up until now, Whitney had not dared call my bluff. She had returned the pictures. I had no way of knowing if she had made copies, of course, but I thought that even she would be embarrassed enough if someone else was permitted to view them. I was still, despite her disappointment, her brother's wife. I didn't hear from or see any members of the Club d'Amour, so I hoped the gossiping had stopped, too. However, as I had told

Professor Fuentes, I was still left with the damage that
had already been done.

Thatcher disappointed me when he called at the end
of the day to say he had been summoned to a very important meeting in Tallahassee. He said it involved the
conglomerate and the men he had met in Nice when we
were on our honeymoon.

"They are working on some state politicians. These
are sort of off-the-record meetings, if you know what I
mean. I'll have to be there the better part of two days.
I'll be back tomorrow night," he told me.

"Oh," I moaned.

"Don't sound so unhappy. It's not even thirty-six
hours," he said.

"I need to talk to you, to have some time with you
without any dinner guests, without any relatives or dis-
tractions, no phones ringing, no interruptions."

"We could fly over to Nassau for the weekend," he
suggested.

"Yes, maybe we should do that."

"Fine. What's it all about? Your brother?"

"No. Not exactly about him. That's only part of it."

"I didn't want to mention it, but maybe I should," he
said.

"What?"

"I think your brother spends hours at a time lurking
outside our door at night."

"Lurking?"

"Last night and once before, I went out after you fell
asleep and he practically leaped for his own door."

"Maybe it was just a coincidence," I said.

"Maybe. Maybe not. He skulks about more than ever,
it seems to me. I know you and Grace think he's made
leaps and bounds in improvement, but I'm still very

concerned, Willow. Please think about it. And be careful," he added.

"He's not going to hurt anyone, Thatcher."

"There are many different ways to hurt someone, Willow. Just be more objective and alert, okay? I've got to get going. I'll call you," he said.

"Thatcher—"

I heard the phone click dead and stood there with the receiver in my hand for a while. Had Whitney gotten to him after all and poisoned his mind? Was Professor Fuentes's suggestion coming too late? I chastised myself for having waited this long, and especially for keeping my confrontation with Whitney a secret. That hesitation might have nurtured suspicions and doubts. If anything was truly the lifeblood and strength of a marriage, it was trust. People loved each other in relation to the secrets they kept from each other. The fewer secrets they had, the more their love grew. I had no better illustration of that truth than my father's marriage to my adoptive mother. The secrets they kept from each other could have filled the Atlantic Ocean, and the love they ended up sharing wouldn't have filled a thimble.

That evening, Mother did not come to dinner. Linden told me she said she had a headache and just wanted to take something for it and sleep. I went to check on her and saw she was already asleep.

"She worries about all of us too much," Linden said when I returned and reported that she was sleeping soundly. He sat there eating with as vigorous an appetite as I had ever seen him have. "I know I am the cause of most of that. I work too much and haunt the house, searching every shadow, but that is all coming to an end," he announced.

"Oh? Why?"

"Today, while you were at class, guess where I was."

I shook my head.

"Where?"

"At your school, too." He was beaming. "I did just what I once told you I would do—I enrolled in an art appreciation class. I'm going every Tuesday and Thursday morning at nine beginning next term. If I like the one class, I'll take two, maybe three the following term."

"That's wonderful, Linden. You should join one of the clubs as well. It will help you meet people."

"Yes," he said. "I might just do that."

How encouraging it all sounded.

"Where's Thatcher?" he asked, realizing suddenly that we were having dinner without him.

"He had to attend a very important business meeting in Tallahassee. He'll be back late tomorrow."

"Oh."

He had a strange look on his face for a moment, the look of someone who had drifted off. I ate and watched him, and then he began to eat again, only faster. I commented on it, and he said he had to get back to work.

"I'm doing something that I really like. It's possessed me," he admitted in a heavy whisper, "but sometimes, being possessed isn't bad. Sometimes, it's what makes my work special. You understand, don't you? Thatcher wouldn't, I know. But you do," he said confidently.

"Yes, I understand. Be possessed, but not consumed," I advised, and he laughed.

"Seems to me," he said, "that's advice you should be giving to Thatcher. He's the one who works around the clock these days."

I said nothing. He was right, of course.

"But we shouldn't worry, should we?" he said, smiling again. "We have each other to keep us company when everyone else disappoints us."

He laughed again, and returned to his dinner.

Afterward, I retreated to my suite to do some studying. I ended my evening by checking on Mother, who had woken and had some tea, toast, and jelly brought to her.

"I'm just feeling a bit on the creaky side tonight," she claimed. "Now, don't go making those big eyes at me and talking about doctors and hospitals. You know how much I hate the thought of it."

"If you're not back to your usual self tomorrow—"

"I'll be back. I'll be back," she promised. She asked after Thatcher, and I told her about his meetings in Tallahassee, and then how Linden and I had enjoyed dinner together.

"He's involved in some new art project," I said. I repeated what he had said about attending college.

"Oh, that's wonderful. If only he does it."

"We'll see to it that he does," I assured her.

I returned to my suite and watched some television until my eyelids grew heavy. I even drifted off while the television was on. Finally I turned it off and put out the lights. In our king-size bed with its massive headboard, I felt more alone than ever tonight. In the relatively short time Thatcher and I had been together, I had grown accustomed to feeling him beside me. Hearing his steady breathing at night, or cuddling up to him when it rained, helped me feel secure.

At UNC and here, I had girlfriends who placed such a premium on their independence that they mocked me whenever I spoke about someone, especially a man, giving me that sense of security, whether it was my father, or my boyfriend, Allan, at North Carolina, or my husband.

"Men lord it over you when they realize that. It makes them feel superior and convinces them you should be beholden to them, be grateful they are there. I'll never let a man think that of me," I heard. I heard it in so many different ways and so often that at times I wondered if it wasn't true, if I wasn't too weak, too dependent after all.

And yet, wasn't it wonderful to find someone to whom you could cling and who would soothe and comfort you? Wasn't it good that we had a soft part to ourselves, a part to be loved and cherished, too? Did we always have to be on guard, ready to stand up for our rights? It gets tiring after a while. After a while you have to wonder what has been gained and what has been lost. There had to be a place of compromise, a place you both came to willingly, seeking ways to become important to each other, to become a part of each other, to lose a little of yourself in each other and move from "you and me" to "we."

I embraced Thatcher's pillow and inhaled the aroma of his cologne. I felt him beside me, and I closed my eyes and without fear let myself drift into sleep.

Maybe it was because of the conflict with Whitney, my worrying about Mother, and my conversations with Professor Fuentes, but my pleasant sailing into sleep on a soft bed of flowers was interrupted by a strangely vivid nightmare. In it, the door to my bedroom suite opened, and silhouetted in the hallway light was a male form. He came closer and closer to the bed. I felt myself cringing, pulling myself in so tightly I was in some pain, but I dared not cry out. I had to pretend to be asleep.

The figure stood there for the longest time, remaining still in the shadows. Then he stepped toward the bed, and I saw it was Linden and he was naked. He reached out to touch my hair. I didn't move a muscle. After a long moment, I sensed his turning and watched him drift away, float toward the door, closing it softly behind him. Still, I did not move. Finally, my body relaxed and I was able to drift back into dreamless sleep.

When I awoke in the morning, the nightmare was still quite vivid, so much so that I began to wonder if it had indeed occurred. I didn't dare ask Linden, and I couldn't mention it to Mother, of course. I just tucked it away in one of the darker places in my mind and hoped it would disappear, like a ghost that had grown tired of haunting the same house.

This is all getting to me, I thought. *I do need a holiday, no matter how short and sweet.* The moment Thatcher returned, I reminded him of his promise, and he made the arrangements immediately.

"We'll have a bit of a second honeymoon," he promised.

"Good," I said. "Ours was too short anyway."

He laughed and hugged me.

"Willow, our marriage itself will always be like a honeymoon," he said.

I was so happy and excited about us going, but in the back of my mind I decided that my going or not would depend on Mother's health. Fortunately, she did improve over the next two days. Maybe she was putting on an act so I wouldn't hesitate to go, but if so, she was doing a good job of it. She ate better, went for her walks again, and even did a little shopping with me so I could get some things I needed for my weekend in the Bahamas.

And what a weekend it was!

Not once did Thatcher mention any of his work, any meetings, any clients. He didn't even bring his *cell phone* along!

"For the next forty-eight hours," he said, "I don't want to know about anything but you."

The moment we landed in Nassau, we were both giddy. As soon as we arrived at our hotel, we went out to the pool, swam, and drank something called a Miami Ice #1 that Thatcher claimed was wonderful. It tasted wonderful, but I had no idea how potent it was. Later I found out it had vodka, peach schnapps, gin, and rum in it, as well as the sour mix and orange juice. We both had three, and I got into a laughing jag that I couldn't stop.

We had a room off the pool but toward the rear of the property, so it was isolated well behind trees and bushes. Thatcher decided that I'd had enough, especially when we realized we had been in the sun too long and were both quite red-faced. I didn't feel a thing and never realized I was getting a burn. He literally picked me up, tossed me over his shoulder, and carried me to our room. Once there, we began to make love almost immediately. My head was spinning from the drinks and now, making love as hard and as fast as we were, I felt I would pass out. I might have, for all I knew.

Exhausted, we both fell asleep and didn't wake up until nearly 8 P.M. I was still groggy, but Thatcher had revived and, before I knew it, he was kissing and fondling my breasts, running his lips over the small of my stomach, and teasing me until we were at it again. Our lovemaking wasn't as soft and sensitive as it had been on our honeymoon and thereafter. It was more lusty and demanding.

"You act like you just got out of solitary confinement or something," I told him. "If we weren't married, it would be more like a rape."

He laughed, then urged me to get up, shower, and dress.

"I'm starving. That's what drinking and making love does to me," he said.

He seemed so different. I wasn't sure I completely liked him like this, but I did appreciate all the attention he was lavishing on me and I did like that he wasn't thinking of anything else. We had a wonderful dinner, overlooking the water. This time I stayed with white wine. Thatcher had a vodka martini and then some wine.

Afterward, we walked along the beach, holding hands. The sky was practically cloudless, the small clouds off on the horizon looking like they were in fast retreat. With the night blazing, my skin feeling so warm, and Thatcher holding me tightly, I felt a sense of contentment and peace.

I slept better that night than I had in a long time. He was up ahead of me, dressed in shorts, and went out for a run on the beach. I found a note on his pillow telling me so. Where did he get his stamina? I wondered, struggling to sit up and think about dressing for breakfast.

My skin was very sensitive and itchy where I had gotten too much sun. *Better spend most of this day in the shade,* I told myself.

I rose, showered, and dressed, finishing just before he returned, hot and sweaty but exhilarated.

"It was wonderful out there. I haven't run on a beach in the morning for so long, I had forgotten how beautiful it could be. You're getting up with me tomorrow, if I have to get you up and dress you myself."

"Then don't wear me out tonight," I warned.

"Moi? Little me?"

He pressed his chest out with male pride, then hurried to shower and join me on the patio for breakfast. I had my juice and coffee by the time he came to the table. We both ordered, and then I sat up, folded my hands between my breasts, and began to tell him of my incident with Whitney.

The small smile on his lips faded slowly and turned into a nasty smirk as I described my confrontation with her, the things she had been saying, and, finally, the acquisition of Linden's pictures of me.

"What were these pictures?" he asked, his eyes drifting to the food that had been brought to us and then up at me. The way he asked, I had the creepy feeling he already knew most of it.

"Linden has been influenced by some artist who believes in consuming yourself with your subject," I explained. "He warned me that he was going to take candid photographs because he wanted to capture the, quote, real me."

"How candid?"

"Candid. He took some pictures he shouldn't have taken. There is no doubt about that, and I chastised him for it, but your sister had no right to pay someone to spy on us and steal those pictures."

"And what have you done with them now?"

"I tore them up and threw them into the garbage. But for her to go about spreading these vile rumors—"

"In this town, people treat the old adage 'Where there is smoke, there is fire' as if it were one of the Ten Commandments, Willow. You have to put an end to this before it goes any further."

"An end to what? There's nothing to put an end to, Thatcher. My brother was following a technique and he went overboard, that's all."

"You know it's more than that. He dotes on you. It's not healthy. I tried to get him interested in other women, but he resists. Look," he said, putting down his fork and reaching across the table to take my hand, "what

Whitney did was inexcusable. I'll speak to her about it myself, but that's not the real problem. Whether it is Whitney or some other snoopy, gossipy person, someone is going to try to make something sensational out of your brother's relationship with you."

"But—"

"He's disturbed. I've been telling you in little ways. I see what's going on in the house. That's why I told you about his slinking about outside our bedroom door. I don't doubt he eavesdrops on our lovemaking, and that picture he did of you . . . we have to take it down. It's just too . . . too revealing. You know I'm right," he added quickly.

"He's not going to understand. He'll be very hurt, Thatcher. It might make matters worse."

"Nevertheless, we've got to do something."

"Let me think about it more," I said.

He shrugged.

"Fine, only I'll make this prediction. I'm afraid Linden will have to have more serious treatment, and sooner than you think," he said.

In my heart of hearts, I knew he was right. I looked away, tears building under my lids.

"Hey, hey," he said, reaching across the table to take my chin and turn my face to him. "Let's put it all aside for now. This is our extended honeymoon, remember? I've rented a Sailfish for us. We're going out for a while."

"But I'm so burned already!" I protested.

"Cover yourself up and put on lots of sunblock. We're going to have fun," he insisted. "And forget everything but ourselves."

In the end I did what he wanted, of course, and we did have a good time. We made love again in the afternoon, slept, and dressed for dinner. It was a wonderful and romantic time, a true escape. It wasn't until we went to sleep the second night, in fact, that I realized I had been so carefree and frivolous that I had not taken my birth-control pills. It frightened me for a moment, but I forced it out of my mind. This was supposed to be a worry-free interlude, a time of magic.

Surely, I convinced myself, nothing bad could happen because of one moment we had spent in our little paradise.

As if we were being punished for being too happy, there was sad news awaiting us the moment we stepped through the front doors of Joya del Mar. Jennings greeted us and, despite his professional demeanor and an aloofness that made him seem mechanical at times, his face betrayed his secret thoughts. I had often caught him looking with amazement at some of the things he saw and heard here, especially whenever Bunny Eaton was present. I also guessed from the way he looked at Mother that he liked her very much, perhaps even romantically, although it was difficult to imagine him that way with any woman.

I had expected to see Mother almost immediately and knew from the vacant air within, the stillness, and the shadows that were draped over the wall like curtains of despair that something wasn't right.

"What's wrong, Jennings?" I asked even before he could say hello.

Thatcher was surprised at my concern and lifted his eyebrows.

"I'm afraid your mother has taken ill, Mrs. Eaton," he began. "It happened yesterday, but she insisted no one call and bother you. The doctor has been here. He wanted her to be admitted to the hospital, but she absolutely refused."

"What happened to her?" Thatcher asked.

"She became very dizzy after dinner, so much so that if Linden had not been standing nearby, she might have fallen. She complained about a pain in her head and weakness in her arms and legs. Linden carried her to her room and we called Dr. Hackford, your mother's physician," Jennings told Thatcher. "He came right away. When she wouldn't go to the hospital, he gave her something to help her relax, but he stated clearly that he couldn't be responsible for her if her condition deteriorated."

"What condition?" I demanded.

"Whatever is causing her dizziness, I imagine," Jennings said.

"I'll go right up to her," I told Thatcher. "Where is my brother, Jennings?"

"He's with her. He hasn't left her side. Last night, he slept in a chair by her bed," Jennings informed me.

"Thank you."

I hurried up the stairs to Mother's room. She had her eyes closed, but she wasn't asleep. Linden was slouched in the chair, his eyes closed as well. I entered slowly, softly.

"Mother," I whispered, and touched her arm when I was at her side. Linden's eyes remained closed.

She opened hers and smiled.

"Now, don't go bawling me out, Willow. I'm feeling much better. Rest was all I needed. In fact, I'm hungry," she said. She looked over at Linden. "Poor Linden has been so worried. He hasn't eaten or slept since I felt ill. Get him to eat and go to his own room, Willow," she urged. "I don't want him having any relapses because of me.

"Did you have a good time?" she added quickly.

"Never mind that, Mother," I said. I knew she wanted

to change the subject as soon as possible. "What happened to you exactly, and what did the doctor advise?"

She smiled.

"Why is it I think you already know the answers to those questions, Willow?"

"Well, how could you *not* go into the hospital if the doctor thinks it's prudent?" I countered.

"I know my own body. I'm fine," she insisted.

Linden's eyes fluttered and then opened. The moment he realized I was standing there, he sat up.

"Willow, when did you get back?"

"Just now. I might have expected Mother would keep it all a secret from me, but not you, Linden. Why didn't you call me at my hotel? I left a detailed description of where we were."

"I was going to call you, but she absolutely forbade it," he said, glaring at Mother. "She threatened to get even sicker if I did."

"Mother."

"Oh, he's exaggerating. What's the difference? No harm has been done and I'm fine. Now, get on with you," she said. "Both of you. Out of here. I'm getting up and dressed and going down to get something to eat, and then I want a detailed account of your holiday. Linden, go wash up and get something in your stomach immediately," she snapped, and he rose.

I shook my head and smiled.

"All right, Mother. You win, for now," I said, nodded at Linden, and left with him. "How bad was she?" I asked as soon as we were sufficiently away from her door.

"She was too weak to stand. And pale, as pale and gray as a wet tissue. If I hadn't insisted, she wouldn't even have permitted the doctor to come here," he said.

"You did well, Linden. We'll have to watch her closely and see that there is no recurrence."

"Right," he said, smiling. "I'm glad you're home. I missed you. And soon I'll have a new work completed for you to see."

Without any warning, he pressed forward to kiss me on the lips, a quick peck, and then he turned and hurried off, truly demonstrating what was meant by "a stolen kiss."

By the time I returned to our suite, Thatcher was already on the phone with business associates. I had unpacked and nearly finished changing my clothes before he was free to ask how Mother was. I told him, and he shrugged and said, "If she feels that good, let her be."

Maybe he was right, I thought. Maybe half the time we make people sicker by doting on their illnesses. In truth, as the days and weeks went by, Mother never showed any signs of being sick. If she had any recurrences during that time, she kept them to herself well. She moved slowly, I thought, and was still not as energetic and as bright as she had been when I first arrived at Joya del Mar, but she was at every meal, listening to our conversations, taking her walks, and sitting out on the loggia reading or just staring out at the sea and looking content.

It was nearly the end of the trimester for me, so I was very busy preparing papers and prepping for upcoming exams again. Professor Fuentes and I continued to have our occasional tête-à-têtes, and Linden returned to his studio, working feverishly on his newest project. All he would tell me was we needed a very large work of art for the wall facing the entrance to the house. The Eatons had taken the tapestry they had bought in Europe, leaving a nearly twenty-by-twenty-foot empty space.

We all settled into a comfortable and pleasant existence, but what I didn't realize was it was more like the calm before a storm.

Six weeks after Thatcher and I returned from our brief but passionate holiday in the Bahamas, I realized I had missed my period. I had been so occupied with my work, worrying about Mother, and the social events Thatcher insisted I attend that I hadn't thought about it. It hit me like a gust of cold wind while I was walking to my car in the student parking lot late one afternoon. I stopped, mentally reviewed the dates, then felt myself go numb, the blood rushing out of my face and down my neck.

With a thumping heart, I stopped at a drugstore on the way home and bought a pregnancy test. When I arrived at home, I hurried up to our suite and closed the door. I went into the bathroom, followed the easy directions, and, with my heart pounding stared at the stick indicator. In just about three minutes, it told me what I had sensed and feared was true. I was pregnant.

For a while I simply sat on the toilet looking at the floor. I had always taken the proper precautions, except for the weekend we had gone to the Bahamas, when I had been so carefree and foolish I had neglected to do so. Now, as if fate had been waiting eagerly at the door to get its grimy paws on me, I was faced with a new crisis, just when I didn't need anything else to add to the burden.

Pregnant!

How could I have let this happen now? I was just getting started on my education. I had Mother and Linden to care for and protect. Thatcher and I had barely started our marriage. I felt like whipping myself.

I spun around and looked at myself in the mirror.

"You," I spit at my image. "You consider yourself a modern woman, an educated woman. You want to be responsible for the welfare and mental and emotional

health of other people, and you, you do this foolish
thing. How could you blunder like this?

"It serves you right. What right do you have even
thinking of becoming a psychotherapist?"

I buried my head in my hands and started to cry.
Then I imagined a knock on the door.

It was Daddy, listening as he had from time to time
when I cried as a child.

What's wrong, Willow?

Nothing, Daddy, I replied—as always, I wanted my
problems coaxed out of me; I didn't want to feel guilty
about telling them so quickly and willingly.

Tell me about nothing, then, he said, and waited pa-
tiently.

I lost control of myself. I'm pregnant. It is not something a responsible person would do, especially someone with my obligations.

*What I have learned is that, although hindsight is the
best sight, it does us no good, even does us harm if it encourages us to wallow in the past and self-pity. What are
the questions I have taught you to ask yourself, Willow?*

What is the problem? What are the solutions? What
are the pluses and minuses for each, and which one will
best serve me and the people who will be affected?

Is there anything else to think about now but that?

No.

*Then why are you wasting your time moaning and
groaning and crying?*

I took a deep breath and flicked the tears from my
cheeks.

The decision that had to be made wasn't only mine to
make, I thought, although I did have the most to say
about it. I wanted to tell Mother, but I thought it was
only right to tell Thatcher first and see his reaction.

He called and started to make an apology for not being able to come home to dinner, when I interrupted him and said, "You have to come home right now. You don't have to stay for dinner, but I must see you immediately."

"What is it this time?" he asked, his voice full of groans.

"It has nothing to do with my brother or my mother. It has to do only with us."

"Oh?"

"Come home now, Thatcher."

He was silent a moment.

"Okay," he said. "I'll swing by on my way to the meeting."

After he hung up, I washed my face, straightened my clothing, fixed my hair, and prepared to have him join me down by the pool. Linden was still in his studio and Mother was in her room resting. I instructed Jennings to tell Thatcher where I would be waiting for him.

Only a half hour later, he came charging down the walkway toward the pool patio. I was sitting under an umbrella looking out at the water.

"What?" he demanded as soon as he was before me. "I hope you haven't demanded my presence on the basis of some Palm Beach rumor."

Funny how it never had occurred to me he would think such a thing, I thought, and for a moment, I was thrown off balance.

"No. This isn't any rumor."

"Well, what is it, then, Willow? This sort of dramatics is more characteristic of my side of the family. You're not taking lessons from Bunny, are you?" he said, softening his face into a smile, but still a smile that masked much irritation.

"I don't mean to be dramatic, Thatcher, only concerned and responsible," I said.

He nodded.

"Okay, you have my full attention." He folded his arms across his chest.

"Just a little while ago, I discovered I was pregnant," I said as dryly as I could.

His eyes widened, and then he reached back for a chair and sat.

"Pregnant? But I thought you were taking precautions and—"

"Except for our wild behavior in the Bahamas," I said.

His mouth opened and closed, and then he nodded.

"Oh. Right." He smiled. "Well, we were a bit wild then, weren't we?"

"A bit—a bit too much, I would say now."

He shrugged, then smiled.

"So, what's the problem? We'll have a baby."

"We'll have a baby? I think it's more like *I'll* have the baby, Thatcher, unless there is some new procedure that involves the father, a procedure I have yet to learn about."

"You know what I mean. We'll have a child. I don't see any major problem."

"You don't? I'm going to school. I am in the middle of developing a career."

"So, you'll put it off for a while. Lots of women do that. And it won't have to be all that long either, Willow. We'll find a good nanny, that's all. Maybe you can even bring Amou back from Brazil," he added, beaming at me.

"I couldn't ask her to do that. She's not a young woman anymore, and she's happy where she is."

"I'm sure there are many, many good and responsible women we could employ."

I shook my head and looked away.

"It's not like we're some poor family dependent on your income to survive, Willow. What good is having money if you don't use it to fix problems?"

I spun on him.

"It's not that. I just didn't envision thinking of my pregnancy and my child as problems to be fixed."

"It's just a manner of speaking," he said quickly. "I don't actually mean a baby is a problem for us. The fact is, he or she won't be." He nodded. "Matter of fact, my parents will be overjoyed, and so will Grace. Have you told her?"

"Not yet. I thought you should know first, Thatcher."

"Of course. I appreciate that," he said, stared at me for a long moment, then smiled, slapped his hands together, and stood up. "Well, for a long time I had trouble believing I was ever going to be someone's husband, and now I have to convince myself I'm ready to be someone's father." He leaned over, grasping the arms of my chaise, and kissed me. "I knew there was a good reason why I married you. You're going to make me a respectable man yet, Willow."

He started away.

"Is that it?" I called. There were so many more things to discuss, but he either didn't hear me or decided to ignore my question.

"Don't wait up for me," he called back instead. "I have to see two different clients in two different places, and I might be back quite late."

I watched him hurry up the steps and into the house.

Was he right? I wondered. Was it all as simple as he made it out to be?

Was that what living here, being part of all this, really

meant? No problem was too big to solve if you just threw enough money at it.

I never used to believe that, I thought, but living here could change you.

Even before you realized it had happened. It was like you never really had a chance to choose.

And even if I had the chance, I had to wonder if I would have chosen differently anyway.

A cloud moved over the sun and cast a long shadow that moved like thick, liquid darkness over the house and grounds. For a moment, even in this warm place, I felt a chill.

It was just a small touch, like the tip of a finger feathering over the back of my neck, sending shivers down my spine.

Why it should be there, I had yet to know or understand.

But there was no doubt that it was there.

16

Something Unplanned

I wish I had kept a scrapbook of pictures showing the variety of reactions the announcement of my pregnancy brought from the people around me: Mother's was the sincerest and the happiest, I thought. Her face filled with a flush of joy that made her look younger, and a brightness came into her eyes that I had not seen for some time. In fact, it was a brightness she evinced only when she spoke about my father and their time together. Surely, then, she placed my pregnancy and her becoming a grandmother in the same circle of happiness she had reserved for so few wonderful moments in her life. I felt I was truly giving her something she cherished and wanted.

"It was obviously not something we planned, Mother," I told her.

"What I have learned, Willow, is that most of the good things that happen to you in this life are not planned. A baby will bring sunshine into this home," she said. "Sunshine so bright that even the darkest cloud won't be able to stop it from lighting our hearts."

She talked about how she would help out. She wanted to be solely responsible, but I insisted as had Thatcher that we hire a nanny.

Linden's reaction was curious. He didn't appear to be surprised or in any way upset about it. In fact, before Thatcher considered it and even before Mother thought of it, Linden asked almost immediately what I would call the child if it was a girl and what if it was a boy. Of course, I hadn't thought about it yet and told him so. He nodded and said he had some names to suggest, and he would write them all on a piece of paper and give them to me. Then he made an even more astounding suggestion.

"I should move out of the bedroom I am in and you should turn it into a nursery. It's closest to your suite, and after all, it was Grace's room. Yes," he decided firmly, "I'll move back to my original bedroom. I'll do it next week."

"You don't have to do that so quickly, Linden. I have at least seven months," I told him.

"Nevertheless," he insisted, "there is planning to do, things to get. Are you going to find out the baby's sex as soon as you can?"

"Probably," I said. "I'll be having an ultrasound, and sometimes they can tell after only twelve weeks or so."

"That's a good idea. Then you will know what colors to use and all that," Linden said.

I couldn't help but be amused by his devoted interest in my pregnancy and the baby. After a while, it seemed to take over a large part of his attention and time. He went into Thatcher's home office and got on the Internet to download information on prenatal care and even infant care, printing out reams of opinions from various child-care experts. I'd find a different set of documents at my place at the breakfast table morning after morning.

Thatcher thought it was all very funny and began calling Linden "Our Nanny."

"What did Our Nanny give you today?" he would inquire when he came home from work. I begged him not to say that in front of Linden.

"Whatever he does, Thatcher, it has helped keep him from returning to his darker places. Mother's happy about it, too, and some of the information he has found is actually very helpful. I am not exactly an expert on childbirth and infant care yet. It wasn't something I expected to face so soon."

"Right, right." He was quiet for a moment, then broke into another fit of laughter at some amusing thought.

"Thatcher," I warned, my eyes wide and furious.

"I'm sorry, I'm sorry, but I just thought of a new career goal for him. Why don't we encourage him to go to nursing school and specialize in maternity nursing? If any woman is having difficulty giving birth, he could show her one of his gloomy, weird pictures and scare her into birthing instantly."

"Stop it," I said slapping his arm.

"Okay, okay," he said, but then chuckled again and ran off.

Sometimes at dinner, when Linden mentioned something relating to child care, Thatcher would smother a laugh or choke down a smile, but only because I sent fire with my eyes across the table at him. At night, when he put his arms around me and joked about Linden's new interest in motherhood, I couldn't help but smother my own giggle and then felt so guilty about it.

"Better whisper," Thatcher warned. "He might have his ear to our wall. This house isn't built as solidly as you might think. I remember catching Whitney listening to my parents through the walls once. She denied it, of course, but then I did it on occasion, too. It was always disappointing."

Thatcher's parents had a typical Palm Beach socialite reaction to the announcement of my pregnancy, I thought. Bunny immediately skipped ahead to plans for a party. She decided that my due date occurring at the heart of the next Palm Beach Season was actually good planning and congratulated Thatcher for it. He accepted her accolades and pretended that we had indeed thought it all out and decided to have a child when it would be most advantageous to social activities. It amazed me how easily he could lie to his parents.

Bunny then went on to give her advice about nursing care and a nanny. She offered to help us choose a name, too, making it seem like that was more important than the child's health.

"I hope you don't go and choose some soap opera star's name, or choose a month. That's so passé, April, May, June . . . all that nonsense. Thatcher's son should have a very distinguished-sounding name. Or his daughter, of course."

"Like Bunny?" I couldn't resist asking.

"What? Oh, that's just a nickname. When you reach my age here, you find that's just a way of showing affection for you. And," she confessed in a whisper, "it makes you feel younger. But a newborn doesn't need to feel younger, does she? I'll work up a list and send it over."

Everyone wanted to offer names. I was beginning to think we should run a contest.

Professor Fuentes had a very mixed reaction. He was happy for me in one sense, but he also seemed disappointed, until I assured him I wasn't going to give up my pursuit of a career.

"I'll just take a maternity leave from it," I told him. "Thatcher and I have already discussed that."

"Good, but don't underestimate the attention and time a child will demand," he warned. "Considering what you have told me about your own early life and adolescence, you know that better than I do."

"I won't," I promised.

"Just be realistic with it all, Willow. Don't overestimate your energy, and be patient with yourself," he advised.

"Thanks," I told him. Then I described the madness orbiting our lives now in relation to finding suitable names.

"If it's a boy, why don't you name him after your father?" he suggested simply.

"And if it's a girl?"

He hesitated for a moment. I could see he had a real suggestion, but he was asking himself, "Do I dare?"

"Go ahead, Professor. Everyone else is putting in his or her two cents, why shouldn't you? Tell me."

"It came to me right after you informed me of your pregnancy," he admitted. "Hannah."

"Hannah?" I smiled.

"I imagine you would like to link her to your mother. Hannah means 'grace' in Hebrew," he said. "I read that the other day."

"I like that. Thank you."

"One more bit of advice," he added quickly.

"Oh?"

"Don't tell Thatcher the idea came from me. Another man, ego, that sort of thing," he said, waving his hand.

"I understand."

"Of course you do," he said, smiling.

It made me blush to think what kindred spirits we had become. Was it all due to our shared love of psychology and our fascination with the human mind and behavior?

Like Pandora, I felt warned not to open this box of mystery, to leave it be. Some things were best left unsaid, untouched, like beautiful but poisonous flowers.

At school, some of my girlfriends treated my announcement as they would a revelation of cancer. Their faces immediately flooded with pity, even disgust. The Butterworth twins couldn't have been more antithetically opposite. Loni thought it was just wonderful and rattled on and on about how she looked forward to a husband and a family. Pet curled down the corners of her lips and talked about the burden of motherhood and how men don't appreciate their wives and the sacrifices they have to make for a child.

"And pregnancy itself! I think I'd rather invest in a surrogate mother to carry my egg," she declared.

"What if she runs off with it?" Loni asked her, wide-eyed.

"Good riddance to them both, then," Pet said.

"How can you blame a fetus?" Loni pursued.

"I don't want to talk about it," she replied. She looked frightened of the whole idea. I assured her I was having a good pregnancy and hadn't even had most of the discomforts women usually exhibit. I didn't want to mention that Linden thought that was a good indication that my baby would be healthy and the birth easier than a first birth often was. They might start calling him Our Nanny too, I feared.

Whitney's reaction to my pregnancy came to me secondhand. I received a phone call from Manon Florette.

She had been inviting me to lunch after lunch with the others, but I had made excuse after excuse.

"We just heard about your pregnancy," she told me. "Your sister-in-law told Liana's mother in the beauty salon yesterday."

"Oh? I haven't heard from Whitney yet."

"No mystery about that."

"Why not?" I asked, my temples starting to ache in anticipation.

"She wonders if it's her brother's child."

"What?"

"I'm just passing on what Liana was told. Whitney wonders, because she says Thatcher would never have a child so early in a marriage. She claims he's too smart for that."

"Oh, now he's too smart for that, but according to her, he wasn't too smart with his choice of women," I muttered, then immediately regretted it. Like some sort of self-creating beast, one bitter remark fed on another until it spun out of control.

"Exactly," Manon said. "We thought you should know."

"Thank you, Manon."

"You should come to our next luncheon in two weeks, Willow. We are not your enemies. We're your allies here."

I was silent.

"I'll call you and remind you," she told me. "Oh, and by the way, congratulations."

"Thank you," I said.

The conversation left me feeling a bit depressed, but I scrubbed it out of my mind like some ugly stain and hoped it wouldn't reappear. Of course, the moment I saw Whitney at an event shortly afterward, it all flashed before me in a red sash of fury. Her first remark, which was almost a compliment, was, "You don't look very pregnant."

"Some women don't really show until their seventh or even eighth month. I take it you were not one of those," I said. I wasn't unfriendly, but there was no warmth in my voice. We were standing among nearly a hundred other party guests in a beautiful garden setting.

"No," she said bitterly. "I even hemorrhaged in my third month with Laurel and almost lost her." Her eyes grew small, suspicious. "If you and Thatcher were planning a child so soon, why did you return to college?"

Conversing with someone close by, Thatcher heard her question, and his eyes fixed on me while he waited to see what I would say.

"What difference does that make?" I replied, assuming what I now called my "Palm Beach personality." "We'll hire a nanny and I'll practically not skip a beat. You had a nanny for each of your children until they were twelve, I understand. I don't think I'll need one that long, but if I do, I do." I gave a nonchalant shrug, then smiled at her and added, "After all, Whitney, it's only money. You don't really wonder why it was no concern for us, do you?"

I saw Thatcher's smile widen.

Whitney, who was stone-faced most of the time, actually blanched.

"That's not the point," she stammered.

"What is the point, Whitney?" I asked, looking as if I really wanted to know.

"I didn't think you were the sort who would delegate those responsibilities to someone else."

"What sort is that, Whitney?" I pursued, stepping closer to her.

"Never mind."

"No, I'm curious. What sort is that, Whitney? More responsible, caring, loving, what?" I asked, my face in her face.

She was flustered now and in retreat, her eyes shifting from side to side, looking for some avenue of escape, someone else to engage in conversation, but no one was close enough.

"You don't mean *neurotic,* do you?" I pursued.

Finally, she hoisted those shoulders of hers, giving her the look of another two inches of height, and looking down at me said, "If you must know, I didn't think you had the social background to tolerate so many servants in your life. It takes some getting used to when you're not born to it."

"Oh, don't worry about that," I said with a hollow laugh that was loud enough to draw attention. "When it comes to being spoiled, I'm just as much a socialite as you are."

Thatcher was unable to contain his laugh now. Whitney glared at him, looked arrows at me, and then walked away.

"You're getting the hang of this thing," Thatcher whispered.

"Maybe," I said, "but I don't enjoy it half as much as you think. Isn't it time to go?"

Despite the front I put up and how easy the first weeks had been, I did experience some discomfort over the next two months. I didn't have any bouts of nausea and vomiting, but I did find my energy sapped more often and took more naps than I usually did.

As soon as I'd told him I was pregnant, Thatcher had taken me to an obstetrician he considered one of the best in the area, a client of his, Dr. Herman Marko, a man in his late forties. Dr. Marko was very good at explaining everything, but he had a contrived pleasantness about him that gave me the impression he was kind and friendly only to the point of necessity. I told Thatcher I thought he was a man who counted his smiles and spent them as efficiently as an IRS examiner.

Thatcher retorted with his standard response to comments I made about the friends and associates to whom he introduced me: "You're analyzing too much. Just relax. Stop being the psychiatrist's daughter."

I was sensitive enough about it to consider that he might be right, so I put aside my negative feelings. After my sixteenth week, I had an ultrasound that Dr. Marko declared proved without a doubt I was going to have a girl. That was when I suggested the name Hannah to Thatcher. He didn't seem very excited about it and simply replied, "We have time to decide."

Whenever I returned home after a doctor's visit, Linden was there to greet me and question me about it. He was, as was Mother, very excited to hear that we were having a girl. In the beginning, I thought Linden's interest in my pregnancy was sweet and loving, and both Mother and I were amused and delighted with his questions, the way he doted on me, and offered suggestions; but gradually, something about the intensity of his questions and the way he reacted to some things I told him—pressing his lips together hard, turning his eyebrows in under the folds of his forehead, stiffening his body—began to concern me.

He was, it became evident, second-guessing the doctor. He began to challenge his opinions, offering me contrary documentation about the recommended vitamins, exercises, and diet, and about the doctor's reactions to my symptoms and complaints.

"You're better off staying away from doctors," he muttered one day. "Get a good midwife."

Of course, I thought he wasn't really serious, but the comments and complaints he made to Mother assured us both he was. Eventually, we had to sit him down and talk to him to try to relieve his anxieties.

"It's going fine, Linden," I said. "I'm doing very well. Nothing I am experiencing is out of the ordinary."

"Some of the things they do can affect the child," he insisted. "Later on, I mean. They treat you like just another statistic, another scientific fact, and nothing more. There's nothing personal about modern medicine. They think we are all here to support the bottom line. *Doctors,*" he spit.

After he left us, Mother turned to me and said she was beginning to understand.

"What do you mean?"

"Linden blames some of his difficulties on the way I gave birth to him. As you know, my pregnancy was something Jackie Lee and I hid from the Palm Beach world. It was her idea that we would try to get people to believe she was Linden's mother, and that way, I wouldn't suffer any disgrace. I think in retrospect it was her way of protecting her own reputation as well, for she didn't want to be known as the woman who had failed to see Kirby Scott's lecherousness and protect her only daughter. People would wonder where she was while all this was going on.

"Jackie Lee found a doctor who would be discreet, and as you know, I gave birth to Linden in the house. I'm sure in his mind he considers all that—the subterfuge, the cover-up, the subsequent lies and deceptions, my condition, all of it—responsible for his difficulties.

"Despite his anger and his refusal to be social, he does understand that he is not mentally healthy."

She dabbed away the tears.

"He has told me many times he knows what he is like and what's wrong with him, but he accepts it, just like any disabled person."

"Yes," I said. "I understand. We shouldn't cause him to feel bad about caring. I'll speak to him later."

She smiled.

"He's so lucky to have a sister like you."

"And I'm lucky to have a mother like you," I replied.

We smiled and hugged each other. Despite the majesty of our estate, the beauty of our property, and the protection it gave us from the problems most people had to face outside our walls, we still felt vulnerable.

We walked on marble floors. We had servants to help us. We had an army of professionals out there to call upon when we needed them, but we couldn't help looking over our shoulders from time to time or pausing to listen for the footsteps of malevolent fate lurking behind the curtain of some shadow, waiting eagerly for an opportunity to lunge at us and steal away the happiness and hope we had so recently enjoyed.

There was no doubt "It" was out there. Like that dark ship Linden often saw slinking over the water in the darkness, It came from the horizon, rising and falling with the waves, relentless, Its prow directed at Joya del Mar, Its ghostly sailors poised, eager.

The buoys sounded in the night.

Warning.

All we could do was wait and hope It would somehow turn and pass by us.

It didn't.

* * *

354 Virginia Andrews

I wasn't deliberately looking for excuses not to join Manon and the women of the Club d'Amour for lunch when they called a few weeks later, but I had a conflict at school that I couldn't avoid. Manon sounded very annoyed.

"I appreciate that you're attending college, Willow," she said, "but we're attending the real world. You should not neglect it."

I had no idea what she was referring to, but I didn't get angry. I apologized and promised to make a real effort to see them all soon. She hung up in a huff, and I did not expect to hear from her or any of them again, but the following Tuesday, Jennings had a message for me when I returned from class. It simply read, *Manon Florette. Call immediately,* and her number.

Figuring it was just another of their dramatic social crises, I did not rush to a phone. I changed, spent some time with Mother, and then returned to my suite and girded myself for what I imagined was going to be some silly conversation. She answered on the first ring.

"I've been waiting for your call. Your butler told me when you were expected," she snapped.

"I'm sorry. Some unexpected things came up," I said.

"You have no idea how unexpected," she retorted.

"What is it, Manon?"

"The others have all set aside whatever they were doing to meet with you. Be at the Rosebud in fifteen minutes. You know where it is and you know it's close by."

"What is this about?"

"Just be there," she said, and hung up before I could offer some excuse. I was annoyed, but I couldn't help

being somewhat curious. This was over-the-top, even
for the members of the so-called Club d'Amour.

The Rosebud was a small coffeehouse, but it had a
very pretty garden patio from which you could see the
ocean, if you had the right table. I had no doubt Manon
would have the right table, but we weren't meeting there
to enjoy the scenery. I could see them sitting on the
patio when I arrived. I was surprised that they were all
there before me. It made me think they had all been at
Manon's home when I called, all waiting with her. That
realization turned my heart into a tiny drum, the beats
increasing with every step I took toward the entrance of
the restaurant. I went in and through the small lobby to
the side door to the patio. They all looked my way, all
with the same intense expression. It took my breath
away.

"What's going on?" I managed, and sat.

The waiter pounced.

"Just coffee," Manon snapped at him.

He nodded and fled.

"We have told you what we do, why we formed our
alliance," Manon began, nodding at the others. They
were all focused on me.

"So?"

"We have rather hard news for you. Naturally, because of your present condition, there was some debate as to whether we should reveal anything at this
time, but after a thorough discussion, we all decided
your condition made it even more essential we don't
put it off."

"Put what off, Manon? All this high drama might be
exciting to you all, but—"

"Thatcher is having an affair," she blurted. "Actually,
it would be more accurate to say continuing one."

"Absolutely more accurate," Marjorie piped up.

I glared at her for a moment and then, my heart now pounding, turned back to Manon.

"What are you saying?"

"Years ago, before you arrived on the scene, Thatcher had what everyone thought was a very serious relationship with a woman named Mai Stone."

"I know all about Mai Stone," I said quickly.

"Do you?"

Their smiles annoyed me.

"Yes. I know he was serious about her, but she left him for a very wealthy prince and—"

"She did and she didn't. From time to time, we heard of her secret forays back to Palm Beach, her sexual assaults on young Mr. Eaton," Manon continued.

"They even had a love nest of sorts," Sharon said.

"A beach house that Addison Steele, a rich friend of his, has here," Liana added, and I felt my face turn so red, I thought the blood would pop the top off of my head.

The waiter brought the coffee and set it down. No one spoke, but everyone stared at me. Then Sharon turned to Manon.

"I told you it might not be healthy for her. She looks like she's going to abort right on the spot."

The waiter raised his eyebrows.

"That's all," Manon said, dismissing him. He retreated quickly.

"Are you all right?" Marjorie asked.

I nodded.

"Why do you say this has gone on?" I asked in a small voice.

"We were hoping for your sake that it wasn't going on. We had our suspicions, and it did take some time to verify certain facts. The first is the most obnoxious of all, we have agreed, right, girls?"

Heads bobbed in unison.

"What is the first so-called fact?" I asked.

The air around me seemed to grow hotter and hotter with every passing second, making it more and more difficult to breathe.

"He had the audacity, the disgusting audacity, to see her on your honeymoon. They met in Nice while you were staying in that château in Eze," Manon said.

"How did he get away from you for so long on your honeymoon?" Sharon asked. "We were all wondering about that."

I sat in disbelief, recalling his sudden, very important business meeting.

"How do you know these things are true?" I asked. My throat was so tight, I strained to speak.

"Marjorie's parents have some friends who are close friends of Mai Stone's in-laws. Some of this came out in ordinary conversation, and then Marjorie began to pursue it for us."

"I followed up with my sources, one of whom is his secretary, Terri Wilson."

"Terri?"

"I know," Manon said, smiling. "You thought she would cut off her tongue before talking about Thatcher's private affairs. Well, she doesn't talk about any business affairs, but I think his behavior finally got to her and she couldn't help talking to someone about it."

"We went to college together," Marjorie said. "She's not any sort of busybody, so don't go telling anyone she is," she warned, those eyes of hers turning into tiny hot coals.

"To continue," Manon said after sipping some coffee,

"we have learned that Mai Stone has been making her raids frequently ever since."

I started to shake my head.

"We anticipated your skepticism, of course. None of us, none of the women we've helped, wants to believe that the man she loves and who professes to love her above all other women would betray her, but they do," she said with a glint of cold, steely anger in her eyes.

"Oh, yes, they do," Marjorie seconded.

"Anyway," Manon continued, reaching down to take a folder from her Gucci bag, "we have from time to time employed a private detective. Everything is done discreetly, of course, and he has proven to be an efficient and effective source of information for us.

"Once we learned of Thatcher's little betrayals, we hired a detective at our own expense, from our club dues, so to speak, to gather the information you would need. It's all here," she said, holding out the folder to me, "dates, times, places. There are even some pictures."

I stared at the folder she proffered.

"It's yours," she emphasized. "A gift from us."

"A gift," I said softly. "Some gift."

"We understand how you feel. We've all felt the same way at different times, but we've all been grateful for the support we lend to each other as well, Willow. That's why we invited you to join our group," Manon said. "You might as well take it and look at it," she added, pushing the folder at me.

I still hesitated.

"You will need this for other reasons, Willow. I don't know what you will decide to do about it, but if you intend to get a divorce, you had better have this, knowing that you are moving to divorce an attorney, who, we assume, has created a prenuptial agreement."

The look on my face told her she was right on target. She offered the file again.

I took it gingerly. Between the covers of the folder was the death of love, the revelation of lies and broken promises. It was filled with tiny arrows directed at my heart. My fingers trembled. I was terrified by the thought of opening the file and looking at what it held, yet drawn to do it as well.

"Are you all right?" Sharon asked, putting her hand over mine.

"No," I said. My eyes stung with hot tears.

"One of us should drive her home," she told Manon.

"Of course."

I shook my head.

"Willow, we hope you understand why we did this for you and don't resent us for it," Manon said.

I looked from one to another. Were their motives so altruistic? Did they do it for the cause of womanhood, as they would have me believe? Or did every betrayal, every little treachery they uncovered, reinforce their own cynical beliefs about loving relationships? Did it help them feel better about their own failures? No one was honest and true; therefore, what happened to them was not unexpected or unusual and they certainly needn't blame themselves.

Maybe that was their true motivation, but I still couldn't blame them for it. Who wants to feel unwanted, unneeded, victimized, and, especially, at fault for it? At least they were doing something to give themselves a sense of self-respect and self-worth, I thought.

"No," I said. "I don't resent you for this."

"It's better that you know all this now, Willow. You're fortunate, in a sense."

"Fortunate? How can you say that?"

"This early, your investment in someone isn't as deep and complete as the investment other women have made and lost."

"We're having a child!" I cried.

All of the glue I had called upon to keep my face together crumbled. The tears broke free of the dam my eyelids had tried to put up against them. My lips quivered. My whole body began to shake.

"I understand," Manon said softly. She reached for my hand, but I pulled it back and stood up.

"I have to go home," I said.

"Sharon will drive you."

"No, I don't need anyone to drive me. I have to go home," I muttered and started away, but in the wrong direction, nearly falling over a couple at another table. They looked up with surprise. I shook my head, mumbled an apology, and turned toward the door.

The members of the Club d'Amour all stood.

"Willow!" Liana called. She took a step toward me.

I shook my head and rushed out of the restaurant. When I reached my car, I fumbled with my keys and dropped them. I got down on my knees and found them, then hurried to insert the key in the door. The girls were right behind me.

"Willow, don't rush off like this," Manon pleaded. "Take your time. Let someone go with you."

I got into the car and threw the folder on the passenger seat. After I started the engine, I looked out at them, all of them standing together, gaping at me with so much pity it made me feel even sicker. My tires squealed on the parking lot pavement as I backed out, and then I shot onto the highway, nearly cutting off another vehicle. The driver leaned on his horn and accelerated, passing me by with a face of brutal anger.

Taking a deep breath, I slowed the car and tried to swallow a lump that threatened to choke the air out of me. Finally, I was calm enough to breathe comfortably. I drove on, but when I reached the entrance to Joya del Mar, I did not turn in. I kept driving until I found a place to pull off the road.

After I stopped, I sat there staring out at the water. I could hear him so clearly now. What was it he had said?

"I knew there was a good reason why I married you. You're going to make me a respectable man yet, Willow."

Respectable?

I started to laugh through my tears. Then I stopped, sucked in my breath, and reached for the dreaded folder. With a shaking hand, I opened it and began to read the documentation. The first few pages delineated the dates, times, and places Thatcher had met secretly with Mai Stone, just as Manon had described. After that were copies of some motel slips, the most recent one being the night he was supposedly meeting those all-important clients in Tallahassee. Then there were the pictures, some of the two of them sitting in a restaurant, one of them walking and holding hands, her head on his shoulder, and one, the most devastating, of them kissing near a fountain in front of some hotel.

Without much warning, my stomach revolted. I had just enough time to open the door and vomit outside the car. I thought I might lose the baby right there and then, the ache was that great in my stomach and chest. When it was over, I sat back with my eyes closed. All

I could see were images of Thatcher looking at me lovingly, saying loving things, telling me how much I meant to him. Each vision was like another sting of the whip.

"Daddy!" I cried, but I didn't hear or see him this time.

This time I was all alone.

I was more alone than I had ever felt or been before.

This time I would have to find the answers all by myself.

17

Guilty

Mother had fallen asleep in a chaise on the rear loggia and looked so at peace, her thoughts and dreams full of contentment, I didn't dare wake her. Linden was somewhere in the house, probably in his studio, I thought. He was one person I didn't want to see me like this. One glance at myself in the hall mirror showed me quickly that anyone could tell I had been devastated by something.

I had no idea how Linden would react to this news. I knew he'd really never liked Thatcher. Keeping the peace between them had always been a juggling act for me, and what kept Linden in check most effectively was my showing him that it would displease me terribly if he didn't continue to get along. This was not the time for me to deal with anyone else's crisis. I had enough of my own.

Anger was still at the forefront of my marching emotions. I went directly to our suite and spread the sheets of information and the photographs in the folder over our bed, laying out the evidence in an orderly and chronological fashion like a homicide detective arranging her presentation for the district attorney. He or she would have no doubt as to whether there was enough to present to a grand jury and get an indictment, I thought. Thatcher, of all people, should appreciate that.

I stood back and contemplated it all for a few moments, revulsion churning my stomach, creating the nausea I had so far escaped during my pregnancy. I needed air, fresh air, and quickly, I thought. This room, full of his things, was closing in on me. I put on a light windbreaker and went out a side entrance so as not to pass Mother and disturb her. I walked down the beach almost to the south end of our property, where I sat with my legs drawn up and stared out at the mesmerizing waves. The sea breeze played with strands of my hair. Terns circled in front of me, studied me, then decided I wasn't all that interesting and flew off. In the distance a single sailboat rode the waves. I could almost see the bloated cheeks of the impish wind blowing and toying with the mast. Of course, that made me think of Thatcher and our many wonderful boat rides, our picnics, and making love out there on the ocean.

Who was this man who had dazzled me with his eyes and smile when I first arrived in Palm Beach, who pursued me with such interest and confessed so much love? Who was this man who had taken me on a roller coaster above and beyond the ordinary world, whose laughter was music and whose kiss was a seal of promise time after time after time? Was it really all smoke and mirrors, elaborate deceptions, lies strung along like fake pearls, so well copied that it would take an expert to deny their value, their truth?

Daddy once wrote an article on what he called "the Don Juan syndrome." I should have taken notes and kept them tied around my neck, I thought. In it, he evaluated a patient of his who, he said, pursued one woman after another, wooing and winning her, not because he was addicted to sex so much as he was searching for a way not to feel unloved and unlovable.

I could understand why Thatcher would have grown up feeling unloved in his home. His parents, especially Bunny, were so self-centered they put his needs and wants well down on the totem pole of importance, below their precious social activities. His sister had grown up in the same household to become a hard, cold person, and like some cancer that spreads into other places, she was turning her children into mirror images of herself.

Thatcher had gone in the opposite direction, collecting small love affairs, conquering innocent women, soaking up their devotion and love, then moving on. I was probably just another exercise for him, just another conquest. He had married me because he thought he should be married. Now, after what I had learned, I truly believed that any other woman who had walked onto the stage of his romances at that moment might have been wooed and won exactly as I had been.

As I sat there thinking, I realized I could analyze him, I could even explain him, perhaps, but I could never forgive him. My heart was like Humpty-Dumpty. All the king's horses and all the king's men couldn't put it together again.

"Hi," I heard him say, and turned to see him standing there on the beach. I gazed up at him without speaking. He blew some air through his lips, ran his fingers through his hair, looked out at the ocean, and nodded. "I thought I might find you out here."

"I needed fresh air," I said. "The air in our bedroom suite was rank and sour with deceit and decay."

He nodded.

"I tell you what surprised me the most," he said. "That you obviously hired a private detective."

"I didn't. Someone else did on my behalf."

"Someone else? Who? You don't mean Linden or Grace? Who do you mean?" he questioned, as if I were a witness he had to discredit in a trial. A frightening thought occurred to him. "It wasn't my sister, was it?"

I was silent, letting him turn over the fire of his own torment.

"This has obviously been going on for some time, this spying, Willow."

"That really isn't the point here, is it, Thatcher? How all that came to be on our bed right now is not what matters. What it says, what it reveals, that's what matters."

He looked at me, and then softened his posture.

"You're right," he said.

He paced for a few moments on the sand. I knew him well enough by now to see him gathering his thoughts, organizing his opening remarks to the jury.

"I'm not here to deny it," he said, turning back to me. "I'm guilty of all of it, but what I want to do if you will listen is offer a defense."

I lowered my eyes and smiled at how well I could anticipate his actions. The man I once had looked up to as nearly perfect, so bright and intelligent, suddenly looked so small and cheap to me. I was immune to all of the techniques, the clever reasoning that made you doubt your own instincts and conclusions. Only he had yet to realize that. He thought he could just switch gears, ratchet up his communication skills, and turn his big guns on me.

"Go on, Thatcher," I challenged him. "Offer your defense."

"You probably know better than I do that Freud

claims there are always four people involved in any love affair," he began.

How clever of him to go right to the subject I loved.

"As in his example," he continued, "that would be the first woman I fell in love with, the first man you fell in love with, and us. We see the firsts in us. We can't stop it, help it, prevent it. That's the power of the subconscious.

"I never got over Mai, never recuperated from that love affair I told you I had. I even told myself many times that I had, but I found it very difficult to deny whenever I was confronted with it, with her. I thought maybe if I gave in to it, I would overcome it, get over her by seeing her as just another woman. When you are away from someone, you tend to fantasize and idealize her. Confronting your dreams, bringing them into reality can end all that. I think that's happened finally.

"I told her this last time that I was very much into our marriage, that you were pregnant, and that it had to end. I couldn't be there for her just because she had gotten herself into a bad marriage. I had a good marriage. We parted with that understanding.

"I owe you an apology, of course. I should wake up every morning with an 'I'm sorry' on my lips and beg your forgiveness until the day I die."

He was quiet, so I turned to him.

"All those times, dates, places listed on those pages? The pictures documenting them? It took you all those adulterous encounters, even on our honeymoon, before you reached this amazing conclusion that you had a wonderful marriage?" I asked, my voice rising.

"She was persistent, and I was weak. I admit that, but I'm stronger now. You've made me stronger, Willow."

"*Moi?*" I said with grand exaggeration. "Little old me? The college girl, the girl with barely enough ro-

mantic experience to fill ten minutes of a soap opera? I
was the one who was able to give you—a man of the
world who speaks three languages, sophisticated, elegant, traveled—give you the strength you needed? To
teach you the truths about a significant relationship?"

"Yes," he said firmly.

I shook my head, looked out at the sea, and laughed
to myself.

"It is the truth," he insisted.

I spun on him.

"The truth? *Please,* Thatcher. You, your sister, your
mother, your whole family are so used to lying, to pretending, to dramatizing and fabricating, that none of
you can even recognize the true and the real anymore,
even if it was hoisted on a flag or set in neon lights on
Worth Avenue. This entire place, the Palm Beach social
world, your precious Season that you treat like some religious period with invitations considered as valuable as
blessings, all of that nonsense has given birth to all this,
made you all who you are."

"Being a bit condescending and superior, aren't
you?" he quipped out of the side of his mouth.

"I don't think so. I'm not a saint, but I won't lie to
myself."

"I thought you wanted to be a psychiatrist. I thought
these things were valid to you, that you would be understanding," he wailed, his arms out.

"You thought very wrong."

He dropped his arms and let his shoulders sag with
defeat.

"Then everything I just told you doesn't matter?"

"No, it matters. It has helped me reach a verdict."

I turned and stared at him coldly, so coldly he actually took a step back.

"What verdict?" he asked.

"Guilty," I said sharply. "Guilty of being false, of betrayal, simply guilty of adultery with no mitigating circumstances. Is that a clear enough verdict? You want me to pronounce sentence?"

He shook his head.

"Don't bother," he said, turned, and walked away. He looked more like he was fleeing. I watched until he disappeared, and then I closed my eyes and lay back on the warm sand so my eyes could swallow their tears.

By the time I went into the house nearly an hour later, he was already gone. He took most of his clothes, but left things behind, especially the folder and its contents, still spread on our bed, the remnants of a crumbled marriage. I gathered up the evidence and shoved it back into the folder, then sat on the bed and finally let the trapped tears streak down my face. I had my hands on my stomach as I wept.

Inside me, our baby was forming. A short time ago, I had thought of our baby as the product of love, thought that, no matter what the timing and the planning, she could never be thought of as a mistake. Our child would be too beautiful, too much a part of us to be thought of that way. But what was this child to be a part of now? A broken marriage? A series of deceits? A home built on a foundation of lies?

What would I think every time I looked at her? Would I see Thatcher and his betrayal? Would I be unable to separate all that from our child? How much of him would be in our baby? Would it be the stronger influence?

I hated myself for my first thoughts, for I was telling myself that I should seek an abortion. I should not permit the fraud to continue. This was not a child born of love, but a child born out of lust. I was just as guilty in that respect. I had no right to her. I gazed at myself in the mirror.

Look at the world, the situation you would be bringing this child into, and ask yourself, Willow De Beers— for that's who you have returned to being, Willow De Beers—ask yourself, do you want to do that?

The rage inside me was hot and wild enough to consume my fetus anyway, I thought. All that bile, that hot blood boiled by betrayal and disappointment, would restructure and remold the infant so that she inherited the bitterness if she did survive. I saw now what Manon meant by offering the information before I had made too great an investment in this corrupt marriage. All of them had sat there and gazed at me, asking with their eyes: Do you want to give birth to this man's child?

I sobbed louder, my body shaking as I rocked back and forth, holding myself.

There was a knock on my door, so gentle at first that I didn't hear or realize someone was there. The knock grew more intense and made me jump. My gasp put a cork in the bottle of my tears. I sucked in my breath and managed a "Yes?"

The door opened and Mother stood there, her face full of concern.

"I saw Thatcher leave," she said. "He was carrying suitcases and he looked furious. I called to him and I know he heard me, but he didn't turn back. What happened?" I shook my head and then burst into a flood of tears that I thought might drown us both.

She rushed to me to throw her arms around me, and for a few moments I became a very little girl again, clinging to my Amou, soaking up her compassion and sympathy and clinging to her words of hope. There was always sunshine in her eyes for me, always enough to help me believe things would get better.

When I was calm enough, I told Mother everything, and then I showed her the folder. She sifted through the documents, stared sadly at the photographs, and sighed so deeply, I felt sorrier for her than I did for myself. She looked like she had aged in minutes.

"How disappointing," she said. "Such hard news. I was always impressed with Thatcher, impressed with how he had managed to overcome his own family to develop into such a respectable, mature young man."

She looked at me.

"I feel like I was part of the deception," she continued. "I feel responsible."

"How could you be?"

"I was so happy about your relationship with him and your marriage to him. I lent my support, my confidence to you and ignored all his philandering."

"I am a big girl, Mother. I didn't do anything I did not want to do. I knew about his past, the way he lived and played. What I was blind to, I was blind to because I closed my eyes myself. No one closed them for me. There were so many hints and little footprints along the way. I think I realized some of this, but lied to myself because it was so much easier to do that. No one is more responsible than I am. I won't let you place an ounce of blame on yourself."

"I am afraid I don't need your permission to do that," she said. She closed the folder. "What have you decided to do now?"

"I can't remain married to such a man," I said.

She nodded.

"And I'm thinking about the baby," I added. Her eyes flew up at me, widening.

"What are you saying? You can't mean . . . you wouldn't seek an abortion?"

"I keep thinking about the life I'm bringing this child into, Mother. Mistakes compounded become so much bigger and harder to live with."

"Oh, no, Willow, no. The child can never be thought a mistake. Besides, whether you want to admit it to yourself now or not, this baby is a part of you. Believe me," she said. "I know."

She reached for my hand and looked into my face.

"Don't you think I went through the same sort of concern, had the same doubts and temptations? But in the end, Willow, I could not deny that the child being formed inside my body was so much a part of who and what I was that I could not place blame on him and I could not deny his existence. This isn't exactly the product of a rape. Mine was closer to that, but I was a young, vulnerable girl who just didn't realize what it all would and could mean."

"Right now, I don't feel any more sophisticated or mature than you were then, Mother."

"This is different, Willow. It's betrayal, it's being taken advantage of, but it's different," she insisted. "Believe me, you will hate yourself more if you stop yourself from giving birth. You wanted this child after you learned of its coming, didn't you? You had worked out all the problems, knew you could afford to have it and still fulfill your responsibilities and needs. What Thatcher has done shouldn't change that, can't change that."

I shook my head, bit down on my lower lip, and closed my eyes.

"No, I guess what he has done does not change that. You're right, of course. It's just that . . . just that it's going to be so hard now, Mother, for so many reasons."

"It's been hard before," she said, smiling. "Somehow, we manage to get through it."

I looked at her and felt so guilty for waving my self-pity in her face, of all faces. If anyone had the right to self-pity, it was she. Abused, sent away suffering emotional and mental pain, having to give up the man she loved and return to a world in which she was considered a leper. And she was the one giving me encouragement and strength.

"Oh, Mother," I cried. "I'm sorry."

"You have nothing to be sorry about, Willow. In the end, believe me, he will be the one who wakes up alone, lost, confused, and very sorry."

She put her arm around me and for a while we sat on the bed, me resting my head on her shoulder, she kissing my hair.

"Let me see about dinner," she said.

"I'm not going to be very hungry, Mother."

"Don't start punishing yourself, Willow," she warned sternly. "I did that for too long before your father helped me realize how foolish and wrong it was. You know if he were here now, he would not approve."

I smiled.

"Okay, Mother. I'll be strong."

"Good," she said, standing. "Good."

She left, her shoulders still sagging with the weight of all this terrible news. I went into the bathroom to wash my face and brush my hair. When the phone rang, I froze. If he was hoping to do better through a phone conversation, he was dearly mistaken, I thought. However, it was Manon.

"Are you all right?" she asked.

"Yes," I said with strength. "I'm fine."

"We all felt so bad for you, Willow. We all had grave doubts that we had done the right thing. Even though it is not the fault of any of us, we would feel guilty if you lost your baby or something," she declared.

"I'm not losing my baby," I said with such determination, I even surprised myself.

"Good. Did you—"

"Confront him with the evidence?" She was silent. I knew that was the real purpose of this call, but I wasn't going to simply fade away into the sunset. Thatcher would have to face the world with all of this revealed. The Club d'Amour would see to that, I thought, and for the first time, I was actually happy about them. "Yes, I presented it to him. He couldn't deny any of it."

"What did he say? I mean, if you want to tell me, that is."

"He said he had an affair with her to get her out of his system."

"What?"

"And he claimed that was just what he had done."

"I don't think I've heard that one before," she said, so thoughtfully it brought a smile to my face. "It's like a serial killer killing one more time to get it out of his system."

That brought a laugh out of me.

"In a way, I suppose it is. It didn't work with me. He's left the house," I told her.

"That's good," she said. "I want you to know we are here for you. We are more than just here for you. Marjorie, having the most bitter experiences with divorce, is our resident expert. She wanted me to give you the name of her attorney, who, you will be glad to know, is a woman, Gloria Baker. Marjorie has taken the liberty of filling her in on your situation already, so when you call, if you want to call her, she will know who you are and what you need exactly."

She rattled off the telephone number. I wrote it down and thanked her.

"In fact, thank everyone, Manon, and tell them I don't blame them for anything or hold anything against them. I never thought I would be grateful to you and the others, if you want to know. I thought you were interesting, but a bit too far left of center for me when it came to male-female relationships. I don't think so anymore."

"I'm glad, Willow. We'll call you and, if you let us, we'll come see you in a few days."

"Thank you, yes," I said.

"As Victor Laszlo, the leader of the French resistance against the Nazis, says in *Casablanca,* 'Welcome back to the fight. This time I know our side will win.' "

I smiled at the dramatics, thanked her again, and hung up.

I actually did feel better and went ahead and called Gloria Baker's office. Her secretary put me right through to her.

"Why don't we meet tomorrow?" she said after I introduced myself. She gave me a time I could manage and, without any words of comfort or any platitudes, she simply concluded with, "We will do what has to be done."

Fortified, I left my suite to go downstairs, then paused when I saw Linden standing in the hallway just outside his studio. He looked like he had been waiting there for some time. He stood so that his face was mostly in the shadows draping the wall.

"Linden? Are you all right?"

"Yes."

"Why are you just standing there like that?" I asked.

"I saw Mother come out of your suite. She was crying, so I asked her why and she told me."

"Oh."

"I'm not surprised," he said, moving into the light. His face was luminous, his smile cold. "When you told him you were pregnant, he wanted you to discover his unfaithfulness so you would send him away."

"I don't know that the baby has all that much to do with it, Linden," I said softly.

"Oh, it does, yes it does," he said. He held his smile, his eyes becoming even more excited and bright.

"Well, what's happened has happened. I don't want to dwell on it," I said.

"Good. We've all got to put the past behind us," he proclaimed. "But now that this has happened, it is the right time to show you my latest work. Tomorrow, I will hang it on the wall."

"So you have finished it. How nice," I said. It took a great effort for me to generate interest in anything at the moment, even to pretend it, but I knew how proud he was of his new work and how important it was to him that I like it.

He went to his studio door, opened it, and stepped back.

"You are the first to see it, of course. Even Mother hasn't been in here yet. I made sure of that."

I nodded, smiled, and walked into the studio. The painting was as big as he had said it would be. He had it up on the west wall of his studio with a light on it. The picture was done in vibrant, almost neon colors, everything as bright as could be. That was startling in and of itself, but what was depicted was so strange, it took my breath away.

It was set on our beach. There was no question the woman walking was I. She was pregnant, but the figure behind her was done in multiples to show movement, and there was also no question that figure was Linden.

He'd painted himself moving up and into me. Emerging from the front of me was an infant, and the infant was shown growing until it was clearly a little girl.

I couldn't help but step closer to the picture. In the background, almost unseen, was the figure of a woman who resembled Mother.

"I don't understand this, Linden," I said. "What's happening in the picture?"

"How can you not understand?" he cried.

I turned and saw his face filling with agony.

"I just want to be sure I'm right, Linden," I said softly. "Please don't be upset. It's remarkable," I added. That seemed to calm him.

"It took every bit of creative energy out of me to paint this," he told me, approaching the picture and gazing up at it with great adoration.

"There's a birth here," I said.

"Oh, there's everything here. This is all of it, love, life, struggles, victories. This is us," he declared. "See Mother? See her watching?"

"And that's you?"

"Yes, of course it's me. Who else could it be?"

"But why are you . . . why are you going into me?"

"Because we're part of each other, always and forever. You know that," he said. "You have even told me so in so many different ways. Isn't that right?" he asked with a frantic note that threatened to explode into full-blown hysteria if it was denied.

"Yes." I nodded. "Yes."

"I'll show it to Grace now. She's been trying to get in here to see this for some time," he added with a smile.

"I bet," I said.

"Then you like it, right? You really like it?"

"Yes, Linden. It's very, very interesting," I said.

"Good. Thatcher wouldn't have liked it," he declared. "He would have wanted it destroyed."

I didn't say yes or no. I thought he would certainly have been shocked.

"I'll hang it tomorrow," he said.

"Maybe we should make this extra special, Linden."

"What do you mean?"

"Maybe we should hang it somewhere special."

"Where's that?"

"Put it in your room," I said.

He studied my face.

"My room? Why in my room?"

"I think it's so much a part of you and who you are that it belongs with you. I'd like to see it there. I'd like to go there often to see it," I added.

"Oh."

He thought a moment, then smiled and nodded.

"Yes, you're right. It's too special for the rest of the world to see. They won't appreciate it like we do, anyway." He looked up at the picture again. "I tried to make her more like you. I know what you want to name her, too. I overheard you tell Mother. I like the name. Hannah," he said. "Perfect.

"Everything," he added, turning to me, "is going to be perfect."

I left him standing there, looking up at the picture as if he could not take his eyes away, as if he was looking somewhere deep inside himself at a place so dark no one else should ever be able to see it, but a place I feared I had just seen.

I knew Mother was as disturbed by the picture as I was, but she tried not to show it because she didn't want to upset me any further. Yes, she said, it was strange, offbeat, but most everything Linden had done to date was. When I asked her what she thought he was saying in the work, she just shook her head.

"I always tell him his work is interesting and very good, but most of the time, I don't understand it. Of course, I remember some of the artwork your father's patients at the clinic did. Your father didn't think of it as art in the true sense. He told me he saw it as a means of bringing troubled or disturbing thoughts up from the dark well in their minds and, by exposing them, beginning to deal with them. There were some very weird things done in that arts-and-crafts room in the clinic," she said, smiling and shaking her head.

"Let's leave it be for now," she concluded. "We have other problems to solve first."

"I'm not worried about them, Mother. I'll do what I have to do."

"I know you will," she said, "but I wouldn't be your mother if I didn't worry, now, would I?"

She smiled at me and held it until I smiled and agreed. But later, when she didn't know I was watching, I saw the heavy weight of it all, my problems and Linden's, furrow her brows and sag her shoulders. Maybe we shouldn't have ignored Linden's troubled thoughts that had surfaced through his picture, but we did. Somewhere deep inside me, regret had planted a seed, and I knew in my heart it would grow into something bigger and, like an insidious weed, curl around whatever flowers of joy were in our garden, choking them until they were gone.

Thatcher's rage at being rebuked took form rather quickly over the next few days, making me even more grateful for the assistance Manon and the members of the Club d'Amour provided.

My attorney reviewed Thatcher's and my prenuptial agreement and advised me that she would challenge any and all clauses not to my advantage.

"He should have had a third party involved, an outside attorney. This is like the beneficiary of a will writing the will and making sure all other beneficiaries are eliminated. There would be and there are grounds to challenge."

"Yes, my attorney from South Carolina wanted me to do that right after it was drawn up."

"You should have let him. If Thatcher calls you and tries to discuss any of this, which I imagine he will do, just have one response: *Call my lawyer.* Understand? I'm the wall between you and him from now on," she advised.

As she predicted, Thatcher did call. He started to threaten me with the document.

"If you're so unforgiving, I have no choice but to protect my rights."

"Go on, protect them, Thatcher. You're the one who included the reference to adultery, which changes everything."

He was silent.

"Very odd," he finally said, "how you have all this so well worked out for someone who is supposedly a victim here."

"Supposedly a victim? Just call my attorney, Thatcher," I snapped. I gave him my attorney's number and hung up on him. He didn't call back, but someone arrived the next day with a list of things he wanted from the house. Most of it was his personal belongings. I had Jennings assist him.

Daddy once told me that bad news travels rapidly because people are so grateful it's not bad news for them.

"It is almost as if they feel that by spreading it, they

ensure that it will stay away from their doorsteps," he'd said. He smiled and added, "Like throwing the garbage over the wall into someone else's yard and keeping it out of yours. I see this as especially true with mental illness. Friends and neighbors can be cruel. Relatives, of course, keep it as hidden as they can for fear someone will think it's in the blood and they or their children are next. How many times have I seen families that hide severely disturbed children, even parents, so no one will know."

In fact, Daddy had written a paper about a teenage girl who suffered from paranoid schizophrenia and was locked in a room without windows for nearly two years until she committed suicide. His thesis dealt with how even the mentally ill had the need for communication and society.

The news of my marital problems found a good home at school, of course. The twins were the first to commiserate, Pet claiming she'd always suspected Thatcher was a heel. Loni felt so sorry for me, she looked sick. Holden Mitchell, who had kept his distance from me ever since the incident on the beach, looked very satisfied and had the courage to approach me one afternoon to say, "I heard about you and your husband. I told you so." I ignored him and walked away quickly.

Professor Fuentes knew about it all as quickly as everyone else, but made no attempt to talk except to ask me if I was all right. I wasn't in the mood to talk about it anyway, but soon after that, I realized I was guilty of the very things we hoped to overcome in prospective clients—avoidance, the ostrich syndrome—only here, it wasn't possible to bury your head in the sand for long. Waves of gossip, intruding eyes, and busybodies washed it away and left you naked with the truth.

Finally, I admitted to the professor that I wasn't all right. He nodded and asked me to join him for coffee, which quickly turned into one of our famous tête-á-têtes.

"How are your mother and Linden taking all this?"

"My mother puts on a good act, but I know she's hurting for me. Linden . . . is behaving strangely again."

"How so?"

I explained how he doted on me even more, and how my breakup with Thatcher had reinforced his idea that it was the two of us against the world.

"He's been insisting I stop going to the doctor Thatcher had recommended. I was never crazy about him anyway, so I might go to someone else. Of course, I'm worried about reinforcing his paranoia."

"Don't worry about that. Worry about what makes you comfortable at this time," Professor Fuentes advised.

I agreed with him, then described Linden's latest painting.

He nodded, thoughtful.

"He literally sees himself in you. Your suffering is his suffering."

"I haven't done enough to help him. For a while there, because of Whitney and her nasty rumors and such, I neglected Linden, actually avoided him when I should have been helping him get stronger and get out in the world."

"Don't try to take too much of this on your own shoulders, Willow," Professor Fuentes warned. "Get him to return to a professional therapist and get back on some essential medication."

"I will," I said, knowing that was a much bigger task than I could envision. There were more storm clouds on the horizon with Linden's and my names on them.

For one thing, the Eatons, especially Whitney,

weren't going to permit Thatcher to be the bad one in this scenario. It wasn't long before new rumors began to blossom like black weeds with sharp thorns. Once again, the Club d'Amour was my source of information. The girls knew when I was going to be home after class, and all burst onto the property together a few days after Professor Fuentes and I had spoken. They were waiting for me when I arrived. Mother had greeted them and sat with them, but Linden, as was usually the case when anyone came to Joya del Mar, had fled to one of his private places on the beach.

The moment I set eyes on them, I knew there was more trouble. Mother, her eyes dark with worry, excused herself and went upstairs. She looked so much more frail and older to me since my breakup. It almost made me wish I had swallowed my pride and accepted Thatcher's ludicrous rationalization for infidelity.

I sat quickly. I could see the urgency and anger in their faces.

"What now?" I asked as soon as Mother excused herself.

"They dropped the second shoe," Manon began.

"Second bomb is more like it," Marjorie quipped.

"They, meaning my in-laws?"

"Yes."

"And the second shoe is what?"

"Thatcher's defense, at least the defense he is floating out there," Manon said, nodding at the front door.

"Oh, and what is this defense?"

"The story they are spreading is that he caught you in an incestuous relationship with Linden, and he is even unsure that the baby you're carrying is his," she said.

"That last part has Whitney's fingerprints on it," Sharon added. "You knew she was circling it for some time, just waiting like a rumor vampire to sink her sharp teeth in it and bleed it all over Palm Beach."

I tried to swallow, to take a breath, but I felt as if there were fingers closing on my throat.

"How could Thatcher permit this?"

"You ever hear 'All's fair in love and war'?" Marjorie asked. "Here, love and war are one and the same."

"They have their image to protect in the community," Liana said. "Thatcher has to be the victim. I've heard they are already being invited to dinner parties so they can tell the sordid tale, and Bunny Eaton is the one eager to do it and do it well."

"I'm disappointed in Asher," I said.

"Why? He was never much of a man, as far as I could see," Manon said. "He's like most of them—he goes whichever way the wind is blowing."

"And Bunny is always doing the blowing," Liana said.

They laughed, but I couldn't find a shred of humor in the moment.

"What will I do?" I looked toward the doorway, the image of Mother hobbling away fresh in my mind. "If my mother hears of this . . ."

"I'd get it all over with as soon and as painlessly as you can," Manon said. "The longer it drags out—"

"—the more the stories will flourish and be embellished," Sharon completed.

"Once it's over, it will become yesterday's news so quickly, your head will spin," Liana assured me. "That's the way things are here."

"Of course, finding another suitable man in this town will be practically impossible," Marjorie said. "I speak from experience when it comes to that."

"So she'll find him somewhere else," Manon said.

"Maybe there is no such thing," Liana mused aloud.

They all gazed at her for a moment.

"No such thing?" I asked.

"As a suitable man."

"There's no doubt about that," Marjorie said.

"My father was a suitable man," I said, hating their cynicism. "I'm sure you all know someone you would hold up as an example."

"Not my father," Sharon said bluntly.

"Nor mine," Liana added.

"Nevertheless, we shouldn't generalize. I have the freshest wound, and I'm telling you, I am not giving up my dreams just because one man brought me a nightmare," I said with heat in my face. "I won't let a man do that to me, and none of you should permit it either. You have a right to be happy. We all do," I insisted.

For a moment, they all looked like little girls again, their eyes full of fantasy and hope, even Marjorie's. Then, as if the magical bubble burst, they blinked, stirred, shook their heads, and laughed with derision.

"What do you expect from someone who wants to be a psychiatrist?" Manon asked them. "She has to be a little crazy herself to understand her patients."

They laughed again.

No matter what happens to me, I vowed silently, *I'll never become like they have become.*

Was I crazy?

I narrowed my eyes at their cynical smiles, my spine turning to steel.

"Laugh if you want, but my father used to say that dreams, that fantasies are as important as vitamins," I said. "If flowers didn't believe that cloudy days would end, they would wilt and die. Bitterness feeds on itself. It consumes you and, in the end, you become the very thing you hate.

"This, too, shall pass," I said, smiling at them. "All of it will end. The clouds will move away. We will have sunshine penetrating the black leaves of our wicked forest and we will be happy. Above all, no matter what, we will be happy. That should be the motto of your Club d'Amour," I admonished.

They all looked like little girls again, but little girls who had been lectured and set straight.

"Maybe you're right," Manon said. "I can't deny I hope you are."

Sharon nodded.

Marjorie looked away like someone who wanted to hide her tears, and Liana smiled.

Despite the terrible and ugly news they had brought me, I actually felt better and stronger myself—until I saw Jennings standing in the doorway. The look on his face told me immediately something was wrong.

Something was very wrong.

"Jennings?"

"It's Miss Montgomery," he said. "One of the maids just called down to me."

"What?" I asked, shooting to my feet so quickly, I felt my heart bob like a yo-yo. I pressed my palms against each other between my breasts.

"She's collapsed by the side of the bed."

18

An Empty House

Mother's eyes seemed to be sewn shut. I felt for a pulse and found a very low, weak beat. Even before I started up the stairs to see what was wrong with her, I had told Jennings to call for an ambulance. Since there was no hospital in Palm Beach, she was taken to Good Samaritan in West Palm Beach.

The uproar brought Linden out of his room. He stood like a stone statue and watched as the attendants lifted Mother onto a stretcher and placed her in the ambulance. Then he came along with me in my car, moving like a robot; his silence made me babble continuously. The girls of the Club d'Amour all went home, each promising to call. From the looks on their faces and the hollowness in their voices, I knew they didn't really want to call. Thatcher once told me that sickness and death were so abhorrent to the residents of Palm Beach that no hospital or cemetery was permitted within its precious boundaries.

Linden was as quiet at the hospital as he had been at home and in the car. He sat with an almost expressionless mask over his face, the only hint of emotion evidenced in the slight trembling in his lips from time to time. His eyes were steely gray, his neck stiff, his hands clasped in his lap as he waited with me in the lounge. When I asked him if he wanted something to drink, he just shook his head. He looked like he was sleeping with his eyes open.

Nearly two and a half hours after we had arrived with the ambulance, the doctor finally came out to see us. He was tall and thin with curly black hair, and so baby-faced it was difficult to have any faith in anything he said, but he did speak with authority and medical expertise.

"I'm Dr. Hersh," he began. "We've examined your mother and concluded beyond a doubt that she has suffered a stroke or, as we say, brain attack. A CT scan has revealed an intracerebral hemorrhage. I'm afraid it's rather massive. We've determined that she has suffered a recent myocardial infarction, which created the blood clot."

"A heart attack? But wouldn't we know if that had happened to her?" I asked.

He shook his head so casually, it was almost as if we were discussing some very insignificant thing.

"The patient suffers symptoms, doesn't report them to anyone, and lives with the damage until a blood clot is created in the heart that breaks off and travels to the brain, cutting off the supply of blood and eventually causing the hemorrhage. It's not as uncommon as you might think," he said.

He looked from me to Linden as he spoke, but something in Linden's face frightened him enough to keep him from looking at him at all.

"What can we expect?" I asked, my heart pounding so hard, I wasn't sure I had spoken loud enough for him to hear me.

"The prognosis is not optimistic, I'm afraid," he said. "She's in a coma, of course. She's not feeling any pain."

"Can we see her?" I asked.

"Yes. We've placed her in our ICU. It's protocol to provide a clear air passageway, of course, so we have a nasogastric tube employed. She's on a heart monitor. I'm just telling you all this so you're not surprised or frightened by what you see," he added with a soft turn of his lips. He glanced at Linden, then shifted his eyes back to me and nodded. "I'm sorry," he said. "My suspicion is, there were some warnings that were ignored. Many people don't even know when they are having a stroke. I read a report yesterday from the University of Cincinnati that indicated 52 percent of their acute stroke patients were unaware they were experiencing a stroke. We've got to do better at making people stroke-smart."

What does all this have to do with us now? I thought. Maybe he was only trying to make conversation, or maybe, in his own way, trying to explain how someone you loved dearly was about to be taken from you and how he, our doctor, a representative of this great medical machine, this expensive infrastructure of doctors, nurses, devices and medicines, was helpless and could offer only a smooth transition to the grave.

I nodded, took Linden's arm, and headed for the ICU. When we got there, the nurse seemed to glide over the floor like a funeral director, gesturing rather than talking, and directing us to Mother's bedside. She looked so small, the bed and the machinery around her engulfing her. I held tightly to Linden's arm. He was still very stiff, mechanical, his jaw taut, his eyes like marbles.

"She doesn't look like she's suffering" was all I could manage.

Linden released a breath, faltered for a second, then regained his poise and straightened his back. I reached for Mother's hand and held it. She already felt as cold as a corpse, her complexion fading as if she were being drawn slowly down into herself, into her own bones, closing like a clamshell.

So she was not going to see her grandchild after all, I thought. She was not going to enjoy the autumn of her life and be part of my accomplishments. All of the promise I had brought, all of the renewed hope was to be lost. I knew that she had wanted to help me and support me at this time of great difficulty. Perhaps, on top of all the pain and suffering she had endured, mine was too much. Perhaps, if I had left her alone, if I had not sought her out and become part of her life, she wouldn't be lying here now. I couldn't help wondering about it.

The tears streamed down my cheeks. I took deep breaths and wiped them away. Then I felt Linden nudging me.

"We've got to get home," he said.

"Get home?"

"You know how Grace is," he replied, smiling. "She won't eat dinner without us."

It felt like an ice cube was sliding down my spine.

He looked up, and I realized he wasn't looking at Mother. He was looking past her. Something in him was keeping him from seeing her like this. He had shut all the doors to reality and retreated to the world he knew at Joya del Mar. Maybe he was better off, I thought. What good would it do him now if I forced him to acknowledge her, dying in this bed?

"Okay, Linden," I said. "We'll go home."

I leaned over and kissed Mother on the cheek and whispered, "I love you."

Then I turned and led Linden away like a blind man. I left all of our information with the medical office before we drove home. As soon as we arrived, Jennings asked after Mother, and I told him the sad news. He looked absolutely devastated and mumbled some consoling remark before retreating. There was no doubt in my mind that the only reason he had opted to remain with us rather than go off with the Eatons was his admiration and love for Mother. It made it all seem that much sadder.

On behalf of the Club d'Amour, Manon did call me that evening. I imagined them drawing straws to see who would be forced to make the call. I told her Mother's diagnosis and prognosis. She muttered her regrets quickly and, with little enthusiasm, asked me to call her if I needed anything. It wasn't difficult to understand. She, as well as her friends and so many other people I had met here, spent most of their time finding new and exciting ways to please themselves. They lived in a world in which they could assign their responsibilities to someone else, even their daily worries. Problems meant only that money would be spent, and money was in such abundance, it meant nothing. Despair, poverty, age, and death itself were persona non grata. They were to be ignored. *Rich people here don't die,* I thought. *They simply stop being invited to parties, balls, and dinners.* That was the extent of facing reality.

Linden was obviously having his own difficulty with the events transpiring. He came by my suite to call me to dinner. I joined him at the table, and unlike his behavior before, he was talkative and animated again.

"Mother isn't feeling well enough to join us," he said. "But she would be upset if we didn't have our dinner because of that."

"Linden," I said softly, "Mother is very, very ill."

"Oh, I know. I've been after her to take better care of herself, you know. Why, if it wasn't for me, she wouldn't eat a decent meal half the time. I'm the one who gets her outside to get fresh air and take walks. She would be content sitting in her room. We've got to get her to help herself more, Willow. I've told you that many times, haven't I?

"She'll listen if you chime in as well. She usually listens to you better than she listens to me these days."

"Linden . . ."

"Yes?" He started to eat.

I watched him for a moment, and then I shook my head, eating what I could while he talked on and on about the things he was going to do with the house to make Mother happier and more comfortable at Joya del Mar.

This isn't good, I thought. *I must make him realize what is really happening. I must make him face the truth.*

"You know she's in the hospital, Linden. You know that we had to take her there in an ambulance. You must not pretend that didn't happen. Please," I said. "I need you to be strong now."

He blinked rapidly and nodded, then smiled.

"I know, but don't you worry about her," he said. "She'll be home soon. Grace hates the very idea of hospitals and clinics and doctors. She's had a bellyful of them. She won't stand for another day there, so get ready to pick her up and bring her back."

He thought a moment.

"I should start something new, do something special for her, don't you think? I'll do something cheerful, something that will bring a big smile to her face again. I know just what I'll do, too," he concluded. He threw his napkin to the table. "I'll start on it immediately. It will be one of the fastest works I've completed.

"You'll be happy with it, too," he declared, standing. "Now, don't you go and tell her and spoil my surprise, Willow. Promise?"

"I promise, Linden," I said.

"Good. Good. I'm sorry I have to leave you, but I have to get to work," he said, and left the dining room.

I sat looking after him.

And for a moment, as fleeting as it was, I wished I had some way to run from it all, too.

Mother died three days later. The call came in the morning just before I was going to leave for a class. I had hoped to go to it and then to the hospital. I hadn't taken Linden back to the hospital since they had brought Mother there in the ambulance. He was still having a very hard time accepting how seriously ill she was, and even that she was in the hospital. Although he had faced that fact with me at dinner the night she was admitted, he continued to make remarks about her resting in her room. I tried to reinforce reality by describing her condition and my hospital visits afterward. He would listen, grow silent, and then beam with new excitement about his current art project.

Overwhelmed by hearing from my attorney about my separation from Thatcher, trying to concentrate on my studies, and thinking about Mother, I decided to let Linden live in his fantasy, but when the hospital called

with the bad news, I had to bring down the curtain on illusions in our house.

The news made me numb. Surprisingly, I didn't burst
into hysterical tears, as I kept expecting I would. I had
sobbed softly on and off during the days after Mother's
collapse, but I think there was a part of me that was very
similar to Linden, a part of me that held on to fantasy, that
dreamed of her snapping her eyes open and smiling up at
me and asking, "What happened? Why am I here, and
when can I go home?" The dream brought a smile to my
face and put energy into my steps, at least for a little while.

Perhaps I had mourned her in advance, I thought
after I received the call, or perhaps I was anticipating so
much difficulty with Linden that I knew I couldn't afford to be devastated. When you have to be strong, when
there is absolutely no alternative to that, you somehow
fish deeper in the well of your very being and find
strength you never knew you had.

Every dark thought I had experienced since Mother's
stroke was thumping at me as I put down my books and
started for the stairway. I was carrying news that was so
heavy, it made me walk like someone with far too much
weight on her shoulders. Before I had come here and
burst in on their world, trailing the past in behind me
like someone with muddy shoes, Mother and Linden
were living an admittedly introverted, secluded life, but
a somewhat contented one. She was living with her happiest memories, dreaming of my father's promised arrival, and Linden was secure in his dark art. Was I the
one who had made him unhappy with himself, opened
up doors he had forgotten existed, made him look at the
blinding light that exposed and reminded him of his failings? Had I brought back the painful memories for
Mother and given her night after night of tortured sleep?

After my father had died, I had felt so alone and frightened. My boyfriend, Allan Simpson, was too self-centered to provide any real comfort for me, and my aunt and my other relatives were not close enough to give me a sense of real family. I was truly desperate myself when I set out to find my mother and have a family again. Maybe I was the selfish one. Maybe I should have left well enough alone.

Now guilt, more than grief, put the darkness in my face and the emptiness in my eyes. Maybe love is too complicated, I thought. Maybe we paint our days and lives with colors that will always fade. We manufacture one illusion after another to keep ourselves from admitting the only truth that has been with us since we began, a truth I had tried to deny and defeat by coming here: We are alone. In the end, no one wants to hold our hands and go with us. They mourn us for as long as they can, but they do not go with us into the shadows.

I knocked on Linden's studio door. He didn't reply, so I opened it and looked for him. He was standing by the window that faced the sea.

"Linden," I began, "the hospital just called us."

He didn't turn.

"Linden."

He shook his head, and then turned to me.

"She's out there again," he said, frowning. "She'll never stop waiting for him. I don't know how many times she has walked to the end of that dock and stood, sometimes for hours, staring out at the sea, expecting him."

He raised his arms and held his hands out toward me.

"How can we stop her? How can we get her to see how foolishly she's behaving? All it does is make her sadder, and that will make her sicker."

"She's not out there, Linden. We took her to the hospital. She had a stroke. The hospital just phoned to say she has passed away. There wasn't anything more that they could do for her. Mother is gone, Linden."

I hated the sound of my own voice. I resembled the walking dead.

He shook his head.

"No. I just saw her," he insisted, refuting my words. "She's out there. Look for yourself," he said, turning back to the window. He stood there. I didn't move. After a long moment, he turned back to me, and this time he had tears streaming down his cheeks. "She was there," he contended. "I saw her. I did."

"I know you did, Linden. I know," I said, and moved to embrace him. I held on to him tightly. His arms hung limply for a moment, and then he clung to me, his tears falling on my cheeks, too.

I pulled myself back slowly.

"I've got to go to make arrangements, Linden. Do you want to come with me?"

"No," he said. "I can't. I have to stay here and finish my work for her."

"Okay," I said. With my handkerchief, I dabbed the tears on his face, and then I wiped them from my own. "I'll be back as soon as I finish."

He nodded and quickly turned back to the window.

I left him standing there looking down at the dock. How I wished that the world he saw was the real one, and the world I moved in was illusion.

Mr. Ross, our accountant, one of the first people I had met when I came here, turned out to be of great assistance to me. As soon as he heard about Mother's death, he called and told me he would take care of all the monetary matters. The Eatons didn't call, but Thatcher did. It was a short conversation. His secretary called and told me to hold on, and then Thatcher came on the line, sounding like he was in his car on his cellular phone and being patched in.

"I'm sorry about Grace," he said. "I was fond of her."

"Thank you."

"When is the funeral?"

"The day after tomorrow at eleven."

"Oh. I'm due in court," he said. "Are you all right?"

"Yes," I said quickly. What I really meant was, if I wasn't, you would be the last to know.

"Okay. I'm sorry," he repeated, and said goodbye.

I called Aunt Agnes to tell her because I knew she would be insulted if I didn't, even though I also knew she wouldn't attend the funeral, nor would any of my relatives. Then I phoned Amou, and she and I had a good cry together over thousands of miles. Her words of comfort were the medicine I needed at the moment.

Manon and the others phoned and told me they would be at the funeral. I thanked them for that. The Butterworth twins and some of my other friends at school paid a visit, those who could promising to attend the funeral.

Linden spent most of the time in his room or in his studio. If I didn't make sure food was sent up to him, he wouldn't have eaten. He certainly didn't want to greet any visitors. The first two nights, I heard him wandering the hallways. I knew he paid frequent visits to Mother's suite. Perhaps it was his way of finally convincing himself she was really gone.

I went to her room myself and sifted through some of her things. It was a way for me to feel closer to her, to hold on to her awhile longer. While doing so, I discovered some photographs she had buried in a small box in a bottom dresser drawer. They were early pictures of her and my grandmother, Jackie Lee. There were pictures of her stepfather, Winston Montgomery, too. He was a very handsome man, and she looked comfortable, even loving with him in the pictures she had.

I could see more resemblances between my mother and myself when we were both in our early teens. Her face was brighter, full of life and joy. This was some time before she was seduced by Kirby Scott, of course. She still held on to that look of innocence and wonder we all see in young girls and remember once in ourselves. It's the beginning of the longing and the regret that comes with growing up and leaving your childhood behind.

On the second night after Mother's death, Professor Fuentes came to see me. He had been down in Miami attending the christening of a cousin's new baby, and said he had just learned the news.

"We have one of those families that comes to events in packs," he joked.

"I envy you that," I told him.

We were in the den off the rear loggia where I had first met the Eatons, and where Thatcher had appeared, surprisingly, after seeing me first at the Breakers. I'd had no idea at the time he was related to these people who were renting the property from my mother. There had been such electricity and excitement between us then. Now, when I sat here and thought about it, I wondered how we could ever protect ourselves against the little betrayals we commit against ourselves. Had I really loved Thatcher, or was I just excited by him, the woman in me stirred so deeply I thought whatever it was would last forever?

Somehow we believe that true love is everlasting in

this life by definition. That was why we said, "To love and to cherish until death do us part."

Professor Fuentes gazed at everything and shook his head. He had been here only for the wedding.

"This is an impressive house," he said. Then he smiled. "For a future therapist, that is."

"I know. I've been wondering now if I shouldn't put it up for sale."

"Don't make any decisions for a while," he advised. "Unless, of course, you have to for financial reasons."

"No, that won't be the reason why I sell, if I sell."

"What about your half brother?"

"I don't know. He's not doing well facing up to the reality of my mother's death. Tomorrow should bring it home to him, and then we will see," I said.

"Where is he now?"

"He stays in his room and in his studio. Mother's death has returned him to a more introverted state."

"You'll have to consider professional help as soon as possible," Professor Fuentes said.

"Yes. It's probably best for him if he is in a structured therapeutic environment. Maybe then I'll sell and go back to South Carolina."

"I hope not," Professor Fuentes said, his eyes full of sincerity, even a little fear that I might do what I said. He kept his eyes fixed on me.

I shook my head.

"I don't really know what I'm saying, what I'll be doing. I have a baby to think about first."

"Of course. You will find the strength, I'm sure. Please," he added, reaching for my hand, which was something he had never before done, "call on me for anything, anything at all."

"I will," I said. Even I was surprised at how sincerely and definitely that came out.

He patted my hand and stood.

"I must get back to the campus."

"Thank you for coming, Professor."

"I think we know each other well enough by now that you can call me Miguel. Unless, of course, it makes you feel uncomfortable to do so," he quickly added.

"No." I smiled. *"Gracias,* Miguel."

He laughed, then hugged me, brushing his lips against my cheek as he pulled back. I walked him to the door and watched him leave.

"Such a property," he said from the front steps.

"Soon, I'll have you back and show you around," I said.

"I'll hold you to that," he threatened playfully.

I waited until he started away in his car, then went upstairs to see how Linden was doing. I didn't find him in his suite, so I went to his studio. As usual the door was closed, only this time it was also locked. I knocked and called to him. When he didn't answer, I knocked harder and called louder. Finally, I heard him unlocking the door. He opened it slowly.

His hair was disheveled, his shirt opened, and some black paint was smeared on his chin. He had a brush in his hand, but it wasn't an artist's brush; it was a house-painter's.

"Are you all right, Linden?" I asked. "I haven't seen you all day."

"Yes," he said. He didn't step back as usual to permit me to enter.

"What are you doing with that?" I asked, nodding at the brush in his hand.

"I'm working," he said.

"But—"

"I can't talk now. I'll see you later," he said, and closed the door.

I heard him lock it quickly.

What was he doing? What sort of work of art was he creating with that? I wondered. I stood there thinking about it for a moment more, and then went to my suite to take a bath and try to relax. Tomorrow would be a dreadful day. I remembered all too vividly how hard it was for me at my father's funeral. Of course, I had been with him so much longer than I had been with my real mother, but the bond between her and me had developed so quickly and tightly, it was as if we had truly been together all my life.

After my bath I lay down and fell asleep. I hadn't realized just how tired emotional fatigue had made me. I slept until nearly seven, then got up and dressed quickly. If I didn't have dinner, Linden certainly wouldn't, I thought. As I was descending the stairs, I heard Jennings and our maids talking in the hallway. The moment they saw me, they stopped, and the maids went about their business. Jennings didn't look guilty as much as he looked troubled, I thought.

"What's wrong, Jennings?" I asked. "I can tell something is."

He shook his head.

"Come with me," he said. "Please."

I followed him through the house and out the French doors of the den. We went across the loggia and down the steps. He continued about a dozen feet or so along the pathway, then turned and nodded at the house.

"What?" I asked, following the line of his gaze.

It was still light enough to see clearly. All of the windows of Linden's studio and all of the windows of his suite had been painted black.

The sight of it made me gasp and step back, bringing my hands to my heart.

"I saw him go to the work shed and get the paint and brushes, so I asked him what he was doing and if he needed any help, but he doesn't speak to me much, Mrs. Eaton, nor does he speak to Mary and Joan, and that spooks them as it is. I mean, he just looks at them with those eyes and makes them feel like they are in his way or something. They have been mumbling about him for quite some time now. Mary is terrified of him, and Joan won't stay in the same room with him. She will actually turn and go in the opposite direction if she sees him approaching. At least, that's what they always tell me.

"Now this," he said, nodding at the windows again. "I'm afraid you're going to lose both of them, Mrs. Eaton.

"Actually," he continued, looking down, "I know it's not the best time to tell you, but I've found a new position myself and will be taking it in a few weeks. I'm sorry."

When he looked up, I saw his eyes were teary.

"With your mother gone and all, and you busy at school and having a baby soon, I know you are worried about costs. I'm sure a nanny could do most of what I do, Mrs. Eaton. You don't entertain anywhere near what the Eatons did when they lived here. It's a waste for you to have a man like me about the house."

"I understand, Jennings. It's all right," I said.

"I'm not the one to give you advice, Mrs. Eaton, but I couldn't leave without telling you to at least think about selling this and finding yourself a more suitable home for your brother and you and your child. These places . . ." He looked back at the building. "Well, these places aren't so much homes as they are stages, if you know what I mean."

"I do, Jennings. Thank you. I am considering it."

"Very good, Mrs. Eaton. Did you want me to do anything about that?" he asked, nodding at the blackened windows.

"Not just yet, Jennings. No."

"Very good, Mrs. Eaton," he said. "Should I see about dinner?"

"Please do," I said, and he walked back into the house.

I stood there looking up at the windows, and then I followed Jennings. Linden was still behind a locked door in his studio. This time I knocked very hard, almost pounding it. I heard it being unlocked, but he didn't open it for me. I did and stepped in. He was seated in a chair to the right, away from the windows. With them painted black and no light on, the only illumination was what spilled in through the opened door.

"What are you doing, Linden? Why are you sitting here in the darkness, and why did you paint all your windows black?" I asked him.

"It's better this way," he replied.

"Why is it better? How can it be better to shut the sunlight out of your rooms? Don't you like looking at the sea when you paint?"

"I don't want to see her out there anymore," he replied. "Every time I look out one of my windows, she's there."

"She can't be there, Linden," I said softly.

"I know, but she is!"

Even in the darkened room, I could see the way his eyes bulged and his temples strained. The tension was palpable. If I pushed him, I thought, he might explode in a rage of some sort. Tomorrow, I told myself, at the cemetery, when they lower her into the grave, this will stop.

Nothing is as final as that.

"Get cleaned up and come down to dinner, Linden," I told him. "You will need strength for what's coming. Believe me, I know."

He seemed to relax.

"Okay," he said. "I will."

"Good. I'll be waiting for you," I said, and backed out of the room, closing the door.

My heart thumped like a sledgehammer, not fast, just heavy, rattling through my bones and giving me a shiver. I tried to calm myself.

"You're pregnant, Willow De Beers," I whispered. "Get control of yourself for the sake of the baby inside you."

I sucked in my breath and went on.

Linden was very quiet at dinner. He ate mechanically, pausing occasionally to glance toward the door of the dining room as if he expected Mother would come walking in any moment, as if waiting to turn to me with a smile and say, "See, this was all just a nasty nightmare."

I almost felt like crawling into his madness and pulling it around me like a warm blanket of security.

It was quite evident on the faces of our maids, Mary and Joan, that Jennings was correct in telling me they had endured all they would at Joya del Mar. After dinner, they informed me of their intention to leave right after my mother's funeral.

"We'll stay to help you with greeting people, but not much longer," Mary said.

I thanked them for that and went to my room, intending to try to get some sleep. Just before I crawled into bed, the phone rang. It was Miguel. Now that he had insisted I call him by his Christian name, I could no longer think of him as Professor Fuentes.

"I hope I'm not calling you too late."

"No, it's fine," I said. "I don't expect to get much sleep tonight anyway."

"Perhaps you should take something to help."

"No, I don't want to be groggy in the morning."

"I understand. I've been thinking about you there in that big house without much family. I'm so used to a houseful of relatives, especially on occasions such as this. I just wanted you to know that I will be there tomorrow at the church and afterward, and I will gladly stand beside you," he said. "If you wish, that is."

"Thank you. I do wish."

"Then it will be," he said. "Good night, Willow."

"Good night, and thank you for thinking of me, Miguel."

What a strange mix of feelings was being stirred in my heart, I thought as I lay back against the big, fluffy pillow. Miguel's phone call had done more than comfort me. It gave me some new hope, some new fantasies and delights, but this came at so sad a time. It was almost like putting candy in a bowl of castor oil. The sweetness was welcome, but for the moment it felt out of place, even awkward, especially as I lay alone in this large suite where my very thoughts seemed to echo.

Now that my mother was gone, this house seemed empty already. How many times had I come upon her unawares and seen her touch a vase or a statue, gaze at a chair or stand by a window looking out, her lips caught in that small smile that comes only with a gentle, wonderful memory. I was sure she heard the click of her mother's footsteps over the tiles, looked up quickly in a mirror or in the reflection off a window and saw her standing there. Memories make ghosts of us all, and

Mother's memories surely brought back so many images, so many moments from the past that she felt ethereal, a body of mist and dreams herself. That restoration of the past at least gave the house some character, some sense of identity; and now, with her gone forever, all the good memories were gone with her. What Linden remembered here, I did not care to know, and what I knew from so short a stay was not enough to give me a sense of place. I certainly was not in the mood to think of it as Thatcher's and my home.

Could I make this a home without Mother? How much would I bury with her tomorrow? I wondered.

Linden put up a quiet resistance to attending Mother's funeral. I had to wake him and urge him to get dressed. I made sure to put out his dark suit. He took so long getting dressed, I thought we would be late ourselves. The limousine arrived and I went up to move him along. He would have no breakfast. I felt sorrier for him than I did for myself. He looked like a frightened young boy.

Whenever we think of funerals, we think of gray days, rainy days, dark and cold; but as if Palm Beach would not permit such feelings, the sky was bright blue and cloudless, the breeze gentle and soothing. Everything glittered with life and freshness. Nature refused to acknowledge death and decay. The only darkness that existed, existed in me and certainly in Linden.

There were just a dozen or so people at the church. Besides Manon and the others, there was Mr. Ross and his wife, some of my friends from school, Miguel waiting for me at the door, and, to my surprise, the infamous Carriage sisters, Bunny Eaton's friends. I had no doubt they were there in the role of social reporters, to fill the coffers of gossip with every detail of the funeral, who attended, what they wore, what was said.

The service itself was relatively short, the minister offering little in the way of a personal touch. It was almost as if he was afraid to say anything real about Mother. He cloaked himself in hymns and biblical readings. Throughout it all, Miguel stood at my side. I held Linden's arm. He was so stiff and terrified-looking, I was sure he provided a great subject for the tittle-tattle the chin-wagging Carriage sisters would pour into the eager ears of the Palm Springs socialites.

Toward the end, my throat closed as I choked back a sob. Miguel seized my hand and held it tightly. Then, when they rolled the coffin out the side door to the waiting hearse that would bring it to the cemetery, we turned, Linden following my lead closely, and walked up the aisle and out to the limousine.

"I'll be right behind you," Miguel said as Linden and I reentered the automobile. Looking out, I saw Manon and the others clump together, all looking somber. I was sure they would rush off to some bistro and have wine or champagne as quickly as they could to wash the mournful sounds of the organ and the scent of funeral flowers from their consciousness. Actually, I couldn't blame them. I even envied them.

I hadn't realized that Jennings was at the church. Besides Miguel and us, he was the only other person at the gravesite. He kept his head lowered throughout the minister's final prayers, then wiped his eyes and left before the coffin was to be lowered.

I watched Linden closely as the coffin descended. Finally, he moaned. For the last twenty years, Mother had been really the only other person in his life. Now every dark and desperate thought he had put into his art surely seemed justified to him. From the way he looked down into that grave, I knew he was wishing he could throw himself over the coffin and be buried with Mother.

Weakened by his sorrow, he began to lose strength rapidly, his legs melting. I wasn't just holding his arm anymore; I was holding him up. Miguel saw this immediately and took a firm grasp on his other arm.

"Better go," he whispered. I nodded, and we turned Linden and guided him to the limousine.

Once inside, he let himself fall to the side, his eyes closed, his body sinking into the seat.

"I'll come along to help you," Miguel said.

He was right behind us all the way back to Joya del Mar. Linden slept during the drive and I had a chance to cry. When we arrived, Jennings came out to help, and between him and Miguel, they were able to get Linden up to his room. They put him to bed. I waited downstairs, pouring myself a good shot of whiskey. Joan and Mary lingered, expecting people to arrive to pay their last respects, but no one did.

When Miguel came down, he asked about the windows in Linden's bedroom.

"They've been painted black?"

I told him why Linden had done it, and he shook his head, his eyes filling with concern.

"Maybe now, now that he has seen her interred in her grave, he will no longer have those visions," I said. "In an ironic and sad way, being at the funeral was probably good for him."

"Maybe," Miguel said, but he still looked concerned.

We had something to eat, then sat out on the loggia. There were a few soft and puffy clouds now, but other than that and a little increase in the breeze, the day had remained one of the most beautiful.

"Mother would have loved this day. She would have spent most of it out here and walking on the beach."

"It's so beautiful here," Miguel said, "I imagine she never really felt neglected or denied much, despite what you tell me about the social world that locked her out."

"I'm sure you are right."

"Excuse me, Mrs. Eaton," we heard, and I turned to see Mary and Joan, dressed to leave, their suitcases in hand. "Since there aren't any people coming, we thought we might as well be on our way," Mary said. "Everything has been cleaned up and put away properly, and Jennings says he can see to anything that you might need the rest of the day."

"Okay," I said.

"We left a forwarding address with Jennings where you can mail us our final pay and anything else that comes for us," Joan said.

"Fine."

"We're sorry about it all, Mrs. Eaton," Mary said.

"Thank you, and good luck to you both," I said.

They flashed small smiles, then turned and left.

"What's that all about?" Miguel asked, and I told him.

"So you're going to be left with no help here?"

"I'll start on that in a day or so. We don't need very much at the moment."

"Couldn't they have the decency to wait a week or so more?" Miguel asked, shaking his head after them.

"I suppose I don't blame them," I said.

"I should go and let you rest."

"I'm fine," I said, "but I don't want to keep you from anything you need to do."

He smiled.

"Don't be a big shot. You're carrying a lot," he said, nodding at my stomach.

I smiled.

"I promise not to be a big shot," I told him.

He held my gaze, and then he leaned over and kissed me on the forehead.

"Take care of yourself, Willow. I'll be by soon to make sure you do."

"I hope so," I said.

"Don't get up unless you're going up to rest. I can let myself out."

"I'll just sit here awhile," I told him. He held my hand for a few more seconds, then pulled his away and walked into the house.

I sat looking at the sea.

Upstairs, behind blackened windows, Linden had retreated to the deepest places in his troubled brain. I had no such escape, nor did I want one.

If my baby and I were to survive, it would be because I had grown stronger from all this trouble and pain, I thought. When you had no one but yourself as Linden had, you could afford to withdraw. I could not. Little Hannah was waiting to be greeted with smiles and joy and hope, not tears, and certainly not gloom and doom.

I don't know why I did it exactly, or even where I drew the strength to do it, but I got up and walked the beach until I reached the dock, and then I went out to the end and stood where Mother had stood so many nights and gazed out at the sea, waiting for my father, waiting for a promise to be fulfilled.

In a real sense, Thatcher's betrayal had left me in the same place that Mother had been. I would be alone here with my child. I would be as unwelcome in the same society out there beyond our walls. Why had she stayed? I wondered. Why hadn't she gone somewhere else to start anew? Wouldn't that have been better for both of them?

Would it be better for me and for Hannah?

I searched my mind, looking for my father's much-needed wisdom.

What do I do now, Daddy? Do I stay or do I go?

What do you want to do?

I'm not sure.

Then why don't you wait until you are?

What if I never am?

Daddy?

What if I never am? I asked more desperately.

But there was only silence in my mind, silence replaced with the sound of the sea and the whispering of the breeze past my ears.

Maybe tomorrow.

Maybe tomorrow I would know.

19

Alone with Linden

Our lives changed in so many ways during the days and weeks that followed Mother's death. Jennings left soon after, as he had previously announced. I had not done much to find new household help, so we were still without any maid. Instead, I closed down as much of the main house as I could, shutting up Mother's suite and all of the guest suites and bathrooms and confining our existence to my suite, the room that would serve as Hannah's nursery, and Linden's suite and studio.

To my surprise, Linden welcomed this shrinking of the property. He said it made our home feel cozier to him, closer to the way he and Mother had lived in the beach house, even though we still utilized the grand dining room and the large den, as well as the rear loggia.

The departure of our servants also had an unexpected positive effect on him.

"Grace and I lived a long time without maids and butlers," he declared when I told him Jennings was leaving us, too. "We survived then, and you and I will survive now."

I was pleased with his new optimistic attitude. A dramatic change came over him. No longer the introvert who spent most of his day locked away in his darkened studio, he decided he would fulfill most of the duties and asserted he would run the house, even cook and do our shopping. His whole demeanor went through a striking metamorphosis. He looked and behaved like a college freshman who was excited about being on his own for the first time in his life, being the one most responsible for himself. Every new responsibility he assumed was exciting to him.

"You're going to cook for us?" I asked with a smile when he declared he would take on the kitchen duties, too.

"Absolutely. I cooked for Grace and me on occasion, and I've been reading up on foods a pregnant woman should be eating, too. And things she should avoid eating and doing!" he added, wagging his right forefinger at me.

"Oh?"

"Yes. After all," he declared with a regal air of authority, "we have more than just ourselves to worry about now. We have our baby, our baby Hannah."

The first time he said that, I thought nothing much of it. It was all part of his new and wonderful enthusiasm about life and our future. But I began to have a worried feeling about it when he pronounced "our Hannah" or "our baby" with a real sense of possession in his voice every time he repeated it. Of course, I told myself I was overreacting and should be grateful for this new demonstration of joie de vivre. It was only rarely that I'd seen Linden enthusiastic and jubilant about anything, and I certainly had feared that after Mother's death, I would never see anything like that in him again.

Now he not only insisted on doing our driving and all

of our shopping, he refused to permit me to carry anything and was continually watching me to be sure I didn't do too much in the house, even though I wasn't quite halfway through my second trimester. If I began to clean something, he immediately took the cloth or the mop away from me and promised to do it all himself.

"Just do your walking," he ordered. "A pregnant woman should do a lot of walking, but no lifting and not so much bending."

"Yes, Dr. Montgomery," I kidded, but he had no sense of humor about it.

"I'm not a doctor, but you would be surprised at how much I know that they don't, or don't care about. They never really care," he stated with conviction. "Not the way I care."

Of course, I thanked him for his concern.

"Why shouldn't I be concerned? You don't have to thank me for that," he practically shouted at me.

Although he moved about with more energy and dressed and took better care of himself than before, he was still susceptible to instant explosions of anger and long periods of pouting if I challenged or seemed critical of anything he said or did. It was truly like walking on thin ice or navigating through a room filled with tissue-thin china, terrified I might bump into something and send a good and happy moment crashing into smithereens.

Nothing, however, seemed to bother him as much as Miguel's now frequent appearances at Joya del Mar. I had decided to take my sabbatical from my college earlier than I had first intended. It seemed to me I had to spend more time at home caring for Linden, although he was convinced it was he who was caring for me, and, of course, handling all the legal problems Mother's death engendered, as well as my pending divorce from Thatcher and my pregnancy.

"How can this college professor come around here so often?" Linden asked me after one of Miguel's visits. "Doesn't he have papers to correct, tests to create, work at college?"

"He doesn't work around the clock, Linden. Don't you think it's nice of him to take the time to see if we are doing all right?" I asked.

"He's not coming here to see if *we're* all right," he declared. "He's coming here to see if *you're* all right. It's disgusting. You're a pregnant woman and you're— you're not even legally divorced from Thatcher. He's like some buzzard waiting to pounce."

"Oh no," I said, disagreeing as gently as I could. "He's not at all like that, Linden."

He simply glared back at me, then huffed and puffed away to do some preparations for our dinner.

One afternoon, Miguel remained longer than usual. He and I sat on the rear loggia talking, mostly about college and his classes. He discussed his students in general and how, even after the few years he had been teaching, he could see a definite decline in their skills and their work habits.

"Everyone wants everything quickly. If they could take a pill that would enable them to learn all they needed in order to get that degree, they would line up for days. No one seems to enjoy the pursuit, the work, the challenge anymore. It's all bottom line: What's in it for me and how fast can I have it? Most of all, how can I get it with the least amount of effort?

"Someday, happiness will be distributed through vending machines—and college degrees, too!"

I laughed at his vehemence, and then he laughed at himself as well.

"I'm on my soapbox again. It takes someone like you, Willow, someone sincere and perceptive, to set me off."

"I don't think it's a soapbox, Miguel, and there is nothing wrong with being enthusiastic about the things that matter the most to you," I said.

He smiled and reached out to take my hand.

"You are truly a lovely, wonderful person, Willow. You don't deserve all these problems."

We held each other's eyes for a few moments, during which he kept my hand closed gently in his. Then I heard a French door slam, and saw Linden standing behind it looking out at us. I let go of Miguel's hand and turned to him.

"Linden, why don't you come out and sit with us for a while?" I suggested.

After a hesitation, he opened the door.

"I have something on the stove," he said.

"Oh, what are you making, Linden?" Miguel asked him.

"It's a pasta dish, a primavera."

"Oh. Sounds good," Miguel said.

"Why don't we invite Miguel to dinner, Linden?" I suggested.

He stared for a moment.

"I didn't make that much," he said.

"Neither of us eats that much, Linden."

"It's all right," Miguel said. "I have to be going. I'm meeting my parents for dinner. Perhaps you will permit me to take you both to Havana Molena one night this week."

"That would be nice. Wouldn't it, Linden?"

"Yes," he said, "but it depends on the night."

"Well, you will let me know what night is convenient, okay?" Miguel said.

Linden nodded and stepped back inside, closing the French door.

"I know you think he's doing better, Willow, but you have no idea how deep some of his mental troubles go," Miguel said, looking after him.

"You're right, of course. Now that the smoke has settled a bit, I'll contact his therapist and get him back into treatment."

"That's wise," Miguel said. He stood. "I'll call you tomorrow, if that is all right."

"Certainly it's all right. I'll be looking forward to it," I said, and he beamed.

Then he leaned forward and kissed me on the cheek. I held on to his shoulders tightly, keeping him from pulling completely away. He looked into my eyes, and then he kissed me softly on the lips.

"I'm sorry," he said quickly.

"For what? Making a pregnant woman feel attractive?"

He laughed.

"I hope that wasn't meant to be charity," I added. His smile froze, and he took on a look of deep seriousness as he came at me again, this time his lips lingering longer on mine.

"Believe me," he whispered. "It isn't charity."

I could feel my eyes brighten. He turned, walked to the door, turned back, smiled, and then left me trembling with happiness I had almost come to believe was forbidden.

A few hours later, we had our reason to go out to celebrate. My attorney phoned to tell me Thatcher had agreed to her proposals for a divorce settlement.

"Because of the reference to adultery, he realizes he

will lose. It will all be far easier than I first feared," she said.

"Oh, how wonderful. I wasn't looking forward to a prolonged battle with him."

"It's over," she said. "We've only got to have it stamped, sealed, and delivered. I don't usually congratulate my clients on their successful divorces. It's like complimenting someone for a good funeral, but in your case . . . congratulations, Willow."

I thanked her, and ran to tell Linden. He listened with that stone-faced expression of his, then said, "Good. Let's think of him as dead."

"We don't have to go that far, Linden. After all, he is still Hannah's father."

"In name only," he declared. "After she's born, I'll help her to forget him."

He said it with such intensity, he actually frightened me.

"It's better we let all of our anger and negative energy go, Linden. I don't want to bring up my daughter in a house full of rage."

He softened.

"Of course not," he said. "I'll always think of Hannah's interests first. Always."

"Good." I smiled. "Why don't we take Miguel up on his offer now and celebrate?"

"We could do that ourselves, here. I'll make something special."

"No, we should go out and have a good time, Linden. We can have another dinner to celebrate by ourselves afterward, okay?"

With reluctance, he nodded, and turned back to his work in the kitchen.

I hurried to call Miguel.

"That's wonderful, Willow. It's changing. I can feel it. Everything's changing for the better for you. I'll make our reservations right now, and we'll go tomorrow night. I'll be by to pick up both of you about seven."

"Thank you, Miguel."

Dared I believe him? Was it all changing for the better? With more bounce in my steps than they'd had for some time, I returned to the dining room where Linden was setting out our dinner and told him about our plans to go to Miguel's family's restaurant. He nodded, still not looking enthusiastic about it.

"You want to celebrate with me, don't you, Linden?" I asked him.

"Of course," he replied. "We'll celebrate. I promise."

He went into the kitchen and returned with our dinner. It was a very tasty pasta dish. He had actually become quite a good cook and always presented the food with an artistic flair. He wouldn't let me have any wine, reminding me that alcohol wasn't good for a pregnant woman, not even one glass, contrary to what some doctors said. He went into one of his lectures about prenatal care. I let him go on and on, reminding myself that at least he was involving himself in something besides his dark art. In a way, he was out of his introverted shell and for that, I concluded, I had to be grateful.

As I ate and he talked, I felt myself growing more and more tired. Lately, I wasn't sleeping as well as I should, and even with Linden rushing about to make sure I didn't do anything strenuous, I was working at keeping the house in somewhat decent shape and appearance. Tomorrow, I vowed, tomorrow I would call one of the agencies and start to interview prospective housekeepers. What I feared was that Mary and Joan might have spread stories about Linden and what it was like working here. That could keep good candidates from applying.

Before dinner was over, I found it more difficult than ever to chew my food and keep my head up. My eyelids grew heavier and heavier. Linden droned on. When he was making what he considered an important point, he raised his voice and slapped the table with his hand, but soon the cadence of his speech was as effective as a lullaby. I was no longer really listening and understanding.

"I'm suddenly very tired, Linden," I announced. "I think I'll skip dessert."

"I didn't make any," he said. "We've got to watch your weight, Willow. You will thank me for that after you give birth because it will be easier for you to regain your beautiful figure."

"Okay," I said. Just to smile seemed to take great effort. When I stood up, I felt wobbly. He rose quickly and came around the table. "I don't know why I'm so tired suddenly," I said. "I'm sorry."

"That's okay. It's normal for you to be tired. You're doing too much. You need more rest. I'll help you to your suite," he said, and held my arm as I walked to the stairway.

When I looked up the stairs, I felt as if I were about to attempt a climb of Mount Everest. It seemed suddenly an impossible task to get myself up to the second landing. I actually moaned a complaint as we began to ascend. I found myself breathing very hard, too, and had to stop and rest about midway.

"What's wrong with me?" I cried, wiping my brow with my hand. I thought I felt clammy. "Maybe I should go see a doctor."

"Oh, you're just tired, Willow. I told you. It's not uncommon. After a night's rest, you'll feel fine," he said.

He continued to guide me up, practically carrying me the rest of the way. When we got to my suite, I stopped to take a deep breath. He helped me to the bed.

"Get me a cold, wet washcloth, please, Linden."

"Of course," he said, and went to fetch it.

I lay back on my pillow and closed my eyes. I don't know if he ever got the washcloth because, seconds later, I was asleep.

When I awoke, it was pitch dark. I was under my blanket, naked. I had no idea how I had gotten undressed and under the covers. My neck felt so stiff. Everything ached. There was a strange new odor in my room, familiar but so unexpected, it didn't register for a few moments. I turned to see what time it was. My clock had one of those illuminating faces so I could see the hands well in the dark. It read seven, which of course meant seven in the morning, but it was pitch dark!

Now more confused than ever, I threw off the blanket and sat up, swinging my legs off the bed and looking at my windows. The curtains weren't drawn, but—

It came like a cold wave of utter shock and terror. My windows had been painted black, just as thickly as the ones in Linden's studio and suite. Why had he done this? How could I have slept through it all? I put my hand against my forehead because I felt myself spinning. My fatigue, my passing out . . . could he have put one of his own medications in my food?

I fumbled about to turn on the lamps, then made my way to my closet to find my robe. It wasn't hanging on the door where I had left it. In fact, my closet was empty except for a few naked hangers. Where were all my clothes? My shoes were gone as well. All I had were my slippers by the bed. What had he done? Why?

For a moment, I staggered. The room took a spin and I had to grab the closet door to keep myself from falling. Whatever he had put in my food still lingered in my body. I had a great thirst and went into the bathroom to get some water. After that, I felt a little better and wrapped a towel around myself. Then I went to my phone. There was no question I had to have Linden committed, I thought. This was too much. Miguel was so right. I decided I would begin by calling him.

When I lifted the receiver, however, I heard no dial tone. I was puzzled about it only for a moment, because I immediately realized the wire from the phone to the wall jack was gone.

"This is maddening," I muttered, and went to my door. I feared it, but was still surprised to discover the door had been locked. A hasp had been installed on the outside. The door opened only an inch or so, permitting a small shaft of light. I put my mouth to the narrow opening and shouted.

"Linden! Linden, where are you? What have you done? Linden!"

I heard nothing. I called again and again and listened, but heard only the same deep silence.

"Linden, please," I cried. "I'm sick. This is no good for the baby. Please, let me out."

Again, I heard only silence. Slowly, I sank to the floor and rested my head against the wall. My eyelids were still so heavy. I closed them and rested, opening them every few minutes to look into the hallway while I shouted for him. Suddenly, I heard the sound of a vacuum cleaner. From the direction and volume, I thought it was being used on the stairs. Shouting over it was useless. I waited and waited. It seemed to go on interminably. When it stopped, I listened and then shouted for him again. Still, he did not respond and he did not come.

Exhausted and very uncomfortable, I returned to the bed. I needed a little more rest, I told myself. Stronger, I would rip that door open if I had to, I thought. I closed my eyes and fell back asleep.

This time when I woke, I found a serving table and a tray beside the bed, the silver dish covered. There was a glass of orange juice, a pot of coffee, milk, toast on a plate, and my prenatal vitamins. Under the silver cover were two poached eggs. I touched them and realized they were still warm. He had just been here.

Hoping he had left the door unlocked, I rose and went to it, but the hasp was still there, the padlock still closed in it.

"Linden!"

I could see only a small piece of the corridor, but I realized that it, too, was very dark. Moving to the right and angling myself, I was able to catch a glimpse of one of the windows. It was painted black.

"Linden, please. Linden!"

I heard music. It grew louder. The stereo had been turned on and one of Linden's favorite Mozart concertos was playing. Shouting over it was futile.

My stomach churned. I returned to the bed and looked at the food. Toast couldn't be harmful, and neither could the eggs, but I was afraid to drink the juice or the coffee. They could easily disguise one of his sedatives, I thought. I drank water from my bathroom faucet instead. The food did give me some strength, and I looked for something to use to pry the door open. There really wasn't anything that recommended itself immediately, but I realized if I could remove one of the metal poles used in the closet, it might serve like a crowbar.

That was easier said than done. A bracket held it on both ends. I found something in my nail-file case that I could employ as a screwdriver and began to work off the brackets. That completed, I pulled and pushed on the metal pole until it came loose. The effort was exhausting. He'd given me quite a dose of his sedatives, I thought. Now I was driven by rage as well as terror. When it came to my health and the health of my baby, I would not be tolerant.

Placing the pole as close to the hasp as I could, I began to pry away. I had just begun to make some progress—I could hear the hasp coming loose—when suddenly, the pole was seized and pulled out of my hands. It happened so fast and so unexpectedly, I gasped and stepped back.

"Stop it," I heard him say in a loud whisper.

"Linden! Linden, what are you doing to me? Let me out of here."

"I've got to help you," he replied. "I've got to be sure you are not disturbed. Our Hannah is coming. We cannot permit anyone to get between us."

"Linden. What did you do with my clothing? You can't keep me imprisoned in here. Let me out now. You're making trouble for us and especially for yourself. Unlock the door now," I demanded.

"You *will* understand," he said. "And later, you will thank me for everything. I have a new idea. I am going to paint something about it. Just be patient," he said. I heard him walking away.

"Linden! Don't do this. Linden!"

The music became even louder. I retreated to my bed and sat sobbing and then screaming my rage. After that, I sobbed again.

"He'll realize what he's doing soon," I told my image in the mirror. "He'll realize it and unlock the door."

The face in the glass that looked back at me was almost unrecognizable. My hair was wild, my cheeks streaked, my eyes frantic. It took my breath away. *Stay calm,* I told myself. *Keep calm, Willow. It does you no good to become hysterical now. Miguel will surely call soon, and even if he doesn't, he's coming at seven,* I remembered. *This won't go on much longer.*

Every hour seemed more like ten. I dozed on and off, afraid that I wouldn't be awake when he opened the door again to bring me something else to eat and drink. He either didn't think of it or didn't remember. By now he was surely so deeply into his own world that what was real and what wasn't were indistinguishable to him, I thought. A madman was my keeper. He dwelt on another level. He might even have forgotten he had locked me in here, I realized. There was no longer any logic. There were no rules in his existence, at least no rules I would recognize.

In order to keep my own sanity more than anything else, by midafternoon, I decided to take a shower. I felt grimy anyway and needed to do something to revive myself. Either he had been watching me and waiting for the opportunity, or he had just happened by when I was in the shower, but after I came out and dried myself, I found a new tray of food by the bed.

"No!" I screamed, and charged the door, pulling and kicking it. It didn't budge. "Linden, you let me out of here now. I swear if you don't . . . Linden, Mother would be very angry at you for this."

"No," he whispered. Again he was just outside and to one side of my door. "She told me to do it."

"Stop it! Stop it!" I screamed. "Mother is dead. She couldn't have told you anything of the sort. Let me out, Linden. I'm getting very sick. I'll lose the baby."

"No, you won't," he said confidently. "You would if

you married Miguel, I bet. He would want you to have an abortion. Why would he want our baby? He would want his own baby."

"Hannah is not *our* baby, Linden. She is *my* baby. Mine."

"You don't have to say that anymore, Willow. It's all right now. It doesn't matter. Everyone can know about us."

"What are you talking about, Linden? The baby can't be yours too. We're brother and sister."

He laughed.

"No, we're not, Willow. That was just a story Grace and you created. She told me. After my boating accident, she told me the truth so I wouldn't be upset. That's why I knew Thatcher and you wouldn't last. So you see, it's all happening as it is supposed to happen. Rest. We'll all be together again and happy."

What he was saying was so upsetting, I couldn't reply for a moment.

"Mother would never have told you such a thing, Linden," I said when I gathered my wits. "You're imagining that conversation. I'll prove it to you after you let me out."

"No, you are the one who is confused, Willow. I'll prove it to you instead. I'll ask Grace to tell you."

"Mother is dead, Linden. She died. You were at the hospital. You saw her. Think, remember."

"No," he said, still speaking in that hoarse whisper. "We did all that just to keep those busybodies away from us, and it worked. No one has come here. No one will come, either." He laughed. "Your professor called to confirm his dinner date, and I told him you were gone. You had decided to visit your relatives and you were gone. I told him we had decided to move after all. He was very disappointed, but he won't be bothering us again. It will just be you and I, Willow, just as I've always planned for it to be. And Hannah, of course. Our Hannah. Rest," he said.

"Linden!"

He walked away. I could hear him descending the stairway, and then a deep and hollow silence fell over the big house.

I wasn't just a prisoner in my suite. I was a prisoner in Linden's very disturbed mind.

When it was a little after seven o'clock and Miguel had not arrived, I began to believe that Linden had told the truth concerning the phone call. Would Miguel have believed him? If he did, I could be in here for days, maybe weeks before anyone realized it. In his madness, Linden could sound logical and intelligent to anyone who called and asked for me, even my attorney. Manon and the girls wouldn't challenge anything he said. I even wished Thatcher would come by for some reason, any reason, no matter how selfish it was.

With little to do except think and be irritable, I paced the suite. Vexed to the point of wanting to tear every piece of furniture apart or beat holes in the very walls that contained me, I fixed my eyes on the painting Linden had done for Thatcher and me as a wedding present. How it had annoyed Thatcher, I thought. I shouldn't have tolerated it above our bed like this. In a surge of rage, I reached up and pulled it from its hooks, tossing it to the floor. For a moment I stood over it, breathing hard, and then my eyes went to the wall where Linden himself had hung it. For a moment it seemed as if all the air had left my lungs and been replaced with hot, steamy vapor. I thought I would explode.

There in the wall was a distinct hole. I stood on the

bed and peered through it. I could see clearly into the suite Linden had once occupied before he decided to move out and permit it to be used as our nursery. What good was a hole in the wall if a portrait in a frame was hung over it? I thought, and then got down and examined the picture. Very clearly, exactly where the hole was located behind the painting, the picture had an area so thin and sheer it was diaphanous. Anyone could easily see through it. From the angle the portrait had been hung above our bed, Linden could easily look down at us and, most likely, was now periodically looking down at me.

So this was how he knew when to come into the room to put down a new tray of food. How eerie and terrifying cleverness and logic could be when they were housed within the walls of madness, I thought.

I struggled to get the picture back on the wall. Surely he would be returning to spy on me. What I had to do now was convince him I was asleep. Then he would unlock that door. I crawled under the blanket, closed my eyes, and waited. Actually, I nearly really fell asleep waiting. Finally, close to seven-thirty, I could hear him in the hallway. I heard him tinkering with the lock and hasp, doing it as quietly and as gently as he could, and then, with my eyes barely open, I saw the door nudged, saw him peer in to study me. I closed my eyes tightly and held my breath.

Practically tiptoeing across the room, he carried a new tray of food to the serving table. He put it down and lifted the old tray away, bending down to put it aside so he could place the new tray on the table. When he did that, I pushed him forward and he went spilling over the tray to the floor. I didn't wait. With the top sheet wrapped around myself, I leaped from the bed and charged at the door.

"Willow, *No!*" he screamed after me.

I didn't hesitate a moment. I was out of the door and down the hallway, but at the top of the stairway, I stopped and stared down in utter shock. Every window before me had been painted over in black. The sight of it took my breath away. I had no doubt that every single window in the grand house had been so covered in black. Linden in his madness was shutting the outside world away, shutting us up in his own little world. The gates and the high walls around our property were not enough to satisfy his paranoia.

I heard him scrambling behind me and hurried frantically down the steps, but in my haste, I stepped on the train of the sheet I had wrapped hastily around myself and lost my footing. I spilled forward, desperately trying to break my fall with my extended arms, but I spun too far to the right, smacking my head against the balustrade and tumbling down the stairway, falling like the Humpty-Dumpty I had considered myself to be after I discovered Thatcher's betrayals. My last conscious thought was, *They will never put me together again.*

I awoke in Linden's arms. He was carrying me back up the stairway. I groaned. My lower back ached where I had wrenched it, and I could feel the bruise on my forehead swelling into a bump. He walked mechanically, his eyes forward.

"Let me go," I whispered through a throat sore from shouting and crying.

He did not respond. I tried to struggle free, but his grip on me was iron firm. I was no better than a goldfish in a plastic bag. We were heading up the stairs, heading right back to my suite, where he would lock me in again.

"No," I moaned.

"You shouldn't have done that, Willow. You could have hurt Hannah. You could have hurt our baby. You have to listen to me. I know what's best for us now," he recited. He spoke like someone in a dream and reminded me of what he was like when I had first returned and he had gone sleepwalking on the beach. He couldn't hear anything I was saying. He was lost in his own dream.

Just as we reached the landing, I heard the sound of breaking glass. He did, too, and he paused. There was more of it, and then I heard the most beautiful sound of all. I heard Miguel call out my name.

Linden's face filled with panic. He turned me as if to start down the stairs again, then spun to continue upward.

"Miguel! Help me!" I shouted.

In seconds, he was at the bottom of the stairway.

"Linden," he screamed. "Put her down. Put her down now."

Linden turned and looked at him.

"Go away," he said. "This is our home. You don't belong here. Go away."

Miguel started up the stairs slowly.

"You have to put her down, Linden. You can hurt her if you don't. Now, just put her down gently. Everything will be all right if you do it slowly, Linden. Go on," Miguel urged.

Linden shook his head.

"Don't come up here!" he cried. "You don't belong here. No one else belongs here but us. This is our home, not yours. Go away."

He stepped to his left, bringing me right to the balustrade. Miguel stopped and held out his right arm. Linden lifted me higher and to the left, as if he was going to drop me over the balustrade.

"Careful with her," Miguel said sharply.

"Go away," Linden cried in response. "Go away," he repeated, his voice full of threat. He lifted me toward the balustrade again, and I cried out.

Miguel held his ground, obviously terrified. His fear revved up my own. My heart was pounding so hard, I thought I would pass out and not even know if I was dropped from this height.

"Okay," Miguel said after another moment. "I'll go away, Linden. You put her down."

He backed down a step to demonstrate his retreat. Linden didn't budge.

"I'm going," Miguel said, "but you have to be careful with her. Remember, she's pregnant, Linden."

"I know she's pregnant. I was the first to know. Don't tell *me* she's pregnant."

"Of course you knew," Miguel said. He smiled. "I'm sorry. I didn't mean you didn't know."

"It's our Hannah coming. *Ours!*"

"Oh, I know. I just stopped by to congratulate you. I want to be your friend, that's all. I'm here to help."

"We don't need your help and we don't need any friends, not from here. Just leave us alone and tell everyone else out there to leave us alone."

"Okay. If that's the way you'd like it."

"Yes, it is."

"All right," Miguel said, backing farther down the stairs. "I'll just be going, then."

"Good," Linden said. "Go."

Miguel and I looked at each other. I gave him a small nod to indicate I was all right and he should continue to placate Linden.

"Call me if you need anything," Miguel said, and turned, walking down the stairs and to the front entrance.

Linden watched suspiciously. Miguel turned again,

waved, and unlocked the door. Then he stepped out and closed the door behind him.

"Good," Linden said. "See? Now they will all leave us alone."

He turned and continued up the stairway. I said nothing. He carried me into the suite and laid me on the bed.

"I brought you a good dinner," he said, "but you made me spill it all over the floor. You'll have to wait for me to get you new food."

"Okay," I said.

He studied me.

"You know I'm doing all this for us, and you know it's right and the best, don't you?"

"Yes, Linden."

He picked up the dishes and put them on the tray.

"I'll be back in a little while," he said. "Maybe I'll sit here and eat with you."

"I'd like that, Linden."

"Good," he said, and walked out. He closed the door and I heard the padlock scrape through the hasp again.

Only a few minutes later, I heard Miguel working at the hasp. I heard him snap it off, and then he opened the door.

"Willow," he cried, rushing to me.

I threw my arms around him and burst into tears.

"I've called for help. The police and an ambulance will be here very soon."

"I don't want him to be taken to jail, Miguel."

"I know. I'll make sure he's taken to psychiatric."

"What's he doing now?"

"He's in the kitchen. He's talking as if . . ."

"What?"

"As if your mother were sitting there watching him."

"How sad."

"But how dangerous and horrible it must have been for you," Miguel said. "When I called and he gave me that story about you leaving, I knew something was very wrong. I actually called the police, but they said they had no justification for coming out here. They phoned, and he answered and sounded very reasonable to them.

"I came as quickly as I could, and then I had to scale the wall to get in. The moment I saw that all the windows in the house had been painted black, I went into a fit of terror and broke through the French door in the den."

I started to cry again.

"It's all right, Willow. It's all right now. I'm here for you. I'll always be here for you," he added.

He kissed the tears away from my cheeks and held me tightly.

I could hear Linden downstairs, moving in and out of his illusions, peopled by the same ghosts that had twisted and tormented him for so long.

It was time to drive them away forever.

I couldn't do it alone, but I had no doubt now that I would never be alone as I had often been before, even after I had come here.

Like Linden, I would drive my ghosts away as well.

Epilogue

Little Hannah proved to be as resilient as I had hoped. My fall on the stairway and my torment and turmoil did not do injury to my pregnancy. Almost to the day her birthing was predicted, she insisted on entering this world. Miguel rushed me to the hospital and she was born at 7 A.M., weighing close to eight pounds.

My divorce settlement with Thatcher provided for his visitation rights, although I had little expectation of his implementing them very much. In fact, when he was called and told of Hannah's birth, he did not appear at the hospital until the following day, and only on his way to a court hearing. Neither Bunny nor Asher ever made an attempt to see their grandchild, probably still clinging to the nasty rumors Whitney had spread.

Hannah was born with hair a shade or so lighter than mine, closer to my mother's hair, actually, which made me very happy, but which I was sure helped fan the flames of those horrible and disgusting stories the Eatons had spread to justify Thatcher's adulterous behavior.

I was too busy now to care. Despite my plans to return to my studies, however, I put off hiring a nanny. I decided I wanted to be with Hannah until she was at least a year and a half. I did hire a new maid, who was an excellent cook as well. Her name was Mrs. Davis, Mrs. Betty Davis, which was, of course, funny, especially when she introduced herself as "the real Betty Davis."

She looked nothing like Bette Davis the actress. My Betty Davis was nearly six feet tall and stout, with rolling-pin forearms and graying strawberry-blond hair. She had freckles peppered over the crests of her puffy cheeks. She told me she was fifty-one, but when Miguel met her, he whispered that he thought she was more like sixty-one. She told me her husband had died more than fifteen years ago and left her with little or nothing. He was a hardworking but mediocre salesman who went from one commission job to another, never, by her own description, very ambitious. They had no children. She had been a librarian in a county library in Virginia before moving to Florida to live with her sister and brother-in-law, but, again according to her, soon felt like a third wheel and went out looking for work as a live-in maid. Her last employer had passed away, but she had excellent recommendations. Most important for me, she was very good with Hannah, so good, in fact, that I had my suspicions about her claim that she never had any children.

Miguel insisted I keep my hand in my studies and enrolled me in a study program that enabled me to pick up some credits after writing a paper. Soon after Hannah's birth, he and I began to see each other on a more romantic and regular basis and then, on Hannah's first birthday, he proposed and I accepted.

My second wedding was far simpler than the first, although Miguel had so many relatives attending that I teased him about it and threatened to hold it at Joya del Mar rather than at church. As it was, we did finally decide to have a reception there. No one but us knew that we had already gone off and gotten married by a justice of the peace during a romantic weekend. There I was, holding Hannah in my arms and pronouncing wedding vows. Needless to say, the judge's wife and the clerk who witnessed were bug-eyed. The way they looked at each other gave Miguel and me many laughs afterward.

During the year, I visited Linden periodically in the clinic we had found for him. I didn't think it was as good nor as well run as Daddy's, but I am sure part of that evaluation had to do with my prejudice. How could anyone do anything as well as my father had done it, especially as regarded mental illness?

They had Linden on medication, but toward the end of the first year he was eased off it, and he settled into an existence that seemed peaceful. He was still quite actively involved in his art, which they encouraged. I had suspicions that some of his work was being stolen. It was always well done and interesting, albeit eerie and strange to most people.

He stopped asking about Mother, but never stopped asking about Hannah. Finally, with Miguel's blessing and even at his suggestion, I brought her with me. I doubt that I shall ever forget the way he looked at her. Thatcher, with all his claims of fatherly interest and love, would never approach such a gaze of admiration and joy. Miguel and I discussed it afterward and agreed that, even though Linden's feelings toward Hannah were caught up in his delusions, they were still sincere and authentic.

"Sort of like a psychosomatic pain. The patient really does feel it, even though there is no reason for it, no cause. It's an authentic complaint, sincere," he said.

Visiting Linden, thinking about all these things, whetted my appetite to return to school and pursue my degree, so when I was ready, I ran a search for a proper nanny, even though Mrs. Davis insisted she was capable of handling Hannah.

"A child of this age can be so demanding, Mrs. Davis," I told her, recalling myself and Amou. "You won't have time for any of your other duties here. In fact, my husband and I are now thinking about opening more of the house and we might be bringing in some additional household help."

She accepted my explanation, but I knew in my heart that she would forever be competing with any nanny for Hannah's attention and love. I was girding myself for the expected criticisms and complaints about anyone I hired, and sure enough, Mrs. Davis would be there to greet me with a list whenever I returned from college or any trip Miguel and I made.

I had found someone who was capable of standing up to her, however, and in time, despite the jealousies, the two of them became good friends. Her name was Donna Castilla. She was from Cuba, someone Miguel's mother had found for us, actually. In many ways she reminded me of Amou, who, with her sister, made another visit to Florida to see Hannah. We had a wonderful visit, and when she left, she told me Señora Castilla would be a wonderful nanny. "Especially with your Mrs. Davis looking over her shoulder, eh, Amou Um?"

It was so wonderful to see her again, and Hannah took right to her the moment she greeted her. All the good memories of my youth came flooding back whenever I saw Amou or heard her voice. She went with me to visit Mother's grave, and then we stayed up late into the night talking. Actually, I let her do most of the talking. She had so many things to tell me about my father, things I never saw or knew, a part of him that I wished I had been able to enjoy back then.

Saying goodbye to her was truly like saying goodbye to Daddy once again.

But I could never say goodbye to Daddy. Even now, with all that had happened, I carried his thoughts and his voice in my heart and my mind.

One night after Hannah had been put to bed and Miguel had gone off to a meeting at the college, I walked down to the dock and stood where my mother had stood so many nights, looking out to sea, hoping for a light on a boat to grow stronger and larger until the boat was there and my father was waving to her. I felt sure she had seen this boat many times.

When do you stop being lonely, Daddy? I asked him.

Are you still lonely?

I have a child and a man who truly loves me, but it doesn't end it. Not forever and ever. There are still nights like this, nights when you can't help but be alone and long for things that are gone forever and ever. You must have been awfully lonely for so many years.

Maybe loneliness in that sense isn't so terrible, Willow. Maybe it's good to remember and long for things that you loved so much and that touched you so deeply. Maybe they will help you provide those things for the people you love now.

Will they?

Will they? he echoed back to me.

I smiled.

Answering a question with a question. Always the psychiatrist.

Always the psychiatrist's daughter, he replied.

SIMON & SCHUSTER
PROUDLY PRESENTS

TWISTED ROOTS

VIRGINIA ANDREWS®

Available May 2004

Turn the page for a preview of
Twisted Roots. . . .

Prologue

I have always felt like someone with a pimple on the tip of her nose because my last name is different from my mother's. First you try to cover it up, and then, when you can no longer do that, you pretend it's nothing and act as if it certainly doesn't bother you.

I have my father's last name, Eaton, and my mother, who remarried a year after I was born, has my stepfather's last name, Fuentes. My father, who is an important and successful Palm Beach attorney, has always refused to permit my stepfather to legally adopt me and thus take on his name, even though my daddy, too, remarried a year after I was born and has twin boys, now fifteen years old, Adrian and Cade.

The irony about all this is my Eaton grandparents have never had anything to do with me, nor has my aunt Whitney, my father's sister, or her children, my cousins Quentin and Laurel, both of whom have their own families. I have seen my Eaton grandparents, my aunt and her husband, Hans, from a distance, and I know they have seen me from time to time, but they have never acknowledged me. I once saw Quentin, but I have never seen his family, and I have never seen Laurel or any of her family. Even when I was very young, it didn't take me long to realize the Eatons built a wall around themselves, so they were the castle-keeps, especially in regards to me.

Whenever I have been with my father, I have been with Adrian and Cade, but I am not very fond of my half brothers. They suffer from 100 percent snob-quotient. I won't deny that they are very good-looking and very good students, but they love reminding people of that, especially me. Even though I am just as good a student as either of them, they often try to make me feel inferior by bragging about how much more they have or how many more friends they have. They have what they call their Invite Board in their game room and they pin up their party invitations on it. They love showing it to me, especially when almost every available space is taken.

My father's wife, Danielle, is polite and nice enough to me, but I have always thought she was afraid to be much more. She gives only about a 70 percent smile and stops short whenever she is about to invite me to do something or give me something that might somehow seem to be extra and above what is absolutely necessary. Perhaps she thinks my brothers would be jealous. I'm sure they would be.

Danielle is pretty, with doll-like features. My father met her on one of his trips to France. She was working for a travel agency. All I know is they had a whirlwind romance and she became pregnant almost the day they were married. She always seems quite overwhelmed by her twin boys. I have caught her looking at them with an expression of astonishment on her face after something they had said or done, making me think she was wondering how two such conflicting and explosive personalities were ever a part of her. I have even heard her jokingly say that they kicked so hard in her womb, she was afraid she would have an unexpected cesarean birth.

Mother calls Danielle my father's trinket wife. She says he has a charm bracelet with pictures of all of his past trinkets, with her excluded of course. I know that's not true and I know that Mother doesn't really believe it, but she likes to say things like that about him. She has what I would best describe as a shaky truce between herself and my father, and I walk the tightrope between them, afraid to say one nice thing about either to either for fear their anger and disappointment will shake the ground I'm on, causing me to fall off and then lose them both.

The only family I really have is what I call my stepfamily, the Fuenteses. They have never made me feel like anything less than a member of their family, making sure to always include me in their celebrations and events. I expect there is such a word in the dictionary as *stepfamily,* but even if there isn't, the word is in my own private dictionary, along with *snob-quotient* and *nongrandma* and *nongrandpa,* which is what my father's parents, Bunny and Asher Eaton, are to me. I suppose I could call the Eatons my nonfamily.

I do have some family on my mother's side: an uncle, my mother's half brother, Linden. He lives in a residency in the Boca Raton area. It is what my mother terms an intermediary home for someone who has spent years and years in a very controlled environment, a mental health clinic, but who is not quite ready to be on his own in the outside world. She never says it, but she doesn't have to say it. She knows I know she doesn't believe he will ever be quite ready. It's not an intermediate place for him; it's a dead end. No matter how deeply set his problems are, however, I believe he loves me very much and I love him.

My father is always warning me about my uncle Linden and telling me things like, "Insanity runs like an underground sewer through that family bloodline," which makes me wonder if he doesn't think I have the mental pollution in me as well. His parents, his sister and even his children certainly treat me as if I do. Sometimes I get the impression that Adrian and Cade think I'm going to break out in mad babbling or stick my finger in an electric socket. They would love that. I know they deliberately do things, tease and shock me with their words and behavior, in the hope that they will bring on a seizure of madness. There is always that slight pause, that hesitation of anticipation, waiting for my reaction. I try to ignore them, but it's like pretending a mosquito hasn't landed on your arm.

My stepfather, Miguel, who is a college psychology professor and whom my mother once even had as her teacher, told me that it's my father's family that has the mental problems. I told him that doesn't help me because in either case, I might have inherited it.

"Not this kind of mental illness, Willow," he replied. "This kind is home grown in Palm Beach. You can't inherit it. You have to wander into those gardens to contact that sort of poison ivy and thankfully, your mother keeps you out of them."

We both laughed at that, me not so much because Mother was keeping me out of that world, but because that world wasn't inviting me to enter. Whenever I walked down Worth Avenue with Mommy, I felt we were both invisible. People who knew who we were seemed too terrified to look at us for more than a split second. Maybe they thought they would be turned into pillars of salt, or if they smiled at us, no one would ever again smile at them. This was especially true about snobby sales people in the better Palm Beach stores who often made us wait or even ignored us for as long as they could or until Mommy put herself aggressively in their face.

"When I tell you these things about Palm Beach, it's not a case of the fox and the grapes, Hannah," my stepfather insisted. "Believe me. You don't want to be part of that social scene. It's cannibalistic. They eat each other for breakfast.

"Pass me that child from Coconut Row. Or, can I have a piece of that young man from Esplanade Way, please?" he added, pretending to be seated at some fancy Palm Beach restaurant. We both roared with laughter.

I really love my stepfather as much as anyone would love a natural father, maybe even more than I love mine. I know my father thinks I do. Whenever he sees me wearing something new, especially a ring or a bracelet, he always says, "I see your mother's Cuban lover is trying to buy your love again with some cheap, imitation jewelry."

I want to say, "He's not her Cuban lover. He's her husband and this isn't cheap, imitation jewelry," but if I defend Miguel too vigorously, it would only convince Daddy he was right, so I usually pretend I didn't hear him. More often than not, when I am with either my mother or my father, I feel like I am floundering in the world of adult quicksand. A critical glance, a sarcastic word, even an innocent question could pull me down into their swampy underworld full of green-eyed monsters.

It's better for me to say nothing, to look bored and disinterested. Both take it as a sign of agreement and I think that's all right. Let them believe what they need to believe. Little silences are like antimissiles I use to keep all the missiles of unhappiness from striking my heart.

I might not be able to do that today, however. Today is one of the strangest, if not *the* strangest, days in my life. My mother is a psychologist who specializes in the problems of young people. She said she likes to get to someone before his or her emotional and psychological difficulties are too comfortably seated. She has been in practice for more than ten years and she is very well known and respected. All during that time, she and my stepfather put off having a child of their own, and then they decided right after my sixteenth birthday to have one. Just a little more than two months later, at dinner, Mother announced she was pregnant. It was the most surprising thing I had heard my whole life. My mother, pregnant? It was so strange to realize she was actually going to give birth. There were girls my age giving birth!

"Your brother or sister might even be born on your birthday," she declared. "Wouldn't that be wonderful? We could have one big birthday party every year!"

I know Mommy was just trying to be excited for me because she never had a brother or sister in her home when she was growing up, but no, I thought. It wouldn't be wonderful. Who wants to share his or her one special day with someone else? I used to feel sorry for Adrian and Cade because they had to do that, being twins. Adrian's solace is his gleeful bragging about being born a good two minutes before Cade. Cade counters by saying that was because he kicked Adrian out of their mother's womb first.

"I couldn't stand the smell," he bellows, and laughs.

"That's exactly why I came out first. I couldn't stand your smell," Adrian throws back at him.

It's hard to believe they are brothers, even though they are mirror images. They so enjoy belittling each other and defeating each other. It's as though they were put on some mysterious starting line and their births came after the report of a starting gun. Cade will always be in pursuit of Adrian, who had that two-minute advantage. However, at least when they are making fun of each other, they are not making fun of me. If I try to stop them from hurting each other, I know they will only turn on me.

Anyway, this morning I was woken by a great deal of commotion, shouting, doors slamming, footsteps on the stairs and in the hallway. My heart skipped a beat when I heard Miguel yell, "We're going to the hospital."

When I went to the door, Miguel turned to me and cried, "Your mother's water has broken."

I knew it was almost a month too soon so I understood why she and Miguel were in a panic about it. Mommy had always been nervous about being pregnant this late in life, so she had been very intense about her prenatal care, her vitamins, doctor's visits, diet and exercise. Now, despite all that, she was being rushed to the hospital to give birth to what I already knew would be my baby brother Claude, named for my maternal grandfather. Even before little Claude, as he would come to be known, opened his eyes and cried for the first time, I was already jealous of him, more jealous than Cade was of Adrian and Adrian of Cade.

After all, my brother Claude would have my mother's

last name. He would be a Fuentes and he would belong in this family more than I did. He would never have a nongrandmother or nongrandfather.

Certainly, he would never feel like a stranger in his daddy's home. He had dozens of real relatives to call his family, not his stepfamily. He wouldn't need little silences to keep him from being too unhappy, nor would he have to worry about saying the wrong things to his father or his mother. He would never think he was on an island, cut off from the sea of society around him.

In short, he would never wonder who he really was.

Lying there and listening to the shouting and the footsteps dying out in the hallway as they left the house, I had one deep regret on this the most confusing of all days for me. Anyone who heard my regret might think it was probably the strangest thing of all, in fact.

Why was I born first? Why couldn't I be the one who was to be born today?